The Mandela Effect

Cliff

Kilmister

Published by Passion Projects

Dedicated to my wife and family,
for their unwavering support, patience, and encouragement throughout this journey. Thank you for believing in me, standing by my side, and making this book possible.

Copyright

The Mandela Effect

Cover Art Designed by Cliff Kilmister

Illustrated by Rebeca Ira

Chapter 1 – The Mystery of Flight 21

It was the evening of November fifteenth, 1945, Fort Lauderdale, Florida. US Navy Captain Max C. Reynolds was enjoying life as a Navy flight instructor. In the tranquillity and solitude of his bedroom, Reynolds reviewed the flight plan for his training mission. He took a moment to breathe deeply, taken by a pair of lovebirds outside that were seemingly singing a personal ode for his ears only. He got lost in the passionate melody, as if Mozart himself had gifted him this moment.

Reynolds fought the temptation to lie down, but fatigue weighed heavy on him. Suddenly, the birds' tones vibrated through the room at a different octave. Reynolds was troubled by the drop in tone of the birdsong, as if a record player had been switched from forty-five RPM to thirty-three RPM. Startled also by the sudden increase in gravity, he fell off his chair and looked up in astonishment.

A small spinning disk entered the room, passing through the outer wall as if solid matter didn't exist. The object reminded him of an item from his favourite comic book character's equipment—Captain America's shield, only unpainted and much more elegant as it glided, bright and smooth, captivating him with its grace. He was shocked and momentarily frozen with fear. A white light emanated from the centre of the saucer-shaped object, cascading beneath it like a waterfall of light.

Reynolds managed to stand up, propping himself against a nearby cast-iron radiator. He looked in the mirror, he screamed at his own alien reflection, then was shocked at the unfamiliar sound of his own voice. His face and hands were black with a slight red tinge, resembling an undeveloped negative, and his dark furniture was glowing white as if the colours had inverted. Reynolds drew parallels to his past experiences as a darkroom technician, experimenting with photographic negatives, which reversed the familiar tones and created a visually striking effect.

A cascade of light illuminated the floor, a vortex formed, and he felt himself being pulled towards it like water draining into a sink. He did his best to resist the gravitational forces as the floor fell away into the vortex.

As he fell through the enigma, a vivid vision struck him. He saw himself at the helm of his Avenger aircraft, lost in an orange fog. Both flight compasses were spinning, and he noticed the cockpit clock was missing and his watch read 7.17 a.m. His radio was full of garbled communication, and the fuel tank meter was reading virtually empty. His instrumentation spun like a compass sitting on a magnet; nothing worked. Before he could see anything else, he lost his grip and exited the vortex. He landed a few feet across the room with a punch, stunned but not physically hurt, aside from a few bruises from the fall.

That night, he suffered, tossing and turning as storms shook the ocean of his sleep.

The following day, Reynolds overslept and arrived late at the Naval Air Station Fort Lauderdale, Florida. He missed the pre-flight briefing with the four pilots and nine trainee co-pilot crewmen. There would have been ten trainees, one was recently promoted and didn't need to re-run this mission. His promotion gave the remaining young men optimism for their career pathways. The training crew was already on the runway, prepping the five Avengers for the flight. Unsettled by his vision, Reynolds had hoped that being late would disqualify him from flying the mission. He reported to the Operations Duty Officer, Commander Kenyon, and saluted.

"Reporting for duty, apologies for my tardiness, sir," he said, out of breath from sprinting.

"It is unprofessional and sets a bad example for your training crew, Captain. Make sure it doesn't happen again, or I will have you on report," Commander Kenyon said sternly.

"Sir, yes, sir!" Reynolds saluted. He paused for a second before continuing, "Sir, who will be replacing me for the flight?"

"Replacing you? Nobody. You know the mission, and you've had plenty of time to prepare, don't you think? Lieutenant Robert Savage ran the meeting, but you can lead the exercise," the commander said, growing short of patience.

"Sorry, sir. I just thought that because I missed the briefing, another flight instructor would have been assigned."

The commander scowled. "Well, Captain, we could do a 'sick, lame and lazy' report on you, but since you're here and you know the drill, I can see no reason why we can't proceed, can you?"

"It's nothing, sir. Request rescinded. Would you mind forgetting I asked? There's no need to file an official reprimand; it's just a bad morning, sir, it won't happen again." Reynolds held his head low in embarrassment. He didn't want to be grounded, and describing what had happened risked having his wings clipped permanently.

"Very well. You are dismissed, and have a good flight, Captain," the commander said. They saluted each other and went their separate ways.

Captain Reynolds met with his flight crew for a pre-flight pep talk. When he arrived, they were all standing beside their planes on the runway, joking and laughing.

"Good morning, gentlemen. I apologize for my tardiness."

"Afternoon sir, bad night, was it, captain?" Lieutenant Stivers said, laughing while straightening Reynolds collar. The crew all laughed at his unkempt appearance and out-of-character unprofessionalism.

"Okay, thank you, Lieutenant Stivers," Reynolds said with a tone of disapproving sarcasm. "Right, as you know, I'll be the flight leader for Flight 21. I'm sure you heard all this in full detail during the mission briefing that Lieutenant Savage delivered in my absence. I just want to summarize the training flight plan so we're all clear on our objectives before we begin. The mission is a routine two-hour patrol and bombing practice. Orders are to fly due east for a hundred and fifty miles, north for forty miles, and then return to base. The entire flight time is estimated to be two hours and fifteen minutes. Any questions before we start our run?"

"No questions, sir," they all said together.

"Very good. Let's have a swell flight, get our payloads on target, and come home. Remember we have live bombs for this training mission, so stay on target. Is everyone clear on the co-ordinates for the bombing target areas?"

"Yes, sir," they all replied simultaneously.

"Excellent. Lieutenant Savage, you'll take point, and I'll follow behind in a tracking position. Gentlemen, I want extra care taken on our pre-flight checks. I want each of you to ensure we have full tanks for this flight. Fall out, and man your planes."

Reynolds felt in control and had almost forgotten about his experience the previous night. The energy of the team encouraged his confidence, and he smiled with pride as he watched them all scramble to their three-seater Avenger torpedo bomber planes.

During the pre-flight checks, all wings reported in. Reynolds verified they each had their cockpit clocks and everything was in normal order. He was relieved. In his vision the cockpit clocks had been missing, thus he convinced himself the vision would not come to pass after all.

By now, their flight was thirty minutes behind schedule. It was a typical clear Florida day, and Reynolds was captivated by the view. The clear skies above gave him self-assurance; he drank up the milkshake sky, manoeuvring the plane's controls without a second thought. The weather in the nightmare had seemed simply out of this world, unnatural and impossible, a stark dissimilarity.

Flight 19 was running the same mission and was already airborne ahead of them. He reassured himself that if there were any trouble, his flight crew would hear about any problems ahead from Flight 19. In any case, any problems and the PBM Mariner rescue seaplane crews were ready to scramble; the rescue crews were well trained.

Each plane was piloted by qualified pilots with two training crew, with exception to one plane missing a trainee. The rookie pilots only had three hundred hours of flight time in the Avengers between them, while Reynolds was an experienced veteran of the South Pacific.

His concerns shifted back to his tardiness, and he shuddered at the thought of dealing with more repercussions from that on their return.

"All right, start your engines," he commanded. "Tower, this is Flight 21; we are ready for takeoff."

"Roger, Flight 21; you are cleared for takeoff," the tower replied indolently.

The first leg of their training mission along the coast went smoothly, and Grand Bahama soon should have been looming.

"Stay on target. Keep an eye out for the Bahamas; it's impossible to avoid. It should be in view any minute," Reynolds radioed across to Lieutenant Savage who had taken point.

The first two target derelict naval vessels came into view an hour later, and they spent the next thirty minutes practicing their runs. After mastering the runs, the forward two planes released their bombs and the two behind hitting the vessels with strafing runs, sinking the dummy ships. Swiftly returning back to formation on completion.

"Nice shooting chaps," Reynolds complimented, and as he said that, a massive vortex tunnel appeared in the air in front of them, leaving no time for evasive manoeuvres.

As the tunnel engulfed their planes, Reynolds addressed the squadron, “Everybody, hold your course. We don’t want to get lost. Don’t panic—we’ll get through this storm front.” He didn’t let on that he was scared; admitting fear in a crisis could have been fatal, and the crew needed Reynolds’ support as flight leader now more than ever.

Reynolds’ compass and flight equipment went crazy. The other crews reported the same instrumentation malfunctions happening on their planes too as they passed through the phenomenon.

Reynolds switched to the emergency channel. “Calling control tower. Emergency. We may have gone off course. We have zero visibility.”

The tower responded with a faint message, ordering him to head west.

“We can’t tell which way is west. Our navigational equipment is malfunctioning. Tower, do you copy, over?” But there was no response. “Visibility is near zero, with heavy, strange, orange fog. Savage, what does your compass read?”

“My compass is still haywire,” Savage replied.

“Okay, we have a little over one hour of fuel left, plenty of time to get back to base. Ease off the power and coast on low revs as much as we can. Ditch any remaining payloads into the drink.”

"Sir, we have less than that, straight route back we have plenty of fuel to get home, from our last known location any way, Sir, sorry Sir," called in one of the rookies.

"Us too Sir," Another rookie called in.

"Great, we have zero visibility, and our instruments are malfunctioning, add to that a fuel problem" Savage shouted in a panic, directing his frustration at Reynolds. "I suggest you inform the tower of it."

"Roger. I'll try and raise them again," Reynolds agreed, but all his attempts failed. "We need to stay calm and, when one of us gets a working compass, call in. We must have gotten lost after the last turn. We can get our bearings when this fog clears."

"I'm picking up another faint distress call from a Navy ship or plane, sir. They sound like they're lost as well," Savage said.

"I read it too, Savage, but it's mostly static. There is no way to know who it is. Maybe it's Flight 19?" Reynolds said, listening in to the call.

Broken communication chatter came from the unknown source, barely audible through the static. "This is the... *Ente...* We ha... visibility and... reddish-orange fog..."

"This is Captain Reynolds, Fox-Tare-Two-Nine. Mayday, mayday. Can anyone read us?"

There was no answer. Reynolds took point and

ordered the members of the squadron to hold their course and fly straight and steady behind him. They maintained course for a couple of hours. Savage continued to voice his frustrations, arguing that they were heading the wrong way.

"I think we must be over the Keys. There's an unfamiliar terrain just beginning to show below—it looks like a canyon or a broken landmass," Reynolds said, relieved that the bizarre fog had thinned for a short while.

The orange-red haze fogged their visibility, but there was enough clarity to see they were still within some kind of vortex.

Reynolds' comms sprang to life. "This is Fox-Tare-Seven-Three, FT-73 Captain West. I stand ready to assist. Do you copy?"

Reynolds reported back their last known co-ordinates and described their situation with as much detail as possible.

"Can you put the sun on your port wing and fly up the coast? That should take you in reach of Miami. I can change course to intercept you?" West said.

"Negative, instruments out, zero visibility, we appear to be in a fog within some kind of vortex, current location unknown." Reynolds looked at his reflection in the glass of his cockpit. His forehead was glowing with what looked like letters. He rubbed at the glass in disbelief, but the reflection remained, the word "Thoth" reflected back. He wondered what it all meant.

A burst of what looked like static from the storm struck his instruments and surged into his dog tags like a lightening streak, heating them with a sudden pulse of energy. He reached for them to remove them from under his clothes, resting them on top of his leather flight suit.

"FT-29, I read you. I am changing course to rendezvous at last known co-ordinates. What is your altitude?" he heard on the comms.

Suddenly something flew between their wing formations at incredible speed, ripping the air. The squadron's aircraft bucked like untamed stallions taking a noose for the first time. It was so fast all he saw was a blur, and the noise reverberated through him with enormous vibration.

"My God, what kind of bird is that?" Reynolds asked in dismay. His comms chatter picked up with confusion, all of his flight crew equally baffled.

"One of ours?" Lieutenant Savage asked.

Reynolds opted to refocus on the problem, despite his reminders, two of the rookies hadn't fully topped their tanks and now their fuel was down to the last quarter, plenty to get home in normal circumstances. But lost, they were running out of time.

"There are some breaks in the fog. Looks pretty

rocky down there. On top of that, we have an unidentified object travelling at incredible speeds. Some kind of jet-powered craft, I think. Listen, if we need to, we'll all ditch together best we can. When the first plane gets to its last couple of gallons remaining, we all go down together. Keep our tight formation so we stay together as much as possible. We will have to start flying low and slow, and if any of you see a good landing site, call in."

Reynolds looked down at the red, rocky landmass appearing beneath him and opened his canopy, trying desperately to improve visibility and find a safe place to land. His dog tags were getting uncomfortably warm again through the flight suit; he launched the chain out of his cockpit into the vortex. As he released it, a jolt of surprise coursed through him, as the high-speed craft roared overhead him at incredible speed once again. He didn't recognize the model or its advanced design; its twin-engine configuration and variable-sweep wings defined its beautiful and terrifying adaptability in high speed.

"Savage, did you see that thing? Is it one of ours? I swear I saw US markings."

Savage's response crackled. "The speed of that thing is incredible! Do you think it was a P-80? Did you really see US markings?"

Reynolds shook his head, his mind racing with possibilities. "It's way more advanced than anything I've seen—something incredible." His voice quivered with awe.

As they exchanged these words, the vortex closed around Flight 21, engulfed in a swirling sea of orange fog.

Chapter 2 – Origins in Chatham the Multiverse Awakens

Almost seven decades later, a young James Knight was about to have his first quantum moment with the Mandela field. He was engrossed in his rare vintage Captain America comic book. His fifth birthday was approaching, and he took a break from reading to dream of the toys he might get.

His mother bellowed from downstairs, "Hurry up and get ready! We want to see Nan and Grandad Knight today!"

"Aw, please, Mum! I'd love to stay and play a little while longer," Jim pleaded.

"Five minutes, and then I'm coming up to get you."

"Oh, all right," Jim said, disappointed.

Before Jim could begin to enjoy his remaining minutes, he froze in amazement as a small luminous disk glided into his room, passing through the wall as if it wasn't there. Jim covered his eyes, terrified, but then peeped through his fingers, unable to contain his curiosity. His mother's call slowed down, and dust particles hung motionless in the air.

A spiral formed within a cascade of light beneath

the disk, a beautiful galaxy swirling in his room. A trumpet sound groaned from the vortex, threatening to pull Jim in and tearing at space-time. Light glowed inversely. Trembling, Jim clung to the bed leg so tightly his hands hurt. His lip quivered, and he broke into tears.

He saw a vision of his parents with another baby in their living room. Jim wondered if he was seeing the future or dreaming. More images came—wave after wave of possible future events. He tried crying out for his mum, but his voice was distorted by the speeding air.

Something shiny swirled closer in the vortex, moving elliptically. Jim grabbed it as it passed, though he had no idea what it was. He slipped it over his neck. He looked at his clock and saw that time in his reality time had almost stopped—no one was coming to rescue him. Five old World War II planes faded into view within the vortex. Then he saw himself through the vision, a little older, playing with a younger child he guessed was his brother, on holiday at a caravan park.

He heard his mum's voice again, muffled and echoed through the vision. "Jeff! Jim! Dinner's getting cold!" The image faded, replaced by another one. Both boys were older now, and Jim was a teenager; he recognized a scar on his arm that confirmed it was him. The speed of the visions increased, and Jim struggled to keep up. Finally, he found himself staring into his own somewhat aged reflection, wearing a white lab coat.

"Jim!" the older version of him in the reflection shouted. "You must remember, Jim. Write it down so you can make sense of things!" The voice was eerie, chilling the little boy.

Jim then saw himself working in an office, supporting computers. One woman in the office vision was particularly striking, with blue eyes and strawberry-blonde hair, leaving a lasting impression on Jim.

The last images were the scariest. Jim saw himself in his thirties standing on a street, hugging the same woman and holding a child, all three staring at the sky in terror as the world began to change. Light was sucked into a dark purple spiral, like a cosmic sinkhole devouring the solar system. A deafening trumpet sound accompanied the carnage. Young Jim covered his ears, thankful the noise did not last long.

The moon grew larger as if clinging to Earth for safety from the anomaly. Planets were ripped from their orbits, swirling into the vortex—a massive brown dwarf, looming like a failed star, threatened to shatter Earth.

From Jim's vantage point, stood with his family in the vision, he appeared to be watching from the top of a hill; he saw across the valley, witnessing changes in the night sky, the stars streamed across the sky as if in a slow-shutter photograph, and in the town below. People were knocked off their feet as Earth's rotation shifted. Meteors began piercing the atmosphere and impacting the town, punching holes in buildings and crushing cars, sonic booms following each hit. There was nowhere to hide.

Jim lost his grip as the gravitational pull dragged him toward the vortex. With the spectrum effect reversed, he was thrown across the room. Then, everything returned to normal.

He looked into his mirror, and for a brief moment, he saw letters that read "Thoth" glowing on his forehead. If he'd blinked, he would have missed it. He had no idea what had happened or why, but he had been sealed.

His mother rushed in, hugged him, and asked, "Did you fall off your bed? Are you all right, Jim?" She picked him up and wiped his tears. Jim, wearing shorts, had grazed his knee from the fall. "It's all right. Let's go and see your Nan; she always makes you feel better.

Jim was relieved she didn't ask questions he couldn't answer. He stayed silent, just enjoying her company, heightening her concern. She asked about his nightmares, and all he could do was hold her tightly, unable to speak of his visions.

"Come on then, Jim, let's get going, shall we?

Jim was different now, quiet as he walked with his parents to his grandparents'. He held his arms in a cradle fashion.

"What are you doing, Jim?" his mum asked.

"I'm carrying my little brother, Jeff," Jim said,

smiling up at her.

Both his parents looked at each other in shock; they had only just found out they were having a baby a few days ago and hadn't told Jim yet. How could he have known? What surprised them even more was how he had guessed the name they had already agreed on, if it was a boy. His mother was speechless, which, for her, was rare.

Chapter 3 – Shattered Illusions of The Prime Reality

Jim was now twenty years old and had never told anyone about his strange childhood experiences. He had tried several times to talk to his parents, but had never found the words. He'd encountered the phenomenon a couple more times over the years, but none of the events was as impressive or intense as the first.

He still had the dog tags that had come out of the vortex that day. He had since discovered they were military dog tags, and he'd never taken them off. His mother often asked where he had found them, and never understood his truthful explanation that he had found them in his room. Four things stood out in his memory of that strange event—being so young, he couldn't remember all the visions, as there were so many. But what left its mark was the carnage he'd witnessed: the premonition of Jeff, the beautiful lady he assumed was his wife, and the World War II planes and subsequent dog tags.

Jim had worked hard to achieve his life goals. In school he had knuckled down to his studies. He had been disappointed that the subject of Flight 21 hadn't come up in his history classes, probably due to that being American history. But that hadn't stopped him reading all the information he could get his hands on in his own time. He had been investigating the name on the tag—Captain Max

C. Reynolds—and eventually uncovered that Reynolds was linked to the mystery of five General Motors TBM Avenger torpedo bombers, circa 1945, infamously lost in the Bermuda Triangle. The breakthrough had given him chills. How could he have dog tags from their mission? He had learnt everything he could about their flight, and even could recognise the missing five planes.

On one exceptionally hot Saturday, Jim was working overtime at Global Tech alone in the open-plan office. Jim was an IT Engineer there, doing office moves, shifting computers from desk to desk. The office needed rearranging, as teams were moving locations. It all seemed rather pointless to Jim, since the same teams and users would still be sitting together, but at opposite ends of the office—a swap of twelve for twelve desks. Some would get a better view perhaps. He pondered what office politics had played out to make such a move necessary. It was easy money, so Jim didn't really care, although he knew come Monday the users losing the view might have room for complaints. He intended to stay well out of those conversations and focus on resolving their IT-related issues and snagging.

While working under one of the desks, unplugging equipment ready to lift and shift, he misjudged the edge of the table and hit his head hard, letting out a yowl, followed by a sharp breath in between the teeth, reacting to the pain.

A sweet voice asked, "Are you all right?" Then a

giggle came from above.

"Yes, I think so," Jim said, rubbing his head. "I'm fine, thank you."

As he emerged from the desk space, he stumbled again in shock. He was staring into the striking blue eyes of the girl from his visions. Her slender yet curvaceous silhouette exuded grace and confidence, creating an enchanting presence, just as he had dreamed of ever since the first vision.

"What were you doing under my desk?" the girl asked.

He couldn't believe it; he'd thought the office had been empty. His possible future wife from the vortex vision had appeared seemingly from nowhere, or perhaps he had just not noticed her presence, busy in his work. He gazed, jaw open, utterly speechless.

"Err, y-y-y-you... you... err..." Jim stuttered, feeling somewhat embarrassed. "I'm working overtime. Desk moves."

"Well, thanks, lumpy. Are you giving me a better view?" She rubbed the sore bump on his head, pouting her lips. He winced as she touched the bump, which made her laugh.

"It just so happens, yes, this kit is moving way over there to the window area."

"Well, isn't that marvellous." She bent down,

exposing her cleavage, and kissed him on the cheek. Jim's pulse raced, and he was captivated by the heaving bosom thrust into his face. He was a blithering idiot. Not knowing what to do, he decided to engage her with some questions to avoid the uncomfortable advances.

"I thought I was here alone today. Where did you come from?"

"I was working late too, but I left as you arrived. I forgot my bag, so had to come back. Sorry if I startled you."

"No, it wasn't you; I just hit my head on the desk. Got up too quickly, is all." Jim noticed his dog tags had fallen out during the motion of hitting his head and standing up. He tucked them back in.

"Ooh, are they Army dog tags? Oh, yes, I like this. Were you in the Army?" she enquired, increasing her flirtations. Her soft hands brushed against his as she stroked his dog tags. "My name is Scarlett. I'm new to this town and don't know many people around here. I would like a... erm..." She contemplated for a moment. "A friend." She tried to look subtly at his work identification badge.

"Jim. My name is Jim," he said shyly, bewildered yet enjoying the attention. He wasn't used to girls being so full-on with him.

"Jim. Oh, I like that name. Very sexy," she said with a slow wink, erotically running her fingers from his dog tags down his chest.

"How old are you? How long have you worked here?"

"Ooh, so many questions. I've worked here a few months now. I thought I was alone too; the place looked deserted until you rattled my desk with your head. I'm nearly nineteen, perfectly legal, if that's what you were worried about," she quipped. "I know I look young, I'm pleased you were still here though, it's been lovely to meet you." She chuckled while packing a few things away into her bag to go home.

As they said their farewells, Jim couldn't help but notice her turn to take a second glance at him before closing the exit.

After that encounter, he found himself magnetically drawn to her whenever the opportunity arose. They began taking their lunch breaks together, slowly getting to know each other. Jim wondered if the relationship would ever blossom as he had foreseen in the visions; would she become his future wife? She was a bit too outrageous for Jim to handle, and at times he wondered if it could last. She would often shock him with some of the things she would come out with. One lunchtime, she opened up to Jim and described how she had got so drunk at the weekend that she had passed out, then woke the next day to find crap in her knickers. Jim thought it was hilarious, and they both laughed hard, but it wasn't the kind of conversation he could have had with anyone else. He felt honoured she trusted him enough to share such a story, and it was refreshing Scarlett didn't take herself too seriously.

He soon got used to expecting the unexpected. Scarlett's outlandishness got her into trouble at work a few times, and many people didn't like her humour. But neither of them was too fussed about what other people thought.

Over the course of a few weeks, and some flirtatious incidents, they finally made arrangements to meet up for an official first date. A double date, in fact, as Scarlett had invited her friend Alice, and Jim had arranged for his friend Chris to come as her blind date.

The evening was a great success; wine flowed as the girls sat and watched the lads kicking a ball around in the park. Eventually, Jim and Chris joined them to chill on the picnic blanket, enjoying drinks and nibbles and the warmth of a beautiful sunset. At the end of the night, Chris and Jim walked the girls back to Alice's house, where the girls were staying tonight.

Chris whispered to Jim, "I hope we get invited in for a bit more than a coffee." But they didn't even get past the front gate.

As they were saying goodbye, for some reason Jim and Scarlett both gazed up at the stars. At that moment, a bright shooting star zipped across the night sky. Both of them smiled, looked into each other's eyes and made a wish. Jim wondered if Scarlett had wished for the same thing, but neither of them revealed.

Jim pondered their future. Even with his insightful glimpses through the vortex, he had no idea what lay ahead.

Chapter 4 – Reality Torn Asunder

Jim, now into his thirties, had worked hard in the gym to sustain his physique, thinking naively that his fitness improved their likelihood of safety. Jim and Scarlett, like fine wine had only improved with age. They had their own place together and were happily married with a baby girl called Jerica, who completed the family. Later their family extended to include a cat called Moopsie, whom Jerica had chosen from the cat protection league rescue centre.

As the years had passed, Jim hadn't been able to shake off the haunting memories of the strange phenomena he had encountered. This was their universe, but he feared a tornado was on the horizon from his visions of another place and time. Reality used to be a friend, but no more; now it was a tormenting question of how long it would last. A few more encounters with the vortex had followed in recent years, and up until now he had avoided being pulled into it.

He had witnessed glimpses of different realities several times, and it haunted him. He recalled the kaleidoscope of past, present, and future, the great noise, gravitational forces tearing at the planet as the Earth died screaming. He worked hard not to dwell on those images, but the signs were there, hinting that, metaphorically, midnight was the hour of reckoning, and the doomsday clock was at five minutes to twelve.

Now, in the present, Jim found a moment of reflection as he put away clothes in their bedroom while Scarlett prepared sandwiches in the kitchen for the next day. It was a typical Thursday night, but something felt off.

Without warning, the anomaly emerged again. The small saucer-shaped object entered the room gracefully, emanating its mesmerizing, magnificent cascade of light, inverting all colours.

As before, time seemed to slow down. Jim knew he was about to experience another journey through the vortex, but he was ill prepared for what horrors awaited him. Fear gripped his heart as he remembered the multiverse of realities he had glimpsed, the different paths his life could have taken. He gripped his dog tags, feeling them start to warm up.

The spinning disk of light enveloped him, and he experienced an exhilarating sensation as he was propelled with velocity through the cosmic vortex, traversing the boundless expanse of space and time. This time, Jim had nothing to grip or secure to, powerless to do anything against the gravitational pull of the vortex; he just had to go with the flow. He fell through the portal, falling through the strange tunnel for a short period. He soon landed on the other side of the same room. He looked around at his surroundings, which felt both familiar yet subtly altered. He noticed new curtains and different photos on display, and called out frantically for his wife and daughter.

"Scarlett, where are you? Jerica, it's Daddy—where are you both?"

In a frenzy, he scoured every room of the house—twice, then thrice—thrashing around outside for her car and dashing back in, repeatedly looking for his wife's clothes, or anything that might offer a clue. He checked the same places for signs of his missing family, uncertain what to do next or if he could even trust his own eyes. He went round in circles, hoping for different results but coming back to the same conclusions. Even their cat, Moopsie, was gone without a trace.

His frantic search revealed nothing but an echoing emptiness within his home. To his horror, not only were his wife and child missing, all of their belongings had vanished without a trace, as if they had been erased from existence. The reality he had once known had dramatically shifted, leaving the house resembling a bachelor pad more than a family home. The house exuded a sleek independence, characterised by minimal décor, a touch of spontaneous creativity in a contemporary style he liked but his wife often rejected. It was missing the harmonious blend of shared tastes and personal touches. What was once cosy and inviting, reflecting a compromise of styles and preferences, with a mix of sentimental items, was now very bland and functional. Even their cosy chair in the snug, a place where they often enjoyed relaxation and togetherness, was missing, everything transformed.

Nothing made sense. Jim phoned his mother in the hope of finding some answers. "Mum, what is going on? Where are Scarlett and Jerica?"

After a pause, his mum said in a tone of genuine concern, "What do you mean? Are you okay? Do you want me to come over?"

"Just tell me where they are, Mum."

"But you know Scarlett and Jerica were both murdered. The police found them in the park near you. You identified the bodies. Why are you asking me this?" His mother broke into tears while trying to get the words out.

Jim collapsed to his knees, dropping the phone. He looked up into the mirror above the fireplace. His face turned red with rage as he screamed at the top of his voice, "No!"

Rage contorted Jim's features, morphing into a heavy sadness that welled up in his eyes, eventually spilling over into tears as the shocking reality unfolded before him.

* * *

He waited weeks, then months, for the anomaly to return so that he could try to put things back the way they were and return to his former reality. He became a recluse; he tried over and over, begging his dog tags and praying to God to help him summon the vortex, but it was in vain.

While living with such crippling loss, he also discovered during his daily existence that in this universe he had won a lottery windfall, and additionally a life insurance policy payment in her death. He found it curious they hadn't moved to a massive house, as he had imagined they might do. He tried to find out when his win had come, and was momentarily relieved to find out that they had had a good eighteen months to enjoy the money together. He considered whether the money had had anything to do with the murders, whether some greedy, jealous people were trying to take it all. He would have gladly given it all to have Scarlett and Jerica back. The money in his bank account was little compensation for the loss he was enduring, and he had no interest in it whatsoever.

In his solitude, he desperately searched for a doorway to other realities, immersing himself in ancient alien theories, portals, time anomalies, and mythological stories. Through online research, library studies, and meditation, he became an expert on phenomena like vortexes and the Bermuda Triangle. He gathered books and documentation about ancient apocalypses and legends such as the fabled ninth planet Nibiru. During the long months that passed, he had taken trips to ancient sites to see for himself the stone carvings depicting the returning brown dwarf causing devastation to Planet Earth, a warning not heeded by humanity, laughed off as conspiracy theories. Each trip had lead him back home with more knowledge, but sadly more questions than answers.

He tore at the dog tags, launching them across his bedroom in anger, then crawled back to hug them in desperation, begging for a miracle.

His research into the Mandela effect gave him some curious insights. There were changes not only in his own perception of reality—other people experienced them too, fortunately for them in much more subtle ways. Most notably, many people remembered Mandela dying in prison in the eighties, yet now he seemed to have lived into 2013, hence the name of the effect. For Jim, the missing Flight 21 in this reality was known as Flight 19. There was a whole host of anomalies, so many it seemed unlikely to Jim that it could be a medley of people misremembering the same things, as the conspiracy debunkers would have him believe.

Jim spent hours, days, months downloading and researching anything he could find related to similar changes in the timeline. Some of the changes were shocking, such as Eric Stolz starring in *Back to the Future*, as Marty McFly, and other films he had watched so many times he had lost count had subtle dialogue changes, notably *Star Wars: The Empire Strikes Back*—it now made no sense, as he vividly recalled Vader saying "Luke, I am your father," in the pivotal moment in the whole saga. Even the economics of this world vastly differed; it was a time of worldwide depression, food was scarce and jobs were hard to come by.

Jim also researched his own predicament more.

Fortunately he found he had kept a diary and soon realised that after the windfall they had kept the win secret. He hadn't even told his parents how much he had won. He not only hadn't moved, he had turned up for work as normal up until Scarlett and Jerica's deaths. He had a new car, but it wasn't an extravagant one. He had always pictured himself driving a Ferrari, but now he saw himself as in a living death. There was little meaning to his life without his family. He learnt from the diary, the lottery windfall had helped clear this realities Jim from being a murder suspect. The insurance pay out was a significant amount, but the detectives ruled it out as motive since he had no need for any more money. Jim's emotional state from the loss of his family and his failed attempts to summon the vortex sank him into depression and drink.

Continuing but merely existing, Jim phoned his old friend Chris for much-needed support.

"Easy, tiger," Jim said to Chris, as this was their customary greeting.

"Easy," Chris replied.

"How are things with you, bud? How's your brother Bullet doing? I haven't seen you all in so long."

"Are you winding me up? You remember we all went to his funeral, right?"

"Sorry, sorry, I'm not myself. This whole thing is making me feel like I'm losing my mind."

"Sure, I understand you've been through a lot, mate, it does mess with your head," Chris said.

"Do you remember our lads' holiday?" Jim asked.

"Of course I do. We had a wicked time. Bullet was such an idiot on that trip to Magaluf, wasn't he? Remember when the coastguard had to rescue him on that £10 inflatable? He tried to paddle out to that tiny island and ended up caught in a current, drifting out to sea. Alex and Chad were on proper *top* form that holiday too—with all the booze, nightclubs, hotties. Man, we had a good youth, didn't we?"

Chris shared a laugh with Jim. It had been a while since he'd felt this kind of joy, and the moment really lifted him.

"Dude, something's off—this timeline is messed up. Bullet, Scarlett, Jerica... they should *all* be here. I'm not feeling right. We'll talk later. I need a night out, a drink. When you're free, let me know," Jim uttered, his voice heavy with confusion.

Jim felt Chris's hesitation through the phone line. The weight of his distress hung in the silence, and Chris's unspoken confusion was clear.

"Err, no worries, dude. We'll catch that drink soon," Chris replied, his tone subtly tinged with concern that Jim noticed. The call ended with Jim hanging up, leaving an unsettled atmosphere in the wake of the conversation.

Jim resolved with newfound determination to find a way back to his former life. However, he grappled with the uncertainty of how to achieve it.

The vortex was an enigmatic force, and though it held the answers he sought, its ways were still mysterious.

Chapter 5 – Fortune's Dark Side

Now that Jim had travelled into this alternate, hellish reality where everything he cared about was gone, he had never felt so trapped and alone. It had been close to two years—he'd lost count of the exact date he'd lost everything—and he hadn't seen any hint of the vortex.

The wealth he had brought mostly superficial comfort; however, it did give him the opportunity to study after quitting his job. He'd relished in paying off his parents' remaining mortgage and ensuring they had enough to enjoy their retirement. He now had his dream Ferrari, kept in the garage, covered in dust, barely used. Driving the nice car wasn't the thrill he had expected without the love of his life to share it with. He'd also helped his brother by paying off his mortgage and surprisingly found more joy in the giving than his car or other toys, such as his collection of motorcycles.

He'd decided to use his money to do as much good as possible. He spent most of his spare time researching every phenomenon he could—astronomy, history, philosophy, ancient cultures, to name a few. He couldn't shake the unwavering desire to get back to the way things were. He wished he had never seen the infernal portal; he would have gladly given it all up to have his family back.

Jim didn't want to donate all of the money to a charity without knowing where it would end up, so he took a trip to London. He invested in property, purchasing three relatively low-priced houses in a row. Although the houses needed some redecorating, they were generally in good order. Jim had no interest in property development; he had a different agenda in mind—a mission of kindness.

He had filled three large wheeled suitcases with fifty-pound notes. He installed safes in each home and filled the contents of the suitcases equally in each of his new properties and took a couple of thousand with him. As he wandered the streets of London, he came across a homeless couple sitting on sheets of cardboard, huddling under a blanket. Placed before them was a hat filled with change. Jim wondered how they had fallen into this situation. He had already decided to help people, but he wanted to ensure his money wouldn't be used for any harmful habits, so he struck up conversations with the homeless people he encountered, trying to get to know them better. However, he found it increasingly difficult to get them to speak honestly. That was when he realised that to truly understand, he would have to become one of them.

Jim bought a new long, thick, warm coat and offered to exchange it for a somewhat smashed homeless man's full-length, smelly, rotten overcoat. The man was grateful for the gift. Jim finally blended in with the crowd and disappeared into the streets. He couldn't help this individual further; the needle marks on his arms indicated he would only descend further into his habit with the money Jim planned to give away. Jim had told him to go to a clinic on the corner of Derby Street, where he had donated money to help homeless addicts and had paid for the soup kitchen next door to be refurbished and to add dwellings for cold nights.

That evening, at the back of Victoria Park, Jim walked through the bitter wind into the unknown. A conglomeration of lost souls awaited him, gathered around a small fire. He might have missed them had it not been for the faint glow visible through the overgrowth. Nervous, but determined, he approached them. They were only interested in keeping warm, just as he was at that moment. As the sun set, the temperature dropped significantly.

Jim noticed that the members of the group helped each other stay warm, and he admired their camaraderie. Staying out of sight, he decided to turn back and visit the nearby coffee shop he had spotted earlier. There, he ordered seven hot baguettes filled with sausage, bacon, and egg, plus three cups of coffee and four cups of tea. He asked the owners to watch where he went within the park, and to deliver the order on a serving tray to the group sitting around the fire—and to wait a couple of hours before bringing it over.

Swiftly returning to the park, he introduced himself.

“Hi. My name is Jim,” he greeted them, a disarming smile playing on his lips. “May I join you?” He acknowledged the suspicious glares with an open, non-threatening stance, inviting trust through genuine warmth and approachability with his humble tone and open body language.

They nodded in unison, but no one was in the mood to talk. He sat with them quietly, almost in a trance as he stared at the fire for quite some time. Finally, he broke the silence, turning to each of them in turn. He engaged each person with the same question: "Can you tell me what's most valuable to you right now?"

Their heartfelt answers revealed their immediate needs and desires. Tasha treasured her large blanket, which she shared with her friends to help keep them warm. Ian valued his relationship with Sammi, finding strength in their love for each other. Marcus appreciated the plastic sheet that now served as the roof of their shelter, keeping the five of them dry on rainy nights. Jana was much quieter and it was difficult to get through her defensive barriers.

Jim had built a rapport with most of them, and they openly shared what had transpired in each of their lives to land them here together. Most of them were victims of the Second Great Depression; he learnt the park was filled with homeless people in this reality. Inflation had brought mortgage rates so high that their once-affordable mortgages were no longer manageable. The banks had foreclosed on them, jobs were lost as the economy collapsed, and here they were. No drug problems, nothing sinister, just unfortunate circumstances and the usual economic greed from those in power. Jim checked his watch; it was nearly delivery time.

"Is there anything to eat? I don't know about anyone else but I'm starving." Jim was unprepared for a sarcastic response.

"Hungry? No, we're never hungry. We eat whenever we want at the most expensive restaurant in town," Tasha replied with a cackle.

His timing was perfect, as behind him the young girl brought the food over within a moment of the foreboding laugh.

In response to the sarcasm, he smiled and decided there was no point in hiding the fact he had paid for their lunches. "Please, my friends enjoy this food; it's a gift from me to you, thanking you for the pleasure of your company." Jim beamed ear to ear.

Their eyes instantly lit up at the sight and smell of the fresh food and hot drinks. Jim let the group choose what they wanted first, and they all thanked the young girl, and Jim for paying for it. They enjoyed the warmth of the fire more comfortably with food and hot drinks in their bellies. Jim felt a sense of contentment as he witnessed the impact of his kindness and their expressions of gratitude. Tasha described him as her "angelic stranger".

After their food, the others drifted off to sleep, while

Jim and Tasha shared an extended moment. The passing hours were marked by a connection that went beyond words. As Tasha continued to convey her tragic story, Jim's attentive listening and the shared vulnerability deepened their bond. Tasha's voice trembled, and her eyes welled with tears.

"I don't normally open up like this. I'm sorry." She nestled her head into his neck, and he felt her tears on his skin. This unguarded display served as powerful evidence of the profound intimacy between them, as his skin tingled with her touch, culminating in a passionate smooch initiated by her. Marcus had just woken up in time to witness their kiss and responded with a whoop that stirred the others.

"I don't know what it is, but when I look at you, I feel like I've known you my whole life," Tasha said to Jim.

"Oooh, we have a new love in the caravan of no-hopers," Marcus joked.

Startled and embarrassed, Jim found himself lost for words, but Tasha had it covered. Jim laughed when she punched Marcus's arm; he could tell Marcus felt that punch, as he soon backed down and the laughter in the group broke the awkwardness.

Jim changed the subject, "Tell me, what are your dreams, what if you had a house to share, what would that be like?"

The question hung in the air as the group fell silent. Jana's gaze drifted to the fire, her eyes reflecting the flickering flames as her brow furrowed in contemplation. The others shifted uncomfortably, their eyes avoiding Jim's and each others, lost in their own thoughts.

Jana's voice finally broke the silence, soft but resolute. "It's not really about having a house. What matters is us. No matter what happens, we stick together, we stay warm and dry together and we share what we have. That's what really counts."

Jim revealed his truth: he had some properties that were fully paid for but needed some work. He wanted them to stay in those three houses, rent-free, to renovate and look after them. In return, he asked them to stay out of trouble and try to find jobs, or work for charity if there was nothing else available. If they succeeded, Jim promised that, one day, he would return and give them the deeds to the houses, making them homeowners. Overwhelmed with gratitude, they eagerly accepted the offer and became resolute in proving themselves. Jim told them to be prepared for the day he would check in on their progress.

"We need to know when, or we'll always be wondering," Jana cried.

"I'll aim to come back in two years, give or take a few months, to see how you're all getting on. However, don't worry if I don't return—it means I'm no longer here, and you just stay there rent free as long as you like." Jim replied.

"What do you mean, no longer here?" Tasha asked.

"I'm hoping to go on a trip. If I do, it could be a one-way ticket. I may not be able to come back."

Tasha was all the more curious and kept pressing Jim for information, but he kept changing the subject. They all spent the night together in the park under the tarp; Jim enjoyed the sound of the rain and the fresh smell of the air, although none of them really slept, the harsh conditions keeping them semi-awake. He could tell, most of them understandably didn't believe the offer was real, their suspicious whispers were not overly subtle.

Tasha was the only one who didn't participate in their doubts. Jim forged a deep emotional connection with her that night, their closeness transcending physical boundaries, finding warmth in simple hugs. For reasons he couldn't quite articulate, Jim chose to share one of his dog tags with her, a symbol of their new bond.

"Wherever we go next, we'll always be connected with our shared half of the dog tags," Jim said as she attached it to her necklace. He too felt like he had known her for years—perhaps another lost reality he had vague recollections, a personal Mandela effect.

The following morning, Jim showed the group the location of the houses, a stone's throw from the park, and handed them the keys. He explained once again the details and conditions of the exchange, encouraging them to stay clean and out of trouble.

As he left the group, an unfamiliar sensation overcame him: a surge of purpose and joy that had been absent since his loss. His fingers tightened around the remaining dog tag, and a subtle yet electrifying vibration ran down his spine, sending tingles through every nerve, as a wave of positive energy enveloped him.

Out of nowhere, the anomaly tugged at him. Time seemed to stretch, and the vortex began to unfold once more, larger and more potent than during any previous encounter. As the colours inverted around Jim, a whirlwind of emotions swept through him, each shift mirroring a different facet of his inner turmoil—warm shades of hope mingling with cool tones of fear, anticipation blending with trepidation in a kaleidoscope of conflicting thoughts as his mind went wild with what-ifs. Yet this was the moment he had longed for, so *excitement* was foremost in his mind.

Taking a deep breath, he spread his arms wide and surrendered to the gravitational forces that propelled him into the vortex, eager to explore the uncharted reality that awaited. He welcomed the anomaly, followed swiftly by a moment of fear at the unknown.

Chapter 6 – Confronting Loss in Hellish Reunions

Jim found himself in an unfamiliar living room, disoriented by the reality shift; he pulled himself together and began looking for any recognisable things. The space exuded a sense of serene simplicity, with sleek furniture and uncluttered surfaces defining each room, not his house but an unfamiliar modern flat.

In the living area, a low-profile sofa in neutral tones provided a comfortable spot to relax, complemented by a simple coffee table and a few decorative accents—a sculptural vase here, a minimalist art piece there. Floor-to-ceiling windows flooded the room with natural light.

The kitchen boasted sleek cabinetry with handleless design, blending seamlessly into the space. A polished marble countertop added a touch of luxury, while a row of pendant lights hung above the breakfast bar, casting a warm glow over the minimalist dining area.

Throughout the flat, Jim's personal items were tastefully displayed, adding personality without overwhelming the space. A selection of books lined a built-in shelf; his doppelganger from this reality had clearly been doing the same research into the Bermuda Triangle and other strange phenomena such as the Mandela effect, the multiverse, space and time, ancient mythology and similar explained and unexplained scientific phenomena. On the mantle, a framed black-and-white photograph of him and Scarlett together caught his eye.

Fumbling with his phone in his agitated state, he finally managed to unlock it and dialled Scarlett's number, but there was no answer. He tried again and again, growing increasingly anxious. The worry that Scarlett and Jerica might not be in this reality overwhelmed him, but he knew there was nothing more he could do at the moment except get home as fast as possible.

Jim called a taxi and asked the driver to take him home—at least the address he knew as home, not this unfamiliar flat. While waiting he went through his phone contacts and noticed that within Scarlett's contact there was an unfamiliar number listed as *Home*. Home for him was always his house with Jerica and Scarlett, even though he had grown up at his parents'; in present time it was a clear divide.

With a mix of excitement and dread, Jim called the home number. To his relief, Scarlett answered. However, when he tried to speak he found himself panic-stricken and struggling for words. Finally, he managed to ask her to meet him at their house.

Scarlett agreed, but her confusion and frustration were evident in her tone. Jim couldn't wait to see her and their daughter Jerica again, and his emotions overwhelmed him.

When Jim arrived, he paid and leapt out of the taxi and didn't have to wait long before Scarlett came out to greet him. He ran to her and embraced her tightly, tears of joy streaming down his face. At first, Scarlett's response was cold, but she eventually hugged him back, trembling.

They sat on the sofa together. Jim wanted to tell Scarlett everything, but he held back for the moment. They shared a passionate kiss, but Scarlett pulled away, asking to talk instead.

"Scarlett, what happened to us and where is Jerica? I can't wait to see her," Jim said.

"Jerica? Who's Jerica?" Scarlett's brow furrowed in confusion.

"Oh, Scarlett, it's... it's Jerica," Jim stammered, his voice tinged with disbelief. Jim's heart sank as he realized the truth. "Jerica... our daughter," he said, his voice barely above a whisper. "So, she doesn't exist here." His vision blurred as tears welled up in his eyes and his breaths came out in ragged gasps as he hyperventilated.

"Stop! Please," Scarlett said, reaching out to him. "Jerica? Who is that? You keep mentioning her. Do you mean Jemima?"

As Scarlett spoke, Jim's heart clenched, a pang piercing through him like a jagged shard. Grief and confusion surged through him like a raging storm. His knuckles turned white as he fought the urge to scream, to unleash the pent-up fury at the merciless hand fate had dealt him. Yet, in the midst of turmoil, a flicker of hope emerged—a desperate wish that, despite the altered reality, his daughter remained unchanged apart from her name, her essence untouched by the cruel whims of fate.

“What the hell are you talking about? Jemima—tell me about her. Could you show me a photograph, please?”

“She’s your daughter, I know not biologically, but in more important ways. You have always been there for her when she needed you.” Scarlett broke into tears, but it was clear she was trying to hold it together to continue the conversation. “Did you call me out here to have this conversation again, or to get back with me, or to torture me? This was why we broke up, don’t you remember?” Scarlett cried as she grabbed the nearest photo frame of the three of them together.

Jim’s features contorted as he tensed his facial muscles, fighting to conceal more tears threatening to escape. The sight of Jemima, bearing no resemblance to him, made it feel more real, like a hazy nightmare becoming reality and punching home the acknowledgement Jerica didn’t exist here.

Scarlett’s fists clenched and the tremor in her voice betrayed her pent-up frustration. The light that once danced in her eyes had dimmed, replaced by a haunting vacancy that sent a shiver down Jim’s spine. He could almost taste the bitterness radiating from her, a tangible manifestation of her hidden anguish.

Summoning his courage, Jim locked eyes with Scarlett, searching for a glimmer of the spirited woman he had fallen for. Yet her gaze, once ablaze with passion, now flickered with a cold detachment that chilled him to the core. Despite the looming discomfort, he knew he had to press on, to breach the barriers shielding her wounded heart. With a heavy sigh, he steeled himself to pose the question that lingered like a dark cloud over their strained relationship.

"I don't understand, if Jemima is your daughter, why am I not—?" Jim cried out in an unfinished sentence.

"Did you hit your head at work again? I can't believe you're saying this! You know why!" she raged. "You were with me for the trial! The animal is in prison for what he did to me!"

"Prison? No. I-I-I don't understand what the hell has happened here. I literally have no memory of any of this. I'm sorry—can you tell me again, please?" Jim was trembling as he spoke.

"How can you not remember this? It's the single most devastating thing that happened to me, and it destroyed us! You just can't forget something like that!" she screamed at him, red-faced and spitting words. "HE RAPED ME! THERE—ARE YOU HAPPY NOW?"

Jim's thoughts careened in every direction,

desperately seeking clarity in the chaos of the moment. Yet all he found was a suffocating sense of betrayal by a reality that seemed intent on unravelling before his eyes, and anger for the person who had done this to his beloved family. He longed to reach out to Scarlett, to find solace in her embrace, but the weight of their unspoken tension hung heavy in the air, suffusing the room with a palpable despair. This place, once familiar, now felt foreign and hostile, a cruel twist of fate that left Jim grappling with the harsh reality before him. The prospect of forging a life in this altered reality, with Scarlett by his side yet not truly the wife he knew, loomed dauntingly. The thought of mourning his own daughter while raising another man's child in her stead was something he was ill prepared to think about in this moment.

"I'm so sorry, Scarlett," Jim choked out, "I don't know how this could have happened. But please believe me when I say that I do love you, and I wish I could do something to make this right."

Scarlett's expression softened slightly. In her eyes, there was a haunting glimmer of sorrow, a shadow that underscored the fragile smile on her lips. Despite the hint of warmth, a deeper pain remained, visible in the sadness that lingered within the depths of her glazed eyes.

"I don't know if I can believe you, Jim. It hurt so much when you pushed me away. I know it was years ago, but I still find it hard to get over the memories of how you shut down completely after the incident. And when you said you didn't know if you could bring up another man's child it nearly destroyed me." Scarlett took a deep breath, trying to steady her emotions. "I want to believe you, Jim, but it's going to take time. I can't just forget all the hurt and heartache we went through because of this. Why can't you just try and think 'he is not her father, only a sperm donor'? It's how I try to compartmentalise it. I didn't want it to happen this way, but I do want and love Jemima."

"I understand," Jim said. "I know I don't deserve your forgiveness right now, but please know that I love you."

"I don't expect you to be able to handle all of this right away," Scarlett said, her voice softened by exhaustion. "But I need you to understand that Jemima does see you as her father. We stayed together for years and in that time you were always there for her. And she needs you, her real father in every sense other than the biological. Even when you moved out, all she talks about is when she'll see you again. I'm grateful you kept your word and made time for her every other weekend—even if it's just for a few hours, she cherishes it."

Scarlett agreed to let him stay the night. Scarlett gently cradled his head against her chest, offering comforting solace as they both let their tears flow. "How strange it is," Scarlett began. "I should be angry, but then I realised we haven't connected like this in ages, not since... well, you know."

As the two sat in the living room, Jim continued to learn the painful truth of what had transpired. It was a harrowing tale. Talking about it appeared to be something his counterpart in this reality had not been able to do and he could understand why. But it was what Scarlett had needed, and the failure to do so that had led to, or at least been a factor in, their broken relationship in this timeline.

Scarlett explained she had been out for a run, only to be accosted by two men in the nearby woods. One was an Irish man called Benson and the other his half-brother Shafto by the same mother.

"You have to understand, Shafto is not like anyone else. He's tall and gaunt, almost like he's starving. It gives him this unnerving, predatory look, like he's always hunting. His teeth... ugh, they're yellowed and jagged, like tombstones, a grim reminder that he doesn't care about himself at all. He tries to appear tidy, but that just makes his unnatural thinness even creepier.

And his skin! It's sallow and sickly, and his eyes—God, those eyes—they're cold and calculating, glinting with this sinister intelligence that makes you want to run away. He moves with this disquieting grace, like every step is planned, like he's always lurking just out of sight, ready to pounce when you least expect it. He's a walking nightmare, but somehow, he always manages to play the underdog."

Jim listened intently, holding his hand over his mouth in shock and unable to speak as he heard how,

Shafto had held her down while Benson had violated her.

"Benson is a monster. Just thinking about him makes my skin crawl. I can't shake the memory of his rotting teeth, stained and uneven, forming that grotesque grin of his. His greasy hair and that perpetual scowl are forever burned into my mind.

He wears that worn-out leather jacket like it's a second skin, and it's clear he crossed a line long ago, becoming something far worse than human. Even now, I can almost smell him—a sickening mix of sweat, stale cigarettes, and the foul stench of decay that lingered long after he was gone.

Those dark, soulless eyes haunt me, always watching, taking pleasure in the fear he instilled. He thrives on intimidation and chaos. I despise him more than anyone. He's a sadist, and I was just another victim."

The tragic event had unfolded almost three and a half years ago. The child's father, Benson Dante, had been identified and tracked down through DNA, while Shafto remained a fugitive. Scarlett recounted the traumatic experience in detail, describing Benson's foul breath and oppressive presence. Overwhelmed by the memories, she shivered, apologizing as if she were to blame. Jim, deeply moved, offered support by simply listening, reassuring and being there for her.

Through this process of communicating and healing, Scarlett's demeanour shifted, her eyes lighting up with a newfound warmth and tenderness. It was as if the first tendrils of love were unfurling within her, evident in the softness of her smile and the gentle way she looked at him. It was obvious it would not be the same love they had once shared. But it had the potential to blossom into a stronger and more resilient devotion, forged through the trials they had faced and the hardships they had overcome. Except it wasn't Jim who had faced these trials—his counterpart in this reality had failed to cope on an epic scale with the tragedy. Jim's mind shifted for a moment; he was torn whether to continue his mission to get back to his own reality or to stay and support his broken wife in this one. He wondered if he even had a choice.

There were two problems. The first was that he would have to give up on ever seeing his own daughter Jerica again. He was grateful that Scarlett hadn't remembered to press him about who Jerica was, for now at least. She hadn't seemed to process the topic, consumed by her own grief. The vortex might have taken much from him, but it had also given him the chance to find what truly mattered—boundless love across time and space. This was the second problem. Would he be able to stay or would the vortex rip him away yet again?

The next morning, Jim awoke to an empty room. He could hear Scarlett bashing pans around in the kitchen preparing breakfast, but he couldn't go to her. As currents of vortex energy pulled at him, Jim grasped for the bedpost—but it was too late. He found himself adrift in an endless void of darkness, lost in absolute emptiness. As he floated, weightless and disoriented, memories flashed by in fragments—a turbulent stream of moments from his original reality and from the myriad alternate dimensions he'd visited.

Glimpses of happy memories with Scarlett, joyous times with Jerica, and the pain endured all merged in a chaotic whirl. He couldn't decipher the tangled timeline of his life. A deep longing gnawed at him to return to his prime reality, the one he'd known before the vortex consumed his existence.

In the midst of this confusion, he held on to hope that this Scarlett he'd left behind might be able to take the healing they had started forward with his doppelganger. It all depended on his other self. Perhaps if he awoke in Jim's place and found her in a good place, they might have a chance, albeit a small one.

Jim stared into the void and saw visions of his own Scarlett and Jerica, holding each other tightly. He cried out to them, but they couldn't hear him. They stared blankly, as if they could see but not hear him—was he a ghost? They were older, and behind them he could see the world in chaos, as he had done many times before. They were outside observing across a valley. Jim saw people and cars floating up from the earth into the sky, and other people falling from the sky in opposition, as gravity came and went. A tremendous earthquake ripped the ground apart, and a crevasse appeared inches away from the family. Jim stood in awe of the apocalyptic scene and observed that Scarlett and Jerica remained safe, and that upon their foreheads were the glowing white letters "Yhwh". He didn't know what it meant, but he was beginning to realise it could be significant and that he would have to remember the letters for research later. As he continued to watch, he saw the ground open up further beneath them. They were floating in mid-air and appeared terrified as the world around them descended into chaos.

In the midst of this confusion, a deep voice echoed in the darkness, like a guiding presence cutting through the chaos.

"James, my child, do not be afraid," the voice said. "You have traversed the boundaries of existence, and in doing so, you have seen the vastness of the multiverse. But fear not, for you are not lost. Your journey is not over, and there is still much to discover."

Jim listened to the voice. It was as if he was being reassured that there was a purpose to his journey, that he was not alone in this vast expanse of possibilities.

"Remember, James, the path ahead isn't set in stone," the voice persisted. "You hold the power to carve your own destiny, weaving a fresh reality from the fabric of your encounters and choices."

As Jim pondered his next move, the oppressive darkness receded; giving way to a radiance that emerged from the very heart of the swirling vortex. Drawn towards this luminous beacon, Jim felt the pull of reality beckoning him back from the depths of the unknown.

Chapter 7 – Uncovering Dark Secrets of Manipulative Agents

As Jim's consciousness slowly returned, he awakened to an entirely alien environment. Unlike previous encounters, where a faint sense of familiarity lingered even in the most peculiar of circumstances, this place offered no such comfort. Panic surged within him as he struggled to communicate through a hazy fog, his pleas for help muffled by the confines of a breathing apparatus, its tubes twisting off to an unknown contraption. His words emerged disjointed and indistinct, obscured by the plastic mask that had accumulated condensation as he gasped in delirium.

Drugged and struggling to focus, Jim realised he was lying on a hospital trolley, dressed in a flimsy paper gown with IV tubes snaking into his arm. The drip beside him was nearly empty, and its contents had left him drowsy and barely able to move his limbs. It took several feeble attempts, but Jim eventually managed to roll off the surgical table, severing the connections and chest monitoring leads. He winced, expecting pain, but the high dosage of drugs left him oddly numb.

Surveying his surroundings, he noticed rows of beds in which were people in similar states, all incapacitated and tethered to IV drips. Instinct told him he needed to escape before someone realised he had awakened. He tried to move his arms, but partial paralysis hampered his efforts. With grim determination, he dragged himself along the floor, keeping out of sight amidst the beds. From the shape of the walls and roof, he surmised he was in a vast aircraft hangar, which once might have been bustling with the activity of airplanes. Now it resembled a makeshift hospital ward. Rows of hospital beds stretched out as far as the eye could see, occupied by individuals clad in hospital gowns, their faces obscured by ventilation masks and tubes and leads winding from machines beside them. The cavernous space echoed with the hum of machinery and the soft murmur of a couple of medical staff attending to the patients in the distance.

As he continued his crawling, Jim noticed the row numbers dwindling in the distance, each one a sobering reminder of the magnitude of the situation, for there were so many. When he reached the marker for "Volunteer 143,895," disbelief washed over him. Had he truly volunteered for this? The revelation struck him with a profound sense of shock, leaving him to grapple with the unsettling reality that he had willingly subjected himself to whatever nightmarish experiments lay ahead, or was it something else entirely? A medical treatment in response to a virus or plague, perhaps?

As he pondered further, doubts began to creep in. Was this volunteer program merely a guise, masking a more sinister agenda? With more questions than answers swirling in his mind, Jim resolved to refrain from drawing hasty conclusions until he had gathered more information. Jim strained to get a better look at the other volunteers, but one of them had already succumbed to whatever was going on here.

Spotting an unopened water bottle on a nearby bed, Jim took a cautious sip before pocketing it. Though he was weakened, the refreshment revitalised him enough to stand. He used the beds for support as he staggered onwards.

"Jana," he whispered to himself, recognizing one of the vagrants from the park he had helped in the alternate reality. He doubted very much they would volunteer for this ordeal; instead, they had been the ideal test subjects for something sinister.

Finally, Jim found refuge for a moment's pause, hidden beneath a conveniently draped table cover. Clutching the water bottle, he began to channel his focus into his breath to regain his strength. Gradually, the effects of the drugs began to subside, and he became more alert.

He had no idea how long he sat there, but during his deep trance, Jim had a vision. He saw multiple disks descending through the hangar's ceiling, reminiscent of those he had encountered before, albeit smaller. They hovered above certain volunteers, and vortexes opened up over specific individuals.

Startled, he snapped back to full consciousness. His

instincts told him this facility was a nightmarish abuse of power, but he needed to uncover the truth. He reached for his dog tag, a symbolic lifeline that somehow connected him to the interdimensional portal and, hopefully, a way out of this nightmare, but when? He couldn't wait years again, not here.

Observing from a distance two men clad in pristine white lab coats, Jim bided his time, waiting for the ideal moment to move. They strolled past him, immersed in conversation, and he couldn't help but eavesdrop on their discussion concerning yet another hangar. A thought crossed Jim's mind—how many more hangars concealed individuals in situations like his own? Jim could still hear the men's conversation. One was having a few laughs at the expense of the other.

"I told you that you wouldn't find that water bottle again—these freaks all look the same after a while. Why did you leave it on one of their beds, you idiot?"

There was a brief and playful shoving, and they shared laughter.

In this grim environment, there was no room for dignity—not for the dead, and certainly not for the living, reduced to a sedated existence.

"Yeah, we should clear out the deceased before they start filling the place with the unbearable stench," the other chimed in.

Jim noticed a doorway at one side of the hangar, leading to what seemed to be a control room above, likely overseeing this nightmarish operation. His gaze drifted to the massive metal doors designed for aeroplanes at either end of the long bay. Sneaking through those inconspicuously was unlikely.

Shadowing the two lab-coated individuals at a safe distance, Jim eventually arrived at a set of steps leading to a sign ↖ marking the control room—a nerve centre that promised to hold the answers he sought. As the lab coats continued on, Jim slipped into the changing room tucked beneath the stairs. Hidden behind the door, he waited anxiously, his heart pounding, hoping that nobody would follow him in.

A lone security guard entered shortly after. He sat down, kicked his shoes off, had a swig of his drink, groaning out loud, “Ahhh, I’m so bored,” switched on a TV precariously placed on top of a couple of shoulder height lockers for background noise, and closed his eyes for a nap. Jim waited for a short while, and it wasn’t long before the snores gave him a prompt to move in. Jim unclipped the guard’s security door swipe card and slipped into one of the spare guard uniforms left on top of a locker. Glancing at the guard’s watch, he was pleased it was three a.m.—a stroke of luck. The guard’s fatigue due to the late hour worked to Jim’s advantage, and it was clear that only a skeleton crew was on duty. He confidently headed out.

As Jim climbed the metal stairs, he found it difficult

to minimize the sound of his steps on the grating. He continued slowly and finally approached the central control room; he was struck by the meticulous organization of the space. At the heart of it all stood the science desk, a marvel of modern technology, adorned with an array of monitors that flickered with real-time data and intricate diagrams. The visual displays and readouts were beyond Jim's comprehension, but he continued to study them, trying to figure out some basics.

Each screen clearly labelled as dedicated to a specific aspect of the hadron collider's operation, providing a comprehensive overview of its complex workings. He figured one monitor displayed the collider's energy levels, while another tracked the trajectory of particles as they hurtled through its vast tunnels. From this vantage point on the mezzanine, high above the patients in the hangar bay, through the windows the hadron collider loomed at the far end, its massive structure a testament to human ingenuity and scientific exploration. He watched from above as the two scientists continued their patrol among the patients below.

The readouts designated the device as a "small" hadron collider, but it dominated the far end of the hangar. Its colossal structure extended from the floor, encircling the far entrance of the hangar. Floor to ceiling, it was an awe-inspiring display of scientific engineering. If this was a small one, Jim contemplated how big a large one would be.

The room buzzed with the hum of server fans and hard drives. The soft glow of computer screens created an atmosphere of focused intensity. It was clear every aspect of the collider's activity was meticulously monitored and analysed in real time.

Papers lay strewn about in disarray, filled with complex equations and diagrams that hinted at the cutting-edge research conducted within these walls. Jim perused the papers scattered haphazardly. The day shift staff had neglected to file their work away, leaving a trove of potentially revealing documents within his reach.

From what he could gather, the scientists believed the anomalies were created with dark matter generated or collected within the collider and used to open portals to other dimensions. Though he was enlightened by this information, Jim couldn't forget the dead people below who clearly hadn't signed up for such experiments. He suspected the agreement had been written in a way that covered their tracks should any future investigations take place.

Among the paperwork he found a folder labelled '*Test Subjects*' where he uncovered the dark truth. Page one gave him pause:

Confidential. Documents to be destroyed at experiment conclusion along with all remaining test subjects.

As he delved deeper, the contents revealed detailed

records of the systematic targeting and exploitation of homeless individuals, their names and personal details catalogued with clinical precision. The document revealed a codename, "the Collectors," their clandestine operations shrouded in secrecy. They lured unsuspecting homeless or vulnerable people with promises of warm meals, fresh clothing, and comfortable accommodations, only to betray them in the cruellest of ways. Jim's blood ran cold as he read accounts of sedation and coercion. It was a harrowing glimpse into a world of exploitation and abuse, where the most vulnerable members of society were treated as disposable pawns in a macabre game of scientific experimentation.

Jim glanced up from the documents back to the science station monitors. A touch-screen display offered the tantalizing option to re-activate the collider with a clearly labelled button. It seemed like Jim's best shot at escaping this predicament. Without hesitation, he pressed the button, and the collider began roaring to life, flooding the hangar deck with its brilliant glow.

As the power surged through the collider, a large vortex materialized within the hangar, its swirling energy centred on the collider itself. Through the window, Jim watched in awe as the vortex expanded, beckoning him toward the unknown.

Jim had no desire to stay a minute longer in this reality. As he made his way, he saw the hangar designation was 20, and he considered that there must have been many more hangars like this, maybe at this base or perhaps across different sites. He ran through the hangar, double-timing it, the opportunity to escape paramount. This was the largest fissure he had encountered, and he had never done so before with others present.

He lost his footing as ran, floating toward the vortex, Jim witnessed a vision of his family facing the turmoil brought about by what he assumed from his studies was Nibiru's return, a brown dwarf visible from Earth with the naked eye, causing chaos to the entire planet.

Jim hovered right on the edge of the event horizon, a shimmering translucent veil that blurred the line between existence and the abyss. It pulsed with an ethereal light, casting a mesmerizing glow that seemed to bend and warp the fabric of reality around it. Swirling tendrils of energy danced along its edge, beckoning with an otherworldly allure. Jim could feel the pull of its unseen forces, drawing him closer to the threshold of possibility and uncertainty.

His resolve was unwavering and there was a smile on his face in anticipation of the impending journey. Despite the underlying fear that surged within him as he stared at the precipice, bracing for impact, he found solace in the thought that he wouldn't be stranded here for much longer.

Chapter 8 – Shadow Mission of the Fleet

As Jim passed through into another reality, he looked down from a great height and to his relief below saw a lake to soften the landing. He held his breath as he fell fully clothed, feet first, hard into the water. Jim went deep and fought his way back up to the surface, gasping for air as he came up, choking up some lake water. He swam towards the nearest outcrop of land with all his remaining strength. When he reached the shore, he pulled himself onto the rocky man-made shoreline and rested on his front for a moment. Then he rolled onto his back, his chest and body still stinging from the impact of the fall. He concentrated on getting his breathing back to normal

Jim looked around for something to dry off with and, to his fortune, saw a towel and a bundle of dry clothes, as if someone had been swimming in the lake. Nobody else was nearby, and he wondered if he was about to steal some dry clothes or if they belonged to his doppelganger in this reality. He moved to dry himself off and change behind some bushes when he heard a vehicle approach, followed by a voice. Jim looked up and saw a man hastily approaching in a Navy uniform.

"Professor Knight, we need you to come back to the base," the voice called out.

Jim quickly made himself decent as the young Naval security officer approached.

“Why, what’s happened, Lieutenant Jed?” Jim asked, reading his name badge to assist with blending in to his new reality.

“I don’t know, sir; I was tasked to retrieve you. That’s all I know. Did you have a good swim, sir?”

“Yes, I did, thank you. How did you know where to find me?”

“What do you mean? It’s Wednesday. You always swim in the lake at this time. It’s not like I was deciphering hieroglyphics,” the young officer replied sarcastically. “Another reason why I knew it would be easier for me to come out here than call you: you’re not exactly answering your phone swimming in the lake, now are you? And you know how pushy our superiors are. It’s all now, now, now.” He chuckled.

Jim found his phone and a set of keys in his trouser pocket and noticed two Army Jeeps parked up on the roadside. He guessed the key must fit one of these two, but he had no clue which one or indeed where they were headed.

“After you. I’ll follow you in,” Jim said, gesturing to the officer with a wave of his arm as he followed behind.

As they drove around the corner, the landscape levelled out, and there were fields and landing strips on both sides, offering a spectacular view. In the distance, Jim could see aircraft hangars on the base as they drew nearer.

As they arrived at the base barrier checkpoint, Jim was instructed by another security guard to have his ID badge visible to pass the barrier. He frantically searched through all his pockets and finally found his ID. Jim stared at the badge for a long moment; the title "Professor Knight." He was a senior research scientist in this reality. The security guard seemed to know him.

"Welcome back to AUTEC, Jim. Would you mind putting your ID badge on?"

"Sure, as soon as I park up. Thank you," Jim replied hesitantly and proceeded to follow Lieutenant Jed's Jeep. They parked up and Jim followed Jed into one of the hangars, saddened by the rows of incapacitated people in hospital beds, all hooked up to drips and breathing apparatus as before. The only change so far was his role, no longer a volunteer, but now a contributing part of the staff here.

Jim followed Lieutenant Jed past the unconscious victims into the control room, where he was introduced to Colonel Truman. Though the layout had been slightly rearranged, much of the equipment remained the same, including the hangar bay designation #20.

"Professor, we have detected some unusual activity in the Atlantic Ocean," Colonel Truman said grimly.

"Why are you here, colonel? Can you update me what has been happening, please?" Jim asked.

"Over the last twenty years, we have seen increased storms coming in over the coast, as you know. When Katrina hit in 2005, we started paying more attention. The sensors you asked us to install in the Atlantic have gathered huge amounts of data since. The last time we had one of these super storms, we picked up something we have never seen before."

The colonel showed Jim the data as he input it into a computer model on the science desk main display. Within the eye of the storm, Jim saw a familiar sight: a massive vortex with the rotating saucer-shaped disk above it. It appeared for only a moment—perhaps only half a second.

"The people we have in the hangar bays who volunteered—" Colonel Truman said.

"Are they aware exactly what they have volunteered for?" Jim interrupted.

"Well, that's one way to describe the rich people who have paid millions for us to save them, volunteers!" He scoffed. "We aren't here to think, Professor, don't think, just do your job and analyse the data. As I was about to say before I was rudely interrupted, I've selected a couple of them to take with you into that area and see if you can muster up a recall of that storm."

Jim realised he should keep his lips tight for now so as not to tip his hand. If this alternate reality was anything like the previous one, they were not likely to reveal it in a heated discussion. He had probably already crossed a line.

"If you don't mind, I'd like to go back to my quarters to study this new data," Jim said.

"Study it where you like. Everything you need is in the usual shared drive area. Lieutenant Jed, please escort the professor to his room."

"Thanks," Jim replied, following Lieutenant Jed away. "Who else has access to these files, Lieutenant?"

"It's all secure, role-based access control depending on your security clearance. At a guess, only you and the other scientists working on the dimensional gateway controls have access, I imagine, but I'm not tech security-cleared, so you would need to check that, of course," replied the lieutenant.

When they arrived at Jim's quarters, fortunately the key ring in his pocket only had a couple of keys and one was for the Jeep, so it was easy to gain access without looking the fool. "Is there anything else?" Jim asked.

"No, sir. See you tomorrow, sir." The lieutenant smiled and left Jim in his room, alone at last.

He now had a new problem. The laptop was sitting on his kitchen table, but what was the password? In his reality he had several variations, but they all contained the name of his wife Scarlett. After a few attempts he cracked it, which gave him pause for breath. So this reality's Jim knew Scarlett, at least to some level, past or present. In Jim's mind, a desire for his simple life with its mundane office job fixing computers and returning home to Scarlett and Jerica momentarily overshadowed his thoughts. He wasn't keen on the idea of being involved in these experiments either, but at least he had an opportunity to try and learn more.

Before he could even begin looking at the video footage and sensor data, he had to know about Scarlett. He found his journal under the bed as usual and flipped through it as fast as he could, scanning for his wife's name. He soon found that she had been murdered in this reality; there were suspects, Benson and Shafto, and DNA evidence they were involved. They had gotten away with it yet again, both on the run. This might explain his counterpart's motivation for being involved with the experiments.

A shortcut on the desktop made finding the shared area very easy. He began to study the data and video footage now available to him. He was convinced that the anomaly was the same as the ones he'd encountered before; even the inverse colour effect and the disk, although larger, were the same. He looked to see if he could find other information on the system. He found his log entries and discovered that this Jim had led this project with his scientific intellect. He had used his scientific contacts and influence to manipulate key government officials and elite families with power and money to investigate the rift. He used fear to motivate them. He'd convinced them there was an end-of-the-world scenario coming and going through the rift was the best way to save themselves. This Jim had logged it all like a timeline of key events where he pompously boasted his narcissistic victories.

Jim found files on disaster management and was intrigued to find that they had prepared an evacuation plan for the people funding the experiments. The test subjects, as before, were not the actual candidates to be evacuated. They were actually trying to create portals to other dimensions in the event of a planetary catastrophe. He found evidence of scans and tests done on the collider, results that suggested that each universe existed in its own bubble. The cosmic skin of each bubble, the scientists hypothesised, sustained itself and prevented any merging or transfer between realities. The universes all existed at once and were all connected, either directly or indirectly. These experiments were creating micro-black holes that were piercing the cosmic skin of differing realities.

Jim already knew that CERN had built a Large Hadron Collider in Switzerland; this was news available to the public. Physicists there were using the Hadron Collider to study the smallest known particles and the fundamental building blocks of all things. However, secretly, there were hadron collider devices in places all around the world. The

AUTEC facility where he was now was only one of them. Next phase of testing was on board the officially retired US Navy vessel *Enterprise* CVN-65, unofficially in the North Atlantic Ocean. He learnt that she was the world's first nuclear-powered aircraft carrier, the perfect testing vessel. She was the eighth United States naval vessel to bear the name and the longest naval vessel of her era.

The Hadron Collider was being tied into the vessel's nuclear twin reactor core. She was the only aircraft carrier to ever have two reactors. The hull was more of a cruiser design, with four rudders, and built extremely well. The *Enterprise* was now deemed decommissioned, which couldn't have been further from the truth, but how easy to cover up if things went wrong, because nobody would notice a reportedly scrapped nuclear vessel going missing.

There was a knock on Jim's door. "Professor Knight?" a female voice called out, knocking slowly, then louder. Jim was focused on his findings and hadn't initially noticed until he heard her name. "It's me, Tasha. I need to talk to you."

Jim jumped up and answered the door, relieved to have some familiar company, although he was certain this version of Tasha wouldn't know him. "What is going on? What do you need to ask me?"

"These experiments, what are they doing specifically?"

"That's classified. I can't talk about it. But wait, I

need to ask you a strange question. Can I ask you when did we meet?" Jim proceeded cautiously, and didn't want to become a security breach.

"We met a few days ago," she replied, looking down as if she was hiding something.

"Didn't we meet before that?" Jim carefully probed.

"Well, I told you that yesterday, and you thought I was insane. Yes, you helped me to get back on my feet," she said hesitantly.

"Please humour me, Tasha," Jim urged her to continue.

"Like I said, we met in a park, but you don't remember that, do you?"

"Tasha, were you homeless at the time?"

"Yes. Jim, is it really you, I mean you-you?" She smiled.

"Yes. I gave you something before I left, do you still have it?" Jim asked, carefully verifying.

She nodded, revealed her dog tag and described every detail of their initial encounter to confirm their genuine reunion. She explained how the vortex had pulled her into another reality shortly after he left. She had been getting by, pretending she knew what she was doing, but she had no clue what was really going on.

"Tasha, you are the first I've met on the other side

of one of these reality jumps who's been through whatever this thing is," Jim said, holding the dog tag in his hand. "In each reality, we might encounter different versions of people we know, but there are always variations to our original universe. I'm trying to get back to my prime reality. I'm sorry. I never should have given you the dog tag and dragged you into this nightmare."

"It's okay, Jim. Honestly, I'm just so pleased I found you. I felt so alone before you arrived and, when you thought I was insane, I thought you were going to get me kicked out of whatever this place is, or worse. That's why I came here to see you—well, the other you," Tasha said. "I don't understand my luck. From what I've learnt there are countless different realities. What are the odds we wind up together again?"

"Maybe their experiments combined with our dog tags have drawn us here together, like twigs in a stream following some kind of quantum current. I don't know, it's just a guess, but the dog tags are the only constant."

"It's hard to grasp, but I've seen enough strange things since arriving here that I'm willing to believe almost anything now."

Jim pulled her closer and gave her a silent hug.

"So you have no clue what's going on either then, I'm guessing?" She laughed.

"I've been doing research—a lot, actually. Best part

of two years before the jumps really kicked in. And these recent realities I've had access to some real data, which backs up some of my crazy theories. But yes, a lot of guesswork too." Jim chuckled. Finally someone he could trust, in it with him. He showed her everything he had found on the computer system and his doppelganger's documents' from this reality to get her up to speed.

"Seems like this version of you knows a lot more about what is going on than you do," Tasha teased and he laughed in agreement. "I don't want to be left here alone, Jim. I want to come with you."

"Look, even professors need assistants. I'll make sure I get you on the next mission. We have to stick together," Jim reassured her, feeling somewhat responsible for her predicament.

Tasha smiled with relief and hugged him tighter than before, as if scared to let go.

"Don't worry Tasha, 'Even in a mine of dark and silent thought, delve deep enough and strange fancies can be found to bring light to the catacombs'," Jim reassured her with a deep embrace.

"More comic book quotes?" Tasha joked, not really understanding.

"Something like that." Jim laughed. "Just don't worry, okay? We've a trip to go on. I hope you have sea legs."

Chapter 9 – Hidden Forces of the Enterprise CVN-65

With the voyage already underway, Captain Alan Malik assumed command of the *Enterprise CVN-65*. His demeanour was like an approaching tempest, carrying an air of brooding intensity. His security clearance did not extend to the full mission details, leaving his ship at sea long past its official decommission date despite his efforts challenging the decisions through the chain of command.

They were enmeshed in a shadowy black ops endeavour. The crew was mostly full of new recruits with no real combat experience, with a few dozen veterans on board to guide them, but this wasn't expected to be a combat mission and they were all well trained. And the younger crew, more eager to please and follow orders without question, was exactly what the mission needed.

The clandestine operation had been impossible to fully conceal from the captain and his engineering crew, who had reluctantly assisted in connecting the small hadron collider (SHC) to the ship's nuclear power source. The aircraft carrier's crew members were not entirely oblivious to the mysterious goings-on, such as their extended tour of duty and the heavy-duty equipment being loaded on the ship along with curious scientific passengers, leading to rampant conspiracy theories. While the collider was smaller in size compared to land-based counterparts, it still filled the repurposed cargo bay.

At over sixty years old, the ship had been deemed expendable by the government, along with its crew. The nuclear reactors had outlasted their expected lifespan by more than a decade. The ship had been mothballed, lending credence to the covert operation's significance. Why risk a new ship when an old one was more expendable?

Captain Malik received orders to anticipate the arrival of scientists at 1600 hours and to ensure his crew was ready to receive them. A helicopter smoothly touched down on the flight deck and disgorged a dozen individuals. Among them were one assistant Tasha, two physicists—Dr Frank and Dr Amin, Professor Jim Knight, Colonel Truman, accompanied by his aide, Lieutenant Jed, and two affluent *volunteers* slated for the experiments.

The colonel saluted. "Captain Malik, I am Colonel Truman. Requesting permission to come on board, sir," he said in a formal tone.

"Permission granted, sir." Captain Malik returned the salute, his attitude respectful and composed. He extended the offer to have his crew assist in moving their belongings to the ship's living quarters, but the colonel politely declined, suggesting his intention not to stay. The others gracefully accepted and followed the assigned crewmen accompanying them each to their quarters.

* * *

After arriving in the relative privacy of their new quarters, Lieutenant Jed notified Jim that his presence was needed on the bridge as soon as he had dropped off his effects.

“Tasha, I need you to wait here for me, okay? I’ll be back as soon as I can. Just stay put, and everything will be fine,” Jim whispered.

Tasha nodded, and he followed the lieutenant onto the bridge and was met by the stern gaze of Colonel Truman and the concerned countenance of Captain Malik. The atmosphere was tense, charged with anticipation and apprehension alike.

“Colonel Truman, Captain Malik, good to see you both.” Jim spoke softly, trying to ease the uncomfortable situation.

“Professor Knight, thank you for joining us. We have much to discuss,” replied the colonel.

“I’m eager to hear what you have to say,” Jim said. “What’s the latest development?”

“Professor Knight, as you’re aware, our mission is of utmost importance. We’ve detected what you have described as a potentially immense dimensional rift in the Bermuda Triangle, and we need your expertise to gather data and conduct experiments.” The colonel handed the captain his written orders with the full co-ordinates.

The captain shuddered. “That is straight into the centre of the Devil’s Triangle!”

Colonel Truman said, “Not today, Captain. Make your course at flank speed, please.”

The captain’s unease deepened as he contemplated their course. The Bermuda Triangle loomed ominously ahead, its dark reputation casting a shadow over the ocean. Known for swallowing ships and aircraft without a trace, it was a realm of uncertainty where the rules of navigation defied logic. At full speed, they were hurtling towards potential disaster, navigating through a labyrinth of dangers that had claimed countless vessels, leaving few survivors to tell the tale. “It’s our turn to bat, so let’s make this one count. We’ve been here before. It’s clearly nothing to worry about.” the captain said, parking his fears and inspiring his crew to sail the *Enterprise* through uncertainty. He chose not to press his concerns further with the colonel on the bridge in front of the crew.

“Sir, is there anything else?” Jim asked the colonel.

“Yes, now you know we are on our way, Professor. Get settled in and then make your way into the cargo bay and get yourself familiar with the gear we have set up for you there,” the colonel replied. “Oh, and Captain, make sure to extend every courtesy and give the professor anything he needs. All other priorities are rescinded, are we clear?”

“Colonel, a word in private, if I may, please, sir?”

“Of course, Captain.” The colonel followed the captain into a room and closed the door behind him.

* * *

As Jim had made to depart, he had noted Captain Malik’s stern expression, the set of his jaw indicating a growing frustration. The captain’s curt request for a private conversation with the colonel had been more of a command than a suggestion. Without waiting for a response, he had turned on his heel and strode away, his brisk steps echoing across the bridge. Despite his outward attempt to maintain composure, there was an underlying tension in his movements, a palpable sense of agitation simmering beneath the surface.

Jim returned to his quarters to meet up with Tasha.

“How are you, my lovely?” she said seductively from the lower bunk bed as he entered the small cabin.

“Tasha, please, now is not the time for this,” Jim replied, trying to resist her charming allure.

“Oh, come on. I’m just trying to make the best of this. One minute I was in the house you set up for us, then a military base with strange experiments, now we’re heading for Lord knows where on a boat.” Tasha slumped backwards on the bed, staring at the bottom of the bunk above, speechless.

“It’s a ship and we’re headed into the Bermuda Triangle—the centre, to be precise.”

“No need to be funny! Oh, more marvellous news. I’ve seen the unexplained mystery programs about the Bermuda Triangle. Isn’t that where all the boats and planes go missing?” she queried. “I wish I hadn’t taken this dog tag off you now.”

Jim countered defensively, “How do we know that it’s my fault? Maybe there’s something greater at play here than you or me. How do you know that your actions didn’t trigger the anomaly and the dog tag isn’t just a mere coincidence?” Jim only half-believed his own words.

Tasha’s manner softened as she replied, 'I’m so sorry, Jim. I didn’t mean to blame you. I just want to go home.' Her voice trembled, and she covered her face, weeping.

“Don’t worry. I understand. We’ll be okay, and the vortex could reappear at any time, whisking us away from here just as swiftly. Everything could change again. In the meantime, I think we have an opportunity to learn more about what’s happening.” He offered her a comforting wink, and Tasha, though she was still tearful, nodded, showing signs of gradually coming to terms with their predicament. Jim held her close until her tears subsided.

“Shall we take a look at the device in the cargo bay?” he suggested. Tasha agreed, and followed him to the cargo deck.

The collider was at one end of the vast cargo area, and its sheer size left Jim astounded. Throughout the bay stood numerous rows of empty surgical trolleys, awaiting their purpose. However, only two volunteers—those who had arrived on the helicopter—were destined to serve as unwitting subjects in these enigmatic experiments.

Tasha was still struggling to make sense of it all. "Why would anyone want to go through with this?" she wondered aloud.

"Those other physicists, Dr Amin and Dr Frank, they were the same two who jeered at a deceased volunteer like he was garbage in another reality. I sincerely doubt they volunteered at all." Jim took a breath, finding the situation difficult to explain. "In the previous reality, they were using vulnerable people as guinea pigs. Something tells me that's likely here too. They'll test it on the lost and homeless, and once the portal is ready, the elite will use it as an escape from whatever's coming. To them, it's likely just an insurance policy, not a real concern. Tasha, when you went through the vortex, did you see any visions of the past or future?"

She thought for a moment. "I didn't see my past, but I did witness something. It was horrifying. The world was in flames—and then I woke up here."

Jim nodded sombrely. "Yes, that's a possible future, at least I hope it's only a possibility, but I've seen it multiple different times from different perspectives. Sometimes I'm alone, other times I'm with my family and I've even seen the pair of us watching it all unfold together.

In this diary it mentions that I informed the government about this end-of-the-world scenario, and pressed the United Kingdom prime minister into discussions with the president of the United States for contingency plans. Seems I came along—well, the other me—and steered them in this direction. I'm convinced they're trying to save people from that future with these experiments. Only the wealthy will be able to afford it, and the less fortunate will perish," he said, a shiver coursing through his body.

"Is there any way we can stop the catastrophe?" Tasha asked.

"I wish I knew. All I want to do is get back to my prime reality, assuming it still exists, and get back to my normal boring nine–five job and family routines." He sighed. "However, if this really is the end times, there may be no stopping it in any reality. If we can find a way to control these reality jumps, perhaps we can find our loved ones and use the portal to escape it just as these aristocrats are planning to do—shift into a safe reality."

"But jump to where?" Tasha questioned.

"Indeed, where and how? At this point I have no idea how to control it or if it's even possible." He shrugged.

The two volunteers were brought onto the cargo deck, attired in the same surgical robes that Jim had worn a few days prior in the previous timeline. They were led into the cargo bay by the two physicists in lab coats from the helicopter. The volunteers were unconscious, connected to drips and wheeled in on trolleys and rested in close proximity to the SHC.

Jim addressed the scientists with a question. "What's going on?"

One of them cruelly joked, "Starting up the collider, then probably nothing as usual. Unless they die unexpectedly, then it's just another corpse for the pile—rich stink this time." They scoffed as they began firing up the machine.

"So these people really did volunteer? You mean these people are rich?"

Dr Amin hesitated before responding, "Yes, they did volunteer for this, with a complete understanding of the risks involved. This time, it's individuals of means, in contrast to our usual participants, who may be less fortunate or marginalized."

"Yes, that guy there, he owns Global Tech, and that lady, well, she's his wife. They both have terminal cancer; I guess they want to hyper jump into some other reality where there might be a cure or something," Dr Amin replied.

Jim pulled the breathing apparatus gently upwards on one of the two volunteers and held his other hand over his mouth, his eyes widened in recognition. He replaced the mask and took a few steps back so Dr Amin and Dr Frank couldn't hear him speaking quietly to Tasha.

“I know these volunteers, in another reality I worked in their company. These were good guys there, they invested in the people and really cared for their workers. It was a great place to work, nobody wanted to leave and if they did they often came back. Tasha, if they are the same here I doubt they are aware of the full extent of their horrific testing programme.”

The machine cranked up, his dog tag began to warm up under his shirt building energy and he exchanged a knowing glance with Tasha before observing the collider as it began to glow. It initially emitted a sound reminiscent of a trumpet, prompting Jim and Tasha to cover their ears. Soon, the noise subsided to a more tolerable level.

The scientists mocked them, pointing at their ear defenders. Jim and Tasha grabbed the two spares and secured them on their heads in case of a repeat. Tasha clung to Jim’s hand tightly, her fear palpable.

The scientists returned to their consoles and Jim followed them, engrossed in studying the data on the screens. He could see the collisions within the SHC, as well as monitoring the vital signs of the two volunteers. He kept a close watch for any environmental changes and simultaneously assessed any possible means of securing himself. Conveniently, there was a sturdy railing behind the scientists.

Tasha squeezed Jim’s hand tightly, apprehensive about what might unfold next. He reassured her, “Don’t worry—everything will be all right. We need to stay and see if there's some way we can control this with their technology. They seem to be able to summon the portal at will."

As she drew closer, Jim's chest warmed with a mix of relief and gratitude. He sensed her seeking solace in their closeness; her head nestled against his chest, her breathing steady and calm. With each moment they shared, he knew he had become her pillar of strength, offering the comfort and safety she clearly craved without a word needing to be spoken. Jim looked down at his dog tags, which began to warm as the machine roared to life.

He gently extricated his hand from hers and guided her to the handrail behind the consoles, allowing them both a better grip. Suddenly, the vortex manifested at the heart of the collider. The SHC unleashed a torrent of magnetic forces, their tendrils swirling and twisting into a visible tunnel, whilst warping the surroundings into surreal shapes and hues. As they danced and coiled, reality itself seemed to distort, casting an unsettling and otherworldly atmosphere. The air crackled with an eerie energy, as if the laws of physics were being bent and reshaped.

The scientists remained engrossed in their work, oblivious to any of the effects, while time seemed to slow down for Tasha and Jim. Again, they struggled to maintain their presence in this space-time continuum against the pull of the realm portal. Both clung to the railing as the vortex pulsed with power, causing the room to continue warping and shifting. Jim's mind raced as he attempted to comprehend the situation. He wondered whether the collider was generating a field around the volunteers; they didn't seem to be affected like Jim and Tasha were. Similarly, the scientists were out of sync with it, while Jim and Tasha both hung on, fighting against the pull of the vortex.

Then, as swiftly as it had materialized, the vortex began to contract. The energy surrounding Jim and Tasha dissipated, and they were lowered back to the floor, staggering as they sought to regain their balance.

"That was close. Did we do the right thing by staying here?" Tasha whispered, her voice trembling.

Jim concurred. "We need to find out what's really going on here. We can't be anywhere near the co-ordinates the colonel mentioned yet, either. This will only get stronger, and the vortex appearances are getting more frequent, so we should be able to go through the vortex again if needed."

While they composed themselves, the scientists cheered and laughed at the successful vortex formation. The volunteers on the surgical beds remained unconscious, seemingly unaffected by the recent event.

Jim returned to the scientists, adopting an air of curiosity. "What just happened?" he inquired, feigning ignorance.

“It’s a vortex formation,” one of the scientists exclaimed, his excitement discernible. “We managed to create a stable one this time. It’s incredible!”

The other scientist chimed in, “We’ve done it before, but we got some more data on this one, and this is the first time on the *Enterprise.* You remember the last one in the hangar, right? Took us ages to get a result like this?”

“Of course, great work, success at the first attempt.” Jim played along, though his concern was growing. “And the volunteers?”

Dr Frank replied in a disappointed tone, “They’re fine. No effect on them. It would have been a real success story if they had vanished into the portal or something peculiar.”

Jim glanced at the volunteers and then back at the scientists. “And what’s the real purpose of all this? What are you trying to achieve with the small hadron collider?”

The scientists exchanged uneasy glances, seemingly uncertain about how much to divulge. Dr Amin said, “We’re exploring the possibilities of interdimensional travel. The collider generates intense energy fields that could potentially open portals to other realities. But this is all largely your work—I’m confused why you’re asking these questions. Very Strange.”

“Just testing you were paying attention.” Jim

furrowed his brow, not entirely convinced. "Are you certain you're not engaging in something more dangerous, like creating a Mandela field outside the collider, potentially opening dangerous por..?"

Dr Frank interjected, "I don't understand all these questions, sir. These experiments were your idea, weren't they? For the greater good of humanity we need to create and control the Mandela field, that's what you told us."

Before Jim could speak, and to his advantage, Colonel Truman and Lieutenant Jed re-entered the cargo bay and stood in front of the collider, observing the test subjects still unconscious. The colonel's stern countenance suggested he had overheard their conversation.

"What's all this about, science geeks?" he demanded.

Dr Amin replied cautiously, "We were just discussing the progress of our experiments, sir."

The colonel shifted his focus to Jim and Tasha. "Progress? Well, at least the two volunteers are still alive. And what *are* you two doing?"

Jim maintained his composure, and approached the colonel, Tasha close behind him as he explained, "We're supervising and reviewing the data with Dr Amin and Dr Frank, getting an overview of where we are, bottom up, sir."

Colonel Truman nodded in affirmation. "Good,

carry on then. We don't have time for distractions. Remember, these experiments take precedence over everything. Is that clear? Now, excuse me—I have a helicopter to catch. I expect full reports emailed to me by 0800 hours tomorrow." He glared at them, leaving no room for dissent. With that, the colonel exited the cargo bay, leaving Lieutenant Jed behind to oversee the situation and integrate with the crew.

Unexpectedly, as the colonel left the room, the two scientists had already fired up the collider again, still charged up it sprang to life instantly, leaving Jim and Tasha no time to anchor themselves.

Chapter 10 – Battling Temptation and Desire

As the vortex took hold of them, Jim found himself looking at a window into the past once more. He called out to his younger self. This time he was on the other side of the looking glass. He recalled the clothing he was wearing today was somewhat similar to his vision in his first encounter. He had to relay the message to his younger self that had been so valuable throughout each reality.

"Jim, You must try and remember, Jim. Write it down, remember what you see! Write it down so you can remember and make sense of things!" He bellowed above the howling wind, and he was convinced he saw his younger self nod in agreement. Jim thought, *Perhaps this is where all the divergent realities branch off, at least for me.* He understood the malleability of time through the vortex, yet he hadn't mastered control, if such mastery were even attainable.

As Jim and Tasha emerged from the vortex, they found themselves in a tranquil grass field bathed in the soft glow of twilight. The rush of energy from their journey left them breathless, and Tasha stumbled, falling into Jim's arms. For a moment, they lay there, caught in the heat of the moment and the intensity of their connection.

"Jim! Thank God. You're still with me!" Tasha

exclaimed, her voice carrying a depth of emotion that transcended her usual playful tone. She reached out and grabbed Jim's hand. As their eyes locked, a silent acknowledgement passed between them, igniting a flame of desire and love that smouldered beneath the surface. With a hesitant touch, Jim brushed a stray lock of hair from Tasha's face. He felt her tremble under his fingertips, her eyes fluttering closed for a brief moment as a soft sigh escaped her lips.

"What are you afraid of?" Jim asked.

"I'm not afraid," she whispered back.

"Then why are you trembling?"

"You're making my skin tingle with your touch," she moaned with pleasure.

In that moment, the boundaries between them dissolved, and Jim surrendered to the intensity of sensation. Their lips met in a fervent kiss as they lost themselves in the heat of the moment.

Wrapped in the embrace of the night, they moved together with a primal urgency, their bodies melding in a dance of intimacy and connection. Each touch, each caress, spoke volumes of the fire that burned brighter with each passing moment as they delved deeper into the throes of their ardour.

As they lay back together, reflecting on what had just happened, Jim grappled with a tumult of affections that tugged at his heartstrings like opposing currents in a tempestuous sea. He was caught between the passionate connection he shared with her and the enduring love he held for his absent wife, Scarlett. It had been years since he had been with his wife and yet guilt washed over him like it was yesterday. Tasha offered love, comfort and companionship in the now, but Scarlett's absence loomed large, a constant reminder of his unfulfilled promise to find her as he suffered his lingering devotion to a wife who might no longer even exist.

"I'm so sorry. I shouldn't have done that, Tasha," he said.

"I'm so embarrassed. Sorry, Jim. I just really like you; I thought you liked me too." Humiliated, Tasha got off him, wiping a tear from her eye.

"I do. My feelings for you run so deeply. I think you're really hot, too- but I have a wife and a child somewhere. I know they're in my original universe, and I have to find them. Sadly, they don't seem to be in many of the alternate realities I encounter. I have to believe that if you put your mind to it, you can accomplish anything," Jim said, angry with himself for allowing himself to become so torn.

"What happens in the future, Jim? Am I there at all?" Tasha asked.

"It's... complicated. I don't really know. There are so many variables, I don't know what is real. God, I'm so confused! I've seen my family with me at the end of the world, and I've seen it happen with both of us together too. So nothing is set. Before I met you, my mission was simply to find the vortex, get back to my prime reality. Now things are changing. If we can find them and then summon the portal when we need it, perhaps we can all leap out of any danger, and if there is no danger, carry on our normal lives. Either way, I have to be there for them, I just have to be. I can't believe that's the end. There are multiple universes; anything can happen. You have to watch the vortex to see your own destiny and believe you can make it whatever you choose," Jim replied, trying to convince himself as much as her.

"So, if there are infinite multiverse realities, there must be one where we're together as well," she said, still totally besotted with him.

"I guess so, yes," Jim said. Then, trying desperately to change the subject, "Let's find out where we are, shall we? We're not on the *Enterprise* any more, that's for sure."

After they walked for a while, Tasha recognized where they were.

"Jim, we're back in England," she exclaimed. "This park is where we met. Lucky nobody was around to see when we, erm—well, you know." She smiled."Come on, let's go to the houses you bought—oh, I do hope we've returned home." Her gaze lingered on him, a hint of longing evident in her eyes. "Maybe you could come home with me?" Her words were filled with eagerness, and Jim couldn't help but feel the tempting appeal of her proposition. "Jim, will you come with me to the houses, please? Then, after that, we can look for Scarlett and Jerica if you really want to—but let's go home for a while, shall we?" As Tasha spoke, Jim noticed a subtle dilation in her pupils, a telltale sign of arousal. She continued, her tone tinged with a seductive undertone. "We can do anything you want."

Jim paused in thought, pondering that if the houses were there, this might be the reality in which he had won the lottery—and his family were dead. His heart sank again, and he looked up into the sky, trying to empty his mind. Perhaps he had at least gotten Tasha home and potentially out of this vortex nightmare. *Perhaps,* he thought to himself, *this could be the opportunity for me to express in a strange way my love for Tasha. If you love someone, set them free. It might be painful at first, but she'll have no trouble finding someone else who's not as damaged as I am. She'll probably be better off in the long run without me.*

"Yes, Tasha, let's find out if this is your reality. I'll come with you, and we can find out how the others have been doing and if they even noticed you were gone," Jim replied, trying desperately to ignore her flirtatious efforts.

As they turned onto the road where the terraced houses stood, Jim was amazed at the transformation. The once-weathered and forlorn row of houses now stood as a testament to meticulous restoration and revitalisation. The facades, once worn and faded, now gleamed with fresh coats of paint in welcoming pastel colours that brightened the entire street. Each house boasted newly replaced windows adorned with ornate, handcrafted frames that sparkled in the sunlight. The front gardens overflowed with colourful blooms and manicured hedges, offering a charming welcome.

Jim smiled as he entered the house behind Tasha, who let them in with her own key. The interior had been transformed into a harmonious blend of modern elegance and historical charm. The original hardwood floors had been lovingly restored. The high ceilings created an airy and spacious atmosphere, and the large windows flooded the rooms with natural light. With a newfound sense of grandeur, these homes had been transformed into havens of comfort and sophistication.

Tasha and her friends had far exceeded Jim's expectations. The remarkable journey from homelessness to becoming the proud owners of these beautifully renovated homes was an extraordinary success story. Jim fondly recalled his promise: if Jana, Ian, Sammi, Marcus and even Tasha, assuming she hadn't been jumping through time and space the whole time, could turn their lives around, he would hand them the deeds to these houses, a pledge he was ecstatic to fulfil.

In the front room sat Tasha's friends, Jana and Sammi, drinking tea and coffee together. When they saw

Tasha come through the door, they went quiet, as if they had been talking about her and had to stop. Tasha didn't care, and couldn't hold back her emotions; she ran over to them both and pulled them out of their seats, giving each of them a hug.

Jim stood and watched, curious if they had known she was missing at all. Sammi's jaw dropped. "Whoa, what is this? Are you guilty about how you've been treating us or something, and where have you been all this time?" she asked Tasha.

"I'm back now. I've missed you guys so much. I'm so sorry if my depression affected you guys."

"We've missed you too. We didn't like seeing you so miserable all the time and taking it out on us, but we didnt want you to run away either," Jana scolded.

Then they looked over Tasha's shoulder and saw Jim.

"Jim! Oh, my, you're back!" Jana pushed herself out of Tasha's embrace to get to Jim, almost crushing him when she did reach him.

Jim gasped as she held onto him tightly. "Easy there, tiger," he said.

Jana eased her grip, but didn't let go totally. "It's so good to see you, Jim. I wondered if you would ever come back. Thank you so much—you turned our lives around." She seemed unable to contain her emotions, tears of joy filling her eyes.

Jim waited for them all to calm down, overwhelmed. He turned gratefully in response to a knock at the door. Ian was on the other side, wearing a suit, and he was speechless when he saw Jim.

Jim held out a hand, and Ian shook it. "It's good to see you, Ian," Jim said.

Ian was still speechless, standing with his mouth open, unable to move.

"Well, come in, Ian. I'm eager to find out what's been happening while I've been away."

Jana prepared more drinks, and they all gathered around. Jim was thrilled to learn that Sammi and Ian were still together and planning their wedding, and that everyone had successful jobs. None of them had fallen into drug use, and they continued to support each other, just as they'd said they would. A year had passed for them, leaving Jim puzzled about the ebb and flow of time in different realities or how the vortex worked in that regard.

"I'll be back in a moment. Excuse me." Jim left the room and headed to the pantry to open the safe he had installed. He keyed in the code and retrieved the deeds to all three houses. Returning to the living room, he handed the deeds to Tasha and said, "I wish Marcus were here for this moment. These are the house deeds. Sammi and Ian can have their own place, and you can decide how to split the other two." Jim signed the paperwork, fulfilling his promise.

"Good luck, all of you, and well done," he said, not wanting to stay around. He made his way swiftly to the door before they could say a word.

Tasha chased him out of the front door. "Wait, Jim—so that's it? Not even a hug goodbye for me? Nothing?"

"Tasha, I can't stay here. If this is the same reality in which I helped you out, then I know my wife and daughter are dead here. I need to get home so I can try and get back into the vortex and find my family."

"What about me? What will happen to me, to us?" she said desperately.

"Tasha, there is no 'us'. I don't know what is next for you. That's the beauty of it—you can live your life now. You're home. Enjoy it," he said, wishing he, too, could be home with his loved ones.

"What if the vortex comes back for me when I'm on my own again?"

"Don't worry. You can give me back the dog tag if you like. It would be like I never gave it to you, and then I'll be free of the thought that I cursed you with that thing. Please give it back to me." Jim paused as he observed her body language shifting.

"No, I'm keeping it. I take back what I said. I *am*

glad you gave me this dog tag—it reunited me with you. It's not over between us. You're in denial. Typical man running off to his cave, that's all this is. I know you do have feelings for me."

"Okay, Tasha, if you won't give it back, at least take it off. Then when you regain your senses, throw that dog tag in a deep river or bury it somewhere." Jim smiled, hoping she would be happy to be home, if not now then eventually.

Tasha smiled through her tears. She thanked him for everything and let go of his hand to wipe her sopping wet face, having chosen to keep her dog tag. "Are you sure you won't come up to my bedroom for a proper goodbye? I am sure round two would be better than we had in the park. Although I have to admit that was pretty intense. Added to the risk of getting caught, exhilarating."

"As tempting as it is, and as much as a life with you sounds appealing, I owe it to my family to keep trying. This is my curse and I release you from it."

"And if you can't get back to them?"

"Then I will regret this decision for certain," Jim replied.

"One last try. Are you sure you won't come upstairs and let me at least try and change your mind?"

"Please, don't tempt me even more than I already am. If I go up there we both know I'll never leave unless the vortex rips me away again."

"Okay then, see you beyond the stars. Look for me, Jim," she said.

"Whenever I gaze at the stars, I shall think of you, Tasha, and pray you are happy," Jim replied, gazing into her eyes.

"*You* make me happy, Jim," she said, hoping that displaying her love one more time might change his mind.

He blew her a kiss, turned, and walked away, hiding his own tears. As she closed the door, he muttered to himself, "What am I doing?" Then, shaking himself, he growled, "Remember your promise, Jim, for Jerica, and for your wife. If Tasha can get back to her reality, surely you can too."

Reluctant to face his own empty home, Jim made a beeline for his parents' place, eager to reunite with family after what felt like an eternity. The familiar surroundings provided a sense of comfort amid the chaos of his journey. Jim rang the bell and called through the letterbox, just like he used to as a forgetful child with a misplaced key.

His mother, Siobhan, greeted him with a mixture of emotions swinging from joy to anger as she slapped him and then held her mouth regretting her actions. "Where the hell have you been? We've been worried sick."

"Erm, travelling. Sorry, Mum," Jim stammered. His recent travels seemed like a dream. But now he was finally home, basking in the warmth of family.

"Well, you should have at least called or sent us a postcard to let us know where you were and that you were okay."

"Sorry, Mum, it wasn't that simple. I had to be alone, that's all. I have been in faraway places with no signal and no way to get a message back to you; I didn't mean to hurt you."

His mum gave him a forgiving hug and made him feel like a kid again. His parents still teased each other like always, and they filled the house with the same love that had always been there. Jim's brother, Jeff, arrived an hour later, and they shared a delightful family dinner, reminiscent of old times. Momentarily setting aside the ache of losing his wife and child, and adding the loss of Tasha, this reunion was a welcome distraction. Being at his childhood home again, surrounded by loved ones, was exactly what he needed. While sipping tea on his parents' sofa, he gazed at the stars through the window and thought of Tasha and the life he'd passed up, hoping she was safe and would soon find happiness.

After dinner, Jim went to the bathroom to freshen up. He heard his mum calling out, asking if he wanted another drink. But as she called his name, the anomaly appeared once more. Her voice deepened and slowed as time unravelled. The colours within the room inverted, just like when the disk had first appeared and cast its radiant light.

Jim stood watching the spectacle unfold. He glimpsed moments from his past as a child, and other events such as his lads' holiday with Chris, Bullet and the gang. He clung to the bathroom towel rail, hoping to spot his wife and Jerica before he could let go and travel through. The visions shifted again, showing the *Enterprise* CVN-65 aircraft carrier in a storm at sea and five World War II Aircraft flying through an orange mist. On instinct, he reached for his dog tag before returning his hand to the towel rail.

From his position within the vortex, Jim beheld a harrowing sight: the entire expanse of the Earth stretched out before him. It was a vision of chaos and destruction, with meteorites bombarding the planet from every direction. Flames engulfed the landscape as fiery projectiles rained down from above. Anomalies in the laws of physics caused gravity to reverse in pockets, sending vehicles and debris floating aimlessly. Some people were torn from the surface, left to orbit helplessly in space along with all kinds of debris, buildings and vehicles, now all space junk. It was a scene of utter pandemonium, a world on the brink of collapse, and Jim watched in horror as the turmoil ravaged the globe.

Jim finally surrendered to the anomaly. Filling his thoughts with love for his, he calmed his mind and focussed on his love and his loss, shutting out all the carnage he witnessed as if it was a mere dream.

“Bye, Mum, Dad, Jeff,” Jim said, as he left their reality.

Chapter 11 – Reuniting with Grief in the Heart of Absence

Jim tumbled to the floor as he transitioned into the next reality. Opening his eyes, he realised he was back in his own house. He sprang to his feet, frantically calling for Scarlett and Jerica, answered only with silence.

But just as despair began to set in, he stumbled upon a simple handwritten note in the kitchen. Its words, though straightforward, filled his soul with a warmth that he had sorely missed.

Hi, my sexy man, I got up early for some overtime. I hope you have a nice day at work, and I look forward to seeing you tonight.

Love you lots, wifey. x

Jim recognized the familiar handwriting, confirming Scarlett's return. He checked his wardrobe, and his old work uniform was there. He looked around and found Scarlett's things; the décor and blend of combined tastes was back. He was finally home, but fitting back into his old life and understanding the longevity of this reality proved a daunting challenge to come to terms with.

In an attempt to wash away negative emotions from the ordeals he had suffered in previous jumps, he took a cold shower. “Is it finally over?” he uttered to himself as he began drying himself.

After all he’d been through; Jim sensed that something was off. Jim dashed into Jerica’s room, finding it eerily tidy and devoid of life, with no photos of their daughter.

Overwhelmed by emotion, Jim dialled his wife’s number, his heart racing with anticipation. After what felt like an eternity, Scarlett’s sweet voice greeted him, filling him with warmth.

“Jim, is everything okay?” she asked.

“I need you here with me, Scarlett,” Jim confessed, his voice imbued with longing. “I miss you more than words can express. Please come home.”

“But Jim, I just left for work this morning. What’s going on?”

Jim struggled to find the right words. “Scarlett, it’s hard to explain over the phone, but I really need you here,” he said, his voice tinged with urgency. “I’ve been feeling... unsettled lately, and I just need you by my side.” He hoped his plea conveyed the seriousness of the matter without causing unnecessary alarm.

There was a soft gasp on the other end of the line, followed by a sigh. “I’ll be there as soon as I can,” Scarlett promised, her love evident in her voice.

An agonising hour or so passed. Finally Scarlett

returned. Jim rushed out to greet her on the driveway, showering her with kisses as she stepped out of the car, taking her by surprise with his unexpected display of affection.

"What's gotten into you?" Scarlett asked, seeming both amused and annoyed.

"I haven't seen you in so long. I had to hold you, to know you're real," Jim confessed sincerely.

"But Jim, we were together this morning. What's going on?"

"Where is she?" Jim asked, suddenly noticing the absence of a car seat in her car.

"She? Jim, I'm really worried. What is happening here?"

"Jerica—where is our daughter?" he said, tears in his eyes.

"Who is Jerica, Jim?" Scarlett asked.

"Can we go inside and talk, please?"

Inside, he proceeded cautiously, having unwittingly reduced Scarlett to tears by mentioning their child.

"Scarlett, I'm having a memory problem. I remember us having a child," he confessed.

"It's been two years of trying, Jim, but it hasn't happened for us," Scarlett exclaimed. "What are you talking about?"

"Okay, I'm so sorry. That's what I meant. Where is she? Why haven't we got our daughter yet?" Jim muttered, sinking into a nearby chair, quickly shifting the narrative. He folded his arms across his stomach as he rocked back and forth, lost in a torrent of anguish. Scarlett moved to comfort him, cradling his head as one would comfort a child. The calming effect helped Jim recover from the traumatic realisation that he was not in his prime universe.

"It could be a boy one day, you know?" she questioned.

"Yes, yes, of course it could. I just have a feeling we were meant to have a girl."

Scarlett hugged him and then went to the restroom to freshen herself up. Suddenly he remembered what he had shouted to his younger self. He dashed into the bedroom to look for the journal under his side of the bed. He hugged the diary for a moment in his gratitude, then began to flip through the pages.

He checked back to Jerica's date of birth, but there was no entry. He flicked back a few months and discovered that in this reality, Scarlett had been brutally attacked by the criminals named Benson and Shafto. She had been raped and beaten. The trauma had caused severe internal bleeding, and in this universe they had lost their baby.

Jim could barely believe his eyes—how could it be the same vile people who had done this to Scarlett? This time, the ordeal had left her damaged and undergoing IVF treatments. He had never imagined things could have gotten this much worse for her. In revulsion, he slung the journal back where he had found it. Everything was starting to become clearer now. Scarlett's presence, after such a long time apart, was soothing, and he desperately needed that sense of harmony.

When she returned, they sat hugging for a time, sharing an emotional embrace that slowly turned into passionate sex. Afterwards, Scarlett asked again why she had had to take an emergency day off and what was going on. Jim avoided the uncomfortable subject.

"Scarlett, let's go out somewhere. We can talk then," Jim suggested.

"Where, Jim?"

"Let's go to where we first met."

They put on their coats, and although the sun was shining and it was a brilliant summer day, there was a chill in the air. Jim walked alongside Scarlett, pausing for a moment to admire her. It had been so long since he had seen her fair complexion, her piercing blue eyes framed by cascading, strawberry-blonde locks flowing over her shoulders. She was beautiful. In awe of her, Jim kissed her forehead. He held her slender hand as they walked together.

Scarlett complimented Jim, "You always provide me with a sense of security, especially after everything that's happened."

Jim responded with a soft smile. "I'm glad I can provide you with that sense of security, Scarlett. It means the world to me. I only wish I had been there to protect you," he murmured, his voice steeped with genuine remorse and shame, a tone he hadn't intended her to hear.

She stopped them in their tracks and looked him dead in the eyes. "Look, it wasn't your fault, and you can't be with me every moment of every day. That is not how life works." She grabbed his hand, squeezing affectionately. Dragging him forward, she continued their walk.

Scarlett led them to a nearby park, where they had first met in this reality. For Jim, it was like experiencing it for the first time, as it hadn't happened this way in his prime reality.

When Jim asked Scarlett to recount how they had first met, her initial reluctance was evident in her shy expression. Gently squeezing her hand, he encouraged her to share the story.

"If you insist." She hesitated, and then went on, "You were in the park with your friends Chris, Bullet and Sid. You were playing football, and I noticed you didn't have a girlfriend, unlike the others, who had brought their dates along."

As she gained confidence, she pointed toward the football pitch, her embarrassment melting away. Jim closed his eyes, captivated by the eloquence of her storytelling, enriched by her enchanting voice. "In reality, it was a setup to introduce us," she said.

Sid's girlfriend had invited Scarlett, her cousin, to join them at the park. Scarlett arrived a bit later than the others. After about an hour of playing football, Sid kicked the ball at the girls as a prank, unintentionally hitting Scarlett in the face. She burst into tears. Jim rushed to Scarlett's side, apologizing for the accident.

Jim and Scarlett were drawn to each other, like protons and neutrons sticking together, forming their own nuclei. Their differences strengthened their bond.

Scarlett and Jim had enjoyed reminiscing about the early days, but it was starting to get colder. They watched the sun set and then headed home. They'd spent much of the day talking, yet Jim found himself savouring the silent moments just as much.

* * *

The next day, Jim awoke to a kiss from his beautiful wife, her presence rekindling his spirit. He cherished the moment, knowing it was fleeting. She urged him to get up for work, and Jim reluctantly attempted his old morning routine, but his negative thoughts returned to the loss of their daughter.

After he had dried off, from his shower, got dressed and started brushing his teeth, Scarlett's voice called out, offering him a cup of tea. But as she spoke, the dimensional doorway reappeared, and colours inverted around him. As Jim gazed into the spiralling vortex, it unveiled a cosmic tableau of primordial beginnings. At its core shimmered a minuscule white dot pulsating with boundless energy—the genesis of creation, a visual echo of the Big Bang. Radiating outward from this focal point was a labyrinthine network of what he could only assume was dark matter, each strand a filament of explosive potential, weaving through the fabric of existence like a celestial tapestry. He reached for his dog tag, yearning for some semblance of control, a paddle for the cosmic currents.

As he hurtled through the vortex, fear consumed him. Terror gripped his soul as he fell through the boundaries of reality. Where would he end up next? His mind wandered into cosmic nightmares. What could be worse than the torment his family had already endured?

Chapter 12 – A Night of Terror Fighting for Redemption

In other parallel universes, Jim bore witness to the aftermath inflicted by Benson and Shafto. In this particular reality, he arrived before the tragic events unfolded. Jim materialised into a nightclub toilet, fortunate to be alone during his clumsy arrival.

Making his way to the bar, he reconnected with his old friends Robbie, Alex and Chad. Their catch-up was brief but exhilarating. As he laughed and reminisced. His gaze wandered to the far end of the club, where he spotted his wife, Scarlett.

Excusing himself, he approached her, only to find her confronted by two familiar faces—Benson and Shafto. Their appearances matched the descriptions and a photo in a newspaper article left in Jim's diary from previous realities, the nefarious Dante brothers.

Benson had rotting teeth and a greasy biker appearance, and he reeked of a foul odour. Shafto was skinny and tall, and exhibited yellow teeth and appeared unhealthy despite his comparative tidiness. Jim couldn't contain his anger for the pain they had caused his beloved in other realities, though he refrained from violence.

Approaching Scarlett, he asked, "Are these two

bothering you, Scarlett?"

Scarlett replied, "I was just asking them to leave me alone."

Jim politely intervened, leading Scarlett to another table, grateful for the opportunity to protect her this time.

"How do you know my name anyway?" Scarlett said with a frown. He quickly realised they weren't a couple in this universe.

Grasping for an explanation, Jim responded, "I'm sure we've met before."

Scarlett thanked him for the rescue, but insisted she had the situation under control. She introduced herself, as did Jim. He tried to jog her memory about their past encounter at a park, but Scarlett could only recall the incident with the football hitting her face, but no names from that day. He inquired if she'd ever worked at Global Tech, but in this reality, she'd applied for a job but decided against accepting the offer. They truly were strangers in this reality.

Jim turned his gaze to the bar, searching for Benson and Shafto, but they had vanished. Despite his desire to find them and get some revenge, he knew he couldn't risk jeopardizing her future in this reality. There were two of them, after all. It made more sense to stay with Scarlett to protect her directly and share another drink.

As the evening wore on, she hinted at wanting him

to walk her home, subtly revealing her unease after the earlier harassment incident and seeking comfort in his presence. Jim was happy to leave with Scarlett on his arm. She looked beautiful in her black knee-high boots, short pencil skirt, and white button shirt. The shirt fitted fine around the waist but was slightly too tight around her breasts. There was a small gap between the stretches of the chest buttons, drawing Jim's gaze. Scarlett seemed to notice his attention toward her visible bra and smiled.

"You like what you see?" she said, teasing him.

"I'm so sorry, they were just there. I mean, sorry, I shouldn't look," he replied, embarrassed.

"It's okay, I'm just messing with you. Trust me, most women wear things like this for the *right* man to look. You're okay, but those other two creeps, they scare me."

"The *right* man huh?" he chuckled.

As they exited the bar into the dimly lit street, Jim's grip tightened around Scarlett's hand, a silent reassurance that he was there to protect her. But their peaceful walk took a sudden turn as they rounded the corner, only to find Benson and Shafto lurking in the shadows, waiting for them.

Without warning, Benson's fist connected with Jim's jaw, sending a shockwave of pain through his body. Given Benson's considerable size and the force behind his punch, Jim inferred that few could endure such an impact. However, his determination, coupled with the surge of rage, kept him on his feet. Jim reacted quickly, catching Benson squarely in the face a couple of times and knocking out one of his teeth.

Spitting blood, Benson said, "You knocked out my tooth! Get him, Shafto!"

Shafto advanced, wielding a bar he had grabbed from a nearby pile of scaffolding. "All I have to do is this," Shafto said as he swung it towards Jim.

Jim avoided the feeble threatening swing. He quickly assessed the situation and decided to grab Scarlett's hand and run. They sprinted down the darkened streets, not daring to look back until they were sure they had lost Benson and Shafto.

Jim was breathing heavily, dangers lurking around every corner—and to make matters worse, they had run into an alleyway with a dead end.

Benson and Shafto caught up, cornering them in the alley. Shafto hit Scarlett on the head, knocking her out cold. Jim grabbed the scaffold bar as Shafto swung it towards him, but Benson grabbed him from behind in an armlock, pulling him away. Jim stamped on Benson's foot as hard he could, then put his left leg through Benson's legs behind him and tried to roll Benson off his back, but he couldn't get away. Shafto hit him in the head with the iron bar, and Jim blacked out.

* * *

When Jim awoke, he was in a dark room with his hands tied behind his back. His shoulder was hurting badly, but he was more worried about Scarlett. As his eyes adjusted to the dark, he could see her in a cage at the other end of the basement.

"Scarlett, are you okay?" he whispered, not wanting to alert his captors to the fact that he was conscious.

"Yes, I think so, Jim," Scarlett whispered. "Where are we?"

Another female voice said, "Don't scream for help. Stay quiet."

"What is your name?" Jim asked.

"Harrietta Amathea, but most people call me Dusty."

In another corner was a man who was suffering terribly, occasionally writhing in pain as he drifted in and out of consciousness. He had no legs, and his wounds had been cauterised to stop the bleeding to keep him alive after amputation.

"I'm Jim. Who is that over there, Dusty?" Jim asked.

"That's my boyfriend, Ken—Ken Arlen. Look what... what... they did to him... He'll be dead soon, and one of us will be next. They're cannibals!" she spat, stuttering and crying as she spoke.

Jim ran over to Scarlett to check she was all right. She was crying too, hysterical with fear.

Jim had a look around and saw that there was a short but wide staircase leading up to a door. He went up to the door to find it was locked, then went back down to talk to Ken.

“Ken, can you tell me anything that might help us get out of this?” Jim asked him, trying to keep him conscious.

“I don’t think it will help, but Benson has a weak left leg. I tried attacking from that side, but it didn’t work out for me,” Ken whispered in agony.

“Thank you, Ken. What about Shafto?”

“That scum raped my girlfriend in front of me while I was tied down.” Ken was so angry that he was gritting his teeth and dribbling, but he still kept his voice as low as he could.

“I’m going to get us out of this, Ken. Don’t give up hope,” Jim said to reassure him.

“Hope! Look at what they’ve done to me! I’m deformed!” Ken rolled his eyes and moved his head back to hit against the wall, as if he had already admitted defeat. “And this is just the beginning,” he whimpered.

Jim asked Scarlett to see if she could undo the knots

on the ropes that were binding him. Shafto had been pretty lacklustre at securing his knots.

"Scarlett, put the rope back on loosely so I can wriggle out of it when the timing is right. The door is locked, so it would be futile right now," Jim said.

He heard the basement door being unlocked and scurried back, pretending to be unconscious, but he kept his eyes slightly open so he could see what was happening. Ken looked scared out of his mind as the door creaked open. He screamed in terror, wriggling and writhing, consumed with dread and fear of losing another limb. He begged for mercy, which only delighted his captors.

Benson and Shafto brought down another man wearing a rubber suit and a gimp mask, tied to a chain. Benson was now wearing a clown outfit with a red wig and a white face with a painted red smile.

Shafto appeared, wearing his skinny jeans and no top. The slave in the rubber suit looked even thinner. Jim was now behind them as they came down the stairs, and he had a look round for anything he might be able to use as a weapon.

"I want her now," Shafto said to Benson, pointing at Scarlett.

"You'll have to wait. Let's see if slave Chuck-Bob is hungry first." Benson walked the slave over to Ken. "Are you hungry, slave Chuck-Bob? Would you like some more of his flesh?"

The slave cried and shook his head. He was clearly a prisoner here too; he couldn't talk because of the ball gag in his mouth.

"I will be replacing you shortly, Chuck-Bob, if you don't start eating again soon," Benson threatened. "Let's have a little fun. The other one is still out cold, so let's have Ken's woman again."

Ken shook his head, pleading with them to leave her alone.

Shafto was disappointed and started to argue. "I want the fresh one. Come on, let me have her—what's the problem?" he said angrily.

Pointing at Jim, who he thought was still unconscious, Benson growled, "No! Because I want him to watch. He's got a lot of spirit, and I want to break him. Maybe he'll be the next slave—we'll see."

Jim's possum act was working well; he peeked cautiously, assessing his options. He noticed Shafto had a gun in his back pocket. Jim's timing would have to be perfect. He had to wait and stay as still as possible.

Ken had given up on himself, but was still begging his captors to let Dusty go. Shafto was holding Dusty down on the table in the centre of the room, and she was putting up a good fight, which provided a decent distraction. Jim wasn't sure if Benson would see him before he had a chance to grab the gun from his trousers, which were now down by his ankles and within spitting distance of Jim. The slave in the gimp mask saw him moving; Jim put his finger up to his lips, commanding him not to alert Benson or Shafto. The slave's eyes were terrified; his body shook in fear, his head shaking. Chuck-Bob closed his eyes, curling into a ball on the floor, refusing to get involved and succumbing to his cowardly instincts.

Dusty got a hand free and scratched at Benson's eyes, drawing blood from his face.

"Hold her down, Shafto—it's my turn first," Benson commanded, enraged by her attack.

With stealthy determination, Jim crept towards the firearm, capitalizing on the distraction engulfing Benson and Shafto. Just as he reached for the weapon, Shafto caught sight of him and attempted to retreat. Yet, hindered by his own trousers at his ankles, he stumbled and lost his footing, granting Jim the upper hand.

Jim had the gun, and he didn't waste any time. He shot Shafto in the top of his leg, near his groin. Shafto writhed on the floor, crying in agony, and Jim dropped to the floor to get Shafto in a headlock with the gun to his head, using him as a human shield in case there were any other weapons he wasn't aware of in their arsenal.

"You're lucky I missed," Jim shouted angrily into his ear with gritted teeth. Then he turned to Benson, who seemed to be the leader. "Now you're going to let us all go."

"What do you mean, 'missed'? You shot me in the leg," Shafto spat, struggling to talk.

"Who said I was aiming for your leg?" Jim replied.

Benson made his move, scooping Dusty off the table by the throat and using her as a human shield, a knife at her throat.

"No, lad, you're letting Shafto go and then we may, just may, let you live," Benson screamed at Jim.

"This isn't living, Benson," Jim retaliated, still holding the gun to Shafto's head. "I think Dusty would rather die than spend another minute in your filthy company."

"Shafto, you idiot, I told you to make sure the rope was tight on his feet and hands," Benson barked.

"Sorry, Benson—I forgot to do his feet. I thought the door was locked so he didn't have anywhere to go."

"Idiot!" Benson shouted again.

"What is it going to be, Benson?" Jim demanded.

"So kill him. Why would I care anyway? There are a million more sickos out there who would love to join in my games."

Benson had revealed his true colours to his half-brother Shafto. There was no honour among these criminals. Jim had never taken a life before, yet felt it was acceptable to take a life of a murderer to save the others, but he was conflicted. The eerie silence confirmed they had reached a stalemate.

Jim turned the gun on Benson, using his arm to choke Shafto.

"Don't get any bright ideas, lad," Benson growled.

"Have you ever read the story of David and Goliath, Benson?" Jim asked calmly.

"I don't believe in that Bible crap. Why?" Benson shouted back, dribbling spit as anger and hatred surged within him. He started pulling the knife across Dusty's throat, drawing a little blood.

Jim knew he was running out of time. "What's it going to be then, Benson? Let us be sensible here. We can all come out of this, right?"

"I'd prefer you all to die," Benson shouted.

But before either had time to act, Dusty had grabbed the hand holding the knife and bit it as hard as she could. Benson let out an almighty scream.

Jim shouted "Duck!" and as she dipped down he took a shot. It hit Benson in the arm and he fell to the floor, cradling his wound.

"Dusty, grab his knife and look for any other weapons," Jim shouted.

Dusty had grabbed the knife, but Chuck-Bob already had taken a meat cleaver from Benson's belt. He stood over his captor, studying him, and mumbled something that was muffled by his ball gag.

"Dusty, help him take that mask off."

She released the mask and ball gag. The slave's words were slurred from prolonged abuse. "You have destroyed me, made me eat your victims to stay alive for months, and now I have the knife and the power. What do you think of that, Benson?"

Benson laughed in his face. "Shut up, Chuck-Bob."

"My name is Adam Caine!" the slave shouted as he hacked at Benson's left foot.

Benson shrieked in pain, but he was made of pure evil and still managed to spit at Adam in defiance.

"Dusty, see if you can release Scarlett and help Ken, please," Jim said.

Dusty took the keys from the pocket of Shafto's trousers, which were still by his ankles because he had been unable to pull them past his wound, which he was still applying pressure to. She unchained Ken first and embraced him. Then she unlocked Scarlett's cage, petrified at the horror that had been unfolding, she helped her out.

"It's going to be okay, Scarlett—we're nearly out of this now," Jim called to her, but she was still in shock and didn't reply.

There was another scream as Adam hacked off Benson's other foot.

Dusty looked at Shafto. "You took my boyfriend's legs, you took our freedom, you took my dignity, and you killed and raped other people in front of us. What shall I take of yours?" She waved the knife back and forth, looking at his genitals.

"No, please, no! You said you would let us live," cried Shafto, begging for his life.

"Wait, Dusty," Ken said softly. "Give me the knife."

"No—he has to pay for what he's done, and he can't do this again to anyone," Dusty cried.

"He will pay. Just give me the knife," Ken begged her.

There was a loud pop followed by more screams as Adam hacked Benson's kneecap off. Adam then started kicking him in the genitals as hard as he could. Dusty joined in, taking it in turns kicking Benson's balls as hard as they could. After a few more repeated attacks, they turned around, looking at Shafto.

"Look out," Jim shouted, as Benson revealed a penknife hidden in his pocket and sliced at Adam's leg. Adam fell to the floor and dropped the meat cleaver; it spun across the room and landed between Ken and Benson. Ken crawled over and grabbed it, and though Benson tried to get there first, he was too slow as he was sliding in his own blood.

They all watched as Ken crawled over to Benson's mutilated figure and a fight broke out between them. Benson was losing a lot of blood and was quickly overpowered. Ken planted the meat cleaver right between his eyes. Red blood flowed down over his clown makeup, and his eyes stayed open, staring blankly at Ken.

Jim looked on as Ken got an approving nod from Dusty.

"No—please, no!" Shafto begged, seeing that his future was in the balance.

Ken replied, "And how many people have shouted those words in your dungeon here, and what mercy did you show them?"

Jim stepped back—he had already seen too much. Scarlett looked away, and Jim ran to her and put his hands over her ears, making sure her back was to the carnage as he comforted and shielded her.

Shafto started moving, shimmying backwards in a pathetic attempt at escape whilst also scrambling to pull his trousers back up, as he still couldn't stand. Ken scrambled over to him and grabbed his arms so he couldn't move. Then Dusty took the knife to Shafto's genitals and slowly removed them, taking several fingers along with them as he tried to protect himself. Ken and Dusty both watched Shafto writhing around on the floor, screaming in agony, blood all over his hands as he held his crotch. Shafto vomited and passed out with the pain.

“Dusty, don’t kill him,” Jim said as calmly as possible. “You have a choice now. Don’t do it, please. Let him live out his days unable to harm anyone again.”

Dusty held her head and cried out, “I want vengeance!”

“Scarlett, we should go and get some help.” Jim grasped her hand and pulled her to his side, hurrying her up the stairs. Thankfully the cellar door was still unlocked. He slowly opened it, looking at Scarlett, a little worried whether there might be anyone else in the house.

Cautiously they crept into the kitchen. There was a phone on the counter. Jim dialled the emergency services for the police and an ambulance to come and help them. As he had no clue where they were, he asked them to trace the call.

As he was on the phone, he heard Dusty calling his name from behind the door. He looked at Scarlett, who was the other side of the room, out of his reach and heading through another door. The strange disk entered the room and the wormhole started to open again; colours inverted and time slowed down. He looked for Scarlett, but she had fled. He figured that she would still carry the scars of this event and that he had failed yet again to stop them from damaging her.

He didn't know when he would see her again, but he was happy she had escaped relatively unscathed in this universe—physically, at least.

He was pulled through the vortex so fast he hadn't had the opportunity to secure himself. The corded telephone was in his hand. He dropped it before it could be damaged, allowing the call to be traced, accepting his fate.

Chapter 13 – Divergent Roads in the Multiverse

Though relief flooded his veins at surviving the ordeal, a shadow of dread still clung to his thoughts like a persistent fog. He couldn't shake the images of Benson and Shafto's victims and the revenge that played out, their cries echoing in his mind like a relentless drumbeat. Despite the element of peace that settled in his soul from knowing help was on the way for them, the weight of the traumatic experience pressed down on him, a heavy burden that refused to be easily shrugged off.

He opened his eyes, finding himself still within the vortex. The transition seemed altered, a zero-G freefall sensation enveloping him as he drifted through a tubular corridor. Eventually, he emerged from the other end and landed on a bed. As he looked around, he realised he was back in his own house once again and the décor had traces of Scarlett's taste positioned all around, such as her annoyingly, excessive scatter pillows everywhere.

He grabbed for his diary beneath the bed—a familiar anchor in his tumultuous journey. A sigh of relief escaped him as he retrieved it. Though he was a traveller through space and time, with no certainty of his destination, at least he had some level of control with his journal.

He leafed through the pages, seeking insights into this version of reality. Astonishingly, he found it was a world that had been restored to a degree of normalcy. Although he and Scarlett had had time apart, they were working through their issues. There was a photo of Jerica on the bedside cabinet too, *the family is together at last* he thought to himself.

Listening to the sounds of the house, he heard a familiar voice call out, "Daddy!" Jerica, his daughter, ran into his arms, and they embraced tightly.

His wife appeared in the hallway. A flood of gratitude overwhelmed Jim for the second chance he had been given. Still holding Jerica close, he relished the touch of his family and savoured the normalcy that had been regained as they all hugged together.

"Too tight, Daddy, I can't breathe." Jerica and Scarlett giggled as Jim released the triple hug.

"Come on now, it's bedtime, Jerica," Scarlett said, her gaze piercing with maternal authority.

As bedtime approached, Jim tucked Jerica in, cherishing the routine he had once taken for granted. In a rare moment of quiet, Jim and Scarlett found themselves alone. Jim felt the weight of the unsaid words that hung in the air, the emotional chasm that had grown between them. He wasn't home yet, but it was the closest he had come.

As the night unfolded, Jim found his evening with Scarlett interrupted by a phone call, and Jim hesitated to answer, longing to stay in this newfound happiness, but Scarlett insisted he answer it. Her patience seemed thin, as if he was an irritation.

Jim picked up the phone, shifting the call from an inconvenience to a welcoming distraction from the sudden discomfort. It was Chris.

"Jim, how are you, matey?" Chris' voice echoed through the receiver.

"Fine," Jim replied. "No, actually, I'm better than fine—I'm great. What's going on with you, dude, and why does the phone sound funny?"

"I'm on the bog." Chris laughed. "Listen, I was phoning to check you're still coming on our road trip to check out Alex's farm."

"What farm? I didn't know he had a farm," Jim said, a little surprised. He wasn't back in his original universe, then. This was close enough, though—his friends and family were alive and well.

"Yes, you do. I told you months ago he bought the farm," Chris said. "He's setting it up to survive some kind of disaster. He won't come here to go out with us, so I'm arranging a lads' reunion at his place. Don't forget, we leave tomorrow. You're still up for it, right?"

The invitation conflicted with the fragile balance

Jim and Scarlett had managed to maintain in their clearly strained relationship, and his heart only desired to stay.

"I need to talk to Scarlett first," Jim said, his voice wavering.

"Again? You told me she was fine with it. That she wanted some alone time."

"Ah, okay. I'd better just check if she's still okay with it," Jim replied.

"Perfect. I'll pick you up tomorrow morning," Chris said, hanging up before Jim could offer any more objections.

After the phone call, Jim discussed the trip with Scarlett. The decision had already been made.

"Jim, I told you I wanted you to go. We need this time apart—well, *I* need it," she declared.

"Okay, I understand." Jim retreated to his room to pack some clothes into a bag along with his wash bag. The wait for the following day seemed endless. They barely spoke.

"Daddy, I can't sleep," cried a voice from down the hall. Jim spent the entire time with his daughter instead, playing with her toys, being silly, lightsabre fights and all sorts of childish fun. They shared much joy that evening, which only irritated Scarlett further, but at this point Jim didn't care. It was the most fun Jim had in quite some time, very refreshing, and when Jerica got too tired to continue he read her favourite story until they both fell asleep.

* * *

When Chris arrived to pick him up the following day, Jim was pleased to escape the cold environment of Scarlett's making, but still experienced a turmoil of emotions, especially leaving Jerica again. On the other hand, he was really looking forward to seeing his old pals again. He leaned in to kiss Scarlett goodbye, but she turned her head slightly, accepting only a kiss on the cheek. The subtle movement spoke volumes, highlighting the rift between them. Sensing the tension, he embraced Jerica tightly, pouring his affection into the hug, silently acknowledging the unspoken complexities of their parting.

"I love you both. Look after Mummy, okay?" Jim said, acknowledged with a nod from Jerica.

After everything he had been through, he had to find out what was going on with Alex and his prepping farm, what kind of disaster he was planning for and why. Jim had many questions. Maybe the guys could fill in some of the blanks as to what had happened. Time hadn't allowed him the opportunity to read far enough back in his journal to learn everything.

Jim took a look at who else was coming on the trip and was delighted to see his brother Jeff was on his motorbike and Robbie and Chris in another and Chad in his own car. Jim was surprised; in his universe, he had known these friends at different times in his life, but here they were, all friends. He was buzzing with excitement. He really liked some elements of this version of reality.

"Road trip, wassup!" Chris screamed, hanging out of the car window with a bottle of beer already cracked open.

"Wooo! Wassup!" they all screamed back in customary response.

"Come on, Jim," Chris whooped, excited to hit the road.

Jim tossed his bag in the boot of their car and went out to his garage. "Wait a minute, guys, I have to check something out, won't be long."

Jim used to have a motorbike in his prime reality. If they were going on a road trip, this was the perfect excuse to put some mileage on his bike, if it existed here. A few minutes later, he emerged in full leathers and a helmet, riding his shiny racing red Suzuki GSXR 1000 K3.

It took them nearly four hours to reach Alex's farmhouse near Hereford, but the journey was not without incident. Jim and Jeff could have cut through some of the traffic to make better time, but he chose to stay with his friends. His brother Jeff was pleased they were both riding, and the trip quickly turned into a friendly competition over speed. They often pulled over, waiting for the convoy to catch up.

At one point, the police flagged them down along the road. An officer approached, asking, “Do you know why you are being pulled over?”

“Speeding?” Jeff ventured.

“No, we’ve had been complaints that you keep overtaking drivers and then slowing down, letting them pass and then overtake them again.”

“Going too slow, now thats funny,” Jim chuckled “we were slowing down to let our mates to catchup—we’re part of a convoy, a road trip.”

The rest of their group honked their horns as they drove past, laughing and shouting “Whasssup” out the windows. The officer saw the humour in it and let them off with a warning to ride more sensibly.

Eventually they arrived at the farmhouse, all impressed by the large Victorian building complete with a two-bedroom annex. As the convoy pulled into the driveway, Alex was already waiting for them, a wide smile on his face, eager to greet his old friends. They immediately asked about the run-in with the police, laughing and ribbing Jim and Jeff for ‘riding too slowly’.

“Jim, how are you, matey?” Alex said, and they exchanged a firm handshake.

“Better now that we’re here, mate,” Jim replied, embracing Alex in a bear hug.

Chad leaned out of his car, a cheeky grin on his face.

"Hey, Alex, you've been holding out on us with this place."

Alex chuckled. "Well, I needed a hideaway from the chaos of the world."

"Chaos, bollocks! This is bloody paradise," Chad chortled, eliciting laughter from the others.

After some introductions and catching up, Alex showed the guys around his farmhouse and annex.

"Shotgun on the big room in the annex," Jim shouted, spotting a spacious room during the tour.

A collective groan echoed as the others realised they'd lost their chance at the best room. Jim pumped his fists victoriously, relishing the small victory. His brother Jeff got the second room in the annex while Robbie, Chad and Chris would be bunking in the farmhouse spare room.

Jim was comforted that his brother had chosen to stay in the annex with him. Jim felt for his dog tag and refocused on his primary mission. Realising in a panic that he hadn't thought about it in a while, and released a sigh of relief, it was still with him. He was strangely glad for the distraction, living in the moment with his friends and his brother, even though he craved time a return to what he considered normal. Even though he knew this wasn't his reality, it was so close that he could see himself finally being at home here, if the dimension-jumping finally came to an end and if Scarlett was willing.

Chapter 14 – A Clash of Past and Present at Midnight

Chad had planned their evening meticulously, wanting to maintain control over the itinerary—that was his thing. It was the main reason he had joined them in the first place. Jim saw an opportunity to talk to Alex privately, and was also looking forward to a fun night out. A seven-seater taxi arrived to pick them up from the farmhouse.

Their destination was a nightclub called Play, though some in the group would have preferred to find a late-night pub. This decision sparked some conflicts, but eventually Chad's choice prevailed. To compromise, they visited local bars before heading to Play as late as possible. This arrangement suited Chad perfectly, as he and Jeff were the only members of the group without a spouse or children. Staying out until six a.m. was no problem for him, though the rest of the gang typically grew exhausted by eleven p.m.

The night was a blast, with nostalgic conversations and Chad's scoring game becoming a topic of discussion, just as Jim had anticipated. Chad would share photos of the girls he was seeing in various states of undress and get the lads to score them out of ten, and afterwards share his ratings. Then Chad gave his scores for bedroom activities as well, afterwards moving on to scoring the looks of the women in the bars they were in. Pretty standard night out for Chad—he was out living the dream, as he called it.

"Do you remember, Alex, back in the day when we were at that club, Zoots?" Jim asked Alex. "We convinced those two girls that we worked as top dance managers for pop bands."

"Oh, yeah, they were so gullible. We even made them balance on the edge of a step to prove their balance skills," Alex responded, chuckling.

"Yeah, we told them to show us their dance moves to assess for potential music video roles. That was absolutely hilarious," Jim said, laughing heartily.

"And what about that time when we told those other girls that we painted lighthouses for a living?" Chris chimed in.

"Ah, yes, that was classic. They totally bought into it, thinking I painted the upper half and you painted the lower." Jim's chuckle was infectious as he watched his friends double over.

"What about when Bullet grabbed that girl's bum and her huge boyfriend wanted to kill him? There I am, his brother, five foot and a fag ash, squaring up to this gigantic fella, not knowing that Bullet had basically asked for it with his silly actions. God rest his soul." Chris giggled with a sigh. Jim's jaw dropped when he realised Bullet was dead here too, but he decided not to dwell on it further and spoil the mood.

The night continued with laughter and amusing stories. Chad's increasing intoxication was evident, and by the end of the night he could hardly stand. The others were surprised at how heavy he felt as he leaned on them, despite his slim build. In this condition, he wasn't exactly attracting the ladies, which provided some entertainment for the group.

Jim and Alex decided to step outside for some fresh air and a private chat. Finally, Jim had the chance to discuss Alex's doomsday prepping activities.

"Alex, what got you into doomsday prepping?" Jim asked.

"It's a hobby, really. I just love it," Alex replied.

"But what's the underlying reason? Have you seen something that led you in this direction?" Jim enquired further.

"Listen, don't mention this to the others, please. Chad already thinks I'm a nutcase," Alex requested.

"Don't worry, Alex—it's our secret," Jim assured him.

"I had a vision of a future where the world as we know it"—his voice faltered, betraying the weight of what he was about to disclose—"was ending, and it was chaos, and another vision was people fighting for survival in a barren world."

Jim offered support, gripping Alex's arm. "I've had similar visions, Alex, through a kind of wormhole."

"Seriously? You've experienced it too?" Alex asked in surprise.

"Yes, mate. I have, and the future I saw... well, it's not pretty," Jim admitted.

"I believe that leading righteous lives is the key to survival. I've turned my life around, have a great family and try to live right. Fortune favours the prepared mind, right?"

"Alex, I hope you're right. Did you pass through the wormhole? What happened to you?"

"I've only seen it twice. When I came back, things were different each time. The first time, I ended up in a world where you didn't even know me. My family didn't exist. I had nobody. It was a lonely world, buddy. The last time, I ended up here."

"Incredible. I've had similar experiences, but it's been happening to me since I was a kid."

"I saw that apocalyptic scenario firsthand, and I figured being prepared is essential," Alex replied.

"Count me in, Alex. But listen, I don't know how long I'll be in this reality. I've been slipping through the multiverse too frequently. I wish my family were with me now; I haven't seen them in a long time. I finally made it back to something resembling normality, and the guys insisted I come up here," Jim said.

"You should head home tomorrow then, mate. Go see your wife and Jerica. But it's been great seeing you." Alex placed a hand on Jim's shoulder reassuringly.

"I think I'll have to do that mate. But definitely count me in with the prepping—as long as I'm here, I'm in, buddy," Jim said, finding solace in Alex's understanding.

"Sure thing, Jim. Keep practising your shooting, or consider taking up archery; that might be useful," Alex suggested.

Their conversation ended as Chad stumbled out of the club between Robbie and Chris. His appearance resembled that of a hobo, stinking of booze, barely able to walk—bedraggled and devoid of life, except for the occasional gurgling noise and slurred words. Jeff soon followed, and Chad, with a moment of clarity, insisted on getting a kebab before they caught a cab back to Alex's farmhouse. The rest of the gang was late coming out of the club and slowly making their way to the kebab shop.

In the dimly lit kebab shop stood Benson and Shafto—two ominous figures amidst the flickering fluorescent lights. Benson, with his menacing presence, leaned against the counter, his burly frame casting a threatening silhouette over the cramped space. His unkempt beard and dishevelled clothing added to his intimidating aura, while the faint scent of stale cigarettes and alcohol lingered around him.

Next to Benson, Shafto stood nervously, his wiry frame twitching with energy. His darting eyes scanned the room, never settling on one spot for long, betraying a constant sense of paranoia, as if he were coiled and ready to spring into action at any moment. The sharp angles of his face, accentuated by a thin layer of stubble, gave him a gaunt, almost skeletal appearance.

Benson shoved Jim for no real reason other than to demonstrate his dominance. Drink had let loose his aggressive tendencies more than usual. Shafto came to his side, ready to get involved in some enjoyable fighting.

Trying the gentleman's approach first, Jim attempted to defuse the situation. "Can you guys just leave it? I'm here for some food, not trouble. Let's all just calm down."

Shafto's response was anything but calm, his hands gripping Jim's throat, his rotten teeth bared. Reacting swiftly, Jim pushed Shafto into the shop window, breaking free from his grip.

"Maybe a toothbrush isn't a foreign concept in any reality," Jim quipped, recoiling from the smell of Shafto's breath.

Shafto swung; Jim ducked and threw a punch, hitting Shafto square in the face. Shafto crumpled to the ground, while Benson was held back by Jim's friends, who had finally caught up. The situation became a standoff, with Chad and the others ready to jump into the action—

though Chad wouldn't have been much help, as he could barely stand and his best move was slurring abuse at the two assailants.

Benson, realising he was outnumbered, chose to retreat, leaving Shafto on the floor as he disappeared into the night. Jim planned to confide in Alex when they could speak privately about his experiences with Benson and Shafto, in case this was only the beginning of the trouble in this reality.

Exiting the kebab shop with a nod from the rather intimidating owners, Jim and his friends walked down the street, surrounded by cheers of approval.

"Great job, man. One punch and he was down," Chad complimented Jim with a hearty pat on the back.

"You're the man!" Their voices rang in harmony.

"I just caught him off guard, really," Jim replied modestly.

"But you had the guts to stand up to them. You're the man," chimed in Alex, beaming with pride.

Their taxi driver expressed his irritation at the ten-minute wait. "Where were you all this time? I was about to leave," he grumbled.

"We had a bit of trouble in the kebab shop. Jim here was busy teaching someone a lesson," Robbie explained with a chuckle.

"It was self-defence, Robbie. I didn't exactly teach him a lesson," Jim humbly replied.

"I did ask him nicely to leave us alone," Jim protested, his cheeks warm with embarrassment.

"Sometimes people like him need a lesson. You did the right thing," Jeff reassured Jim. "With any luck, they'll think twice before bothering others. I hope we never see them again."

"So do I, bro, so do I," Jim affirmed.

Back at the farmhouse, the members of the group headed to their rooms. Jim waited until the others were settled in bed before he knocked on Alex's door.

"Can we chat briefly, mate?" Jim called through the door.

Alex cracked it open. "It's quite late. Can it wait until morning?"

Jim hesitated, but nodded.

As he turned to return to the annex, he heard Alex's faint voice, calling him back. Just as he began to turn around, a small saucer-like object entered the stairwell. The familiar effects of the Mandela field began to manifest, and Jim instinctively gripped the staircase's railing. The landing's colours shifted and the pull of the vortex grew stronger. Jim's feet left the floor, and his grip weakened. The desire to stay in this reality and reunite with Scarlett was overpowering. He needed to speak with Alex too, and had countless questions.

The force of the anomaly was relentless, and Jim struggled to maintain his hold on the banister. Desperately looking around, he noticed his belt. With one hand holding the railing and the other fastening his belt around the staircase spindles, he improvised a means to anchor himself against the pull. Jim pulled his legs onto the spindle, clinging on with all his might.

As he held on tight, he witnessed a series of bizarre visions. Old warplanes flying through an orange fog, glimpses of himself in different years, and the glowing dog tag warmed against his chest.

The vortex revealed more sights. In the midst of the swirling vortex, Jim witnessed something astonishing—the Twin Towers of the World Trade Centre in New York. He wondered whether this was a reality in which the towers hadn't been attacked by terrorists, or whether this was a glimpse into the past. Jim held on, desperate to stay in this reality and get back to Scarlett and Jerica to sort things out.

As the vortex closed in on itself, he released his grip on the bannister belt with a gasp of relief.

Chapter 15 – Tension and Doomsday Preparations

Jim staggered, his muscles trembling with exhaustion from the fight against the pull of the vortex. As time resumed its normal speed, he slowly regained his senses and heard a voice calling.

"Jim? Jim!" Alex's voice cut through the aftermath as he hurriedly made his way to his friend's aid. "Are you all right, mate?"

But Jim struggled to breathe, clutching his stomach in distress, unable to respond. He closed his eyes for a moment, overwhelmed with adrenaline.

"Jim, what happened?" Alex released Jim's belt from the staircase railings. "Why are you attached to my banister?" But Jim, in a daze, still didn't answer. A solid slap to Jim's face brought him back to normal awareness.

"Easy. Easy! I'm fine, just fine," Jim exclaimed, his voice shaky with shock and his mind still reeling from the ordeal. He reached up to gingerly touch his sore cheek, feeling the sting of the impact linger beneath his fingertips. "Cor, did you have to hit me so hard?"

"Sorry, mate," Alex replied with a chuckle. "But still, what was all that commotion? What's going on?"

"Why do you think, Alex?" Jim paused, hoping Alex

would connect the dots. “It was the vortex again,” he explained, frustrated that his friend hadn’t fully shared the experience.

“No way! That’s insane,” Alex exclaimed. “I heard this weird noise and thought it might be that vortex again. But why would it come after you and not me?”

“I don’t know. Maybe it’s because of these,” Jim said, revealing the dog tag. “I think they carry a vibration frequency that matches the spiral, acting as a magnet through space and time. I gave the matching one to a friend of mine and she got sucked through a portal as well.”

“Oh, *she* did, did *she*?” Alex said.

“Yes, just a friend, Al. Perhaps it’s my destiny to be dragged through perdition’s flames for the rest of my days. Am I already dead, maybe? Is this my hell?” Jim asked desperately.

“You’re not dead, old friend—and remember, I’ve been through it as well. You’re not alone,” Alex reassured him.

“I’m still in the dark. Do you not have a pendant or something that ties you to the vortex?” Jim asked.

“I can’t explain it. One day it just happened. I don’t have dog tags like you do. Maybe that’s why it’s only happened a few times. Mine happened by these rock formations, like a small Stone henge formation out back.

That sound, man, it goes right through me every time."

"All right, listen, the thing I wanted to tell you... Those guys from the kebab shop today, I've met them before. Their names are Benson and Shafto. They were rapists and murderers in other realities. Cowards in this one, but bullies nonetheless. They always seem to be evil. They've become my nemeses. I seem to be dragging their presence across realities, or maybe they just exist everywhere, I don't know. I never came across them in my original reality. I just wanted you to know how vile they can be so that you can protect your family."

"Understood," Alex said his tone resolute. "I'll make sure we're prepared for whatever they throw at us."

"Listen, don't underestimate them. I barely escaped with my life. They had me and Scarlett tied up in some kind of torture room with other victims they had raped and mutilated."

"You and Scarlett were targeted?" Alex's voice tightened with anger, his brows furrowing. "We can't let them get away with this. Let's track them down and make them pay."

"That was another reality, and I'm not sure it's wise to confront them directly. We have no idea where they live in this reality, and we have no proof they're even that evil here. Just be aware if they ever show up again," Jim cautioned, trying to dissuade Alex from a dangerous manhunt.

Alex reluctantly agreed and extended his hand to help Jim to his feet. He guided Jim back to the annex. Still tired from the intensity of the vortex, Jim appreciated the support from his old friend.

* * *

The next day, Jim was awakened by Alex. It was midday, and Jim was surprised at how long he had been asleep.

"Come on, Jim, get up," Alex said. "We have a job to do."

Jim's mind was still foggy. "A job? What job?"

"Training. We need to let off some rounds, Jimmy boy. Are you going to join me? Nothing makes you feel better than getting your guns off," Alex said with a grin.

"Of course, mate. Let me get showered, and we can head out to the field, let off some rounds, and then I should get home," Jim replied with a smile.

They spent a couple of hours shooting targets on Alex's homemade practice range; he even had an area for clay pigeon shooting. Alex had a shotgun and a couple of rifles, and he was a crack shot with any weapon. Jim had many talents, but unfortunately he felt shooting wasn't one of them. He had a sixty-five per cent success rate, which Alex said wasn't bad for his first attempt.

As the day wore on, Jim found himself relishing every moment spent alongside his friend. With each shot,

Alex's patient guidance led to an improvement in Jim's aim, hitting the clay pigeons with greater accuracy than before. Jim couldn't help but feel a swell of pride at his progress, and he turned to Alex, wrapping him in a warm, genuine embrace of gratitude. "Thanks, mate," he said, his voice tinged with appreciation for the invaluable lessons his friend had provided.

As they were putting the safety cartridges into the rifles and zipping them into their bags, Jim enquired about Alex's guns. "Do you have licenses for all these?"

Alex laughed heartily in reply.

"Surely you could end up in jail for five years or more if you get caught with no licence?" Jim asked, concerned.

Alex's laughter subsided, and he looked at Jim with a mischievous glint in his eye. "Of course they're licensed, Jim. Well, most of them. We won't talk about the hidden ones that are unmarked and untraceable," he said with a wink.

"You've got to keep quiet about this gun situation, Alex. And if Benson and Shafto do come here, you can't use weapons," Jim warned, trying to reason with his friend.

Alex responded with a silent, intense gaze that communicated a thousand words.

"All right, just be careful, okay?" Jim said softly.

Then, attempting to appeal to Alex's reason, he added, "Responding to violence with violence usually leads to more violence."

"We haven't finished yet." Alex pointed at the lake and a run-down shed nearby. "Time for a spot of fishing. I'm teaching you how to hunt and now fish so you can survive if everything goes tits up."

The shed was loaded with fishing supplies and rods, and they spent the next few hours setting up and relaxing with varying success. Alex loaded him with information, but Jim realised he would need more lessons if he was to master shooting or fishing.

"We only fish for food to eat, or if we practise and there is no need for food we throw them back in." Alex explained.

"Got it, mate, cheers," Jim said.

"Hey do you think the others are up yet?" Alex said.

"Are you kidding? The amount those guys drank if they are awake they will not want to moving about much." Jim chortled.

An hour later, they headed back to the farmhouse, and saw an old white van approaching in the distance.

"We need to make sure whoever that is doesn't see these guns," Jim said.

"Don't worry," Alex replied confidently.

"Do you know who that is?" Jim asked.

"No, I'm just saying you worry too much, Jimmy."

Unamused, Jim said, "Don't mess about. Do you recognize that dodgy old van?" he asked again, hoping that Alex might recognize it now that it was closer.

"No," Alex admitted.

"Let's be cautious, all right? They can't have seen us yet, I hope. Let's stay low," Jim suggested.

Alex nodded, urging them forward. They approached the house carefully and quietly, moving like stealthy predators.

"I recognize the people in that van," Alex said through gritted teeth. Jim had to grab his arm to prevent him from acting recklessly. Two men emerged from the van, and there was also a woman seated in the middle. She appeared older than them, and her expression exuded misery.

"I wonder how they found us?" Jim whispered out loud.

"I reckon they must have had beef after you got the better of them, and followed us. There were a few other taxis in that pickup area; maybe they told one of them we were together and to follow us," Alex replied, surmising.

The woman's snarl cut through the air with a nasty bite. "Benson, you useless oaf! Get back in the van and take me home. You wretched pig, I can't believe I wasted my time giving birth to you."

Jim and Alex crouched, prepped and loaded their weapons keeping out of sight. Jim saw Alex's grip tighten on his shotgun, and threw a glare of warning his way.

"What? It's just a precaution," Alex whispered. "I won't shoot unless things get out of hand, I promise."

Jim decided to make his stand. "Wait here and cover me. I'll find out what they want," he said, and made his way over towards Benson and Shafto, who still hadn't noticed him. He drew their attention, saying, "Can I help you, gentlemen?" He tried to project confidence, which was a little easier with his old friend covering his back.

"You! I've been looking for you," Benson shouted.

"Right. Well, here I am. How can I help you?" Jim said.

Benson reached for a handgun; it looked like the same one Jim had seen in the previous reality. He had to think fast; he didn't want Alex getting in trouble for murder, and he certainly didn't want Benson to shoot anyone.

"Those guns are illegal and hard to get in the United Kingdom. A guy could do a lot of years having one of those out in public even if it fires blanks," Jim said.

"It used to fire blanks; I fixed it up so it shoots live rounds now. And I have a bullet in the chamber just for you, lad."

Jim raised his rifle, prepared to use it in self defence. Out of nowhere, a crowbar hit Benson's head from behind. It was Benson's mother who had dealt the harsh blow to her own son.

Shafto seemed surprised by her actions. "Mary, why did you do that?"

"Call me Mother. And why? To teach this piece of crap a lesson in humility, that's why. As long as I'm alive, I'll keep him under control. Now get me home and leave these people alone. So what, you lost a fight in a kebab shop? Big deal. You just lost another one. Are you going to kill everyone who dislikes you?" Mary's voice dripped with disdain.

"I just wanted you to be proud of me, Mama," Benson sobbed.

"Proud!" she scoffed, sniggering at his pathetic attempts to show off. "You want to impress me, then why don't you start by getting a job and leaving these people alone? Now shut up and get back in the van. Where did you get that gun anyway?"

"Oh, it's easy to get a weapon in Weedswood, you just gotta know the right people, drug dealers there are very well connected. Hooked me up with the guy to fix it up too," Benson replied.

Mary shot a piercing glare at Jim, her eyes

narrowing, before settling back into the centre seat of the van. Benson swiftly returned to his spot, and Shafto wasted no time in accelerating away, leaving Jim and Alex visibly exhaling. Their shoulders relaxed as a sense of relief washed over them.

Alex had joined Jim, and Jim turned to see his friend's expression. "At least we know now they're after me," he commented.

"You say that as if it's a good thing," Alex responded, puzzled. "If you ask me, he was lucky his mother whacked him. I had him right in my sights. If that hand rose another few inches, he would have been leaving here in a body bag, or staying a long time in a shallow grave."

"I am glad it didn't come to that, thank you for having my back Alex. Quite honestly I am not sure I could have taken the shot myself."

"Oh I could have. If it was you or him there was no choice, no dramas bud."

Jim was reassured the events were over. "Trust me, Alex, it's all good. Nobody died, they left fearful of their mother's retribution. You need to stay safe and stop dwelling on these evil monsters. I'll be leaving soon, and that should be the end of it."

"Do you think they'll come back?" Alex asked.

"I doubt it. Did you see Benson cry like a child in

fear of his mother? You should be fine. And if he does return, tell him I've already gone. That should settle things," Jim said hopefully.

They returned to the farmhouse. Time had flown that day, and with a little persuasion from his friends Jim agreed it was too late to head home. He wasn't in the mood for a four-hour ride. The opportunity to have a couple of beers with his friends and stay one more night was a welcome comedown from the stressful confrontation earlier. He refrained from drinking too much, switching to orange juice after a couple, knowing he had to ride his motorbike home tomorrow. It was a good, chilled session.

Chapter 16 – Acid Rain Apocalypse

The following morning, Jim revelled in the thrilling ride home, and his heart quickened in response to the wind that raced past him. The engine of his motorcycle roared with power, propelling him past a hundred and forty miles per hour, and he held his breath with the exhilarating rush of speed.

He eased off the throttle, taming the powerful machine to a more controlled pace. As he continued to navigate the road, he imagined a reality devoid of human presence, in which he could unleash his bike's full potential without the constraints of road laws and drivers pulling out or not seeing them at high speeds.

The journey back home was not just a return to Scarlett but a test of endurance, one that he welcomed. His friends had been less enthusiastic about an early start, still feeling the effects of last night's drinking session. Jeff was the sole companion who matched Jim's eagerness for an early departure, and they had set out at first light to secure quieter roads.

Jim cherished his bike in this reality, a beast that could accelerate from zero to sixty miles per hour in under three seconds. As their engines roared and the road blurred beneath them, the brothers shared a moment of freedom as they got away with some speeding on an open road with good clear views and no junctions for miles. The outside world dissolved into the rush of wind, the hum of the engines, and the joy of two siblings in pursuit of unbridled exhilaration. Jim let out a noise expressing his euphoria—"Wahoo!" His smile was wide as that of a child offered ice cream for the first time, completely overtaken by excitement. He and Jeff both shared a deep love for motorcycles that had its roots in their childhood, riding with their dad in their fair-sized garden, tearing up the grass, much to their mother's dismay.

Jeff's Suzuki 1200 Bandit fell short in terms of top speed, making it a test of rider skill to keep up with the GSXR. Jim's bike, capable of hitting a hundred and eighty miles per hour, outmatched the Bandit not just in top speed but also in acceleration. Jeff had lovingly nicknamed his Bandit the "wheelie monster", as what it lacked in speed it gained in torque.

Jim approached a small hump bridge and seized the moment. Channelling the spirit of Evel Knievel, he accelerated, taking flight and soaring at least a metre high before landing smoothly. He couldn't help but chuckle as the thrill of conquering the jump washed over him.

In his rear-view mirror he saw Jeff take the air, and as gravity reclaimed him, the back wheel thudded on the road, turning his machine into a bucking bronco. With disaster inches away, the bike wobbled precariously before he regained control.

Jim let out a sigh and checked in with Jeff on their two-way intercom system. "Are you okay, little brother?"

"Yes, I'm fine—a little squeaky bum time there, but I held it up all right. Don't you worry, bro."

About halfway into their journey, the clear sky turned into an unusual, thick fog. Jeff warned his brother through the helmet communication system to slow down due to the drastically reduced visibility. Even with his lights on, he struggled to see more than fifteen feet ahead. The fog grew denser, transforming into an eerie orange haze, more like dust or a sandstorm, unlike anything he had ever seen in England.

In a state of shock, Jim witnessed the unimaginable unfolding before them—the quantum vortex materializing right before their eyes with him careering towards it.

"Jeff, can you see that?" Jim shouted, but the helmet communication system was plagued by static.

Jim surveyed his surroundings, observing in the sluggish movement of the ground beneath him that time was slowing down. The speedometer remained fixed at thirty miles per hour, while the colours around him distorted into strange hues. The orange fog began to emit a blinding white light at the centre, leaving Jim with no choice but to ride straight into the heart of the anomaly. He eased off the throttle, gently applying the brakes to slow down and keep control.

He turned to make sure Jeff was still behind him. "Stay calm! Slow down, Jeff! Brace yourself for a turbulent ride!" he yelled, hoping Jeff could hear him, as he entered into the dimensional anomaly.

Jim knew that maintaining balance would be crucial upon re-entry, as quite often he materialised on the other side at a height. He anticipated the need for rapid manoeuvres to dodge potential obstacles or vehicles in this new realm.

Upon emerging on the other side, colours returned to normal, but the fog persisted. Their bikes, initially travelling at thirty miles per hour, experienced sudden jolts, as if gravity had amplified their velocity. Jim's bike lifted off the ground, performing a wild shimmy before landing on its rear wheel, the impact far more ferocious than the comparatively small jump they had both manoeuvred. With his extensive motorbike experience, Jim managed to handle the situation, recovering from the perilous wobble and regaining control. Jeff, on the other hand, came out of the anomaly in a chaotic slide, eventually disentangling himself from his bike before it came to a halt.

"What just happened?" Jeff's voice trembled with shock.

Jim, rushed over to help Jeff's, and replied optimistically, "You seem okay; thank God you made it through. I had hoped you might have experienced this before."

"Are you kidding me?" Jeff exclaimed incredulously.

"I've wanted to talk to you about this for years—well, other versions of you."

Jeff's wide-eyed, bewildered gaze spoke volumes. "So you've seen this before? What the hell is it?"

"Yes—it's some kind of doorway to other versions of reality."

But Jeff's perplexity only deepened, rendering him momentarily speechless.

"Don't worry, Jeff. We'll navigate this together," Jim said confidently.

"What did you mean by other versions of me?"

"It's hard to explain. Let's talk when we get back to my house," Jim replied.

The fog began to lift slowly. Jim's apprehension grew as he checked his mobile phone, finding he had no signal. "Come on, Jeff. I need to get back home to see my family."

"What's bothering you, Jim?"

"Nothing, let's just get back to my place, okay?"

Jim's reply was gruff, having intended to avoid discussing the possibility that he might have lost his family once more. Jeff recognized the tone and opted not to press him, especially as his own anxiety mirrored his brother's.

As they resumed their journey home, the landscape revealed signs of death—lifeless birds and animals littered the surroundings. Their approach to a traffic jam further highlighted the eerie change. Jim deftly manoeuvred his way through the immobilized vehicles, stealing glimpses into the lifeless interiors. The scene was a grim testament to the ravages that had befallen this reality. The cars stood as corroded relics, succumbing to the onslaught of time, decay, or something else entirely. The majority of the cars were occupied by lifeless corpses, suggesting that whatever tragedy had unfolded here had done so swiftly. In the distance, the sun hung like a withered orange in a sky turned black, as though the Earth's orbit had veered off course or some other unimaginable catastrophe had occurred.

Now at a solemn pace, Jim stole a glance towards Jeff. Their eyes met briefly through the visors of their crash helmets, a silent exchange of understanding passing between them as eyes widened. They shared a moment of empathetic shock at the devastation surrounding them. Together, they wove through the macabre gridlock of death.

Hours later, they arrived at Jim's home. Rain was beginning to fall, yet its scent was foul. As Jim extended his gloved hand, he watched in dismay as the leather discoloured. They sought shelter on the porch from the ominous rain. Jim fumbled with his keys desperately as he tried to open the front door.

When they finally entered, they were greeted by a dishevelled house. The photos on the wall appeared to have been collected up as only a faint mark where the paint had faded left a hint their used to be a picture there, anything of value was nowhere to be seen. In the kitchen were open cupboards, revealing their emptiness, an unsettling sight.

Jim's frantic search led him to his diary, which was, strangely, lying open on the floor. When he flipped through the pages, his gaze settled on the final entry, sending a shiver coursing through his veins. The entry recounted a planet Earth poisoned to a cataclysmic extent, and life struggling to endure amid societal collapse. Acid rain had become commonplace. The lifeless bodies on the road, the corroded vehicles—they all bore witness to the Earth's tragic fate. His thoughts turned to his loved ones, dreading the uncertainty that loomed ahead. In the diary's final entry, the few sentences were ominous and incomplete, its smudged words a testament to the haste with which he had written, *The survivors are all turning on each other, fighting for resources. I am heading to my parents', and Scarlett has gone to the f...*

"I think Scarlett might have gone to Alex's farm, Jeff. What do you think?" Jim asked, his voice tinged with despair, showing him the diary entry.

"Maybe, yeah, would make sense, but what about Mum and Dad—do you think they're all right?"

Jeff's question elicited a pang of shame in Jim's heart. Across countless realities, he had searched for Scarlett and Jerica, often leaving no time to search for his parents. However, he reminded himself that his primary goal had always been to find his original universe. But with nothing else to try, it seemed a feasible suggestion. He also considered the possible benefits of the rock formation Alex called a small henge, assisting him with opening another vortex to get out of this nightmare.

"You're right. We should check on them. However, we need to focus—our main aim now is to get back to our own realities. Well, my reality, which is different to the previous one, which is better than this one, but when in Rome..." Jim conceded.

"What do you mean, 'our own realities', and what did you mean earlier about 'other versions of me'? What the hell is going on?" Jeff's scepticism was palpable.

"Do you remember how Scarlett and I were together, do you remember how we got along over the course of our relationship?" Jim asked.

"I do, yes. You got on really well. That was before her accident, of course. You two had a lot of problems after that," Jeff replied.

"Accident? What accident? You see, in my reality we

didn't have any accident or major dramas to contend with."

"So you're from a different reality to me?"

"Yes, originally, yes. Let me ask you a question—have you heard of the Mandela effect?"

"Yeah, sure, why?"

"Great, can you remember another turn of events that was a significant change for you? Let me show you. We used to play Monopoly as kids every Christmas, in my reality. We knew it well, right? Is that the same for you?"

"Yes, why?" Jeff questioned.

"Okay, good, does the Monopoly man have a monocle?"

"Of course he does."

"Well, let's see what's real in this universe. Help me find the game." After a brief search Jim showed him the game and Jeff was shocked. No monocle. "How about one of our favourite films, *Forrest Gump?* Is the phrase 'life is like a box of chocolates' or 'life was like a box of chocolates'?"

"'Life is'," Jeff said.

"A little harder for me to prove since there is no power here, but most realities I have been to since my own it was 'life was like', which makes no flipping sense to me. There are hundreds if not thousands of examples. If we had power, we might find here it's back to normal and the scarecrow in *The Wizard of Oz* might have lost his gun again."

"Wait, Scarecrow has a gun? Get out of here."

"Yup. Weird, huh? And remember that terrifying scene where the witch unleashes her flying monkeys', what did she say?"

"'Fly, my pretties, fly'. I remember that scene vividly it terrified me." Jeff answered.

"Most realities, she just says 'Now fly, fly' but to me, it loses the evil emotion, there is no weight to it anymore. Anyway, look—each reality has its own differences. Sometimes they're so small, you barely notice when the Mandela effect kicks in. But when we pass through the dimensional rift, it's like we skip straight into a reality that's totally different from our own. The weird part is, as I grew up and experienced the effect without going through a portal, the more similar or connected the reality was, the more the changes felt familiar. So we don't notice a shift we just accept it—even if it feels wrong—and we don't make a fuss about it. I only realised this after I did some research. Take Vader, for instance—he doesnt say 'Luke, I am your father,' any more. Now he says, 'No! I am your father' and it just loses something. The original feeling is gone."

"No way, has that changed too?" Jeff asked, eyes wide.

“Yup, in some realities, it has. But look, our main focus right now is survival. We'll wait out this storm, and then ride to see if Mum and Dad are okay at home. After that, we'll head to Alex's farm. If we're lucky, we can get everyone out of here, or at least find out if his lake has turned into its own self-sustaining ecosystem, we might be able to get some fish to eat. For now, though, let's find some food, grab some water, and rest for a bit.

The air hung heavy, suffused with mysterious convective forces that seemed to exert an unsettling influence on Jim like a static charge warming his skin. He couldn't shake the strange sensation of vibrations rippling through his body, as if his very being was resonating with an unfamiliar energy in this reality. He hoped it would pass when the storm subsided.

Despite its terrifying intensity, the storm's roar was almost mesmerizing. Jim found himself entranced by the astonishing might of nature. He stole a brief glance at Jeff, who was clearly captivated by the storm as well, his focus unwavering as he remained fixed on its tumultuous display. Amidst the tempest's fury, Jim's thoughts ran wild, his gaze fixed on the sky illuminated by bursts of energy, captivated by the raw power on display.

Chapter 17 – Trapped on a Forsaken Earth

The unending storm showed no signs of easing. Hunger and thirst compelled them to continue their search for sustenance. Jim's relief at finding water in the toilet cistern was short-lived and gave way to amusement. The water was surprisingly clean and odourless. They couldn't help but chuckle at the absurdity of contemplating drinking from the toilet. Jim replaced the lid, turning down the option for now.

Jim's search for his cat yielded no results, leaving him to wonder if Scarlett had taken him, or if they had met a grim fate. Stumbling upon a stash of cat food in a kitchen cupboard, the brothers guffawed at the thought of dining on cat food and toilet water. Although unconventional, having options provided a degree of comfort. Their mirth echoed through the house, and their sides ached.

"Cat food for dinner?" Jim managed to choke out between breathless fits of amusement.

After their laughter subsided, they returned to the window, the storm's unrelenting fury mirrored their emotional roller coaster. The captivating spectacle continued to draw them in. The thunder and lightning surpassed anything they'd seen in movies. While the storm raged outside, their sense of wonder remained undiminished. There was an unspoken understanding that they were each grateful not to face this awe-inspiring might alone.

“We could risk going out in it and check on Mum and Dad or see if they left anything,” Jeff suggested.

“You saw what it did to those cars and our motorcycle gear. I don’t think so, Jeff, let’s stick with the plan and wait it out.”

The night sky continued to transform into a dazzling spectacle, a celestial dance in which darkness and pure brilliance collided as lightning streaked across the heavens, illuminating the horizon with veins of vivid light. Red and blue bursts occasionally joined the symphony of thunder, painting the clouds in volcanic hues. In this cosmic theatre, the moon made sporadic appearances, casting an oddly magnified, blue-tinted light. The laws of physics seemed different here. The otherworldly panorama proved irresistibly captivating, drawing attention like voyagers to an uncharted horizon.

Seeking rest, Jim and Jeff gathered in the living room, where they arranged mattresses closely to keep an eye on the enthralling storm through the window. Uncertain of what lay ahead, Jim insisted they stay together, prepared for the return of the wormhole.

“Jim, can you explain it again? I’m still trying to grasp it,” Jeff said.

"In one reality I visited, I worked with scientists as their lead physicist—I had to bluff my way through that one. There, I discovered a link between what they called the Mandela field and experiments with a large hadron collider. Look at this dog tag." Jim displayed the tag from the leader of Flight 21 in the past. "They're somehow connected to this phenomenon. Think of it as a doorway to other universes."

"That sounds unbelievable," Jeff replied sceptically.

"Scientists discovered the Higgs boson and dubbed it the 'God particle'. What I read said it exists everywhere, all the time. Collisions in the collider might have caused fractures in space-time, creating temporary openings between realities. Whether these experiments made realities collide, merge or destabilize—or whether something else caused it—I don't know. But our priority is survival, we need to find a way back to the portal and locate our loved ones. Any better ideas?" Jim said, his eyes meeting his brother's, acknowledging the mysteries they faced.

"All right, so you don't have a clue what's going on either," Jeff replied, a sly smile on his face.

Jim nodded. "I can't say I fully understand it, no, not really. What I know for sure is that the phenomenon will return, and we need to be ready. You have to stay close to me from now on, little brother. I found some research papers that suggested the Higgs particle could be linked to a fifth-dimensional membrane that connects different universes. The wormhole might be created by negative energy from the Higgs boson experiments. When I transition into other realities, I never see my other self. I think we can't coexist in the same universe as our counterparts and there are always differences...” Jim's voice trailed off as he observed the faint creases of fatigue on Jeff's face—the slight sag of his posture, the occasional flutter of his eyelids, and the weary lines etched around his eyes. It was evident that Jeff was putting up a valiant effort to ward off the overwhelming exhaustion.

“Jeff, did you get all of that? Am I boring you with science nonsense?” Jim asked. Jeff's eyes were closing as he drifted toward sleep. “Are you hungry for cat food yet?” Jim smirked, trying to raise a smile.

Jeff's humour shone through. With his eyes still closed, he playfully motioned towards the cat food with a finger, and then flipped Jim the bird. They both chuckled before succumbing to sleep.

* * *

The next morning, the early sunlight disrupted their slumber. Hunger and the idea of breakfast had stripped away the humour of the cat food. Jim hesitantly took a bite, then was unable to prevent his expression revealing his true feelings. “It's not that bad,” he claimed unconvincingly.

Jeff replied, “Yeah, right. It looks delicious. Not,”

neither of them was laughing now. They managed to eat some cat food before deciding to drive to their parents' house in Jim's car. The toilet water offered little refreshment, other than washing away the flavour of the cat food.

When they arrived at their parents' home, they found it empty. Their parents' neatly made bed hinted at an unrushed departure.

"That's just like our mother. End of the world and she can't be rushed. Made the bed and I bet she did the washing up too while Dad was getting annoyed at her dilly-dallying," Jeff said as they continued searching the house.

"Chocolate!" Jim remembered suddenly. He dashed to the bottom cupboard to retrieve his dad's secret stash. Opening the concealed Tupperware box, Jim was relieved to see it was empty.

"They got out, Jeff. Dad took the chocolate stash, I saw him hiding it here from Mum once because otherwise she eats it all before he gets any. He told me to keep it as 'our secret'," he explained, showing the now-empty container.

Jeff offered a less optimistic possibility: "Or maybe they just finished it all before leaving?"

Jim countered quickly, "No, you don't understand. Either way, it means they were here for a while and then decided to leave. They must have left when they realised the situation wasn't getting any better. There's hope they found safety somewhere."

"Let's check the garage." Eagerly, Jim rushed ahead, nearly knocking Jeff over in his haste.

In the garage, his jubilant reaction told the tale. "Yes!" he exclaimed.

"What happened?" Jeff asked, catching up.

"Don't you see? Their car is gone. It means they must have made it out. Dad took whatever water and food they could, and they left before things got too dire. There are no signs of panic or haste in the house," Jim explained, a hopeful smile on his face.

"But where could they have gone?" Jeff pondered.

"I'm not sure, but we have to believe they made it out. Where would *we* go?"

"That's easy—back to Alex's farm. I would have told them about Alex's preparations. It's our best chance of finding them, it's a safe bet my doppelganger would have told them too."

"That's where we need to head," Jim said. "I'm confident one of us would have told them to go there, and Alex wouldn't have turned them away. He always said our parents were like a mother and father to him too when we was growing up."

Jim's resolve was reinvigorated now that they had a

clear objective in mind. They had driven his car in case his parents needed it, knowing he and Jeff would eventually return to their bikes—navigating the car through the barricaded main roads would have been impossible. On their way back to Jim's house, they kept an eye out for stores or potential sources of supplies.

Upon returning to Jim's house, they reluctantly consumed another serving of cat food, their distaste for it growing with each bite. They also filled a small bottle with toilet water for later. Jeff packed the essential supplies into a pack secured to the bike and patted the tank affectionately.

"Ready, little brother?" he inquired.

"Yup," Jeff replied.

And so their adventure in this new world continued.

Chapter 18 – Lost Brothers Torn Apart by Fate

Jim and Jeff approached the jammed motorway, navigating the congestion on their bikes. Cruising steadily, Jeff called over the motorcycle intercom, signalling he wanted to stop. They pulled up under a bridge and removed their helmets.

"Jim, what if our parents' car is among all these vehicles?" Jeff asked, gesturing at the abandoned cars.

"Trust me, they're not here," Jim said confidently, dismissing the possibility.

"Shouldn't we at least keep an eye out for their car?"

"When you've experienced as many different realities as I have, you realise that there's nothing you can do, Jeff. Suppose their car is here. Do we just give up? Look, I think naturally if one of us spots their car we should stop and check they aren't in there. But let's stay positive, okay? Mum, Dad, Jerica and Scarlett are at Alex's farm, or we find a way out of this reality together. Most importantly, you stick by my side, you understand? Besides, they are positively alive in another reality. Who knows how long we'll stay here? Just stay close to me in case that vortex reopens," Jim explained.

"You're right, let's stay positive, but keep an eye out

anyway," Jeff conceded, still adjusting to this shift in perspective. "Look at that. What a sweet-looking ride," he exclaimed, changing the subject with practised expertise. "Is it wrong if I take this dead guy's Harley Davidson for a spin?" He pointed at a deceased biker.

"I just had an 'aha!' moment," Jim remarked. "This guy doesn't look too decomposed, and the bike is in good shape aside from a few scratches. This tragedy can't have happened too long ago, Jeff. He's been sheltered by the bridge."

With a furtive look around, Jeff mounted the bike. Jim chuckled at the natural reaction, and watched as his brother rode around on the Harley.

"*Easy Rider*, Yeehaa!" Jeff exclaimed above the deep roar of the bike's powerful engine. Then he glanced at the dead biker and offered a respectful apology.

They set off together, navigating the maze of vehicles. Jim gazed at the sky painted with shades of red, blue and grey, an indistinct yet picturesque summer's day in an alien world.

A few miles from Alex's farm, the anomaly reopened, leaving Jim in shock as he glanced towards his brother in the rear-view mirror—he was further away than Jim had hoped, and seemingly frozen in time. Fearing leaving Jeff behind in this unfamiliar reality, Jim leapt off his bike, desperately trying to avoid plunging into the temporal portal without his brother. The thought of abandoning Jeff tore at him. He landed on the ground and watched his bike spin off the road, slowing down unnaturally until it was motionless. With his own momentum propelling him forward, Jim overtook the frozen bike and the field captured him. He knew he had limited time before he spiralled into another reality, and he feared his brother was too far away to come with him this time. His loyalty to his brother compelled him to stay in the cursed Earth.

Frantically, he clawed at the concrete, attempting to find something to anchor himself. He seized an old metal bumper that had fallen loose from someone's vehicle and pounded it into the ground, but his efforts were in vain. Desperation welled within him as he shouted, "No!" and his voice burned with pain during the transition into the vortex.

Jim landed harshly on the road. Narrowly avoiding an oncoming car, he rolled off the road. He rested his head on the grass verge for a moment, struggling to hold back tears. Then, surveying his surroundings, he hoped against the odds that his brother would come through as well. Unfortunately, that wasn't the case, and he became numb, powerless to do anything about leaving his brother trapped there in that dead world.

After some time, Jim regained some semblance of composure. He remembered his earlier conversation with Jeff. He couldn't save everyone across the multiverse; it was an impossible task. Recalling his own words, he muttered to himself, “Do you believe you can change the universe and improve it? I don’t believe it can be done. This is not my fault.” Jim realised the situation was beyond his control.

Jim’s bike hadn’t made the transition, and neither had the supplies secured to it. He was grateful that his own motorcycle leathers had protected him from major physical injury, leaving him with just minor scrapes.

As he walked toward his friend’s farm, the thought that solitude was the last thing he needed gave him pause. He stopped and clung to a signpost as if hugging it for some comfort. He knew he had to regain his composure; he couldn’t remain a statue of despair forever. As daylight faded, he accepted that he needed to rescue Jeff if and when the opportunity presented itself. Closing his eyes, he visualized the event in his mind, letting go of the pain yet longing to bring his brother back. The power of his visualisation was so intense that a wave of emotion swept through his body, as if every cell resonated with a positive vibration, as if he was manifesting a reality.

When he opened his eyes, he couldn’t believe his luck. The event horizon of the portal appeared before him, summoned intentionally for the first time. He gazed into the interdimensional gateway. Its immense power surged through his body. He saw himself in the past, and other realities he had visited, but he was looking for the previous reality. Jim was concerned that the visions within the vortex didn’t always match his destinations; however, he realised this was his best chance of returning to the wasteland to rescue Jeff. He watched intently, waiting for glimpses of his brother. He finally succumbed to the gravitation of the dimensional rift, but it closed before he could reach the event horizon. He had lost his control over it and the anomaly just collapsed out of existence.

Jim fell to the floor, but refused to admit defeat. Through gritted teeth, he declared, "You only fail when you quit."

Hungry and determined, he walked the remaining miles to his friend's farm, constantly trying to call upon the anomaly. Reflecting on his past successes, he thought about the time he'd returned to a universe where Jerica was alive and tried to recapture that feeling and other successful reunions with loved ones. Stopping to focus on a specific point ahead of him, he concentrated all his energy on his goal. But this time, nothing happened. He continued walking, resolute and more focused than ever on learning how to control, or at least call upon, the oddity. He was beginning to believe that with practice, anything was possible.

Upon arriving at Alex's farm, Jim observed that everything looked the same as during his previous visit. The ancient monoliths were present and still fallen in the nearby field, and the same cars were parked in the driveway, indicating his friends were still here, providing some much-needed familiarity. He had no clear plan in mind—all he wanted was rest and food, hoping for a fresh start the next day.

Alex's surprise upon seeing him was tinged with concern about Jim's motorcycle leathers, prompting questions about Jeff's whereabouts and the bike's fate.

Jim wasn't in the mood for an interrogation. "Where in the world indeed," he replied cryptically, not yet willing to confess he had left Jeff behind in another reality.

Alex pressed him for answers, asking about the bike and the accident.

Jim, desperate and needing shelter, explained, "I had a motorcycle accident. One moment he was there behind me, and the next I was dragged into the infernal vortex. One moment I was with him, and then I was here. I just need a place to stay, mate."

Understanding Jim was in shock, Alex ushered him inside and settled him on the couch. In a flurry, he provided comfort and a quick meal, and Jim devoured the food so rapidly he felt a bit queasy. It had been a while since he'd eaten well. Exhausted, he collapsed on the couch, where Alex had left him a blanket, and rested.

Chapter 19 – Celebration Amongst the Lost

The rising sun cast a tranquil glow through the window, creating a serene atmosphere for Jim to awaken calmly. He took a deep breath of gratitude, it was a welcome contrast from the previous reality.

Amber, Alex's wife, entered the room and was surprised to see Jim on the sofa—it appeared that Alex hadn't informed his wife that Jim had stayed over.

"Oof! You made me jump." She flinched, slightly embarrassed.

She was dressed elegantly, wearing an ivory and black flock chemise with a long slit revealing her firm thigh. Startled, Amber quickly grabbed a blanket to cover herself, and let out a scream when she inadvertently saw more of Jim than intended due to his boxer shorts.

Jim couldn't help but laugh as Amber, in her flustered state, covered her face with her hand. He grabbed a nearby pillow to maintain his modesty.

"Sorry, Amber, I didn't mean to scare you," he said, still smiling and secretly enjoying the playful tease, a welcome distraction from the burden of guilt that had kept him awake half the night.

Amber rushed out of the room, her face still

concealed, and Jim heard her raise her voice at her husband, blaming him for the encounter. *Alex probably should have informed Amber before she ventured downstairs*, he mused to himself, a wry smirk tugging at the corners of his mouth as he heard her scolding Alex. With effort, Jim pressed his lips tightly together, his hand rising to cover his mouth in a futile attempt to contain the laughter threatening to spill out, all the while wary of Amber overhearing his mirth.

Jim got dressed quickly and fetched breakfast from the kitchen. Alex soon joined him, wearing a cheeky grin on his face.

"I hear you had an encounter with Amber this morning?" he said.

Jim couldn't resist sharing a laugh. "Yes, I'm sorry about that, mate," he replied.

"It's all right. She's a bit miffed with me for not telling her that you were here, and embarrassed about the whole situation. The other lads all moved into the annex after you two left—if she had known, she would have worn a dressing gown. Please don't tease her, Jim," Alex requested. "I'm already in hot water, so don't wind her up."

"Oh, I won't," Jim responded. "But I have to say, she's stunning. You're a lucky man," he added, winking at his friend.

Alex chuckled in response and nodded in respect of the compliment.

During breakfast, Jim opened up to Alex about his experiences over the past day. He shared the story of Jeff, lost in a world with acid rain, and his deep concern for his alternate brother. He also talked about Scarlett and Jerica, expressing his worries for his family's future. He talked about the Bermuda Triangle and the missing Flight 21 where his dog tag had originated from. When Alex replied he knew the story of the missing planes but in his reality it was Flight 19 that went missing, Jim acknowledged another Mandela effect. He admitted to feeling confused about what was real, and whether any of it truly mattered. He questioned how he would recognize his real family if he kept leaping between realities to find other versions of them.

Alex didn't have concrete answers, but Jim appreciated having a friend to confide in. It allowed him to discuss these problems without fearing he might sound crazy, which helped clear his mind. It only struck him halfway through their conversation that this version of Alex might never have experienced the vortex, making him even more grateful for his friend's understanding.

Alex suggested they go for a walk and led Jim to one of his fields, where the ancient monoliths lay. Each stone bore the scars of millennia, worn smooth by the relentless caress of the elements. Moss and lichen clung to their surfaces, lending an ethereal green hue to the weathered grey. Like Stonehenge, these colossal stones had once reached towards the heavens, but here and now, they had collapsed.

"I wanted to learn more about this part of the field and I found the tips of these stones, and so I excavated and uncovered them as best I could. Look at this." Alex placed his mobile phone against one of the stones. The phone's screen started flickering with intense interference. Alex quickly put it back in his pocket. Jim reached for his own phone and the same effect occurred, displaying patterns of energy rippling across the screen.

"I often wonder, were ancient people deliberately hiding them? Not only had they fallen, they had been deliberately covered up as well. It seems unlikely to me nature covered them. I guess we will never know," Alex said, sealing his lips in a tight line across his mouth in contemplative thought.

"Be careful, Jim—it's some kind of magnetic energy field. It's damaged one of my phones, so don't leave yours near it for too long," Alex said.

"Why did you bring me here, Alex?" Jim asked.

"The first time I went through the vortex, I landed here. When I returned to my original reality, I felt this place was significant. I couldn't get it out of my mind. Imagine how I felt when I saw it for sale. I had no choice but to buy it. First thing I did was come here and dig." Alex's expression was one of chilling intensity.

Jim was intrigued by the concept of having an anchor point. "I see. So you think the stones drew you here? That's fascinating. I don't have a fixed point like that when I go through. It seems completely random for me, although it's linked to my dog tag. I've managed to control it a few times to a limited extent."

They talked for hours, discussing theories and experiences, and exploring the monoliths—at least, the exposed remains of them. They questioned their own sanity, but concluded since they had similar perspectives it was not a mental illness, but actual temporal effects.

"Would you mind giving me a moment Alex, please?"

"Sure, I need to go and check on the other reprobates any way and see if they want any breakfast or if they will be lying in until the afternoon again."

Jim walked around the henge, searching for the ideal spot. One stone featured a convenient natural hollow, worn by centuries of weathering, which provided the perfect place to secure his grip. He was ready to practise controlling the rift. Placing one hand on the stone, he closed his eyes and focused his thoughts on his reunited and happy family, including Jeff safe and sound.

Gradually, Jim relaxed his concentration, his mind and body to enter a state of deep relaxation, reaching an intense emotional state as tingling sensations of energy coursed through him, his dog tag held in his other hand.

He sensed the changing atmosphere. Opening his eyes, he observed a translucent, silky mist forming around the base of each stone and at the top, creating a halo effect. A vortex started to manifest overhead, accompanied by a slight gravitational disturbance, noticeable from the shifting of tiny stones and loose dirt scuttling towards the rift. Jim checked the time on his watch, which was moving at a slightly slower pace, but not drastically so. Within the centre of the vortex played out visions of past, present, future and alternative realities.

As he waited for the perfect moment to enter the rift, he witnessed an event he hadn't noticed before. In the vision, everyone he cared about was gathered at a party: his wife, child, parents and most of his friends and their wives or girlfriends. Even Jeff was there. A birthday cake with Jim's name on it suggested this was his own upcoming celebration, still months away by his reckoning. Realising it was an opportune time, Jim loosened his grip on the stone and allowed himself to drift upward into the gateway between realms.

The transition seemed notably calmer, but Jim's arrival on the other side was less so. As he emerged from the portal he bumped his head on a urinal. Cursing in pain, he rolled onto the floor, clutching his head. Laughter from someone entering the toilets echoed around him.

"What happened, you lightweight? Why are you on the floor? Are you drunk already, you pussy?" His old friend Chris held his sides while he howled at his friend on the floor, in pain. Jim didn't know what to say, so he just looked at his friend and smiled. "Oh, man, that's so funny. I wish I'd come in a second ago and seen you fall over, mate. That's prime YouTube click bait." Chris moved nearer, offering his hand to help Jim up. Jim took his offer and grabbed his friend's hand to stand up, still holding his head with his other hand. He was still a bit stunned from the rough landing, but he was glad to see Chris.

"Chris, how are you, man? It's good to see you," Jim said, wincing and rubbing his head.

Chris passed wind loudly, and they both chortled uncontrollably. Amazingly, Jim couldn't feel much of the pain from the bump after that.

"You haven't changed a bit—still as warm and smelly as ever," Jim chuckled.

"Hey, and neither have you. A couple of drinks and you're on the floor in the toilets. Man, you must have hit your head harder than I thought. You already said all this at the bar earlier," Chris replied, sighing from the breathlessness of their humorous outburst.

"What do you say we go and get some more drinks then, buddy?" Jim said, excited to see all the people he loved again.

"Sure, it's your birthday after all, Jim. Do you think you can handle it, lightweight?" Chris teased.

"Let's find out. Mine's a whiskey and Coke—thanks,

buddy," Jim said, his lips curling into a grateful grin.

Upon re-entering the party hall, Jim stood for a moment and took in the scene, observing the various special people from his life gathered in one room, alive and well, all enjoying the party. As they danced, mingled and celebrated, they seemed unaware of his recent absence, while he had missed each of them intensely.

Then a sweet, angelic voice rang out. "Daddy, Daddy, Daddy, happy birthday, Daddy!"

Jim's gaze dropped, a whirlwind of emotions stirring within him as he beheld his three-year-old daughter, Jerica. There she stood, her small frame framed by the vastness of the room, her arms reaching out to him in a silent invitation. In that instant, a surge of warmth spread through Jim's chest, mingling with a tingling sensation that prickled along his skin.

"Jerica! You look beautiful. Oh, I love you so much," Jim exclaimed, sweeping her up and spinning her around in his arms.

Her happiness emanated from every inch of her being, evident in the sparkle of her eyes and the dimples that deepened with her beaming smile. Jim was caught in the moment, fully immersed in the joyous reunion with his precious daughter.

Scarlett approached next, and he ran to meet her halfway, still carrying Jerica, paying no mind to onlookers.

He held them both tightly for as long as they would allow.

"Happy birthday, Daddy. Would you like a drink?" Scarlett asked.

Jim fought back tears as he replied, "Yes, I definitely need a drink, but I think Chris is getting me one."

Scarlett asked, "What's wrong?"

"Absolutely nothing—I've never been happier. These are tears of joy, my love," Jim assured her as they made their way to the bar.

The entire evening seemed like a dream to Jim. He spent quality time with his parents, and even his brother Jeff and Bullet were present in this reality, which was a huge relief. Jim enjoyed having a drink with his parents, and couldn't help but chuckle as he observed his mum indulging in chocolate again.

"Where does she put it all, Dad?" Jim asked curiously.

His father replied, "I have no idea; she's as slim as ever. It's probably because she doesn't sit still."

Jim's mum laughed and playfully swatted his dad, all while taking another bite of chocolate. Within minutes, she assumed her role as a grandmother, chasing after Jerica and joining her in running and dancing around.

Jim was the star of the party, and he relished the

attention. Robbie, Chris, Alex, Bullet, Sid and Chad surrounded Jim at the bar. In high spirits, they shared laughter and jokes for hours. Chad, as always fashionably late and ready to party, took full advantage of the offer of shots for two pound. They ended up in a shot-drinking competition, but Jim wisely abstained, determined to savour every moment. In typical Bullet fashion, he managed to skip paying for his round of drinks. Engaging the bar man in conversation he distracted him just enough that the bill was forgotten. Grinning, Bullet handed out the shots, nearly spilling them as he struggled to contain his laughter.

Jim spent the evening conversing with old friends and family, savouring the time with these wonderful people. Although he was enjoying the festivities, he ached to return home with Scarlett and Jerica, away from the attention of others. The paradox was that he was eager for the party to continue and yet also desperate to leave.

As the night's end approached, the DJ selected one of Scarlett and Jim's cherished romantic tunes. With a tug, Scarlett pulled Jim onto the dance floor, craving a slow dance, and he acquiesced without hesitation. Amidst the tender notes of their wedding song, they found themselves enveloped in an intimate embrace, sharing a passionate kiss that spoke volumes without a word. Lost in each other's gaze, they swayed to the music, immersed in their own world.

By the end of the night, Jim, tired, took a seat with

his dad, watching the final moments of the celebration, and couldn't take his eyes off his beautiful wife. Even as the party wound down, Scarlett and Jerica continued to dance together. Jim bid farewell to his friends with a sense of melancholy as he contemplated the uncertain future, and the question of when he might reunite with these wonderful people again.

Scarlett joined Jim, collapsing into a chair beside him, clearly exhausted. Jerica had fallen asleep in her pushchair beside them. She had a lot of energy; it was nice to see her so peaceful.

"She's grown so much." Jim could barely stop looking at her, regretting the lost time.

"Are you ready to help me tidy up this hall?" Scarlett asked Jim. She looked utterly drained.

"Okay, let's do it," Jim replied, grateful for the distracting shift in thoughts. His parents and his brother Jeff also pitched in to help with the tidying. Together, they had the hall looking quite orderly within an hour.

Jim grew fearful this respite wouldn't last, but he was determined to make the most of this gift of time, however fleeting it might be. *At least I had some element of control over the vortex this time,* he thought to himself.

Chapter 20 – The Enterprise's Quest into the Triangle

In the early hours of the morning, Jim awoke beside his beloved. A sense of tranquillity enveloped him. He stroked her strawberry blonde hair as she slept, basking in their togetherness. A smile graced her face, and Jim couldn't help but smile too, grateful for the enchanting evening they had shared. His affection and concern for her ran deep. His thoughts turned to protecting his family from the terrors he had witnessed in other realities.

Jim contemplated the toll the anomaly was taking on his emotional state. He'd finally made it home and yet an overwhelming unease bubbled in his stomach. He left for the bathroom, a knot of apprehension tightening in his chest as fears of being whisked away gripped him. He did some deep breathing exercises to help him gain some level of control back, and after a few minutes returned to their bedroom. He didn't want to wake Scarlett, so he decided to read his journal. Curiously, he reached for the hidden compartment under the bed, wondering if this version of him had experienced any encounters with the vortex.

"What are you doing?" Scarlett mumbled, her voice laden with frustration in her semi-conscious morning state. "You woke me up. What's up? You seem restless."

Jim whispered, "Nothing," settling on the floor, cross-legged and hidden from her view. She closed her eyes, allowing him to continue his research. Fortunately, enough morning light etched through the corners of the curtains to allow him to read.

He leafed through his journal, searching for any signs of changes or vortex-related incidents. This version of him had lived a normal life—similar, yet noticeably different; he had his own technology company, for starters. This wasn't his reality, but it certainly felt like home. As he continued reading, he felt the pull of the anomaly behind him. He watched helplessly as Scarlett lay in her bed, unaffected by the disturbance. So many repeated losses had made him feel numb, a denial of grief and a reluctant acceptance that he wasn't quite home yet.

As he passed through the vortex once more, he still harboured a degree of confidence earned from the previous success. To his surprise, Jim found himself in a familiar, small, swaying room with battleship-grey metal walls. The logical assumption was that he was back on the *Enterprise*.

He sat at a small desk, searching for his journal. First he found his scientific logbook. A quick skim through confirmed he was in a reality in which he worked as a quantum scientist again. He wondered if he had been in this reality before or if it was another similar one.

Reflecting on the jumps he had experienced, he

realised the mysteries were growing stranger. He thought about the holiday with friends, the world in which his friend Bullet had died, the world with abundant wealth but no loved ones, and the darker realities and sinister villains he had encountered. Things could certainly be worse.

He needed answers, so he made his way to the ship's bridge, fortunately no guard was on duty to prevent him entering.

"This is no place for a civilian," Captain Malik said to Jim with a scowl.

"I need to know what's been happening for my scientific research, Captain. I think I might be able to help," Jim responded, trying to exude confidence.

"Dr Knight, I will respond in due time, unless you have any specific questions—clear the bridge," Captain Malik commanded with a finger pointing at the door.

But Jim was determined to buy time, so he brought up the experiments that were causing strange readings on the sensors that started the whole excursion in the first place. The captain, intrigued by these unusual events, granted Jim a brief reprieve. Jim asked for a private conversation, but Captain Malik declined.

"We detected sensor readings over the Bermuda Triangle in the co-ordinates Truman has us heading towards. The onboard particle accelerator, is creating the similar readings on a smaller scale, designated as the

Mandela field, and the experiments are exploring the possibility of creating doorways to different realities. When the Mandela Field on this ship comes in contact with whatever it is out there, we don't know what will happen." Jim said.

"Sounds like it's about time we shut these experiments down," Captain Malik declared.

"Colonel Truman won't allow that, Captain," Jim warned. "The government wants control of this doorway. Shutting it down now could end your career."

"Fine, if a court martial is what's needed, I welcome it."

"Remember what Colonel Truman said? Ship and crew are expendable on this mission. They would just replace you, sir, and carry on with someone else. By the time you have your court martial it would be too late. Now isn't the time, but perhaps later things may change when we have more intel."

"What is the status of the drone?" Captain Malik asked his bridge crew.

"I had it on standby in anticipation of your command, sir. She launched and is on route with clear skies, checks five-oh, Captain."

"Good work, CAG—that's why you're the best," the captain complimented.

"Checks five-oh?" Jim asked.

"US Navy speak, Doctor. This is why you don't belong up here. It means excellent, in proper order."

"I see," Jim said, stepping back.

After a few moments, the radar technician reported, "Wait—it's gone, sir. It just went off the radar."

"Did she go down?"

"Unknown, sir. The UAV was at eighteen thousand feet and suddenly vanished off the radar. There was no indication of any drop in altitude and we've lost communication," the young officer replied.

Jim was fascinated by what he was witnessing.

"Was she shot down?" asked the captain.

"Negative, Captain, no other birds in the sky according to radar, and electronic countermeasures did not fire before we lost contact. Looks like a massive storm suddenly formed on the radar out of nowhere."

"CAG, I need my best man in the air. Find out what the hell is going on. Don't make me send out the angels. We only need a single sortie—I don't want to take any more risks," ordered the captain.

"What does CAG stand for? And the angels?" Jim whispered to one of the lower-ranking officers.

"It's Commander Balfour's designation, stands for Commander Air Group, sir. Angels are our SAR team, Search and Rescue," the officer said, anticipating another unknown Navy term.

"Captain, taking a jet into that cloud at this time is an unwarranted gamble. We don't know enough about it," Jim interrupted, earning himself the captain's death stare, fearful this move could lose the captain his commander.

"Double Nuts has already been prepped and I am set to go, sir," replied the commander, saving Jim from the captain's wrath.

"Double Nuts?" Jim whispered to the young officer again.

"CAG's plane designation is zero zero, sir. Hence double nuts."

Captain Malik was losing his patience. "What are you still doing here? Shut it down, Dr Knight!" the captain commanded, prioritising the safety of his crew.

"I can put a few spanners in the works and buy you some time until you find out what is going on in the Triangle, but we may not be able to permanently shut it down," said Jim. "I may be able to cut power on this experiment for now and we can see what happens from there. Can you keep me posted about what you find out, please, sir?"

"Good, get down to the cargo bay and do what you need to do. I'll call you on the bitch box if we find out anything useful," said Captain Malik. He turned his back and went towards the ready room.

He didn't notice Jim following him, staying at his side for as long as he could. "Thank you, on your way, CAG. Dr Knight, you too. Get down to engineering. If these experiments have anything to do with this, I want that thing shut down. Do I make myself clear, Doctor?" the captain commanded.

"You can call me Jim, sir. Oh, and I'll need something to subdue the other scientists." Jim winked at the captain and smiled.

The captain's expression changed to one of curiosity and amusement.

"Fine. CAG, on your way to the flight deck, can you make sure the good doctor finds his way, please, to sick bay. I'll inform them to expect you for some pussy pills and bilge juice," the captain said with a smile.

"Bilge juice?" Jim asked. The reaction from the bridge crew was raucous.

Jim left sheepishly and made his way to sickbay, where he was given the seasickness pills by the medic on duty, and the assistant gave Jim a litre flask and a metal cup.

* * *

Commander Balfour escorted Jim into the sick bay on his route to the flight deck and went in with him to ensure he had everything he needed.

"Be careful with this bilge juice, Doctor. When we

can't get hold of branded booze, we make our own moonshine. The captain turns a blind eye, but it's powerful stuff. He'd throw us in the brig and put us on report if he felt we were taking the piss. I wouldn't recommend using it with those pussy pills." Commander Balfour said.

"I'm almost afraid to ask, what is bilge juice? Could it kill someone?" Jim queried.

"The bilge juice on its own can be dangerous—be careful, sir. Not every swinging dick on this boat can take it, and I'm talking about some of the few hardened lifers still on board who can't touch this stuff. You could call it Navy moonshine, our own homemade alcohol, Doctor." The sick bay medic warned.

"I need to incapacitate the other scientists, not kill them. And why do you call them pussy pills?"

"If you are in the Navy, and you get sea sick you are a pussy." Commander Balfour chuckled.

"It's rare these ever get used on this ship. Okay, look, I'll give you one of these pills for each person. How many are there?" The medic said.

"Only two."

"Here you are, take this bottle and don't let them drink more than a glass each. Honestly, it's all they'll need. If they start having a reaction, call me on the bitch box. I'll have a stomach pump and a med team on standby." Furthermore, the young medical officer pointed out the warning on the accompanying leaflet of the captain's so-called 'pussy pills'.

Kwells (hyoscine hydrobromide)

This medicine is prone to cause drowsiness, may cause blurred vision and other side effects that may affect your ability to drive.

You should not drive or operate machinery if you experience these symptoms. Alcohol should be avoided as it can worsen these side effects.

As Jim left, he smiled and said, "That's perfect. I'll let you know if we need you.""Do you have everything you need, Doctor?" asked Commander Balfour.

"I believe so, yes, thank you, Commander."

"I need to get going, but what is your plan?"

"Incapacitate the scientists and cut the power on the experiments."

"That's it?" the commander said with a frown.

"That's all I've got, unless you have any better suggestions?"

"Okay, do you know your way from here? I need to get to the flight deck."

"Get going, Commander, I'm fine from here, thank you."

Chapter 21 – Allies United to Disable the Collider

As Jim entered the cargo bay he observed everything was strikingly the same as the last time he was here.

Keeping out of sight, Jim poured three cups, then added a pill to two. Suppressing laughter, he swirled the contents of each before approaching the scientists, giving the pills time to fully dissolve.

"Dr Amin, Dr Frank, could you use a pick-me-up?" Jim asked with a grin.

"What is it? What's so funny?" Dr Frank inquired, scowling at Jim's demeanour.

"This stuff is amazing." Jim pretended sipped his own unadulterated cup. "You wouldn't believe what I had to go through to get this," he added, swallowing hard.

"That looks good," Dr Amin replied.

"We're about to activate the collider. Maybe afterwards. Let's see how this run goes. Have you forgotten we need to get a report back to the colonel?" said Dr Frank.

Jim closed his eyes, recalling Tasha's presence on the *Enterprise*. Everything seemed the same apart from her presence; she couldn't be here though, she'd returned to her own reality.

As he opened his eyes, the vortex was opening. He gripped the handrail behind the console, the scientists froze and time slowed to a crawl. A gust of wind emanated from the wormhole, carrying with it a myriad of sensations. The atmosphere shimmered and crackled with energy, distorting the space around the vortex in mesmerizing patterns. The vortex moved closer, unveiling a figure cloaked in white. With a trumpet-like blast, Jim was knocked onto his back, his head spinning from the impact.

Awareness seeped back, he heard a familiar voice. “Jim, are you all right?”

Blinking and reaching for his head, Jim found Tasha straddling him as he lay on the uncomfortable metal floor of the *Enterprise*’s cargo bay. His head throbbed, leaving him momentarily dazed and groaning.

“Where are we?” Tasha asked, scanning the cargo deck.

“Back on the *Enterprise*. Am I relieved to see you! But would you mind?” Jim gestured for her to move off him.

“Oh,” she said, taking a moment to breathe in. She stayed put and smiled into his eyes.

“Just follow my lead, okay?” he said, attempting to deflect the awkwardness.

“Follow your lead? Just when I thought I had you

right where I wanted you," she teased, feeling his bicep. Her fascination with Jim persisted.

Jim, sat up as she adjusted herself. Time was still disrupted for the scientists, which gave him a moment to collect himself.

"I don't have time to explain, but we need to get these two scientists to drink this stuff so they pass out. They won't agree to switching off the machine, they live up the colonel's butt. I'm hoping they won't question where you came from. But if I'm right, it won't be an issue," Jim declared, confident that this would just be an unnoticed Mandela effect for them.

"Let's do it, Jim. I was just thinking about you right before I went through this thing again, you know?" Tasha said, taking every opportunity to touch Jim.

"Stay focused; we can talk after. Just help me get them to drink this stuff," Jim said, a bit flustered and embarrassed.

As they rose to their feet, time suddenly normalised, and the unstable deck due to the ocean waves caught Jim off guard, causing him to stumble. He steadied himself against the desk, eliciting laughter from the two scientists.

"That must be good stuff," remarked Dr Amin, not seeming to notice the addition of Tasha to this reality, as if she had been there all along.

"Oh, it *is* good stuff," Jim laughed, maintaining the

camaraderie.

Tasha took the cup from Jim and had some herself.

“Come on, gentlemen, join us for a drink, take a break,” Tasha said in an almost seductive manner, her big blue eyes focusing on one of the doctors while she touched the arm of the other. Jim was surprised at his twinge of jealousy, an emotion he couldn’t control despite having no reason or right to feel that way.

He reminded himself of his wife somewhere in the multiverse. He shouldn’t have been lusting after Tasha, he knew it was wrong, but her beauty was captivating, and he had missed her company. He had deep feelings of love for both his wife and Tasha.

Soon enough, the two scientists were both downing bilge juice like they were at a party. They were out cold within minutes; Tasha had convinced them to drink full cups straight down. Dr Amin, in the midst of laughter, began passing out first. Jim instinctively checked their pulses, praying he hadn’t overdosed them.

“Thank God they’re alive,” he said to Tasha.

Her expression remained unimpressed. “What was in that drink?” she asked.

“Don’t worry, it’s mostly alcohol and pussy pills,” he said with a cheeky smile. “You didn’t drink from the bottle, did you?”

“No, uh-uh, nada, not me, no,” she said, flustered.

“You did, didn’t you?” Jim asked in concern.

“Well, maybe a small swig, but I didn’t drink it like they did. Straight up, whoooa! What are pussy pills?”

“It’s what the captain calls the seasickness tablets. Here’s the leaflet. Take a look. It’s hyoscine hydrobromide. It wasnt in the bottle, but that’s moonshine! Are you sure you’re okay?”

“Don’t sweat it, jeez, relax, I can handle it,” she slurred, her words betraying her less-than-sober state.

“Okay, well, let me know if you feel you need to rest,” Jim said, preparing himself to take her to the sickbay. “We need to buy the captain some time and shut this experiment down. Can you start looking for a way to sabotage the collider while I try and contact him? We need to get some help moving these two into the sick bay.”

Jim keyed the intercom to call the bridge; it took him a minute or so to convince the junior officer on the bridge to let him speak directly with the captain.

“This is the captain; go ahead, over,” the intercom chirped.

“Captain Malik, we need some help in the cargo bay. There’s a problem with the scientists, and we need to get them to the sickbay,” Jim reported in an urgent tone.

“I read you, Dr Knight. Continue with the operation and stand by for assistance, out,” Captain Malik replied.

Jim glanced at Tasha, curious why she was back from her own reality, but before he could contemplate anything, a rhythmic thumping of marching feet echoed through the ship's deck plates, growing louder. Several security officers and a medic charged into the cargo bay, their faces serious. The medic checked the two scientists, and one of the security team approached Jim and said sternly, "Report, sir."

Jim's jaw dropped as he noticed the captain was with them. He wasn't prepared for that and was unsure what to say.

"Stand down, son," Captain Malik commanded. "I'll handle this."

"Captain, we need to get these men to sick bay. I think they're drunk—well, incapacitated at least. They were drinking the bilge juice, sir." The medic reported.

Before the captain could reply, four more men entered, carrying stretchers, checking the two scientists and swiftly taking them away. The crew's efficiency was admirable, disciplined, and a credit to the captain, whom they clearly respected.

"Already under way, Doctor. I won't tolerate this behaviour on my ship, even from civilians. When they come around, they will be confined to quarters," the captain announced, directing his junior officers. It was a clear display of authority, ensuring word of this event would circulate among the crew. It also granted Jim the time needed to shut down the experiments without interference as planned.

The captain gestured toward the collider, silently instructing Jim to proceed as discussed.

"We're working on it, sir," Jim replied.

"We?" Captain Malik asked.

"Yes, my assistant is working with me. It must be easier to turn this thing off than to turn it on," Jim said. "What do you say, Tasha?"

"Erm… well… you could be right. I found an emergency shut-off button. And these components look important," Tasha replied, her words coming out somewhat more sensibly than earlier. The seriousness of the situation, Jim surmised, was perhaps helping her focus.

"A hangover from hell and escaping a lockdown—that should take care of the scientists a while. It's perfect. Hit it, and then we can try this sabotage while it's off," Jim suggested.

They looked around and tinkered, assessing before taking action.

Jim paused; once again, the dilemma struck him. His mind circled the predicament. What if he became ensnared in this alternate reality, torn between his attraction with Tasha and the unsettling prospect of being unable to return to Scarlett and Jerica? Lost in thought, he turned to Tasha. His lips slightly pursed, he looked into her eyes. “It’s good to see you, my partner in time, or whatever the hell you call this.”

“I told you to keep an eye out for me. I’m not done with chasing you yet, across time, realities or wherever the hell we end up.”

“Okay, Tasha, we need to focus. You heard the captain. If we remove these components but need to put them back later, do you think we could do it?” he asked.

“Right now, sure, but an hour or a day from now, I don’t think I could remember how it all goes back,” Tasha replied.

“It’s just a precaution—we need to photograph the fittings in case we need to repair this thing to get out of here. Take it apart and at each stage we change it, take more photographs. Until the thing doesn’t work and only we know how to put it back together.”

They worked together. There were a few cameras—digital and a Polaroid—on the desk for scientific recording purposes. They used both and the Polaroids they stashed in Jim’s journal.

Jim watched her take the photographs. Whether she was a ragged beggar or a scientist’s assistant in a white lab coat, Tasha’s beauty was a beacon of light illuminating any room in any reality.

“I think that should about do it,” Jim said. Their

sabotage seemed to successfully rob the device of power even after disengaging the safety stop button. "Let's go up to the bridge and report to the captain, and see if we can get some answers."

They tidied up and headed out of the cargo bay towards the bridge. As they traversed the passageways, Jim noticed some crew members casting strange glances their way. The crew seemed uneasy with civilians on board, and their lab coats only heightened their visibility. It wasn't just the captain who harboured discomfort about the experiments on board.

* * *

Upon their entering the bridge, the officer on station announced their arrival. The captain approached them immediately, uttering not a word but conveying through his body language the fact that he expected information.

"We have disabled the experiment for the time being, Captain," Jim said, taking a half step back as the captain moved forward into his personal space.

"Very good. You've earned my trust. Join us, Doctor, would you?" The captain gestured toward the radar station. "Ensign, would you repeat what you just told me, please?" the captain instructed.

"Yes, sir. If you watch the radar, sir, you'll notice that it's getting interference. About an hour ago, the radar started behaving strangely. Possibly this is due to our location in the Triangle, or your experiments, or both. It springs back to life for a few passes and detects our plane. On the second pass, there's nothing, and then we get into a whole new level of weird—similar readings to a huge storm. Then there seems to be, for a moment, a small group of other planes." The ensign's voice quivered, a trace of fear seeping through his words.

"You better have good news for me, because we lost contact with CAG." Captain Malik frowned.

"Okay, now let me try to explain what I think is happening," Jim began. "I've been looking into this for some time and reading up on what those two have been doing in the cargo bay with the God particle. Our planet is alive with magnetic forces; it is entirely electromagnetically driven. There are places where you can actually feel something, described by some as a power—Stonehenge and other historic monuments, for instance—certain areas on the planet where magnetic forces, if they converge at the right frequency, time and space, can open up a doorway. If you happen to be there at that precise moment, you can travel through it.

"The Navy knows about this, but it's all classified—they've done it before with the USS *Eldridge* in Philadelphia. Any hints of this information leaking get dismissed as conspiracy theories. Like the enigma of the Triangle, it gets attributed to weather or some other arbitrary hypothesis for the unknown. What if there's more to it than what they release to us?" Jim was mostly addressing the captain, but also attempting to reassure the young officer that he had some insight into what was happening. It felt as if he was tapping into the knowledge of his doppelganger from this universe and filling in the blanks from his own experiences.

"So, are you suggesting there's a doorway to another time, space or dimension, and the radar is picking up a flight of unknown planes or objects from this other reality? That sounds..." The young officer paused.

The captain finished his sentence for him. "Crazy."

"Captain, these experiments are being conducted worldwide in places where magnetic forces are augmented," Jim replied. "There are dozens of particle accelerators or hadron colliders in key locations. According to the journal I found, a secret elite group has been running these experiments for decades. There's even a historical collider on public display in the London Science Museum, hidden in plain sight. I've visited and seen it myself. Security around the active experiments is high, but I can show you the documents in my quarters—obviously technology has advanced since the forties. It's no coincidence that we have a hadron collider on board the *Enterprise*, being tested in the Bermuda Triangle. You may think it's crazy, but here we are."

Jim looked at Tasha for support. She nodded in agreement. A shared smile gave him comfort. She hadn't said a word while they were on the bridge, but her presence was bolstering Jim's confidence.

There was an incoming transmission on the communications channel. "*Enterprise*, this is Commander Balfour. Come in, *Enterprise*, over."

The captain grabbed the microphone before the communication officer had a chance to respond. "CAG, what happened? We lost contact. Report!"

Chapter 22 – The Experiments that Bind Us

CAG reported, "It was incredible sir, a vortex appeared ahead, and I went into it. There was an orange fog around the plane and electrical discharges. The plane's instruments went crazy. I couldn't tell if I was flying up, down or straight. I just kept my arms as still as possible to maintain a straight line and went with my feelings. The plane felt like it was accelerating, and at one point, it felt like I hit mach 3. Now I'm miles out from where I started, an incredible distance in a short space of time. I may need a drink to get back. My instruments are functioning normally now, sir. I need an IFR. Over."

"Roger, I'm sending a Super Hornet to rendezvous for in-flight refuelling. Hang tight, CAG," the captain said, and closed the communication. He looked at Jim. "Well, Doctor, it looks like my flight commander has inadvertently corroborated your story, at least in part. What the hell is going on here?" he muttered, scratching his head under his hat.

"I wish I could tell you more. Maybe the moment we shut down the hadron collider, the doorway closed long enough to bring him back," Jim suggested.

"Get back down to the cargo bay and get me some more information," the captain said firmly. "I need answers."

"I can, yes, sir, but that would require more testing. Surely you don't want me to turn it back on?"

"No! Do not turn that thing back on, especially while I have birds in the air. You turn that thing on, and you'll end up in the brig," the captain warned.

"Can I make a suggestion? Take the ship to the location where the commander first encountered the anomaly. If there's a connection, maybe we can find some answers at that source."

"What happened to your 'unwarranted gambles'?" the captain asked.

"At this point, we have no answers, only more mysteries. If I'm right, this is our best chance at taking the crew to safety."

"What makes you say that?"

"To get more information, to save Commander Balfour, it makes sense to follow after him and we can take a look for ourselves. What are your options?"

"Very well. Helmsman, set your course and proceed at flank speed," Captain Malik ordered. "It will take us time to get there anyway. CAG should be able to meet us there with an in-flight refuel plane on the way."

Jim headed towards the cargo bay along with Tasha, frustrating a crewman behind him, who huffed and pushed past them, muttering profanities.

“I need to do some research,” Jim said. “In this reality, I’m a scientist, so I think it’s the same reality we were in before. I’ll delve deeper into the project notes and tap into my doppelganger’s knowledge.”

“I could help you in your quarters if you like?” Tasha offered, fluttering her eyelashes. Preoccupied with the task, he was trying not to dwell on her, racked with guilt from previous encounters and continuing lustful thoughts. He needed space and solitude to explore the answers in his journals.

Jim said, “Tasha, check out the cargo bay, see if you can find out anything on the consoles there that might help us track the anomaly they’re picking up on the radar. I’ll join you in about an hour.” He kissed her on the cheek. “Everything will be fine.”

Tasha clenched her jaw, her eyes flashing with resentment as she turned and stormed off without uttering a word in reply.

In his quarters, Jim sifted through his counterpart’s project notes and stumbled upon a personal journal. Tempted by curiosity, he flicked through the pages, searching for references to Scarlett. He found a piece of paper with a photo of her, and a chilling revelation swept over him as he read the funeral eulogy: Scarlett was gone, her absence starkly evident in the haunting words on the page. He couldn’t get past the first line.

Beloved wife, gone but never forgotten.

Remaining in this reality meant never reuniting with his wife. He checked the date; it was before Jerica's birth too, so she wouldn't exist here either. Having endured these losses countless times, he found himself growing increasingly numb to the ache of it all.

Skimming further, he discovered a darker side to this version of him—a controlling and jealous nature that had driven Scarlett to suicide. He learned from the journal that his counterpart revelled in the control as he watched Scarlett tiptoe around him, careful not to upset him. He had dictated her every move and monitored her interactions with others, increasing her dependence on him. He even described satisfaction in belittling her in front of her friends and how he drove them away, leaving her completely isolated. She was nothing more than a pawn in his game of dominance, an obsession of his. Jim surmised that she must have seen death as her only means of escape.

More disturbingly, this Jim had successfully created the vortex using the hadron collider in an attempt to reclaim Scarlett, or at least another version of her, seemingly as a possession. Jim, imagining himself as a lonely soul driven by fear, acknowledged that the portal could drive a man to insanity. Despite examining the diary carefully, he couldn't pinpoint the final straw, but deduced the effect might have been cumulative, or perhaps that version of him had always been like this. The journal was too one-sided to reveal the truth, so he tossed it aside, too emotional and revolted to delve deeper into the dark version of him, and instead focussed on the project notes for preservation of his own sanity.

His counterpart had performed extensive research into archaeological sites and had visited most of the sites himself, trying to find a way to get back to Scarlett. Jim was fascinated by the reference to a site in Peru known as the Puerta de Hayu Marca, known in legend as the Gate of the Gods. Excerpts of text had been highlighted.

The notes described an ancient story about a doorway believed to be a portal. The story began when the Spanish conquistadors arrived in Peru, then looted gold and precious stones from the Inca tribes. An Incan priest named Aramu Muru fled from the Temple of the Seven Rays with a sacred golden disk. The disk became known as the Key of the Gods of the Seven Rays.

The priest hid in the mountains of Hayu Marca and eventually came upon an incredible structure carved into the red rock, shaped like a doorway to nowhere. It had no visible openings, and most interesting was its size, big enough for massive beings to pass through, at seven metres in height and seven metres wide. In the middle, at the bottom, was a smaller door, human-sized at two metres in height.

According to the legends, the doorway was guarded by shaman priests at the time of Aramu Muru, and it was said they only let him pass because he had the golden disk, which he placed in the small indentation in the centre of the door. When the disk was inserted into the doorway, a portal opened, according to myth. Aramu Muru handed the disk to the shaman priests and entered the portal, never to be seen again, and, according to the myth, a strange light emanated from a tunnel inside the portal.

It sounded a lot like the vortex phenomena Jim had encountered. There were descriptions from folklore as well, recounting strange experiences such as visions of stars, columns of fire and the sounds of peculiar rhythmic music or trumpets. Interestingly, there were still, to this day, exceptionally high numbers of sightings of unidentified flying objects in the Puerta de Hayu Marca.

Jim slumped back in his chair in amazement; if this phenomenon was related, it was extraordinary to learn that these gateways had been around for centuries. His whole body vibrated with excitement at the possibilities. If ancient civilizations and indeed Aramu Muru long since gone had harnessed these energies, then there must be a way to control it now too.

He sat forward and pored over more of the research. Some theories suggested that the Mayan and Egyptian pyramids also functioned as early particle accelerators, engineered to harness the Earth's natural energies from the Earth and attract positive energy and protons from the universe. This was something the scientists working at CERN near Geneva and on board the

Enterprise, his other self had been determined to find out more, fuelled with ambition and the desire to get his wife back. Jim could tell his alternate self was no quitter; even death was not reason enough to let Scarlett go.

Jim discovered by reading the project documents that the Mayans had predicted that humanity would try to harness the power of the God particle, and the pyramids were designed in preparation for the end times. It was speculated that gods or beings from another world or dimension had helped humans create these spectacular structures. Sadly, over time, the majority of such structures had decayed into ruin. His counterpart had visited some of these sites, and in his project notes he described, during physical contact with the ancient architectures, energy flowing through his body. Jim thought back to his experience with the monoliths on Alex's farm and wondered if these structures could all be linked in some electromagnetic way.

Jim became engrossed in the journal's reference to a 1943 research project, the infamous Philadelphia Experiment, which the Navy denied all knowledge about. The experiment had aimed at perfecting radar invisibility using phased generators on the USS *Eldridge*. An overload had allegedly created a powerful energy field, causing the ship to disappear briefly. Crew members reported strange events and phenomena, including instances of time travel and the appearance of a vortex. Some of the crew had even ended up physically embedded into the ship's structures, as if the deck plate had gone soft and then re-solidified, merging the crewmen with the ship's hull. Something was affecting the laws of physics in that experiment. For the crew who made it back alive, many struggled with mental health issues, and the secrecy surrounding the experiment fuelled conspiracy theories.

The entries highlighted the striking similarities between the *Eldridge* incident and missing airplanes and vessels in the Bermuda Triangle. Notably, Flight 19 in December 1945 had experienced instrument issues and an orange fog before disappearing, echoing the accounts of the Philadelphia Experiment.

Jim, in a frenzy, checked his dog tags, confirming the names were different. The flight numbers and flight crews were completely different in this reality, but most of the other details such as locations and flight plans remained similar—another Mandela effect variation in this reality, Jim noted.

* * *

Jim, realising the time, returned to Tasha. At first he couldn't find her on the cargo deck, causing a surge of concern. Eventually, he heard her sobbing and discovered her crouched behind a part of the machine. Jim approached her and offered comfort, but she quickly composed herself, insisting she was fine. Jim respected her privacy, reminding her that he was there if she wanted to talk. But she avoided his gaze, sat back and tightened her grip around her legs, curling into a ball. She rested her head on her knees, attempting to hide her tears.

Shifting the subject and attempting to break the ice, Jim sat beside her to discuss the experiments and expressed an interest in Tasha's own discoveries. She began to loosen up, took a deep breath in and slowly exhaled, visibly shaking off her momentary emotional incapacitation, stood and approached the computer. Jim followed.

"Sorry, Jim," she whispered with a low tone, suggesting she was somewhat embarrassed for her outburst. "Via the computer, I uncovered information about attempts to open a wormhole using particle accelerators, but I can't say I understand it all."

Jim leaned in, intrigued. "What did you find?"

Tasha continued, her fingers tapping on the keyboard as she spoke. "Those two scientists made references to the creation of something called a Higgs boson at CERN. They were attempting to control and harness its energies here, I think."

"Look here." Jim pointed to the screen. "You notice the energy release recorded during the time you came through the vortex?"

Tasha leaned closer, frowning and squinting as she examined the data. "Yeah, I did. I don't know how they could have missed it. Maybe our diversion tactics paid off.

Or it means nothing and this is normal to them."

Jim and Tasha spent some more time looking at the files. Then, for a moment, their eyes met. Jim couldn't stop himself. His desire and longing had grown so strong that he no longer knew what to say.

As she leaned in closer, her gaze lingering on his, her playful smile returned and she brushed her breasts against him as she initiated a passionate kiss. He was caught in this complex web of emotions, torn between his feelings for Tasha and his unwavering love for his family in another reality that might no longer even exist.

The kiss ended naturally. Neither really knowing what to say or do next, they finally decided to make their way back to the bridge to update the captain with the information they had found. The crew needed to know what was happening, and it was clear that there were significant connections between the experiments onboard and various historical mysteries.

Jim and Tasha strode side by side, sharing a sense of urgency and purpose. As they made their way through the dimly lit corridors of the *Enterprise* CVN-65, Jim couldn't help but think about the strange and dangerous journey they were on. The mysteries of the multiverse had become all too real, and their quest for answers far from over.

Chapter 23 – The Pyramid beneath the Waves

On the bridge of the *Enterprise*, Captain Malik faced growing tension. The refuelling plane sent to assist was now lost, and CAG was attempting to return with an empty tank. Frustrated, the captain sought options.

"We've lost contact with the IFR plane, sir," reported the air boss. "Commander Balfour is on his way back, but he'll need to eject soon. We're en route, but even at full flank we won't make it in time."

With limited choices, the air boss suggested deploying the SH-60 Seahawk for a rescue mission. The junior officer's support sealed the decision. "Affirmative, sir. From my chair here, this is our last option."

"Agreed. Proceed with caution," Captain Malik ordered. "We can't afford another loss, tell CAG to ping his co-ordinates repeatedly until the last possible moment before ejecting, and let him know we are scrambling the angels. Standard rescue procedures."

"Do you mind if I join the rescue mission sir? I mean as an observer" Jim asked.

"All right join the party, but, be careful, stay secured and buckled in your seat at all times Doctor." Jim nodded.

The Captain turned to the Search and rescue team

leader who was now on the bridge. “If I can get you all back in one piece I will only have the missing IFR plane to worry about and that bird has plenty of drink time. Those other intermittent blips on the monitor whatever they are will have to wait for now. Your mission is to bring CAG back safely. Keep an eye out for any other flights in distress secondary, and if you make contact call it in and we will decide how to handle it.”

Jim left and followed the search and rescue team lead to the seahawk rescue helicopter.

It took them about twenty minutes to locate Commander Balfour. Fortunately, the co-ordinates came through accurately and it was easy to spot the floating Pyrotechnic red smoke flare the Commander had released.

The rescue team swiftly winched the Commander out of the water, sat him down and gave him a towel to dry off with and a foil sheet blanket. After he had settled for a few moments Jim asked if he was okay.

Commander Balfour recounted the event, his voice steady but filled with wonder. “While I was waiting for the Seahawk to rescue me, I decided to swim down a few meters and take one last look at my aircraft. In the distance, I saw it—an underwater pyramid, massive, like something out of Giza. And there was a sphinx too, its face larger and more feline than anything in Egypt. And I have been there so I know Doctor.”

“Is there any way I can see it, from up here maybe?”

"No Doctor, the water is too choppy from up here to see it, and we aren't diving down there right now. We need to get back to the *Enterprise* and report and start scanning for the IFR plane. Take my word for it, it's there."

Returning to the *Enterprise*, CAG was taken to sickbay for a check-up. He reassured the medics about the refuelling plane's fuel supply—after all this crew was a tight-knit family. He informed them that the search was underway, which eased their concerns.

Dismissed from sickbay, CAG changed into dry clothes and headed to the bridge for debriefing. Captain Malik welcomed him back. As a former pilot, the captain understood the sensitive nature of such reports. The Seahawk continued its search and rescue mission for the missing IFR plane, for the moment and there was no immediate danger of running out of fuel. Meanwhile, the crew remained fascinated by the discovery of the pyramid. After CAG's report, Captain Malik decided it was time to consult with the scientists again.

"Where is Dr Knight?"

"He headed to the cargo bay after we landed, captain," CAG replied.

"Get him up here on the double," he commanded. "We must find out what additional information he has, I don't like these experiments being conducted on my ship, especially when air crew go missing."

Commander Balfour acknowledged with a quick, “Aye, sir,” and signalled for a security officer to fetch Dr Knight and Tasha from the cargo bay.

“Commander, I want that refuelling plane found. Top priority—work with the radar station,” ordered Captain Malik.

* * *

In the cargo bay, Jim and Tasha observed a familiar security guard approaching.

“I have orders to escort you to the bridge, sir,” Lieutenant Jed informed Jim.

Upon reaching the bridge, Jim observed the search for the missing refuelling plane intensifying. With limited options, Captain Malik addressed the crew, urging them to stay vigilant.

“Ahh, Dr Knight, good, please tell me you have some information.”

“From what we understand, based on our interpretations, this has been tried before. Have you ever heard of the Philadelphia Experiment?”

“This is what I know, Dr Knight: I know this ship was fake-decommissioned, and we have a top-secret mission that we are in the midst of,” Captain Malik said in a frustrated tone. “But now what you’re telling me is we’re involved in another Philadelphia Experiment?”

"Yes, sir, something very similar. The government and military consider the ship and crew expendable. All they care about is finding a way to control these portals through time and space,"Jim replied.

Jim's eyebrows shot up in surprise as the captain's laughter echoed across the bridge. But beneath the hearty chuckle, Jim detected a blend of disbelief and concern woven into the timbre of the captain's voice. It was in the way the captain's shoulders tensed slightly and the fleeting shadow that passed across his eyes before he regained his composure. Jim knew there was more to the captain's reaction than mere amusement; it carried the weight of uncertainty and worry. "Captain, consider this for a moment. What's the cost of another decommissioned ship lost at sea for the government? Now compare it to the expense of demilitarising and properly disposing of the *Enterprise* and her nuclear reactors."

"Interesting point, Dr Knight. I'm in command here. I don't care what my orders are, I won't blindly or unnecessarily put my crew in harm's way. I hope you're with me on this, Doctor," the captain warned.

"You can count on us, sir," Tasha assured him.

Jim nodded in agreement. "Of course, but right now, Captain," he added, pointing at the storm in the distance. "Your pilots need to come back through whatever it was CAG came through."

"Agreed. Okay, you've both earned my trust. Now I

need your help. I still have a missing bird out there. I need the crew all back in one piece. What else can you tell me that could help?" Captain Malik asked.

"Commander, briefly, what else happened to you, please?" Jim inquired.

"In essence, Dr Knight," Commander Balfour began, "the instrumentation malfunctioned. I was shrouded in an orange mist or fog of some kind. I saw something that matches Dr Knight's description of a vortex, flew through it, and I thought I saw other planes up there with me and then I was being fished out of the drink by the search and rescue angels."

"I have a theory. When the device is activated, it may invoke the anomaly, causing the planes' instrument troubles. However, it's not the only way these portals open. My theory is, if we get the ship to the underwater pyramid location where the commander was rescued, and activate the hadron collider in the cargo bay, it could act as a focal point for the refuelling plane to come back through." Tasha looked to Captain Malik for his reaction.

Captain Malik was poker-faced as he considered the suggestion. His lips tightened as he appeared to be processing the information. Jim knew he was resisting having to turn the machine back on.

"I support Tasha on this. I think she's right," Jim added. "This portal that the commander saw, he mentioned other planes... Have you ever heard about the mystery of Flight 21, sorry Flight 19 for you guys?"

He had directed his question to the captain, but it was Commander Balfour who answered. "Every pilot worth his salt knows about Flight 19. It's an unsolved mystery—five planes on that flight went missing in the 1940's. No wreckage, no explanations. I swear I saw some planes from that era in the fog for a moment. Does Flight 21 have any connection to all this?"

"Commander, you saw the planes. Were they TBM Avenger torpedo bombers?" Jim asked.

"It's possible. I didn't get a good look—they were flying much slower than I was—but they were definitely of that era, and in mint condition. But how could they still be in the air? It sounds impossible those ancient pilots they would be dead by now." Commander Balfour replied and Jim interrupted.

"I think this doorway has been opening and closing on its own for decades, possibly even centuries. I believe it's the same thing that Flight 19 encountered and possibly other lost vessels and aircraft in the triangle. To them they just went through the doorway, and they must be low on fuel too. We can save them."

"We should turn on the collider to reopen the vortex," Tasha said excitedly, gripping the captain's arm to get his full attention.

It was clear the captain was unimpressed. "That

sounds crazy. Why in the hell would we want to do that?" he bellowed.

"To bring our missing plane back into alignment with our reality, sir, give them a doorway home," Jim explained, attempting to simplify the idea and strengthen their suggestion.

"Well, that's as good as anything else I've heard. But do you have any evidence to back up your theory?" the captain demanded.

Jim reluctantly took off his dog tag. He looked at it lovingly, hesitating to share it, then threw it to the captain.

"What is this, Doctor?" the captain asked as he examined the dog tag.

"Just read the name tag, sir—see if you recognise the person it belongs to," Jim replied.

After a moment's examination, the captain threw it to Commander Balfour, who assessed it. He checked the ships computer for historical records, "I don't believe it, sir. It can't be," he exclaimed.

"CAG?" the captain said, urging him to continue.

"Sir, its confirmed, this is the flight leader's dog tag from Flight 21," Commander Balfour said, unable to contain his excitement.

"Fakes?" the captain said, still sceptical.

"I don't think so, it looks genuine," Commander

Balfour confirmed as he handed the dog tag back to Jim. “Where did you get these from, Doctor?”

“I pulled it out from the vortex during one of my earlier encounters with the anomaly years ago. I think there’s a very real possibility the flight leader and those planes are in a much larger rip in the multiverse. They’re probably still alive. In my reality it was Flight 21 that went missing. It’s got to be Flight 19 or 21 or possibly both out there.”

“Alive! After all these years? Preposterous,” the captain piped up.

“Captain, you’re thinking two-dimensionally. What you can see and feel is only the beginning, and time doesn’t always flow at one speed. It’s more like a river, which ebbs and flows, travelling in multiple directions, or perhaps everything happens at once. This vortex... it’s the beginning, it’s the end, it’s everything and every possibility. Everything that ever was and everything that never was. Time doesn’t follow any laws there. As far as those old flight crews are concerned, their fuel is low, and they need to find somewhere to land right now. If I’m right, only a few hours have passed for them, but for us it’s decades, with the turn of a new millennium having been and gone.”

“I’ll believe that when I see it, Doctor. Right now, I have a missing plane of my own to worry about. And we have a little over an hour to find them.” The captain’s jaw clenched in determination as he turned towards the viewport, gazing out at the sky, his mind already strategizing the next steps in the search and rescue mission. I don't want to activate that device unless it's the last resort. Commander, I want you to try and get our boys back the traditional way, please. See to it, CAG. Standard search and rescue tactics. Calculate the search distance circle and get started from the last known co-ordinates. Dr Knight, you'd better start putting that thing back together so we have a backup plan. Make sure that if we need to turn the machine off, we can easily unplug the damn thing. CAG, make sure the other scientists are secured in the brig. I don't want them interfering. Navigation, let me know as soon as we're on top of that pyramid. Let's move like we have a purpose, gentlemen."

The captain's decisive commands spurred the crew to action, and the bridge was buzzing with activity once again.

"Captain, what do you plan to do about Colonel Truman?" Jim asked.

"Thankfully, he's not on this ship. He transferred aboard the clipper ship, which has been shadowing us for days. Look, you can see her on our port bow. I'll just give him some vague updates about his out-of-sorts scientists, our missing flight crew, and direct them to stay at least forty miles out of the danger area. No need to risk them getting lost as well. It won't be far from the truth, since we don't really know what the hell is going on. I need to consider all alternatives before we turn that thing back on," Captain Malik said. "We need to get some control over the situation, minimize risks. I need the hadron collider in a semi-ready state in case we have to try your plan. Get back down there, Doctor, and stand by for orders. You are plan B—got it? You're dismissed."

"Actually, it was Tasha who did most of the sabotage on the collider. Can you take care of it? I will meet you there shortly," Jim said to Tasha. The captain nodded in approval.

"Don't be too long, Doctor, please," Tasha said, turning away. She swiftly left the bridge to begin the work.

"Commander, you've been up there in the middle of this thing, what are your thoughts on reactivating the collider?" the captain asked.

"It's risky, sir," the commander replied. "We don't know what could happen to the ship, but I believe the crew would want to do everything possible to bring our boys home. If they have gone down, I hope they're in brown water, sir," he added, referring to shallow waters.

"If they've gone down, why didn't they activate their transponder for us to find them on the radar?" The captain didn't wait for an answer. "No, Commander, they're still airborne. If the doctor is right, they could be lost in that soup that had you. We have to get them back. Put the ship on high alert. I'll address the crew. Get the rescue angels back to the co-ordinates where they found you, on the double. Are there any other options?" He looked around at his bridge crew with only blank faces or shaking heads in response.

"None that we can think of, sir. There's nothing on the radar—no visual sign, no distress call, no beacon. We don't know where to look. I agree: standard SAR tactics, starting from the rescue co-ordinates, sweeping pattern outward from there. It could take hours. Commander Balfour replied.

"We don't have hours!" the captain shouted in frustration, not wanting to take any further risks. Leaving it to the last moment was not an option.

"Then the collider may be our only hope." The Commander replied.

"Proceed with SAR, standard procedures, for now."

The crew scrambled to get under way with the rescue. Within thirty minutes, with the ship at full flank speed, they were in the pickup position of CAG's crash co-ordinates. The Seahawk had been expanding its search.

"We're right on top of the co-ordinates given by the commander for the underwater pyramid location, Captain. This is also within visual distance of the refuelling plane's last known co-ordinates before she went missing," a young helmsman reported.

"Excellent work, everyone. I want lookouts to report back any sight of the plane, flares or smoke signals our missing plane might have left for us. They still have well over an hour and a half of fuel left, so there's plenty of time." The captain was praising them all, but he deliberately directed his gaze toward the young officer, detecting he was in need of a confidence boost.

The time passed swiftly and there was not more than a faint blip on the sensors that vanished as quickly as it came. Jim noticed the Captains face and posture drop as he acknowledged the SAR mission had failed to locate his missing crew.

Then the captain announced to the entire ship, using the intercom so that his message could be heard on every speaker. "We are on high alert due to our missing refuelling plane. Stay mindful and focused, stay on battle-ready alert. Rescue crews have been recalled but will be going back up after refuelling. Prepare for a storm, batten down the hatches, and Godspeed."

"CAG, tell the angels to stay on ready alert, I don't want them in the air while we reactivate this bloody thing. The second it's all clear, we can get them back up there."

"Aye, sir," Commander Balfour said, his movements swift as he sprang into action, relaying the captain's orders to the rest of the crew.

"Doctor, you're up. Get down there and start up the hadron collider experiment, I hope this Mandela field of yours makes a welcome doorway for our boys." the captain commanded.

Chapter 24 – Echoes of What Could Be

When Jim arrived in the cargo bay, he was pleased to see that Tasha was almost finished.

"Do you need a hand finishing off?"

"No, almost there. The photographs we took made the job easy." Tasha smiled as she placed the last component back where it belonged. She joined Jim at the console. "Are we ready?"

"Hit it," Jim replied. She didn't hesitate, and the hadron collider roared to life, summoning the familiar dance of the temporal vortex in the cargo bay, this time in sync with another spiralling rift that reformed outside the vessel. Jim grappled with the unseen forces, but as the gravitational pull intensified, his grip faltered. Through the void, he witnessed fleeting glimpses of his past, his present, and a hopeful future with his family.

Tasha, better prepared than Jim, had access to the railings behind the console and instinctively held on.

Jim was surprised at the speed with which the vortex appeared, instantly succumbing to the inexorable force. As he levitated and then plummeted through the time tunnel, he contemplated his purpose. Amid dual portal interactions on the *Enterprise*, he refocused on his paramount mission—a quest for a reality in which love, peace, and joy defined his family's existence. Thoughts of his losses weighed on him. He wondered if Scarlett ever missed him during his time of absence, or if time flowed differently in alternate realities, thoughts of his daughter and Tasha crept into his mind.

* * *

After travelling through the multiverse rift, he was surprised to find himself back in their bedroom—but this was a different reality, as his belongings were present.

He was startled to see photos of him with another woman—Tasha. Before he was able to explore further, Tasha entered the room, a smile playing on her lips as she revealed a hint of eagerness in her gaze. Her steps were slow and deliberate, the silk of her nightie clinging to her curves as she subtly emphasized the length of her legs with each languid movement. Jim was thrown onto the bed, unable to resist her advances as she pinned his arms down and straddled him.

The unfamiliar sound of a passing train snapped him back to reality. He pushed Tasha away.

"Wait, what is going on here? Where is Scarlett?" Jim questioned.

"What are you talking about? She died years ago. I thought you were over this—well, not over it, but, you know, moving on with us."

In disbelief, Jim headed to Jerica's room, the building layout was all wrong but her bedroom layout and things were very familiar. She was alive and well but asleep. That was a pleasant surprise. Returning to the kitchen, he sought solace in whiskey. Tasha's attempts to comfort him were met with silence. Frustrated, she followed him, demanding an explanation.

"Will you please talk to me, Jim? For God's sake, what is your problem?" she said quietly, trying not to wake Jerica but doing a terrible job of concealing her anger, which was contagious and began to affect Jim.

"My problem? Scarlett is dead again. Tell me what happened," Jim exclaimed.

"She was horribly raped and killed—you know that," Tasha replied.

"No! No!" Jim said hysterically. "Not again. Was it Benson and Shafto?"

"So you *do* know what happened. Jim, baby, please let me help you," she begged him.

"Nobody can help me, Tasha—nobody." He grabbed his coat and put his shoes on, which was quite difficult as he was shaking badly due to the negative energy and uncontrollable emotion pulsing through his body. He stormed out of the house, hoping to clear his head in the fresh air. He paced, releasing endorphins to counteract his adrenaline-pumped rage, hoping to find some serenity in relentless striding.

The recurring cycle of torment bewildered him, and he questioned why Benson and Shafto relentlessly targeted him and his wife across alternate realities. Tasha's presence intrigued him, and he wondered if she was a different version of the woman he knew, unaware of the multiverse's complexities, or if she had travelled through the vortex again to find him.

As Jim wrestled with his thoughts, he oscillated between rationalization and furious resentment toward Benson and Shafto, a desire for revenge. He contemplated the consequences of eliminating them across universes. Recognising the potential futility of such actions tempered his rage, yet the urge for retribution lingered. He questioned if it was even possible to break this cycle and ensure the safety of his family, at least in one reality they could settle in.

Jim decided to confront Tasha, to find out if she was playing games with him or if his counterpart had a genuine connection with her in this reality. He found her in the kitchen. "What's going on, Tasha? Be honest with me. Do you still have the dog tag I gave you?"

"What are you talking about? Dog tag, what dog tag?"

"So where and how did we meet?"

"In the park with my friends, of course. You were

there with Chris."

"Were you homeless, with Ian and Jana?"

"Homeless? No, God no, what an absurd thing to say."

"I'm sorry, Tasha, for a moment I thought... Well, it's nothing. I think I'm losing my mind. I need some air. Just give me a moment."

"Of course, Jim, I'll be waiting for you. I love you," she replied with a sincere tone, and went back indoors.

"Yeah, I love you too," he replied.

He stayed outside, deep in contemplation. *So we were destined to be together, Tasha and I, at least in this reality.* He pondered over his recent journeys and realised he had been successfully calling upon and, to a degree, controlling the vortex appearances. He had to try again, and as he gazed at the moon, a profound connection to the universe washed over him, and he experienced a tingling, electric sensation like static tingle surge through him. Jim reached for his dog tag. Without realising what he was doing, his thoughts turned to Benson and he was overcome by deep-seated rage. His negative thoughts were paralleling negative energies within the vortex, which this time glowed red with matching fury.

Bracing himself, Jim surrendered to the portal, ready for the twists awaiting him in the ever-shifting multiverse.

Chapter 25 – Allies in a Forsaken World

Jim awoke on cold asphalt, battered and aching from the turbulent transition through the wormhole. The stillness of the surrounding cars hinted at a hauntingly familiar, desolate reality.

Dim sunlight struggled to penetrate the perpetual fog, and unlit streetlights added to the eerie atmosphere. Droplets materialised, forming an acid smog that seared Jim's exposed skin. Seeking refuge, he grabbed at the nearest car door, unlocked, with a corpse slumped in the driver's seat. Despite the overwhelming stench and revulsion, he gritted his teeth and forced himself to unbuckle the lifeless body, each movement accompanied by a wave of nausea. He dragged the corpse onto the road, heaving from the smell. *Not this place again? Why am I here—unless I can rescue Jeff from this torrid wasteland?* he thought to himself.

Jim sought refuge in the driver's seat of the now-vacant car, leaving the front passenger window on the opposing side open a crack to allow some air to flow in. He was relieved to find the car keys in the ignition and still working. He drove onward, navigating through a landscape littered with vehicles laden with the dead, until he could no longer find a clear path forward. He sat and waited for the bizarre weather to pass, viewing the road full of rusted cars, so similar to the road and reality where he had last seen his brother Jeff.

He spotted a motorbike in the distance. Hope surged within him; perhaps he *was* back where he had left Jeff. Jim watched the fog transform into the beauty of the tempest, reminiscent of the bizarre lightning storm he had witnessed with his brother. As the storm's fury eased off, the rain transitioned into soothing white noise. He drifted off to sleep.

* * *

When he woke, the storm had passed. He left the car and came upon the motorbike that matched his own from that previous hellish reality. Despite minor damage, the bike carried him away through the desolate realm. He headed back on towards Alex's farm.

En route, Jim noticed a holiday complex. It was the first place he had seen that appeared to have electricity. Lights were on; smoke billowed from one of the roofs. Perhaps they had a stove to keep warm or a place they were cooking. Hunger led him to investigate, and there he encountered a dozen people in the courtyard, seemingly waiting to greet or warn him off. Wary but hopeful, he slowly rolled up, preparing for any trouble. Hand ready on the clutch and accelerator, he planned to stay on his bike until he was satisfied it was safe.

He recognised Ken. The last time he had seen Ken was in another reality, somewhat the worse for wear, tortured and beaten with no legs in Benson's basement. Here Ken was in good health, wearing a park manager uniform emblazoned with a name badge.

"Hi, Ken, do we know each other? You seem familiar," Jim said, intrigued at the prospect of any potential connection within this world.

"I don't believe so, sir. Here people call me Kenneth." He pointed at his name badge. "What's your name, and what brings you to our little community?"

"Ahh, sorry, you must have one of those familiar faces. I'm just passing through. Call me Jim. I need shelter for the night, and if it's not too much trouble, some food and water would be greatly appreciated."

"You're not with *them,* are you?" Kenneth asked with a hint of suspicion.

"Them? No, I travel alone."

"We don't have much, but we can offer you a roof over your head, limited solar and generator electricity for essentials, and the luxury of a hot bath. We don't have a lot of food, but we can share some with you in exchange for your help. Those howling dogs will return in the evening—they scavenge our food and take what they want. If they're unsatisfied, they punish us. They come and go as they please, even assaulting some of our women. We need help to get rid of them for good. Is there any way you can help us?"

"I'm just a simple man trying to find my family, Kenneth. I'm not sure how much help I can provide, but I'll do what I can around here to help in other ways," Jim explained regretfully.

"It's a real pity. Benson and his sick gang of Reapers will never leave us alone," Kenneth said, his voice filled with sorrow. His head dipped.

Jim's anger flared. "Wait—did you say Benson?"

"Yes—why? Do you know him?" Kenneth asked.

"No... well, yes... sort of. It's complicated," Jim replied, his emotions in a jumble. He rubbed his hand over his face. "When was the last time they were here?"

"Several days ago. They never stay away for long, but they always return to plunder our supplies. We have to find a way to get rid of them permanently," Kenneth said.

"Now I understand why I'm here. Yes, I need to help you."

"So, you'll help us now? Why the change of heart?" Kenneth asked.

Jim struggled to justify his newfound resolve. Finding it difficult to explain, he went quiet for a moment while he gathered his thoughts. "Benson and some of his associates... they've brought immense suffering to some of my family."

"Do you know Exodus 22:2? In that verse, God

declares that if someone breaks into your house at night and you kill them, you're not guilty of murder. We need to prepare in case they return to inflict more terror and rape and pillage," Kenneth said.

Jim didn't know quite how he would help, but the universe seemed to have landed him with a unique opportunity. He had allies here with a common enemy. "Do you have a wife or girlfriend?" Jim asked.

"Well, erm, yes... I... err..." Kenneth broke down, his shoulders slumping in defeat. He was rendered speechless by grief. One of his friends moved closer, wrapping her arm around him as he struggled to find his voice. Finally, through choked sobs, he managed to whisper, "Benson took her."

"Dusty?" Jim asked.

That got Kenneth's attention. "You know her? Have you seen her? Is she okay?"

"We have to believe she is. 'Never, never, never give in. Never give in except to convictions of honour and good sense'," Jim said.

A woman in the crowd smiled and said, "Winston Churchill?"

"Indeed," Jim said with a sympathetic smile.

"Wise man," she replied.

"Wait—when did you see Dusty?" Kenneth

interrupted.

“I haven’t. It’s difficult to explain. It seems like a lifetime ago. I met Dusty; it was another reality—I mean it seemed like another reality, before the world died, that’s how I thought I recognised you, through her. Listen, we have to believe she is alive, Kenneth. Nothing else matters. She will make it out of this,” Jim said, regretting some of his rambling explanations, but it was interesting that Kenneth and Dusty were together in this reality as well.

“Wait, how do you know Benson? Are you sure you’re not one of his goons messing with us, a new recruit on a mission?” Kenneth asked, paranoid in his mistrust.

“Not in the slightest. I’m as much a victim of that evil crowd as you,” Jim answered.

“Not likely. The last time I saw Dusty, she was in a barred trailer, caged like an animal for their amusement. She was so skinny, like she was being starved, and practically naked, stripped of all her dignity. How long can a person survive like that?” Ken said, tears welling.

“With water, faith and hope, she could last a couple of months. Depending on her physical condition, of course,” the girl comforting him reassured him.

“Look, let’s focus. We know we can’t fight evil with evil. But if we were to turn evil onto itself, there should be a destructive result, like a rabid dog attacking its own limbs. We must come up with a plan before they return,”

Jim said.

“What are we going to do?” Kenneth asked.

“I don’t know, yet.”

“I hope you have some ideas, because we are desperate and have none,” Kenneth said, frowning.

“I need to know more.” Jim pointed at the petrol tanker. “Is that thing full?”

“Pretty much. We found it not long ago, and the Reapers come back for fuel whenever they get low, around once a week,” Kenneth replied.

“Reapers?”

“It’s what the gang call themselves.”

“Okay, how many of them are there?” Jim asked.

“Seven.”

“Only seven? That’s a slim crew. Perfect. We’ll leverage that. Benson’s our ticket to disruption, and with such a small gang, we can manipulate them to provoke Benson’s short temper. Shifting that tanker and generator is a good start to light the fuse. I know a place that will be safe, but you’ll have to trust me.”

The community present sighed heavily, and then started talking amongst themselves.

“What’s the matter with them, Kenneth?” Jim asked.

"Losing the generator is one of our biggest fears. To hand it over to a stranger, if that's what you're suggesting, isn't going to be a popular idea."

"No, I don't want it, but it's going to be a key component in our plan because it's something the Reapers want," Jim replied. "Okay, if they are the Reapers who are you guys and what do you call yourselves?"

"We are the fortunate, or unfortunate survivors who have lived to witness the aftermath of the apocalypse and must now work to survive through it together. We refer to this group of a couple of dozen people and this place, as the colony." Kenneth replied and then turned around to address the crowd and calm their uncertainties. "My friends, the time has come to make a stand. We have the beginnings of a plan, we must help in formulating it. Jim may be on to something. Let's at least hear it out, consider and contribute to the planning. We have to do something; Jim may be our salvation," he shouted, motivating each person to cheer for the cause. "Can we agree to moving the generator and fuel tanker temporarily as long as we move it ourselves, so we know where to find it afterward."

"Yes!" A unity of affirmation roared from the crowd as Kenneth's speech served its purpose.

Jim agreed and asked to see their water supply. They took him around the back of the buildings, into what had once been a kids' play garden, now a lush vegetable area. He was impressed that they had made a large water-catching system with a filter. They had devised a way of neutralizing the acidic water and purifying it with a scientific process that would have made Louis Pasteur proud. Jim gratefully received a pint of the refreshing beverage, the lifeblood of this colony, and found it possibly the best water he had ever tasted. The large plastic sheet provided protection to the plants from the acidic rain, and a greenhouse environment and also served to catch the water for the purification process, which was ingenious.

As he observed the community's anxious faces, he pondered the challenges and secrets of this desolate world and admired how they had overcome such adversities. The universe had granted him an opportunity for redemption, and he was determined to seize it. Thoughts of his lost brother Jeff lingered, since this was the last place Jim had seen him; thoughts of his wife, daughter and parents swiftly followed. This moment was not about him though; it was about freeing these people from Benson's tyranny.

Chapter 26 – Turning the Tide with Strategic Deception

Jim was giving instructions to a pair of young lads, Mason and Blake, who had volunteered to help. Their camaraderie was evident, and they clearly found joy in each other's company amidst the desolation. One was lean and agile, and possessed a mischievous sparkle in his eyes that accompanied a devil-may-care grin. His movements were as fluid as a dancer's, exuding energy and spontaneity. The other, solid and steadfast, radiated a quiet strength. The colony had commented how pleased they were with his skills as a cunning huntsman which added the occasional flavour to the table. His observant gaze and precise actions suggested thoughtful determination. Jim found their unique qualities complementary, making them an ideal dynamic duo to assist with whatever plans he could muster.

Jim was taking a gamble that Alex would be alive in this reality, or at least the farm he knew would be an ideal place to hide the tanker. He led them to move the petrol tanker. Mason drove the truck. Jim and Blake took the generator, which was on a trailer hooked up to the back of the truck Jim was driving. The journey to the farm unfolded smoothly, offering a brief reunion.

"Hey, Alex, good to see you," Jim said with a smile,

relieved to see his friend did still live here, and still recognised him for that matter.

"You too, buddy," Alex said, shaking his hand. "But they can't stay," he said, pointing at the two young lads.

"Don't worry, Alex, they're not staying, we just need somewhere to hide this fuel tank and their generator. Just for a little while, is that okay?"

"Yeah, I guess so. Will they mind if I take some juice for my generators?"

"I don't think so, as long as it's less than four cars would normally take."

"I have four or five twenty-litre metal fuel storage cans that could do with a top-up. Why four cars?"

"That's how much Benson took the last time they came round to torment these people," Jim said. "Anyways, have you heard from Jeff? Last time I saw him he was on his way to you."

"Benson? That guy again?" Alex asked.

"You know him?" Jim questioned.

"Errr, sure, you got in a fight with him in a kebab shop and then he turned up here, before the skies turned to acid."

"So you do know him. Have you travelled through the vortex again?" Jim asked, risking sounding mad.

"Unfortunately for me yes, but this time was different. Seems everyone in my house travelled with me—oh, and then someone else turned up at my door not long after."

Before Jim had a chance to reply, his brother appeared from the farmhouse front door, which Alex had left wide open.

"Thank goodness you're okay, little brother," Jim exclaimed, rushing forward to embrace Jeff tightly.

Their parents, who had been inside the farmhouse, emerged at the sound of their voices. Jim pulled back slightly from the embrace, meeting his parents' eyes with a sense of urgency. They came out and enveloped both Jim and Jeff, enhancing their family reunion. Jim and Jeff made time to have a conversation and Jim confirmed it was the same Jeff whom he had lost in this putrid reality before.

As he glanced around anxiously, Jim added, "Has anyone seen Scarlett and Jerica and what happened to Chad and the boys? Are they safe?"

His parents, now standing beside him, exchanged a glance before his mother spoke. "There's no sign of them," she said, her concerned voice carrying a subtle tremor beneath its usual steadiness.

"The boys left before the vortex opened, lucky for them they didn't wind up in whatever this place is." Alex said.

“Listen, I need you all to stay here and protect the tanker. I’ll be back as soon as I can, I promise.”

“Want any help?” Jeff and Alex chimed in unison. “Jinx,” they both said together, chuckling again.

“Yes, you can help by making sure the Reapers don’t get hold of the fuel or the generator. Stay here and keep each other safe, all of you. I’m going to take care of Benson. I’ll be back.”

Jim had to explain who the Reapers were to Jeff and Alex before he made his farewells and took Blake and Mason back in the car to the holiday village; Jim prioritised rest, recognising that the hours ahead would be critical. His plan revolved around secrecy—Benson mustn’t discover that they’d moved the generator themselves. Jim instructed Kenneth to establish a cover story: the equipment had been stolen, and blame would be placed squarely on Benson or his affiliates. The plan was simple—create division and misdirection so the Reapers would turn on themselves. Observe for opportunities to further drive wedges using jealousy and subterfuge, taking sides where it benefitted to fuel their egos, and then let the Reapers do the rest with their own bad karma.

Kenneth escorted Jim to his lodging. Jim settled into the bed, having found the holiday chalet surprisingly comfortable. Despite its tired condition, it had a shabby charm; there was undeniable warmth about the place. The creaks in the floor and the rustic, well-loved furniture added a certain character.

They had agreed to let their thoughts simmer overnight and reconvene the next day to meticulously craft their plan and explore any known weaknesses of the Reapers. The first was already in play; greed would fuel their rage when they realised the fuel was missing. It just needed guiding back on themselves rather than the colonists, that was the risky part.

* * *

The next day brought a sense of purpose and clarity. Despite the looming threat, Jim experienced a surge in confidence. He took a hot shower in one of the chalets with solar panels and, clean, dried and refreshed, decided to mingle with the members of the community. He got chatting with a couple of friendly old ladies who shared gossip about their neighbours. He learned more about Kenneth and others and came to understand the dynamics within the group. Jim then discovered that two lads had walkie-talkies, which Jim felt might be useful communication tools.

Returning to his apartment, Jim reflected on the plan that he had been formulating in his mind, which he soon needed to discuss with the villagers to get their insights. He was about to sit down and make a few notes of ideas when he observed the second hand of the clock on the wall seemed to slow and raindrops outside the window were suspended in the air. Jim, feeling the need to stay and see things through, grabbed at the radiator nearby to secure himself. To his surprise the gravitational pull didn't manifest, and the ominous anomaly seemed different; it wasn't in the living room, but he could see it down the hallway in a reflection of a mirror.

Suddenly, a crash came from the bathroom door; time resumed normal speed. He was relieved it was over, albeit in an unfamiliar way. It didn't seem like a normal transition.

His eyes widened as his bathroom door opened and Tasha walked out wearing nothing but a towel.

"What do you think, Jim? It's not like I have control over this thing. One minute I was on board the *Enterprise*, taking a shower, and the next thing I know, the multiverse vortex engulfs me and I end up here." Tasha moved in and kissed him passionately. Jim tasted flavoured lip gloss.

"Wait a minute," he said. "You have lip gloss on. I thought you were in the shower?"

"Hmm... very observant, big boy, aren't you? Yes, I was applying it as I got out of the shower, and then it happened. We girls don't always dry ourselves first, you know."

"Oh, why is that?" Jim asked.

"You never know who will be lucky enough to walk in. It's important to look your best, wouldn't you say?"

Tasha laughed.

Jim found himself staring blankly into space trying to make sense of it all. How bizarrely illogical the mind of a woman, particularly Tasha, could be.

"Wait—what were you thinking about when you came through into this dimension?" Jim asked.

"Not *what*, Jim, more like who. I was thinking of you, hoping you would come in the bathroom and find me all aroused... and now here you are." She dropped the towel and approached to embrace him, but he moved away half a step, his eyes running all over her delicious body. He was fighting the temptations her hot, wet, nubile young body offered. He was very aroused, but he was also trying, and aware he was failing, to maintain some level of faithfulness to his beloved wife, who in almost every other encounter didn't reciprocate his feelings or often didn't even know him.

"What's the matter, Jimmy? Don't you likey me any more? We can have a lotta fun, you know?" Tasha said in a playful tone, with a terrible attempt at a Chinese accent, whilst moving one hand suggestively to her loins, a mischievous glint in her eye. Her other hand made a come-hither gesture.

Jim chuckled despite himself—her playful antics were hard to resist. "Tasha, as tempting as that sounds, we need to stay focused on the task at hand. We have to help these people defend themselves and prepare for Benson and Shafto's arrival. This is serious—pull it together."

"Oooh, pull it together, now *that's* what I'm talking about," she laughed, chasing after him round the bed, still naked.

Jim started getting frustrated. Knowing he needed to discuss the plan with Ken and the others, he shouted at her, "Tasha, stop it. I have things I need to do—Benson and Shafto could be here any time now and I need to work out a plan to deal with these people here. Get some clothes on and perhaps you can help me."

Tasha stopped immediately and her mood became low. She had a sullen look on her face and her playful banter disappeared. She snatched at the towel to dry off and make herself ready. Clearly, she was disappointed that she had failed to seduce Jim once again.

"Tasha, your arrival seems to have carried a Mandela field effect into this reality. Something's different, that mirror has moved to a different wall and some of the curtains have a different pattern on them."

Her interest in Jim's sudden and tactical change of subject was noticeably disappointing.

"Oh, how lovely" she said sarcastically.

Chapter 27 – Tempest Rising in Chaos

Disturbed by a frantic banging on the door, Jim looked through the spy hole and saw Kenneth. He opened the door and noticed Ken instinctively looking up at the sky, no doubt checking for signs of acid rainfall.

Jim greeted him and invited him inside. As Ken walked past him, he took a moment to look himself. The sky in this timeline always appeared alien, changed by the cataclysmic event that had altered their world. Even when it wasn't raining, unnatural shades of violet tainted the heavens. The sky bore visible scars in the ionosphere, resembling Vincent van Gogh's brushwork, creating eerie yet captivating patterns that struck fear into anyone who dared to gaze upon its surreal beauty for too long. Fear for when the acid rain would strike next and whether it would ever pass. Fear and wonder. Would this world ever return to its former glory?

"Hurry up—the others are getting impatient. Lunch will be served in thirty minutes, with or without you," Kenneth urged Jim. He noticed his dishevelled appearance. "Tasha keeping you busy again, is she?"

"Wait, you know Tasha?" Jim's voice carried a note of disbelief, his brows knitting together as he struggled to process the unexpected connection.

"Have you been drinking? She arrived here with you in that sweet red machine you found. That's an odd question. Actually, it's weird because I have this feeling that you were here alone and also a memory that Tasha arrived with you."

"A Mandela effect feeling?" Jim asked hoping he might understand what that meant.

"Yes, I've heard of that, yes a lot like that. I swear he died in the eighties in prison, but he didn't. False memories, I guess, right?" Kenneth said, but Jim's jaw dropped as he stood there speechless. "Anyway, thirty minutes, both of you, don't be late. Let's get lunch and get this plan ironed out, please."

Jim closed the door as he left, leaned against it and muttered, "What the hell is going on here?" Then he refocused on the more pressing problems. "Will you please speed up making yourself look pretty, Tasha? The whole community is waiting for us."

"Us?" Tasha replied curiously.

"Yes—they know you." Jim hesitated. "We arrived together, apparently."

Tasha's face lit up mischievously. "Well, isn't that something, gorgeous? These people think we're together. Oh, wow, this is going to be fun."

"That's the least of our problems. They're expecting us to have a plan. If we're in a different reality again, it could be for anything. Hopefully it's to deal with Benson and his cronies, and nothing has changed," Jim said in concern.

"Well, let's go find out what it's all about then, shall we, lover?" Tasha smiled. "Oh, Jim, look at this beautiful thing I found in the wardrobe," she teased, slipping her naked body into a little red dress, commando. "Who needs underwear anyway? Let's go, darling."

Jim felt the heat rising as he struggled to contain his desire, and he was thankful to leave the apartment and the tempting situation behind him—for now, at least.

Jim and Tasha arrived at the old clubhouse, where the community had gathered for midday lunch. The building, though weathered, was sturdy. Inside, dim lighting and candles on the tables cast long, eerie shadows on the walls, creating an unsettling yet strangely comforting ambience. The room buzzed with conversations as people shared stories and laughter—a stark contrast to the tension they had left behind in their chalet.

The residents had done a splendid job in laying out a feast on a long table. The food comprised canned foods, MRE military rations and nicely prepped Mountain House-branded freeze-dried foods, bolstered with some home-grown vegetables. The chef was clearly very talented despite limited resources; the spread was magnificent. Jim was directed to the head of the table, and Kenneth sat nearby. Fifteen seats lined each side of the table plus two at each end: the entire village population was present.

As they entered, the group fell silent, all eyes fixed on Jim and Tasha.

"Jim, Tasha, glad you could make it," Kenneth said to break the awkward silence. "This is Pauline and Betty, the gossip queens, as we affectionately call them."

Pauline and Betty, the two elderly women Jim had met earlier, exchanged knowing glances and smiles. "Oh, we've heard so much about you two," Betty said with a wink. "Welcome to our little community."

Jim nodded politely, and Tasha offered a warm smile, trying to put everyone at ease. "Thank you for having us. It's quite a place you've got here," Tasha said.

Amidst the lively atmosphere, wine flowed freely. The two boisterous young lads in their twenties, Mason and Blake, drew attention with their crude behaviour, fixating on Tasha. Unfazed, Tasha engaged in friendly conversations with the residents, skilfully navigating the dynamics. Jim, strategically gathering information, listened attentively to the challenges faced by the community.

"It's a shithole old holiday village, but we have made the best of it, thank you. We do plan to revamp it some more when we can, but right now we desperately need some help," Kenneth replied, redirecting the spotlight toward Jim so that he could describe his plan.

Now the ominous truth unfolded—Benson held not one but two girls hostage. Stripped down, caged, and exposed to the harsh elements, their survival hung by a thread. The revelation hit Jim even harder when Kenneth mentioned the other girl's name: Scarlett. In shock, Jim explained that his long lost wife's name was Scarlett.

His outburst echoed through the room in a collective gasp as he grappled with the realisation that his wife was suffering once again at the hands of Benson in this alternate reality. In the aftermath, Jim, overwhelmed with anger, left the room to collect himself. Tasha intervened, holding Kenneth back, recognising Jim's need for a moment of solitude.

"It might not be her," Tasha shouted as he left the room.

"Oh, it's her." Jim had become familiar with reality's way of tormenting him.

Jim took some time to calm down and eventually returned to the table, revealing the truth of his outburst about Scarlett's predicament, rooted in his painful history with Benson and his experiences with the vortex and other realities. Jim got the impression some of the colonists were beginning to think he was mad, but at this point it didn't matter to him. As he gathered more information about Benson and Shafto, it became evident that the community had firsthand experience with them. Again, they had a gang called the Reapers who kept taking the fuel from the tanker. Yesterday in this reality Mason, Blake, Tasha and Jim had taken the tanker to Alex's farm. The situation was practically the same here, only there were now nine Reapers they had to deal with. There was now Conrad and Marvin too. Another shift in the timeline.

Kenneth was forthcoming with information, diving into the grim details about the Reapers and their ruthless leader, Benson. Villagers painted Benson as a monstrous figure, wielding power through fear and cruelty. He took delight in inflicting pain and death without a shred of remorse. Benson's mother, Mary Burge, was likened to a nefarious character straight out of a gritty crime drama—a femme fatale with a chilling aura, capable of manipulation and deception. Her husband, Steve Burge, was depicted as a deceitful and subservient simp, contrasting with her commanding presence. Through the tales of the community, Benson's dysfunctional family dynamics came to light, revealing a disturbed individual capable of betraying even his own associates—a fiery personality, easily provoked and impossible to please.

As Jim absorbed the vile descriptions of the gang, the villagers shared a particularly disturbing incident. Benson had brutally attacked one of the Reapers, Morgan, in a fit of jealous, obsessive rage, because Morgan had looked at Mary his mother "in the wrong way". The assault left Morgan with one eye permanently damaged, a grim consequence of Benson's violent outburst. Jim heard that the reconciliation took days—largely facilitated by Benson's mother, who tried to mend the rift her son had caused.

Dental problems were prevalent among the gang, with missing teeth, cavities and gum diseases haunting them. The foul-smelling breath that emanated from their unhygienic mouths added to the unsettling aura surrounding the Reapers. Additionally, the villagers spoke of unusual abnormalities in a couple of the gang members, like missing fingers and scars, injuries rumoured to be inflicted by Benson to instil fear and control. Given that Morgan had almost left the group over his incident, Jim reflected on the missed opportunity for the colony to recruit Morgan as a potential powerful ally in their fight against the sadistic gang leader. Kenneth understandably revolted at that suggestion.

In the grim roster of Benson's gang, there was also his half-brother Shafto, the older of the two but lacking authority. With their father's disappearance and having both endured years of abuse, especially Benson, they had become corrupted.

Marcos Weeks, a gang member, was described as very tall and lanky, with large ears, cocky but lacking substance. Conrad was marked by childhood chickenpox, carrying a lifetime of scars on his pockmarked skin and missing a few fingers. Briana Mills, known simply as Mills, stood out due to her chic appearance and her volatile relationship with Morgan. Despite her yellow teeth, her beauty intrigued lustful admirers. Lastly, Marvin Case, ruddy and stocky, had an oily and creepy demeanour and carried a Chelsea smile courtesy of Benson.

Jim envisioned a strategy to exploit Benson's weakness, but knew he needed assistance. Stressing adaptability, he urged the villagers to expect the unexpected, emphasising the need for improvisation.

The primary goal was to mislead Benson but first, he needed him to be blinded by lust, hate, and vengeance. Though he was uncomfortable about it, he enlisted Tasha to play up to Benson's desires, recognising it as a risky but necessary tactic.

He noticed an old photo shop with Polaroid cameras and film, which would be essential for misdirection. Cable ties and the use of spare keys to Benson, Mary and Morgan's usual apartments were also crucial elements. Jim decided to work the bar with Kenneth so he could calm Benson should the need arise. The plan was to spike Benson's drink to extract valuable information and feed the Reapers' paranoia.

"It's a pretty thin plan, isn't it? Basically, we're gonna mess with their already warped minds and see if they self-destruct," Kenneth said, unimpressed.

"Pretty thin," Jim agreed with a confident smile.

"This is the best you got? Hide the fuel and generator they want to benefit from, fuel their paranoia and hope they don't just kill us but attack each other instead?"

"I don't know. I'm making this up as I go. Look, if anyone has any better ideas, now's the time. But since you've endured this, for how long I don't know, I'm going to guess you don't. They terrorise you anyway, what's the difference?" Jim paused for a moment as silence swept the room. "Okay, we need a backup idea, this is the bottom line—plan B. We stick together. They attack one of us and they attack all of us. We outnumber them. Plan B is everybody fights for their freedoms. We rush them all at once—the element of surprise. Let's just hope it doesn't come to that, but everyone in the colony needs to be prepared for it." Jim glared at him.

"Plan B seems scarier than wafer-thin," Pauline said.

"Indeed, but fear must be overcome if plan B becomes necessary. Stay flexible and enjoy messing with their minds, they've done it to you long enough. If it comes to Plan B, Kenneth, you need to talk to everyone outside of this meeting and get them ready for it. I want you to come up with a battle cry. If anyone starts getting maimed, they must shout the battle cry and the power of the crowd will overcome the Reapers. But blood will be on our hands then, it doesn't need to be—plan A will work, trust me."

Kenneth nodded, his eyes glazed and wide with fear of what was to come.

“Mason, Blake, I want you to gather any weapons you can—spare knives from the kitchen, baseball bats, broken chair legs, anything you can find. Turn one of the empty chalets into an armoury. If it comes to a full-on battle we need to be ready.”

The colonists’ dispersed, and Jim hesitated about returning to his apartment with Tasha. Wary of renewed attempts at seduction and fearful of discussions regarding her part in the misdirection, he went quiet.

In fading candlelight, their conversations dwindled until the last flicker disappeared. They left the clubhouse and enjoyed the warm, peaceful night, illuminated by the glow of the moon with the skies often-purple haze of toxic clouds partially shrouding it. Seeking solace, Tasha linked her arm with Jim’s, and he found comfort in the silence.

“Is something wrong?” she asked finally.

Jim redirected the conversation smoothly, assuring her, “nothing’s wrong. Let’s just take a moment to savour the moon together. It’s truly extraordinary tonight. Look at the beauty of the moon, Tasha, it’s closer to Earth than usual, that’s why it looks bigger tonight. They call that a supermoon, did you know? We’re lucky the clouds cleared enough for us to see it tonight,” he said softly.

“You are such a nerd.” Tasha smiled reaching for his hand, as they both became immersed in the enchanting scene.

Chapter 28 – The Reapers' Reckoning

Jim and Tasha stood at the doorway of their dishevelled apartment. Tasha, seizing the moment, pressed her body against Jim's, engaging him in a passionate, seductive kiss.

"Isn't it time to carry me over the threshold, my enticing, and nerdy man?" she teased.

Jim, captivated by her allure, yielded to her charms. However, guilt flooded him. Remembering his wife locked in a cage prompted him to pull away and lift Tasha through the doorway, only to pause and place her down.

"Stop, please," Jim pleaded softly, looking down and avoiding eye contact.

"One day, Jim, you'll surrender, and when you do, you can have anything you want," Tasha declared. She put her index finger in her mouth, sucking it slowly and provocatively.

Jim closed his eyes, swallowed deeply, shook his head, and, in a last-ditch effort to do the right thing, persisted in resisting the temptation.

They each vacated to their separate bedrooms. Before closing his door, Jim turned for one last glimpse. Tasha had done the same, and their eyes met across the dim corridor, burning with desire, wanting more, needing to consume each other. They both closed their doors and in vain tried to sleep, tossing and turning. Each of them repeatedly peeked at their bedroom doors, wondering if the night was truly over.

Jim's head was full of overactive thoughts and possibilities, many of which involved his wife, or at least the version of her that was caged up, undergoing a terrible ordeal. He refocused on the plan to destroy Benson. He took deep, slow breaths, closed his eyes and cleared his mind. Imagining floating in the vastness of space with only the spectacle of the solar system for company was liberating.

* * *

He was woken by the surprising warmth and brightness of daylight beaming through the cheap curtains of the apartment. *There's hope for this broken world repairing itself in time,* he thought to himself. He got out of bed and put on his dressing gown. As he made his way to the kitchen to make himself some food, he stopped suddenly, noticing Tasha had prepared breakfast already.

"Kenneth gave me two freeze-dried scrambled egg with cheese, prepping pouches. I made them for us." She smiled.

"Why, thank you, Tasha, that's kind of you."

After breakfast, she went to her room, for a few minutes later. "I found this in the wardrobe—do you like it?"

She stepped into the room wearing a striking, form-fitting dress that clung to her curves with an almost liquid sheen. The material was a sleek, glossy red, catching the light as she moved. The dress was already short, but it was cut daringly higher on one side, revealing a toned leg partially covered by a stocking. The neckline plunged low, accentuating her cleavage, while thin straps crisscrossed her back, leaving much of it bare and adding an air of sultry elegance.

"What are you doing to me?" he begged.

"Well?" she insisted.

"It's... er... yeah, it's great. A little *too* great. You look like you're about to go to work at a pole-dancing club. You need to get dressed, Tasha—we need to get focused on the task in hand."

"Oh, don't worry, I am dressed. This isn't for you, big boy—this is for Benson. It should get his attention, don't you think? It looks like it got yours," she added cheekily.

"Don't you think that's going a bit too far? You could get yourself into real trouble with him if you're not careful," Jim warned. "He is a rapist, you know."

"Jim, be careful. I might start thinking you care," she said, wagging her finger disapprovingly and tutting.

"Of course I care. This man is dangerous. I don't

want to see you get hurt, Tasha. I have strong feelings for you, you know I do. I think I've made a terrible mistake. We should just go with plan B."

Tasha didn't seem to be listening. "A little jealous, are we, *Jimmy*?" she said, emphasising his name.

Jim hesitated, realising he absolutely was, but his concerns were genuine. If he admitted his feelings, he knew it could lead them back to her bedroom, so he decided to avoid answering. "Listen, I know how dangerous these men are. You remember what happened in the basement, right?"

"No, I wasn't there—that was your wife, remember?"

"No, it was Scarlett, but she wasn't my wife," he corrected her.

"Okay, okay, and yes, you did tell me about it. I can take care of myself, Jim. I was doing just fine until you came along. Life was simple: stay warm, stay dry and find food. You may not believe it, but I was quite happy. My friends and I always found a reason to laugh or cry, the same as everyone else. Some of them found love to keep them warm. That could have been me too."

"You wish you had never met me, then?" he asked.

"No, Jim, I wish—" She hesitated. "I wish I had never fallen in love with you," she said as she left the room. She turned to address him from the doorway before she left. “Nothing bad is going to happen to me, and we both know plan A is the safest way for success without any of the colonists here getting hurt.”

After a brief pause, Tasha continued, “would you try and remember, even if it is Scarlett out there, that doesn’t mean it’s your wife either, now does it?”

A void of emptiness dawned on Jim’s consciousness as he battled his fears for her safety, the love he felt for both Tasha and the loss of Scarlett. Was it even possible to love two women? He wondered, *am I chasing a lost cause, is this driving me crazy.*

As he rose from his chair to follow her back out to the colony, the fading sunlight captured his attention. The sky darkened abruptly, a strange purple cloud transforming the brilliant late morning into dusk, reviving memories of storm clouds he had witnessed with his brother.

At the same time the roar of a V10 engine echoed, announcing the arrival of a mint Audi R8, a V6 Grand Cherokee Jeep with a trailer, and a couple of other cars. Jim pulled his curtains together, kneeling to observe undetected. Recognising Benson, he knew he had to stay put and study his enemy. A fresh scar on Benson’s face hinted at a tough encounter, perhaps with a strong-willed captive defending against an attack.

As Morgan and Mills emerged from the Audi, Jim couldn’t help but notice Morgan’s possessive demeanor.

With his arm wrapped tightly around her waist, he guided her steps, leaving little room for her to move independently. Shafto and Mary, accompanied by an older man—Steve Burge—stepped out of the Cherokee. Jim saw two girls in the trailer and yearned for an opportunity to comfort Scarlett, but Shafto's lewd behaviour near the trailer kept him at bay. Jim watched as Shafto taunted the girls, provocatively wagging his tongue at them.

Noting the trailer's sturdy roof, reminiscent of a circus lion's cage, brought a degree of comfort. The presence of a plastic sheet for cover offered its occupants a meagre but crucial refuge. Jim remembered the colonists assuring him that there had been no prolonged heavy acid rainfall during their captivity, hinting at a degree of safety. The well-maintained condition of the cars suggested sufficient cover, possibly a barn. Despite the looming threat of a thick rain cloud, for now they seemed relatively unscathed at least.

"Tasha, here they come! We need to get to the bar," Jim called to her anxiously. "Let's—"

Before he finished his sentence, she interrupted. "Let's go?"

She seemed amused at having stopped him in his tracks. She was wearing knee-high boots, and her makeup was particularly seductive. Her long, dark hair was swept into waves, seeming effortlessly sexy. Jim could make out stockings beneath her white fur coat, which was only partially done up to allow visibility of her cleavage. He had no doubt that Benson would take notice of her. The plan was already in motion.

Jim strolled past the impatient Reapers, settling behind the bar. Benson met him with instant aggression, warning against keeping him waiting. Jim, with a degree of sass, assured him it wouldn't happen again, passing over a glass of neat whiskey with a confident smile.

Benson's gaze shifted to Tasha, captivated by her beauty. In high spirits, he said, "Well, well, well, this place has taken a turn for the better. And who might you be?"

Tasha responded with a sultry silence. Closing in, she whispered playfully in his ear, leaving him intrigued. Turning her attention to Jim, she ordered whiskey, mimicking Benson's choice with a flirtation tactic.

Kenneth entered, distracting Benson with apartment keys. Benson, revelling in his control, taunted Kenneth. "The usual apartments all cleaned and ready for us, I hope, geek boy?" Silently seething, Kenneth handed over the keys; Jim clocked the flaring of his nostrils and the clenching of his fists.

Benson, examining the keys, made a crude comment aimed at Kenneth: "Don't worry, geek boy, you can have your bitch back soon. I'm nearly done with her. Oh, by the way, I've made some improvements to her. She had a filthy mouth, but you won't have to worry about that anymore." Benson let out a loud, evil laugh that filled the room.

Mills, Marcos, Mary, and all the others followed suit, laughing along wholeheartedly, their eyes full of venom. Jim was concerned by what that meant. Unfortunately, Benson picked up on Kenneth's anger as well.

"Oooh, Kenneth," Benson enticed him, clearly hoping for conflict. "Upset, are ya? You want to try it with me, lad? Come on, then, let's be having you." He stood and stared at him. "Well, go on, lad, if you think you're man enough—or are you a chicken shit?"

Kenneth looked to Jim and saw him shaking his head and raising his hand, instructing him to wait. Kenneth reluctantly backed down and released his clenched fist, dropping his head back into a pose of submission.

Benson clocked Jims subtle guidance. "That's what I thought, lad. You better get our supper sorted, me lad. Me and the crew want one of your banquets laid on. You got that, Geek boy?" Benson demanded, poking him in the shoulder so hard he nearly lost his balance.

"Yes, sir," Kenneth muttered. A glint in his eye was the only hint of defiance.

"I'm glad you have a new barman working here, you pussy. He just saved your puny little life. Now get out of my sight." Benson snatched the keys and pointed to the door.

Jim had to stop himself from reacting to the taunting as well; he knew he needed to watch and study them first. He realised he shouldn't show weakness to Benson; he gambled Benson would have more respect for him if instead he showed strength. But he had to be careful not to push the boundaries too far and be made an example of for anyone who opposed him.

There were other things Jim noticed too; Benson's mother, Mary, was a flirt and didn't much care if her husband Steve Burge was there or not. Jim continued pouring their drinks and observed her humiliating people—lover, friend or foe she didn't care. Her attention was firmly on Morgan now, whilst her husband had nothing to do but watch through jealous eyes, his squint giving away his contained rage.

Burge sat at the bar, knocking back one shot after another, seemingly trying to drown his feelings while Mary leaned against the counter next to him, engrossed in whispered conversations with Morgan. Her laughter echoed through the room, drawing the attention of everyone nearby.

"You're too funny, Morgan," Mary exclaimed, her hand brushing against his arm in response to something that had been whispered in her ear.

Burge clenched his jaw, the muscles in his neck tensing as he watched Mary's flirtatious display. He tried to drown out the sound of her laughter with another shot. Mary leaned in closer to Morgan, her breasts pressing into him as she continued what appeared to be an intimate conversation out of immediate earshot, shrouded with moments of laughter. Burge's face flushed with embarrassment and anger, his grip on his glass tightening with each passing moment.

Finally, Mary turned to Burge with a smirk. "Steve Burge," she said, her tone dripping with condescension, "why don't you do what you're good at and just sit there quietly? It's clear your brain isn't needed for this conversation. Piss off and give us some space, would you, micro dick?" she scoffed. Jim observed Shafto, the quiet one, lurking in the shadows smirking at the drama that unfolded like it was all for his own personal entertainment.

Jim now understood Kenneth's perception of Morgan and concurred with the colonists' evaluation, finding Morgan's participation even more unsettling than anticipated. Mills—Morgan's girlfriend—sat at a nearby table, her gaze fixed on the shot glass in her hand. Without a hint of emotion, she tilted her head back, downing the contents in one swift motion. Her face remained impassive, revealing nothing of the turmoil Jim suspected she was feeling. As she reached for another shot, her movements were methodical, almost robotic, as if detached from the world around her, lost in silent contemplation, perhaps already high on something else.

Benson's disapproval of his mother showing

interest in Morgan was clear. He stormed over to Mary's stool at the bar and started pointing, his expression a mask of anger, red-faced as he raged through gritted teeth. "What the hell are you doing? You're an embarrassment."

Mary turned to him, a surprised expression on her face. "Benson, darling, what's gotten into you?"

"What's gotten into me? Are you serious right now?" Benson's voice rose. "You're flirting with Morgan, making a spectacle of yourself and Burge. Have you no shame? You're old enough to be his mother, maybe even grandmother."

Mary's demeanour shifted from surprise to defensiveness. "Benson, don't you dare speak to me like that. I am your mother."

"Yeah, well, maybe you should start acting like it," Benson retorted, his tone dripping with contempt. "Burge has been nothing but loyal to you, and this is how you repay him? By acting like a tart in public?"

Mary bristled at his words, her facade of indifference crumbling. "You don't understand, Benson. This is none of your business."

"None of my business?" Benson scoffed. "You're my mother. When you behave like this, it becomes my business. Grow up. You're nothing but mutton dressed as lamb." He glared at her and returned to his own stool.

With that, Morgan stepped away and joined Mills at

her table. She served him some awkward silence and he began apologising, insisting that there was nothing in it, just a bit of harmless banter. “She was just flirting, there’s nothing going on. Look at her, she’s way too old for me. Besides, Benson would probably kill me. I would have to be stupid to risk his wrath, and then there is Burge too. We was just messing about, baby, it’s you I love.”

Mills took a sniff of some white powder and after seemed to quickly forgive, or at least move on from it, with a weak hug. Their conversation began to flow again, in a slurred fashion, as did their drinks.

Jim noted the fear in the eyes of the lower-ranking members of Benson’s Reaper gang. They lingered in the background, avoiding attention. Perhaps they were relieved not to be the recipients of cruel manipulation, whether mental or physical, for once, Jim silently surmised. But they were close enough to provide direct support, proving their worth to the leader who clearly ruled with fear. The others had barely said a word apart from chatter amongst themselves he couldn’t fully hear.

Chapter 29 – The Reaper's Temptation the Edge of Deceit

Jim skilfully kept his guests at ease, serving spirits while monitoring the escalating tension within Benson's group. The volatile atmosphere was palpable, and Jim navigated it by engaging Benson in conversation, sharing stories without overshadowing him but still earning respect.

Tasha played her part flawlessly, her eyes locking onto Benson's with an intensity that bordered on magnetic. With each word she leaned in subtly to get her drink from behind him, breathing on his neck as she grabbed her drink. She noticed the goosebumps on his skin as she withdrew. She brushed a stray hair from his forehead, her touch lingering for just a moment longer than necessary. A playful smile danced on her lips as she teased him about his drink choice. "So I guess you are the leader of this ragtag crew? Very commanding," she complimented.

"You could say that."

Her body language spoke volumes, every movement designed to keep him engaged and entertained. A quick quip here, a playful jab there, all delivered with impeccable timing and a sparkle in her eye that made its impact on Benson evident; he licked his top lip with delight, a sinister grin spreading across his face as he unwittingly fell deeper under her spell.

"Come on, Benson, there's still some juice in these batteries. Let's see if we can get that jukebox to play something decent." She nudged him with her elbow once again and Benson, caught in her spell, happily followed along.

Benson selected "I Wish It Would Rain Down" by Phil Collins, his favourite eighties love song.

"Oh, come on," she chided, her voice laced with mock indignation. "Your taste in music is absolutely rubbish. Let me show you how it's really done."

Tasha's hand was on the jukebox, ready to change the song. But Benson had other plans. With a swift move, he grabbed her hand away from the jukebox and pulled her close, wrapping his arm around her waist. Without missing a beat, he guided her into a slow dance, their bodies swaying to the melancholic melody.

Caught up in the intimacy of the moment, Benson leaned in to kiss her, his lustful passion evident in the way he pressed his lips against hers. And Tasha played along, their kiss deepening with each passing second. Unbeknownst to Benson, it was all part of Tasha's plan, a calculated move to keep him occupied while the real game played out around them.

As Jim watched from behind the bar, a mixture of

emotions swirled beneath his composed exterior. His hand covered his mouth, a feeble attempt to conceal the jealousy that gnawed at him as his stomach turned with regret for suggesting this plan. It was a sensation that caught him off guard and left him unsettled.

With each passing moment, the realization sank in more profoundly: he was grappling with feelings for Tasha that went beyond mere friendship or lust. It was a revelation that stirred a lingering conflict within him, one that he was ill prepared to confront. Perhaps, buried beneath the layers of concern, grief and despair, there lay a love that he had been denying himself too. His Scarlett in his original reality might be gone forever for all he knew. His commitment after years apart had been tested and in this moment he was failing on all levels.

"Kenneth, did you inform everyone what the battle cry command is?" Jim whispered.

"I did, but of course, the others still want to try Plan A first," Ken replied, careful not to be overheard above the music.

"What is the battle cry, Kenneth?" Jim asked.

"For the Colony!" Kenneth whispered. "We will wait."

"That's right stay patient, and think of Dusty and Scarlett in the trailer. If we fail, they die out there. Let's wait and see where this goes."

Another song started on the jukebox and Kenneth nipped out of the back entrance of the kitchen into the courtyard.

After several songs, dancing and playfulness, Benson and Tasha soon returned to the bar, and Jim continued feeding them drinks. Benson, in a fit of laughter, remarked, "That weasel Kenneth better have laid on a nice spread for us, or else his woman will take another beating." In a venomous tone, he added, "Kenneth's bitch was a mouthy one. I've improved the dog, and Kenneth can have her back soon. She won't ever backchat anyone again, I can tell you that."

The room fell silent, and Jim felt a growing sense of concern. Benson's comments hinted at something even more sinister, but he didn't really understand the comment.

As the evening progressed, Benson's impatience grew with his hunger. He downed his drink in one gulp, slamming the glass down with a pleasurable sigh. The burning whiskey left him momentarily speechless, evident with his croaky gasp as he gestured for the Reapers to follow him into the main hall, where tables were set. Like an alpha in a troop, Benson ensured the gang didn't go hungry for too long, which revealed a concealed reliance on Kenneth's community.

With no alternative—her arm was grabbed forcefully—Tasha joined Benson. She offered no physical resistance, but annoyance was evident in her facial expression, her forehead tense as she was yanked to his side.

Meanwhile, Jim left the bar and joined Kenneth, Mason, and Blake in the kitchen. Kenneth stood by the stove, his posture tense as he slammed pots and pans. His face was flushed as he measured out portions of freeze-dried food with sharp, deliberate movements.

Do you guys need any help in here, Kenneth? Are you okay?" Jim said.

Kenneth shook his head, his hands trembling with frustration.

"Forget I said anything," Jim replied, realising he might have overstepped by asking the blindingly obvious. It was clear Kenneth was deeply concerned about what Benson had done to Dusty.

"Did you hear any of that, Kenneth? They're already at odds with each other. Stick to the plan, they only need a nudge and they will destroy themselves," Jim said, attempting to console Kenneth.

Kenneth shrugged off Jim's attempt at comfort. Without warning, Kenneth's control snapped. With a primal roar, he grabbed a nearby plate and hurled it against the wall with all his strength. The ceramic shattered into a thousand pieces, scattering across the floor like shrapnel.

“I popped out to see her, tried to speak to her in the cage while Benson was distracted. She wouldn’t even look at me. What have they done to her?” he muttered through gritted teeth. “I’m going to kill him.”

Jim reassured him, “We need to stay calm. You don’t have to take matters into your own hands, Ken. We’ll get them out soon enough. Killing him won’t stop all the Reapers—we need them to tear themselves apart. Stay the course. Think of the consequences for the girls if you do anything drastic that backfires.”

“You’re probably right. When they’re safe, *then* I’ll kill him,” Kenneth replied.

“You stay here and out of the way of them. I’ll go back and keep them boozed up. Mason, Blake, you two serve their food when it’s all ready. We need to give Kenneth a break from them,” Jim said.

“Sure,” Mason answered, “and then it’s go time with the Polaroid cameras, getting evidence of Mary banging Morgan, yeah?”

“We only need a photo of them leaving together. When you see them leaving together, make sure the flash is off so it doesn’t draw their attention. If it’s safe to get more photos, through a window or something, sure, but if you think there’s even a chance they’ll see you, abort the mission. We only need the Reapers to know they have gone off together, then we hide their car.”

“Got it,” Mason replied, reaching for the camera to check the flash was off and film was loaded. Jim double checked the flash setting was disabled, just to be sure.

* * *

The food, hastily prepared and served in the main hall, was devoured with little regard for decorum. The Reapers tore into their meals with voracious appetites, devouring them with the ferocity of wild beasts. Plates were emptied within moments, the remnants of their feast scattered haphazardly across the table. Shafto was ignoring the noise; he mentioned he was tired and left almost immediately after the food back to his room.

“Pah! What is this crap anyway?” Benson spat out the last mouthfuls, remnants of food falling out of his mouth.

“Kenneth was a big-time doomsday prepper before the skies went dark. Lucky for us, he has years of long-life freeze-dried emergency food options to get us through when crops aren’t ready to eat,” Mason said.

“Dog food would taste better,” Shafto said in support with no appreciation from anyone in the gang.

“Here, wash it down with this.” Jim served them each a red wine.

The evening sped by, marked by more free-flowing alcohol and escalating aggression among the Reapers. Marcos, Conrad, and Marvin seemed to all be getting along just fine among themselves. Jim took a guess that they were mere sheep along for the ride, skimming whatever they could from Benson's spoils, such as the meal they had just enjoyed. Benson and Morgan, in particular, were embroiled in petty disputes. Jim noted Morgan's proximity to Mary, and her strategic avoidance of conflicts—until Benson brandished a knife, prompting her to intervene.

"Sit down and shut up, Morgan," Mary scolded him. "Benson's deliberately provoking you, can't you see that?"

As the night concluded, Benson, in a fit of anger, flipped a table before storming off, instructing Tasha to follow him. The tension lingered as they exited, leaving the remaining Reapers discussing the evening's tumult. Morgan, out of Benson's range, began laughing, met by a stern look from Mary.

Mills, Morgan's girlfriend, was barely coherent, lost in a haze of substances and alcohol, and appeared bewildered by Benson's abrupt exit. Jim nodded at Kenneth, signalling it was time to put their plan into action. Kenneth smiled genuinely for the first time.

"Be careful, Morgan. Benson has a temper to rival the Devil himself," Mary warned.

Burge had left the room in a huff earlier following some scathing remarks from Mary. Shafto and Marcos, Marvin and Conrad had gone with him—Jim wasn't sure why, but they were clearly discussing something as they left. Mary was unconcerned about their departure, her interest in Morgan growing visibly. Only Mills, Morgan, and Mary remained in the room.

"You need a mature woman, not a child, Morgan," Mary suggested seductively, licking her top lip slowly. "If you want me, you can have me tonight." She grabbed his hand and sucked on his finger.

"We can look after Mills here tonight?" Jim suggested.

Morgan eagerly accepted. "Yeah, look after that silly bitch, would ya?" he slurred. "She's completely wasted. She won't wake up until tomorrow, I doubt." Morgan and Mary left the venue impatiently. Passing Mills' unconscious body on their way out, Morgan spat on her back and laughed, much to Jim's revulsion. When they left he got some napkins and rubber gloves from the kitchen, cleaned her back, laid her on one of the benches and covered her with a blanket.

Mason and Blake knew their mission with the camera and successfully captured photos of Morgan and Mary leaving together, holding hands. Jim heard their laughter echoing as they snapped pictures from the kitchen window. Fortunately Morgan and Mary didn't hear it.

Their excitement grew at the prospect of taking dirty pictures through the window of Morgan's ground-floor apartment as they made their stealthy approach.

“Jim, come in. We are in position; we have a clear view. They are leaving the lights on, over.” Mason whispered to Jim on the walkie-talkie.

“Great. Take one or two pictures; we don’t need loads. Get out of there as soon as you can. If they see you, run. Take Morgan’s car; the keys are in the ignition, and drive to the farm. You tell Alex I sent you and that Benson’s after you. He will look after you. Over”

Fortunately, there were no net curtains and Morgan and Mary hadn’t bothered to pull the curtains, so the show was taking place in full view of the window. Jim and Kenneth were keeping a watchful eye on the surrounding area, to keep the lads safe.

Jim’s anxiety for Tasha’s safety only intensified. Each moment she spent with Benson felt like an eternity to Jim, his mind consumed by the fear of her potential vulnerability. Despite her necessary efforts to distract Benson, Jim remained gripped by a profound sense of dread, unable to find solace until he knew for certain that Tasha was out of harm’s way.

“Look, look, look, quick,” Mason exclaimed, keying the mic, his excitement palpable, as he took a peek. “Jim, she’s wearing stockings and sexy underwear, and now she’s kissing Morgan.” Mason continued as Blake snapped pictures for evidence.

Jim's heart raced as he imagined what Blake and Mason were witnessing. He felt a mixture of disbelief and discomfort at the sight.

“Jim, come in! We have some great photos—more than two!”

Jim's frustration flared. “That’s great, now get the hell out of there and come back now!” he replied on his walkie-talkie, trying to keep his voice steady.

They retreated, their mission accomplished, holding in fits of laughter until they were out of earshot on their way back to meet with him. Jim felt a knot in his stomach as he wondered how this would play out, hearing them howling uncontrollably on the walkie-talkie wasn’t helping his calm.

“Well done, boys. I hope they didn’t hear you laughing so loudly.”

“Nah, we were well out of earshot and they are far too busy to care about us.” Mason replied, his face lit up with a mischievous grin.

“Give me the photos. There’s one job left to do—take Morgan’s car, drive it down a lane somewhere, and ditch it where it can’t be seen too obviously. He left the keys in the ignition; I checked earlier. He probably thinks nobody would be stupid enough to steal a car from the Reapers,” Jim said.

“Yeah, sure,” said Mason. “Come on, Blake, let’s do it.”

“Great stuff, then just walk back and go to bed. And

for God's sake, don't get seen. And be quiet!"

Jim and Kenneth embarked on their stakeout mission, it wasn't long before Mary left the chalet, presumably to return to Burge. They had gathered rope, a taser, cable ties, and some old material to use as a gag and blindfolds for the abduction. Jim observed Kenneth's demeanour closely. As they approached Mary there was a tense set to his jaw, his muscles coiled like a spring ready to snap. Jim recognized the signs immediately—the clenched fists, the furrowed brow, all telltale indicators of Kenneth's surging fury. Without hesitation, his pace quickened to reach her first. Kenneth lunged forward, his anger clearly driving him to silence Mary's screams permanently.

Jim moved swiftly, realising that Kenneth's emotions were running high. He saw Kenneth's arm clamp down on Mary, his grip tight and unyielding, as if trying to extinguish a flame. Jim's heart pounded in his chest as he intervened. Jim eased Kenneth's grip off her face, allowing the now-unconscious Mary to breathe. He could feel the tension radiating off Kenneth, his body trembling with pent-up rage. With Mary now subdued, Jim acted quickly, seizing the opportunity to restrain her, binding her hands behind her back and gagging her to prevent any further outbursts when she came around and blindfolded her. As he worked, Jim couldn't shake the feeling of unease that lingered, knowing that they were treading a dangerous path, one that could have unforeseen consequences.

“Ken, let go, we need her alive,” he commanded urgently as Kenneth moved once again to strangle Mary. Reluctantly, Kenneth released and carried her to one of the furthest apartments, then secured her to a bed and made her as comfortable as possible.

Jim left and slipped the incriminating photos under Benson’s door. As he turned to leave, the door swung open, startling him. “Jeez! You scared the life out of me,” Jim hissed.

Tasha, gesturing for silence, whispered, “Shhh, come on, let’s go.”

They swiftly met up with Kenneth, who was still with Mary.

With a mix of jealousy and genuine worry in his voice, Jim couldn’t help but ask Tasha, “What happened with you?”

A sly smile appeared on Tasha’s lips. She whispered mischievously, “Nothing to fret about. He slipped some Rohypnol into my drink, or something of the sort, but I switched the glasses so he drank it. His performance didn’t last long, but he sure had a memorable night, even if it was rather brief.”

“Oh, right,” Jim said, discontented at the thought of Benson enjoying any time with Tasha.

“Don’t lose sleep, Jim. Nothing happened. You can keep dangling me on your bit of string a while longer yet,”

Tasha replied, starting to get annoyed.

Relieved that nothing had gone wrong, Jim smiled back at her, though a hint of jealousy lingered. "Why didn't you leave earlier?"

Tasha's expression turned serious. "I needed to ensure he wouldn't wake up and grow suspicious."

Jim nodded, understanding the necessity of her actions. "I was just worried about you," he admitted sincerely. "You had the most dangerous part of the mission, being alone with him."

"As I've said before," Tasha declared, pushing herself up from her seat, "I'm a big girl, Jim. I can take care of myself just fine." Her tone was assertive, with a hint of exasperation. "I didn't need your help in the park, and I sure as hell didn't need it with Benson. Trust me, dealing with guys like him was just another day in my life back when I was on the streets. He's a pushover compared to the real troublemakers I've faced." She paused, meeting Jim's gaze squarely. "I appreciate the concern, but I had this covered."

"So I can see," Jim said, firmly put in his place.

The stakes were growing higher as they moved into the next phase of the plan. Now they needed to abduct Morgan, restrain and gag him and move him to one of the other apartments so he couldn't be found.

Kenneth quietly unlocked the apartment door, to let

Jim and Tasha in first. Jim noticed Kenneth's face twist with anger, as he picked up a baseball bat he had taken from the armoury in the nearby apartment. They stealthily entered Morgan's apartment. The dimly lit room made it easier to approach Morgan's bed. Before he fully awoke, Kenneth pushed by them both and struck Morgan with a powerful blow to the head, causing a large gash and rendering him unconscious. Blood spattered across the bed, and Jim's expression soured.

"We were supposed to take them both down with the taser," Jim hissed, brandishing the electroshock weapon Blake and Mason had found in Kenneth's prepping stash.

Kenneth's response was laced with malice. "I wanted to hurt him and her, okay?"

"I think he's still alive. He's breathing anyway. We need to move him," Jim said, still in shock at the unforeseen brutal assault. Jim shook his head disapprovingly. "You better clean up this place, get new bedding, and leave no trace of the blood behind. If Benson suspects foul play, it's all over for us."

Meanwhile, Tasha stepped in to assist Jim. They gagged Morgan and secured him with cable ties.

Jim shot Kenneth a glare for complicating an already precarious situation. "Okay, Tasha, hold his legs to prevent them from bumping on the floor and help me carry him. If we can get him to those apartments across the way and ensure he's fully secured so he can't signal for help, then we're in business. Kenneth, you'd better do a thorough job cleaning up in here."

As soon as Morgan was secured and the room was cleaned up, the three of them ran to the cage to check on the girls. But they were nowhere to be found.

"Where are they?" Kenneth said rather too loudly.

"Shh, quiet, Kenneth," Tasha reminded him. "Now is not the time to go waking the Reapers up. This needs to unfold naturally tomorrow. One of them must have taken the girls into one of the apartments. Better that, than left out here to the elements, don't you think?"

"I guess so."

"One more night, which is almost over, by the way. One more check of the room for any blood spatter or clues and then we get back to bed. It's a big day tomorrow," Jim said.

Chapter 30 – Crafting the Perfect Misdirection

Kenneth reluctantly began to clean up the blood in Morgan's apartment. Jim was far from pleased with Kenneth's actions. Morgan's death was not part of the plan, though luckily that hadn't happened.

"Kenneth," Jim said, waiting for eye contact with Kenneth, "are you going to continue to be a liability to the plan?"

Kenneth, seeming to feign ignorance, replied, "What, what? What was that?"

Jim repeated his question with more intensity. "Are you going to be a liability to the bloody plan? Can you handle this?"

Kenneth hesitated, his confidence wavering. "Erm, of course, yes, yes. I just lost it for a minute, that's all. I'm fine now. Are we all fine here?"

Jim sighed. "I guess we'll have to trust you, Kenneth. Just don't let your emotions control you. We could all end up dead, or worse, your actions could have terrible consequences. Think about what might happen to Dusty if we get found out. Remember, clean sheets are great, but leave them a mess; he doesn't seem the type to make his bed."

"Of course, you're right. I'm sorry, Jim. It won't happen again."

Jim nodded, though he remained unimpressed. He knew they couldn't dwell on this now. They had a plan to execute, and there was no room for further missteps.

After they had finished cleaning up, they returned to their apartments. The sun began to rise, casting an eerie and beautiful red glow throughout the toxic sky. Jim and Tasha were exhausted, but needed to rest before the impending drama.

Jim and Tasha found sleep elusive, and they both ended up in the small kitchen, stumbling into each other in their weary daze. They brewed coffee on one of Kenneth's camping stoves, relishing the invigorating warmth as it spread through their bodies.

"Damn, that's a good cup of coffee," Jim exclaimed, a dribble escaping his mouth, which he quickly wiped away with his hand. Uncontrollable laughter followed, momentarily dispersing the tension of their situation. The more time he spent with her, the more confused he was about his feelings for her. It had been so long since he had lost his old life with his wife and daughter, it had started to feel like a dream. Had any of it even been real?

After their first brew, Tasha offered, "Would you like me to make you another coffee?"

Appreciating the offer, Jim replied, "Yes, please."

As Tasha turned to make more coffee, Jim was mesmerized by her beauty in the red peignoir and matching thong, and found himself lost in an erotic daze.

Tasha caught him in the act. “You like what you see, do you, Jimmy?” she teased, smiling at his attention.

Struggling to regain composure, Jim said, “Tasha, you’re stunning, there’s no doubt about that, and I do have strong feelings for you. I’m so confused with all this travelling through realities, I don’t even know what’s real any more. I am so sorry.”

“Jim, don’t be ashamed. That’s the most honest thing you could have told me and it makes sense. Unfortunately, it only makes me want you more. And since we’re a couple in this wasteland, it’s all the more confusing.”

“I mean, the brief party with my Scarlett and Jerica there and all my friends and family too was practically the only time I’ve really been close to them in the best part of two years. I’ve spent more time with you these last few months, and then seeing you with Benson, it really made me worried,” Jim said.

Her voice trembled. “Benson is a pig. He takes what and who he wants, and doesn’t care about anything or anybody. You know he’s going to be coming for me now, don’t you, Jim? I can’t just drug him every time he makes a move on me; he’ll catch on.”

“He’ll get what he deserves, and it might be today. Besides, you can handle yourself.”

“That’s true, he wouldn’t know what hit him if he tries it with me. It’ll start as soon as he wakes up,” Tasha said, for the first time admitting some concern. “The side effects of the drugs can last up to twelve hours. He had a lot to drink, so I doubt he’ll be up before noon.”

“Yes, but when he sees those photos and their car gone, you’ll be the last thing on his mind,” Jim said, reaching out to grab her hand in comfort.

“I hope so, Jimmy, I hope so,” Tasha said, handing him his coffee with her other hand.

“Now, we wait for the right opportunity to introduce more misdirection and watch their gang tear themselves apart. We might not need to do anything.”

She nodded. “There’s already a rift in the gang. We didn’t even have to do anything to expose it last night in the bar. And whenever Benson wakes up, he’ll be groggy and hopefully easier to influence. All we have to do is give them a little nudge and the photos should do that.”

“We should get some rest.”

“I’m not in the mood for sleep, Jim. Take me to my room and hold me.”

They only managed to drink half a cup before putting them down and, despite his reservations, Jim allowed himself to comfort her in bed. Soon she was asleep, feeling safe in his arms. Jim found himself deeply aroused and more stimulated than ever. He noticed the scent of perfume in the room and kissed her neck gently. She responded with a heavy breath, seemingly aware of his touch, and his breath on her neck even in her semi-sleep raised some goosebumps.

Jim whispered, "You smell divine. I recognise it. Is it Frederic Malle, Tasha?"

Her response was a half-conscious murmur. Moments later they were both fast asleep.

* * *

Jim had set an alarm to ensure he'd be up before the Reapers. Later that morning, he awoke to the sound of the alarm and, along with the others, swiftly made his way to the clubhouse. Mills was still asleep in the bar, and Mason and Blake were having an early drink and seemingly enjoying themselves. Jim wondered if they had even gone to sleep or carried on partying through the night.

"Man, I wish I could have another look at those photographs." Mason chuckled. "Did you see her breasts?"

Blake reached into his back pocket and revealed one of the photos he had kept. Both of them erupted into laughter that made them hold their sides in pain. Blake turned and saw Jim entering the bar.

"Jim, can we have another look at the other

photos?" Blake said, grinning.

"Shhh! Be quiet. Mills could hear you. Don't be foolish," Jim said, pointing angrily towards the sleeping Reaper girl.

"Sorry, we just wanted another look, that's all," the boys said, almost in unison.

"This is the last time we mention it. Do you understand?" Jim stood and waited for them to respond. After a brief pause, they nodded their agreement. He then dragged them both by the arm into the kitchen area and closed the door behind him. "Listen, the photos have been slipped under Benson's door. He'll go ballistic when he finds out Morgan has been tapping his mum. Burge will be hacked off, too, when he sees the evidence, and when they don't show up today. Then we can sit back and watch their anger burn. Adding fuel to the fire at every opportunity should be enough. They'll destroy each other."

"That's what you think. I kept one photo back," Blake said, bouncing on the balls of his feet with excitement, tongue out and eyes wide.

"Let me see it!" Mason urged.

"When this is all over, you can have the photo. For now, just hand it over," Jim said. Reluctantly, Blake handed it over. "I let you in on this because I trusted you. I don't want to see you getting hurt on account of this silliness. Now come on. You know what will happen if he finds out we took the photos."

"Yeah, plan B, right, 'For the Colony'?" Mason said, and Jim responded with scolding eyes and a stern look and moved his finger to his lips instructing them to both quieten down.

Jim heard a noise from the bar. Mills was awake but in a real mess, sitting on a bar stool and leaning over the bar.

"Can I have some water and painkillers, please?" she said, her speech slightly slurred. "My head's pounding. What the hell happened last night?"

Jim dashed to the bar and fetched her some water, having readied some aspirin for her as well. "You drank too much and slept here. Burge left early because he was annoyed with Morgan and Mary flirting in his face."

Mills, still groggy and disoriented, interrupted Jim's narrative with a disbelieving scoff. "Do me a favour. I can't remember much from last night, but I don't believe he would do that to me."

"Haven't you seen them together before?" Jim pressed.

She seemed to be struggling to recall the events of the previous night through her hangover fog. "They flirt a bit, but that's all it is. She's way too old for him, he told me. He said he loves me."

Jim knew that Mills' condition could be an

advantage in their plan to sow discord among the Reapers. Her lack of clear recollection would make it easier to manipulate her perceptions of what had occurred. However, he needed to tread carefully to avoid raising suspicions among the group.

"I feel sick," she said, hunching over, grabbing her stomach with one hand and her head with the other. As Mills attempted to make sense of the situation, Jim kept a watchful eye on her, ready to guide her perceptions in the direction required for the plan to succeed.

"He's telling the truth—they left in Morgan's car," Kenneth chimed in, pointing towards the car park area. "Go and see for yourself."

Mills' anger flared as she rushed outside to confirm that Morgan's car was indeed gone from the parking area. Jim followed Mills outside, concerned about Kenneth's next move. Hiding the car had turned out to be a smart move.

"Morgan, you scum—open the door, you pig!" Mills shouted as she pounded on their apartment door.

"Mills, we need to be careful here. We don't know for sure what happened yet." Jim stepped closer to Mills, trying to calm her down and give a false sense of support.

But Mills was beyond reason, and her rage continued to intensify, seemingly aiding her hangover recovery with adrenaline surging. She continued pounding on the apartment door, demanding that Morgan answer. After waiting for her knuckles to bleed, Ken finally opened the door with the spare key. Inside the apartment, Mills' tirade continued when Morgan's absence became apparent.

It was a tense moment, and Jim knew they had to tread carefully. Kenneth, still observing the situation with a subdued grin, was ready to add more fuel to the fire if necessary. Jim realised that they needed to control the narrative and redirect Mills' anger toward all the Reapers, not just Morgan.

Mills, in a state of fury and disbelief, was desperate for answers. "Where is he?" she demanded through gritted teeth.

Kenneth, playing his part to perfection, spun a tale designed to further enrage Mills and manipulate her emotions. "He's been planning this for months, Mills. The two of them came the other night, and next thing we knew, the fuel truck was gone." He gestured toward the empty spot out back where the truck had been parked.

Confused and overwhelmed, Mills couldn't fathom what Kenneth was suggesting. "What the hell are you talking about, geek boy?" she snapped.

"They were having it off, and you're too self-involved to even notice. You're an immature, spoiled little girl, and Morgan's been taking you for a ride." With each word, Kenneth pushed Mills closer to the brink. Tears welled up in her eyes.

"No, it can't be... it makes no sense. I've never seen them behave like this before, and we've been on the road a long time together. Sure, a bit of harmless flirting, but he told me that's all it was. Why would he want that old hag instead of me?" she mumbled in disbelief, her voice quivering.

Jim saw a glint in Kenneth's eyes and a smirk as he relished in the role of the tormentor, continuing to twist the knife. "Maybe because she gave him attention. You just talk about yourself, whining constantly, and nothing he did for you was ever good enough," he taunted. "Besides, Mary is pretty hot—you know, for an older woman—and not a crackhead like you."

Jim, recognising that Kenneth had pushed Mills' emotions to their limit, intervened. He couldn't afford to have her completely broken, as she still had a crucial role to play. "Ken, that's enough," he cautioned.

Unable to cope with the emotional turmoil, Mills collapsed onto the bed. She was too distraught to notice the subtle details and implications of the situation. In her mind, she was now convinced that Morgan and Mary had eloped.

The Reapers' internal conflicts were beginning to unravel. Jim knew that this was just the beginning of the chaos they had set in motion, and he needed to tread carefully as they moved forward.

"Benson is going to be raging when he finds out Morgan has taken his mother and the fuel tanker," Mills spat.

"You need some time to recover. Lie here for a while and I'll get you a bowl in case you need to be sick," Jim said, covering her with a blanket and fetching a bowl from the apartment kitchen. Mills barely glanced at it, shoving it aside.

"I'm not that bad. More angry than sick. I've had worse benders than that so—called 'light session' last night. What, you think I can't handle my drinks?"

Kenneth snorted, arms crossed. "Handle it? You were so far gone they had to haul you over to a bench to sleep it off like some washed-up hobo. Half the bar got an eyeful while you drooled all over yourself." He smirked, letting the words sink in. "Face it, Mills—you're a walking disaster."

He leaned in, voice dripping with disdain. "No control, no self-respect, and not a single thought for the people left cleaning up your wreckage. You disgust me!"

Chapter 31 – A High-Stakes Game Against the Reapers

Mills' emotions were a maelstrom, her tears flowing freely. Jim, sensing the aggression had gone too far, shielded Mills protectively. "Kenneth. Give us a moment," he implored. He reassured Mills, "It's not your fault. Morgan is the one in the wrong. Don't listen to Kenneth."

She sobbed, "I could understand this happening in the old world, before the skies turned to acid. But I thought... hoped... he would be devoted to me in these wastelands. All we have—well, had—was each other. There's nothing left."

Calmly, Jim asked about Dusty and Scarlett's whereabouts. Mills suggested checking Burge's room, suspecting he might have taken them for company. Then she asked, "Why would you care where the two skanks are anyway?"

Jim explained, "Can't you see it's wrong what Benson has done to them, Mills? What if that was you in the cage?"

She looked down, acknowledging the truth. "I know. The Reapers just take what they want without fear of consequences. I guess that makes me a skank too. The only difference is I don't live in a cage."

“There are always consequences, Mills. They just don’t know it yet.”

“Maybe, Jim, maybe. I just want to be on my own for a while,” she said, burying her head in the pillows.

Jim rushed to Burge’s apartment with Kenneth. Jim cautioned against impatience as Kenneth fumbled for the master key.

Burge opened the door, scowling at the interruption before he opened it.

“Mary and Morgan are missing. Have you seen them?” Jim asked nervously. Inside the room, he spotted Dusty and Scarlett, gagged and bound to old office chairs.

Burge was immediately angered by Mary’s departure. “That slut whore has left with Morgan, huh?” He turned towards the two captive girls and continued with a sleazy expression on his face, “Looks like I’m on the market again, girls. It’s your lucky day.”

Noticing Kenneth’s squared shoulders, lifted chin, and clenched fists—clear signs that he was ready to charge—Jim subtly stepped in front of him, preventing him from acting. Burge was busy declaring his discontent with Mary and dragging the captive girls to the cage, bumping their chairs along the concrete road, their muffled screams echoing.

Burge vowed, “I’ll put the skanks back in their cage and find the whore. She can try and explain herself before

I tear her a new one."

Jim exchanged a knowing glance with Kenneth; intervention would have to wait. The stage was set for Benson's explosive reaction, and they couldn't afford to disrupt the plan.

As Kenneth prepared to confront Burge, a disturbance echoed from along the street, where Benson had kicked a bin over in a temper and confronted Burge in the main square of the holiday village. "What the hell is going on out here? What are you doing with my girls?" Benson shouted.

"None of your business. That skank whore mother of yours has gone off somewhere with Morgan."

"What did you call my mother?" Benson demanded. His fists were clenched, ready for bare-knuckle combat. When Burge stayed silent, Benson raised his fist and shouted, "Say the wrong thing, Burge. Did you know that when I was in the ring, they used to call this the Hammer? This destroyed Reggie Pickering back in the day!"

"Who is Reggie Pickering?" Jim queried.

"You never heard of the Pickering brothers', Reggie and Ronnie both bare knuckle fighters the pair of them were. They had a reputation in the White Road estate area back in the day. They were no match for me sunshine, now do I need to hammer your face Burge, explain yourself?"

Burge snivelled a pathetic apology, and then

revealed Morgan's car also was missing. When questioned about the girls, he callously admitted to mistreating one of them.

"I only used one of them, the mouthy one. I used her mouth, that's all, and the other had to watch. You're right—it's a very different experience. Quite incredible, actually," Burge said with a vile smile.

As Burge pointed at Dusty, Kenneth's posture changed, as though he was a deflating balloon. "Why?" Kenneth shouted at him.

"Because I wanted to try it out, geek boy. Now shut it. She isn't so mouthy any more, at least. We've improved her, now keep your mouth shut or I'll improve you as well," Burge replied, laughing in Kenneth's face, enjoying the confrontation with a weaker adversary.

Suddenly, Benson punched Burge, breaking his nose.

"Get out of here, mate, please," Jim whispered, directing Kenneth away. "You're not doing any good here. Go and plant the Polaroid camera in Burge's room."

Meanwhile, Benson sought more answers about Mary's whereabouts.

"She left with Morgan last night. I don't think they're coming back," Jim explained.

Enraged, Benson demanded an explanation for the photos he had found slipped under his door, and kicked

Burge in frustration. "So who took these? What is going on here?"

"Nothing to do with me, is it?" Burge spat some blood as he spoke from the kick in the kidneys.

Benson's eyes darted around the courtyard, searching for answers, his gaze piercing and intense as it landed on each person present. There was quite a crowd by now; most of the village community had come out to see what all the commotion was about, including Blake and Mason, who were now very quiet, unlike them. Jim wondered if they were preparing for Kenneth's battle cry.

Jim stepped up to take the heat and delay any foolhardiness from the crowd. "I don't know, Benson. Maybe Morgan set a timer on the camera and wanted to rub your nose in it before he left. Or maybe it was Burge in his jealous rage last night, and that's why he took the girls from the cage?" Jim pointed at Burge, lying on the floor. "Maybe he wanted to show you what he thought of your mother?"

Burge, holding his bloody nose, protested and denied the accusation, earning another kick in the ribs from Benson.

"Listen," Jim said, "several nights ago, Morgan and Mary came into town. They stopped for a few beers in the bar, then forced Kenneth to give them the keys to the gas truck and drove off in it. Honestly, Kenneth told me he wasn't expecting you to come back again after that. He was quite relieved when the gang rolled in yesterday."

"Why would he be relieved?" Benson asked.

"Well, because of his wife, of course, and there is the missing tanker the colonists were hoping they might get back."

"Why didn't Morgan and Mother just drive off that night and not bother to rejoin our gang, or bring the fuel truck to me?" Benson asked.

Jim hadn't considered that question, and had to think on his toes. "I don't know. We thought that they'd driven it back to you last week. Now I'm thinking they hid the fuel truck somewhere and were waiting for the right time to leave you. Maybe one more night of hot food, drink, a comfy bed here before driving off forever was all they wanted. And when Mary saw you hooking up with Tasha, maybe she thought it was the right time to move on."

"What! That's ridiculous," Burge said squeakily, the sound muffled by his bloody nose.

Benson kicked him in the stomach. "Is it?" he said, spitting on him as he walked past him towards his apartment. "Because it's starting to make sense to me. Someone bind his feet and hands behind his back and drag him to the bar and wait for me there."

"Let's search his apartment. I'll help you if you like," Jim offered.

"No, you lot can tie him up for me instead," Benson commanded, pointing at Kenneth, who had just returned from planting the evidence. Fuelled by anger and betrayal, Benson charged off on his own. Kenneth asked the colonists to stay in the courtyard with him. A handful followed Jim back into the bar, where he poured them all and himself a drink.

“A bit early for drinking, isn’t it?” Pauline jested.

“All things considered, I just need to take the edge off,” Jim replied, smiling. “Cheers.”

It wasn’t long before Benson was storming out of Burge’s apartment clutching the Polaroid camera—a damning piece of evidence that Kenneth had planted.

“You were right again,” Benson raged as he re-entered the bar. “The camera was in his room. I’m going to shove this camera up his arse.”

“Okay,” Jim said neutrally, trying to stay out of the fight as he poured another double shot, this time for Benson.

“You seem like a down-to-earth bloke, Jim. Wouldn’t you do the same?” Benson asked, seemingly seeking his approval.

“I don’t know. I suppose I might want revenge, yes,” Jim agreed.

Shafto hadn’t been present during the earlier confrontation, but his brother had followed him dragging

Burge along the ground by his collar. Benson updated him in the bar. Without warning, Shafto spat at Burge, who was tied on the floor. "What did you say about my mother?" Shafto demanded.

"Great, just what I need, the retard brother on my case as well," Burge replied.

Benson straightened his posture and moved towards Burge. "Are you kidding me? First you insult my mother and then my brother? Do you have a death wish, Burge?" Benson said venomously. "You are ridiculous. And if you ever, *ever* slag off my family again, you'll be eating meals through a straw for the rest of your miserable life—have you got that?" Then, unexpectedly, Benson turned his aggression toward Jim. "What are you smiling at?"

"Nothing. Nothing at all, Benson. He had it coming, that's all," Jim said.

The bar had filled with colonists, all watching the Reapers' karma erupt.

"I like him." Benson smiled and then his face turned red, his eyebrows shifted inwards and he pointed in Jim's face, shouting through gritted teeth, "But that's none of your business now, is it? And as for the rest of you, get the hell out of here! All of you!" Benson said, swinging his finger around ninety degrees at the sea of faces, people standing around like kids encircling a fight in a school playground.

They slowly started to disperse, and Jim decided it would be wise to make a move as well. He checked in with the colony and swiftly returned back to the bar, anticipating Benson wanting a drink when he discovered the tanker missing from the back yard.

Benson and Shafto left together through the back doors in the kitchen to discuss and investigate the validity of the allegations about the missing fuel tanker out back.

Mills and Conrad freed Burge as soon as the brothers hastily left the bar, exchanging quick, terse words. The three of them moved toward the other exit, their footsteps too quick, too quiet—like they were trying to outrun something that had already caught up with them.

Chapter 32 – Wrath Unleashed

As anticipated the brothers soon returned from the yard. Benson was infuriated to find Burge was no longer tied up and the fuel tanker *had* been stolen. Tasha and Jim kept Benson entertained for the moment, getting into his head.

Jim inquired, "Who do you think will join your cause?"

Benson's face twisted into a mask of fury, his brows furrowed in a menacing scowl. His normally composed demeanour had dissolved into a storm of anger, his fists clenched and unclenched at his sides repetitively. Every movement was charged with tension, his jaw clenched so tightly Jim could see the muscles flexing beneath his skin. "Shafto and the Reapers will follow us. Burge won't stand a chance."

"So it's them *against* Burge? Interesting. You're sure? Because they released him as soon as your back was turned."

"Who?"

"Mills and Conrad"

Benson looked at Shafto, who was throwing back a neat whiskey. "It's time," he declared. Pulling a five-and-a-half-inch knife from a concealed sheath, Benson left the bar. Jim followed discreetly, avoiding being seen. Making sure Benson had left the bar first, Tasha subtly hugged him from behind as they hung back far enough not get in the way of his wrath but close enough to watch.

As he walked through the streets of the holiday village, Benson shouted, “Burge! Where are you, you coward? Face me!” He pounded on doors, with an insatiable desire for vengeance.

The search was interrupted by a cry from up the street. Burge, Marcos, Mills, Marvin and Conrad confronted Benson and Shafto.

“Benson! You think you can take us all? We’ve all had enough of your attitude,” Burge shouted.

The Reapers were turning on each other as planned. Living in fear of Benson had brought them to this moment. Without the mother to maintain some semblance of balance within the group, this outcome was inevitable. “Oh, you think they’re on your side? Oh, that’s funny. We’ll see. They’re either with me or they’re dead,” Benson declared. “Come on, Shafto, let’s take down these pigs!”

Then they charged. Shafto, who was swift but less bulky than Benson, struck first, ending Mills’ life with a quick, fatal blow to the neck. Conrad, witnessing the gruesome scene, hesitated for a moment before swinging a metal pipe at Shafto’s head with all his strength. The pipe connected with a sickening crack, and Shafto staggered, slashing wildly as he fell. In the chaos, the blade found its mark, cutting deep across Conrad's abdomen.

As Shafto crumpled to the ground, his blade clattered away, but the damage was done. Conrad gasped, hands trembling as he tried to hold his guts inside, collapsing after a brief, desperate struggle with Benson.

Burge faced Benson, armed with a kitchen knife and Shafto's blade. Marvin and Marcos, the cowardly duo, fled to their car, leaving only Burge and Benson in the bloodbath.

"They always were cowards—they'll be back soon." Benson locked eyes with Burge, he asked, "What about you?"

Then Burge surprised Benson by elbowing him in the eye socket, following up with a stab in the side with the small blade, and punched him in the face with his other hand. Blood filled Benson's left eye and trickled down his side. Fuelled up on rage and adrenaline, Benson roared, overpowering Burge swiftly, retaliating with a head-butt that floored him, and repeatedly stabbed him, blood spraying all over them both, up close and personal, eyes locked until the final inevitable moment.

Crawling towards Shafto, Benson screamed upon realising the blow to his brother had been near fatal. Though Shafto was still breathing, his severely damaged skull hinted at a grim prognosis. With no medical aid available, survival seemed bleak.

In the distance, Jim saw Kenneth approaching the carnage. When Benson looked up and saw him with Dusty and Scarlett, he stood up and demanded, "What do you think you're doing, letting my skanks out of their cage, geek boy?"

Kenneth didn't answer. Instead, he took the two girls into an apartment in the distance for safety. He came back out a moment later, dragging the gagged and bound Morgan from the apartment in which they had hidden him. Kenneth slashed his throat in the street with his machete. The body dropped to the floor with a huge thud. Jim covered his eyes and turned his head in shame for Kenneth. Benson had turned him into a murderer in two realities now, and this time it wasn't even in self-defence; it was pure hatred and vengeance.

"Tasha, he killed Morgan," Jim exclaimed, moving towards Kenneth.

"Leave him. I want his head on a stick." Benson glared at Jim, driven by adrenaline and endorphins from the intense fighting.

Still from a distance, Kenneth shouted, "BENSON! I made you kill your friends, made your friends kill your brother, and now I've killed your mother's toy boy! How does that feel?"

"Where is my mother?" Benson screamed, his voice strained.

“I see why you enjoy torturing people, Benson. It makes you feel powerful, doesn’t it?” Kenneth taunted.

“Where is she?!” Benson’s words, punctuated by flecks of spittle, propelled from his mouth in a storm of crimson rage.

“Wouldn’t you like to know? I wonder what ideas we could cook up for her?” Kenneth retaliated, becoming the venomous thing he hated most.

“What’s our next move?” Tasha asked.

“Get Mary,” Jim replied. “If Benson sees her alive, it might prevent Kenneth from putting himself in more danger.”

“Okay, let’s do it.” Tasha ran off to get Mary, while Jim stayed and calmly made his way over to see if he could defuse the situation, or at least buy some time.

Before Jim could intervene, Benson’s measured walk transformed into a full-on charge at Kenneth, reminiscent of a soldier going over the top in World War I—an all-out frontal assault. Demonstrating impeccable timing in defence, Kenneth yielded skilfully, turning Benson’s own momentum against him. With a deft sidestep, he swung his machete, cleanly severing Benson’s right hand.

As Benson writhed falling to his knees in agony, clutching his stump, Kenneth gave a dark chuckle. “Oh, look who’s decided to join us—your mother. Did you know she never left this complex at all? She was our special guest," he gloated, pointing towards Mary, whom Tasha ushered into view, arms behind her back.

"Do you like what we did to your mouthy bitch wife?" Benson spat back.

"She hasn't said a word to me since I rescued her from your filthy claws. What did you do?" Kenneth replied, his features contorted with raw fury as he stood before the person responsible. Jim could hear his teeth grinding so hard it seemed as though they might shatter under the pressure of his tight jaw. His eyes blazed with an intensity that could sear through steel, the fire of vengeance burning bright within them. "She turns her head away and won't even look at me."

"She will never, ever speak again, geek boy—but she does have half a tongue left for some use. You see, we ripped out her tongue with pliers and a knife—quite painful, I should imagine, judging by the noise—and then all of her teeth. Quite an improvement to the sk... *aghhhh!*"

Before Benson finished his sentence, Kenneth cut off his other hand, unable to contain himself. Hatred had fully taken over.

"Kenneth, please stop," Jim pleaded. "This won't bring anything positive for Dusty."

Dusty, now wearing shorts and a T-shirt,

approached her former captor, wielding a small but lethal knife she had found on the floor. With a final sprint, she delivered a powerful kick that sent him sprawling onto his back, utterly defenceless. With no hands or strength to resist, he lay there as she unzipped his fly.

"You want another go on it?" Benson asked, still hoping to torment his former victim and smiling as she drew out his penis. She thrust the knife in and cut his penis in half so he could never hurt anyone else again with it. She attempted to speak, mumbling and muttering, and pointed at Kenneth to make him go away. Kenneth was shocked and devastated by her dire predicament. She spat on Benson as he lay on the floor, mutilated.

Mary cried out for her son, struggling to free herself from Tasha, her hands still bound behind her back. She ran to Benson's side, sobbing, offering him support as he battled the agonies inflicted upon him. "How could it have come to this? I love you. Don't you dare die on me, son."

"I'm sorry for not believing in you," Benson grovelled. "They tricked me into thinking you had left me."

"No, son, I would never leave you," Mary said, leaning over him and comforting him in his final moments. Unexpectedly, blood started flowing from her mouth as her lungs filled with blood. She died and slumped onto her son's chest.

Dusty had made a move to kill Mary, and Jim had stopped her—but while he was holding her back, Kenneth had plunged his machete deep into Mary's back. Dusty ran off, emotions getting the better of her.

"Mary won't be providing comfort any more, Benson," Kenneth said viciously. "Look at you—alone and frightened, just like so many of your victims. It's your fault your mother is dead now, too."

"You son of a bitch. I'll kill you!" Benson retorted.

"Oh, and how will you kill me? You're pretty helpless now," Kenneth jeered.

"I've already done far worse than kill you. I've hurt you and your lover; you'll both go on suffering long after I've died," Benson wept, still attempting to get into Kenneth's head.

Dusty returned, gripping a red-hot poker. Jim noticed fresh burns on her legs—likely from the same poker, used on her during the torture the night or early morning before. He figured Burge must have left it heating on one of the multi-fuel stoves, the main source of warmth in the chalets. Without hesitation, she thrust the glowing iron into Benson's open wounds, sealing them to stop him from bleeding out. The agonised screams of their former captor echoed around the courtyard.

Benson turned to face Dusty, who waited a moment and Kenneth held his face so he couldn't move away. She calmly put out one of his eyes with the poker, and he cried out in terror.

“Remember this well, because her face will be the last thing you ever see, Benson,” Kenneth said with intense hatred.

Dusty took his other eye. Benson shrieked as the smell of burning flesh filled the courtyard.

“We should nail you up and see how long you last,” Kenneth continued. “Oh, no, even better than that. We could let you writhe around the streets, scared and alone, forever in the dark, with no hands or strength to provide for yourself. Don’t worry, we’ll feed you some scraps, just enough to keep you alive. Maybe we could get you a chain, like the animal you are. Everything you had, everything you knew, everyone you cared about is lost.” He kicked Benson in the back as hard as he could.

Dusty looked around to take her revenge out on Burge, but his lifeless body lay face down in a pool of his own blood. Shafto lay unconscious in a pool of his own blood, barely alive and awaiting whatever fate Kenneth and Dusty felt like inflicting on him.

Overwhelmed by the brutal scene and unable to instil mercy in those involved, Jim turned to Scarlett and Tasha. The situation had deviated significantly from his expectations and Jim didn’t know what to do. He couldn’t leave Tasha or Scarlett here. He followed his instincts and walked them away from the horrors in the courtyard.

Chapter 33 – Navigating Fate's Crossroads

Jim, his heart still burdened by the gruesome spectacle in the courtyard, guided Tasha and Scarlett into the car park. If they could get to Alex's farm at least they might begin to have a chance of some normality. He turned to face them. "Come on," he urged them. "We don't need to see any more."

"Why?" Scarlett questioned.

"Because it's not right, what they're doing," Jim replied firmly.

"But Jim, didn't you plan this?" Tasha asked, surprised he wasn't revelling in the victory over the Reapers.

"No, Tasha, this was never the plan. I wanted them to fight amongst themselves, destroy each other maybe, or drive each other off, but not like this," Jim explained regretfully. "Kenneth turned it into a savage act of retribution."

Scarlett clung to Jim's arm, her shoulders sagging with exhaustion. Her breath came in ragged gasps, and her once-defiant eyes now held a hollow gaze, reflecting the horrors she had endured. Each movement was tentative, as if she were navigating through a fog of fear. Yet, despite the tremble in her limbs, a quiet determination remained in her posture. When she looked up at Jim, her expression conveyed a mix of gratitude and weariness, silently acknowledging the debt she owed him for her freedom. "Who are you, and why did you save me?"

Jim looked at her hand—there was no ring—and then back into her eyes, his voice tinged with sadness. "So, you don't know me or Jerica?"

"Who is Jerica?" Scarlett asked, puzzled.

Jim hesitated, and then stammered, "It... it doesn't matter. The important thing is you're safe now. We should get going."

"Where are we going?" both girls asked almost simultaneously.

"To my friend's farm. We'll be safe there," Jim replied.

They circled Jim's car, and the girls approached the passenger and rear seats, while he headed for the driver's seat. But just as he opened the car door, Marvin and Marcos careened back into the complex in their car. It collided with Scarlett, smashing her frail, malnourished body into a mangled mess of broken bones, blood and flesh. Tasha managed to get into the car just in time, narrowly avoiding a similar fate. Their car wheel spun off into the courtyard, where Jim anticipated yet more carnage would unravel.

Jim knew Scarlett was dead. He approached her lifeless body and kissed his ill-fated loved one's forehead goodbye. This wasn't his wife—she didn't even know him—and yet he mourned her as if she was.

In a daze, Jim climbed back into the car, his mind reeling as the world around him fell into a suffocating silence. He stared at his hands, turning them over repeatedly, speechless as he took in the blood that stained them—Scarlett's blood.

He closed the car door and his eyes, lost in the overwhelming impact of it all. His chest tightened, and goosebumps prickled his skin. He opened the door, leaned out, and vomited on the road.

Tasha's screams were distant and muffled by Jim's subconscious terror.

"Maybe it's me, Tasha," he said in desperation. "My neurosis could have created all of this." His senses slowly came back to normal as Tasha's screams merged into sobs.

"That's impossible, Jim," Tasha replied. "What are you talking about?"

"Something must be driving the vortex. What if it's the power of my mind?"

"But what about me?" Tasha asked, her voice trembling.

"Those infernal dog tags. I wish I had never touched them, or shared them with you. It's not fair for you to suffer either. Maybe we're suffering from the same neurosis then, I don't know," Jim said. "Or maybe you don't exist at all?" He was questioning everything now.

"I don't believe that, not for one second," Tasha insisted. "Not since you saved me that day in the park. That was real, Jim. I remember it, and I still feel it. I'm real, got it?"

"You said you didn't need saving."

"Not like that, I mean from the loneliness. We're all lonely and we spend the rest of our lives trying not to be lonely." She reached from the rear seat to uncomfortably hug him best she could to comfort him. Jim glanced through the window at Scarlett's lifeless remains.

"It's not over," he declared, reaching for his dog tag.

At that moment, the vortex enigma began to manifest itself again in front of the car, and Tasha's expression turned bitter as she anticipated what was coming next.

"Tasha," he began, then paused, looking her straight in the eye, both hands on her beautiful face, "please do not follow me this time. You still have your dog tag, right? Please wait as long as you can before going through. I don't want to put you in any more danger. Focus on getting home and this time please stay there and get rid of that dog tag."

He kissed her forehead goodbye, stepped out of the

car, and stared in awe at the anomaly, welcoming it like an old friend arriving to save him. He offered no resistance. Keeping his eyes closed, he avoided glimpsing any possible realities and instead concentrated on his family. For a fleeting moment, Tasha's love tempted him like a distant, forbidden dream, but he quickly steadied himself, focusing on the bond he shared with his family.

As the vortex pulled him in, Jim clung tightly to the memory of Jerica and Scarlett from his prime reality, yearning for their warmth and love.

Jim landed heavily on a carpeted floor, winded from the fall, gasping for breath. He looked around, relieved to find himself back in his own bedroom. The warmth of the room embraced him, a stark contrast to the chilly reality he had left behind. The comforting hum of the central heating—the simple pleasures he'd once taken for granted.

Suddenly, the bedroom door burst open, and a familiar voice called out, "Daddy!"

Jim felt a small hand grab his arm and opened his eyes to see the face of his daughter, Jerica.

"What are you laughing at, Daddy?" she asked.

Jerica's presence filled Jim with joy, and he laughed as he hugged her tightly. "Nothing, Jerica, nothing at all," he replied, kissing her forehead. "Where's your mother?"

"She's in the bath, Daddy," Jerica answered

innocently.

Tentatively, Jim made his way to the bathroom, only to find Tasha in the bath. Shocked and confused, he stammered, “Tasha, what the hell are you doing here?”

“Well, lover, I was taking a bath. Did you have something else in mind, big boy?” Tasha replied cheekily.

“But... but... where is she?” Jim asked, his distress growing.

“She? Who’s she, the cat’s mother?”

“Okay, let me ask you another question. Where is Scarlett? And where exactly did we meet?”

“Jim, you’re scaring me,” Tasha said, genuine concern in her voice. “Is this some kind of joke? Because it’s not funny.”

“Just answer the damn question,” Jim shouted, his frustration boiling over.

“Okay, okay—in the park. It’s me. Listen, I didn’t mean to follow you, Jim. I’m sorry. I waited in the car park until the vortex began to close before stepping out of the car to be taken. I was pulled through and landed here just before you arrived, and the bath was already drawn. After that last place, the hot bathwater was simply irresistible, I guess my doppelganger must have run it before I jumped into her reality. To be honest, I didn’t even know you were here. Where are we, Jim?”

“This is my house! You’re in my house, in our bath!” Jim said, shocked and concerned about the possibility of his wife coming home and finding him in such a compromising position. He washed the blood off his hands as they spoke.

Jerica’s voice interrupted their conversation as she asked for some milk. Jim, not knowing how to respond to the situation, followed her into the kitchen on autopilot.

After tucking Jerica into bed and reading her a bedtime story, he asked her, “Listen, Jerica, who is that in the bathroom?”

“It’s Mummy, silly,” Jerica replied with an innocent smile that could hide no lie.

“Are you sure, darling?” Jim asked.

“Yes, Daddy, silly Daddy. Milk, please.”

Jim passed her the fresh bottle they had just prepared for her bedtime routine, kissed her goodnight, and turned to his bedroom, where Tasha was drying herself on the bed.

Feeling utterly defeated, Jim got down on his hands and knees, searching for his journal. He flipped through its pages, and his heart sank as he found a dreadful entry—the worst he could have imagined. In this reality, his wife had died during childbirth. Tasha had been the only mother Jerica had ever known. He dropped the book whilst Tasha had re-entered the bedroom and sat beside him.

Jim found his head resting in Tasha's bosom as he vacantly stared into her eyes. "She's dead. Why does she always die, not know me or not want me?" he said. "She passed away during childbirth. Is it time to give up on finding my way back to her through the vortex, or am I condemned to this forever?"

"We could all have a nice life here together." Tasha said, holding him closer.

"Can we? And how long before it rips us away into some new nightmare?"

As if summoned by his subconscious mind, the vortex rippled open behind Jim. Glancing at Tasha, he couldn't miss the downturn of her lips and the crease of disappointment on her forehead. Her eyes, once bright with hope, now held a glimmer of resignation. In that brief instant, he saw a silent acknowledgement of the life she had hoped for with him and Jerica, slipping away before her eyes. Reality hadn't even given him the chance to glimpse what it might have been like. Before he could make a choice, Jim was pulled into the swirling expanse.

Alone, he faced the vast and unforgiving multiverse portal. He considered his other realities. Powerless to do anything about the visions of the end of the world, and the losses he had endured, he wondered if he should be more focused on the experiments. Perhaps if he couldn't save himself or his family he could help save others.

* * *

Tasha clung to the bed as long as she could, trying to respect Jim's wish for her to stay away this time, feeling jealous of the memory of Scarlett. Eventually, she lost her grip and was pulled through.

As Tasha transcended time and space, she purposefully aimed to steer clear of Jim with her mind. She avoided any thoughts, emptying her head completely, avoiding the familiar temptation that had ensnared her in countless realities.

In what she hoped was a distant reality from Jim's fervent pursuit, Tasha found herself back on the aircraft carrier *Enterprise*, nestled in her quarters. Sighing deeply, she let her thoughts return to Jim, hoping he'd discovered solace in another realm.

As she went about her day, she reluctantly checked the cargo bay, convincing herself it was to check the status of the experiments, though deep down she sought Jim, even though, paradoxically, she hoped not to find him. Her heart was a dormant void, but held the potential to become a radiant enigma, devouring everything in its path. She aimed to spare Jim further pain, hoping her absence would pave the way for his reunion with family and happiness.

As their destinies intertwined yet diverged, both of them sought answers, redemption, and a place to belong in the ever-expanding tapestry of realities.

Chapter 34 – The Earth Dies Screaming

Meanwhile, weightless in the swirling void, Jim slowed his breath, settling into a rhythm. He closed his eyes, cleared his mind and focused on the love he had for his lost family. This time, his thoughts remained steady—Tasha didn't intrude, and his connection to his family anchored him in the chaos.

He went deep into a trance like state, relishing his favourite family memories. Jim's transition into reality was smooth, a rare occurrence that brought him unparalleled joy. His room, now filled with familiar surroundings and family photos, felt more like home than any other jump. Scarlett's melodious voice filled the house as she sang along to her favourite tune, its echoes dancing through the hallway between rooms.

"Yes! Yes! Yes! I'm home!" Jim rushed, practically skipping. Inside, Scarlett was arranging a salad in the kitchen.

"Hey, sexy," Scarlett greeted him, her voice like honey. They embraced tightly, and she almost choked with the intensity of the squeeze.

"Sorry, sorry." Jim chuckled. "It's just been so long since I've been home."

"That's true," Scarlett acknowledged. "You rushed home from Global Tech, but you wouldn't say why."

Jim was taken aback. "I still work at Global Tech?"

"Did you hit your head again at work, lumpy? Apart from..." She hesitated.

"What is it, Scarlett?"

"I have this really weird memory of you working somewhere else, like a hazy dream that you worked at some AUTEC facility, and then you didn't."

"That's a Mandela effect. In another reality, I did work there."

"What are you talking about?"

"More importantly, does the name Benson or Shafto mean anything to you?"

"What are you chatting about? I've never heard of those names, no."

"Oh, thank God, I'm home!"

"Jim, what is going on?"

"All I know is that I'm home, and I'm happy." He kissed her passionately, his hands wandering. They laughed, and she pushed him away, teasing, "Later," casting a promising glance.

Jerica entered the room. "Kiss," Jerica said with a smile, holding her arms up. Jim picked her up, and they enjoyed a family embrace.

"Daddy, telly, please," Jerica requested as Jim put her down, grabbing his hand and leading him toward the living room. "Kids' telly, please, Daddy," she repeated, her cute smile lighting up her face.

"Good girl. Of course, yes, come on then," Jim replied.

As he turned on the television, the news channel came on. He stood frozen in front of the screen.

"Mr Tumble, please," Jerica said.

"Wait a minute," Jim shouted.

Scarlett entered the room, concerned. "Jim, what is it?"

Jim pointed at the screen. "This is it, Scarlett, the end of days. Look!"

"I don't understand. How in the world?" Scarlett asked in shock as they both watched a news report of boats in the harbour getting launched into the air and people trying to jump out who kept travelling upwards.

"Shhh, Scarlett, listen," Jim insisted, turning up the volume.

The news reporter confirmed the phenomenon was happening worldwide—a brown dwarf, a failed star they called Nibiru, had come into close proximity to Earth, its massive magnetic and gravitational field impacting the

Earth in strange ways. The report went onto confirm that NASA said the orbit of the object was at such an elliptical orbit it had been obscured by the position of the Sun and the naturally dark colour didn't reflect much light.

"I don't know exactly why, but I've been having visions of this since I was a child, and I hoped it would never come to pass," Jim replied.

"What do we do now?" Scarlett asked. Then she screamed as she saw cars and people crushed by an invisible force.

"We can see most of the Medway Towns across the valley from outside our house. Let's go outside and have a look. But above all else, we must stay together. Don't either of you let go of my hands, understand? I'm going to try and get us out of this through a vortex, come on," Jim instructed them.

"I have no idea what is going on," Scarlett said, voice trembling.

"Just trust me."

"Yes, Daddy, I trust you," Jerica responded.

"Good girl. Listen, Jerica, it's just a new game, that's all. Do you trust me, Scarlett?"

"Of course," Scarlett replied.

They went to the front of the house, mesmerised by the surreal spectacle before them. Exactly as he had foreseen in the vortex as a child and on the news reports, houses crumbled and cars levitated, challenging the very laws of science. Their neighbour Bob, out walking his dog, met a fate that defied comprehension—hurled skyward, seemingly into space, with no hope of return. Desperate to shield Jerica from the unfolding chaos, they tried to avert her gaze, but her curiosity persisted, drawing her eyes inexorably to the evolving cosmic drama.

"What's happening, Daddy?" Jerica asked.

"Just hold on to me, sweetheart; we'll be fine. I'm going to get us out of here," Jim reassured Jerica.

"I'm not a baby, Daddy," Jerica protested.

"Of course not." Jim smiled at her, finding solace in the beauty of her pure soul amidst the chaos surrounding them.

"Look, another moon!" Jerica pointed up.

"That's no moon. It's a brown dwarf," Jim explained, staring at this marvel in the night sky, looming larger than any moon he had ever seen.

The Earth was transforming into an alien world, with pockets of gravity behaving in extreme and unpredictable ways, and they were bearing witness to its effects across the valley. Various areas experienced crushing pressures, flattening everything and creating massive sinkholes, or the reverse, throwing people, vehicles and debris upwards. In other places, gravity and relativity seemed normal.

Jim felt an overwhelming sense of guilt. Could his shifting through dimensions have caused this? He recalled the research at the AUTEC facility; they had punctured holes in the delicate balance of the entire multiversal bubble structure. Were the multiverses now collapsing, pulling this brown dwarf into the solar system as well? Had his experiments opened a singularity, one that was all-consuming?

Jim thought to himself, trying as hard as he could to create another portal. As he imagined one appearing in front of them, just a small one, he tried to reach for his dog tag, but both arms were occupied with his loved ones.

"My cat!" Jerica screamed, attempting to wriggle out of his grip.

"No, Jerica! Leave it!" Jim shouted, tightening his hold as she struggled to pull away.

As he glanced around, he witnessed a rapid transformation in the sky, cycling from day to night and back again in mere moments. The star field streaked across the heavens, zipping by in a blur of motion. They all fell down with the disorientating effect. Jim picked himself up and grabbed Jerica with his left arm and reconnected hands with Scarlett as quickly as he could. Jim shuddered at the thought of leaving anyone behind again.

They held each other, captivated by the marvel in

the sky, their own familiar moon, which was now visibly growing in size and spinning in the wrong direction through the astral sphere, illuminated by a stunning aurora. The moon appeared alien, its dark side visible for the first time to all on Earth. Jim missed the familiar craters and features, the seas of Tranquillity and Serenity that had been visible to the Earth for billions of years, now completely out of sight. Jim wondered if humans would ever see its beauty again.

"What's happening to the moon, Daddy?" Jerica asked, tugging at his hand. Scarlett looked at him, waiting for an answer to their daughter's question, but they were interrupted by loud sounds reminiscent of a trumpet echoing across the entire area.

"Jim, is this Armageddon?" Scarlett asked, tears welling up in her eyes. She quoted a passage from the Bible: "'And immediately after the persecution of those days, the sun will be darkened, and the moon will not give light; the stars will seem to fall from the heavens, and the powers overshadowing the Earth will be convulsed.' This is it, isn't it? The trumpet has sounded, and the Earth will soon disappear? Jerica and I visited Sunday school for a long time, and we learned this verse too, she liked it: 'And I shall send forth my angels with the sound of an almighty trumpet blast, and they shall gather my chosen ones from the farthest ends of the earth and heaven.'"

"We will get through this—you have to trust me," Jim reassured them. "Stay positive, and stay close, okay, you two?"

"Are you an angel, Daddy?"

"No, darling, I'm just your dad, but I will get us out of this, I promise."

Scarlett's eyes fixed on the Medway Towns below. She was silent with terror.

"Okay, just stay with me," Jim said, his voice steady amidst the turmoil. As they stood atop the valley outside their house, a sense of dread hung heavy in the air, suffocating them with its oppressive weight. Below, the Medway Towns were engulfed in chaos. The ground convulsed violently, buildings crumbling like sandcastles beneath the relentless assault of seismic upheaval.

In the distance, the brown dwarf star cast an ominous glow over the Medway Towns, its presence a harbinger of destruction. A deafening roar echoed through the valley as a monstrous tidal wave surged up the river Medway, a relentless force of nature consuming all in its wake.

From their vantage point, they watched in horror as the tidal wave swallowed everything with merciless fury. The torrent of water crashed through the streets of Chatham, tearing apart homes and businesses with abandon. People ran frantically, their cries drowned out by the roar of the rushing water.

The ground beneath their feet trembled, sending

shockwaves through their bones. "I need both of you to stay close and focus on your favourite family memories, any happy thoughts you have," Jim said. "Just imagine all of us safe and happy together."

A girl in her twenties, with pink hair, covered in tattoos and piercings all over her face and body, out walking her dog, stood, oblivious to the world, her eyes glued to her phone until the signal was lost. She screamed, "What the hell is happening?" Her trembling finger pointed across the valley.

A tremendous crack echoed across the valley, reminiscent of thunder, though no clouds were in sight. Jim and his family looked down as the ground shuddered, followed by another cracking sound beneath them, like the gates of hell were opening to unleash its horrors. Meteors streaked overhead, threatening to barrage the planet.

Jim clung tightly to his family.

"I'm scared, Daddy," Jerica said, quivering. They could see Rochester Castle, a testament to centuries of history, slowly crumbling in a cataclysmic crash that reverberated across the valley. The sky was veiled by broken black clouds that rolled in suddenly, their ragged edges creating an ominous backdrop, their shadows spreading like a dark omen across the horizon.

"Daddy, look at the fireworks. They look strange," Jerica exclaimed, pointing skyward. All three of them were fixated on the surreal heavens above. The entire sky crackled with electricity, an intricate web of pure energy suspended in an eerie stillness, as time's flow no longer had its natural rhythm. At half speed, a torrent of forked lightning descended in simultaneous bolts, striking the earth with relentless force.

Jim and Scarlett exchanged anxious glances before fixing their attention on the dog walker. From Jim's perspective, she appeared ensnared in a peculiar time distortion, as if confined within a bubble that isolated her from their reality. Her movements seemed frozen in time, caught mid-stride in unnatural positions one wouldn't normally hold. The dogs, typically brimming with energy, moved with a strange lethargy, their barks muted and distant. It was as if they were all ensnared in a dreamlike state, where time flowed like thick treacle, resistant to any progress.

Instructing them to close their eyes, Jim embraced his family as the pandemonium unfolded. Jerica, her curiosity piqued, peered at the young girl walking the dog.

"She's crying, Daddy," Jerica exclaimed, fear in her voice despite her confusion. Jim shielded Jerica's eyes, sparing her from the unfolding horror.

The unfortunate soul screamed in eternal agony, frozen in a moment of perpetual pain. She resembled a flickering candle, her clothes serving as the wick, ignited by a nearby lightning strike. Flames licked around her ankles, a cruel and drawn-out torment. Jim couldn't help but wonder how many years or decades it would take at this altered speed for the fire to ascend her legs and engulf her entirely. As he watched, a tear slowly formed in her eye, a testament to her suffering. The lightning effects illuminated the sky once more as another colossal strike built up, as they experienced the bizarre sensation of time, gravity, all the laws of nature behaving differently above and below.

"What can we do to help her?" Jim asked.

"You said we need to stick together," Scarlett reminded him. "She's beyond help! Look at her, we need to do something about our own family!"

"Time seems fairly normal around us for the moment. We have to try, and we still have time—the vortex isn't here yet. Okay, we hold hands and work together. We run to the kitchen, fill the bowl with water and run back and throw it on her. Me in the middle carrying Jerica with my left arm. You fill the bowl?"

"Vortex? What vortex? Never mind. Okay, let's try and help her, how do we carry it?" Scarlett asked.

"At that point you use both hands, but we link arms, the vortex could come any minute. The vortex is our way out of this nightmare. Whatever happens, we must stick together, okay?"

They exchanged a quick nod of understanding, ran to the kitchen and filled a bowl of water, maintaining linked arms. When they returned to the front yard they were dismayed to see the girl had vanished. Scarlett dropped the bowl.

"Scarlett, we need to swap. You take Jerica and hold my hand with your other hand." They swiftly changed positions and Jim, with his now free hand, reached for his dog tag, closed his eyes and began summoning the vortex with positive thoughts and emotions.

"All of you, close your eyes and focus on a time with all of us together happy, somewhere safe!" Jim guided them.

Chapter 35 – The Enterprise's Descent into Chaos

Jerica looked up pointing towards a vortex forming above them. "What is that, Daddy?"

"You can see that, baby? What does it look like to you?" Jim said anxiously.

"It's a pretty swirly thing, Daddy. What is that?" Jerica replied.

"We did it!" Jim looked at Scarlett. "Open your eyes. Please tell me you see it too."

"Oh, yes, I see something. I don't know what it is, but I see it."

"A vortex?" Jim asked.

"A swirly thing and colours seem to be shifting into a funny glow," Scarlett replied.

"You sound just like your daughter, yes that's the vortex," he laughed at his family's cuteness.

"Is this it? Are we going to die?" Scarlett asked.

"Not this time. Everybody hold tight. We'll be pulled up through into this thing soon. This is what I have been waiting for my whole life," Jim said as their cat approached from behind and started rubbing himself on Scarlett's legs.

"Jim, can you hold that cat tight with your other hand now?"

"I think so," he replied. He let go of his dog tag and scooped the cat up. "Good. Now, both of you continue to imagine us somewhere safe together. I think it works on emotions."

Jim struggled to focus as the visions flashed before him.

"It's incredible! And what is that on your face?" she asked, looking at his forehead.

"I don't know, Scarlett. What is it?" Jim replied nervously.

"It looks like a word or something glowing on your forehead. I don't recognise it. It spells out 'Yeshua,'" she said, confused. "What does it mean?"

"I have no idea, but right now it's not important. We're getting out of here."

"But it's miles high. How will we get up there?"

The vortex soon answered. The pull swept them off their feet, lifting them high into the sky, higher than Jim had ever ventured before, almost reaching the lofty heights of the clouds. Peering downward, he observed the Earth below, but his awe was interrupted by another ominous sound emanating from the ground. A tear formed in the Earth's crust beneath them, and another chorus of trumpet-like noises echoed as the planet continued to convulse, its death throes reverberating with what sounded like agonised screams. Scarlett and Jerica screamed as the three of them continued levitating toward the dimensional energy rift.

"This is it. Hold tight, girls, this could get a little bumpy," Jim shouted.

As Jim, Jerica, and Scarlett plunged into the swirling vortex, a cacophony of colours and sensations enveloped them. The family wrapped around each other tightly so as not to lose one another. He stole a glance at Jerica, his daughter's face a mixture of awe and apprehension, her eyes wide with wonder as she took in the surreal surroundings.

Amidst the chaotic whirl of energy, Jim could feel the pull of the vortex tugging at his senses, disorienting and exhilarating all at once. The air crackled with electricity, sending shivers down his spine as they hurtled forward through the maelstrom of swirling light and shadow. But amidst the chaos, there was also a sense of unity and purpose. Scarlett's reassuring presence in his embrace grounded Jim, her warmth and strength providing solace in the tumultuous sea of uncertainty. And Jerica, his precious daughter, radiated a quiet resilience that filled Jim with pride and determination. Together, they navigated through the swirling vortex, their path illuminated by flashes of brilliance and obscured by veils of darkness. And as they emerged on the other side, Jim felt a surge of relief wash over him, knowing that they had faced the unknown together and emerged unscathed, and their bond stronger than ever.

They landed on a battleship-grey metal floor. Jim looked around and felt the wind on his face and the sea all around them. They were on the deck of an aircraft carrier. They had landed near the edge, and the wind had blown Jerica too close; she was in danger of falling into the waters below.

"No!" Scarlett screamed in panic. Jim had tears in his eyes; he had come so close, losing them again was unthinkable. Jim dashed as swiftly as he could and grabbed Jerica before she fell.

"She's—she's okay, thank God. Where are we? What happened?" Scarlett stammered.

He looked around. "CVN-65? Yes! We're back onboard the *Enterprise*!"

Overhead, a storm was unnaturally and rapidly forming. There was a metallic taste in the air, and orange-red dust blew across the flight deck in the crosswinds. The air smelled thinner, which was strange to Jim because he had never known any better air quality than during sea voyages. Jim wasn't really watching the storm; it was just in the background. He became tense and almost stopped breathing. The flight deck of an aircraft carrier was a dangerous place to be with no safety railings and the risk of jets launching or landing, it was certainly no place for a civilian family. The deck crew quickly directed them towards the safety of the ship's interior.

Just as they were about to go inside, the deck lit up, and they turned to watch a meteor fill the sky overhead with brilliant, blinding light. After it flew by, there was a shockwave and sonic boom that almost deafened everyone. Two more meteors flew overhead in the same fashion. This time, everyone was already covering their ears in preparation for the noise as the massive meteors broke the sound barrier. Lightning and a fierce crack of thunder were followed by tremendous deep tones of what sounded like trumpets again.

Jim looked astern and there it was. Miles off, the familiar, yet eerily unpredictable, energy vortex reappeared, its ominous presence seemingly fixated on Jim, as though it were pursuing him with relentless determination.

"Is it happening again, Jim?" Scarlett cried in terror, clutching their little girl with fear.

"Girls, listen to me. We aren't out of this yet, but I have an idea," Jim said, closing the hatch behind them. "I'm going to take you to my quarters, assuming they are still my quarters here. You'll be safe there, besides the Captain won't allow you on the bridge. All of you, including the cat, you need to stay in that room for now until I come back or you hear from me, okay?"

Scarlett shot Jim a questioning look. "Your quarters? What is all this? Shouldn't we stay together?"

“We tried that, but this reality is now in danger too. I don’t have time to explain, I need to speak to the captain. Just trust me, I need to save us all this time, not just our family,” Jim said.

Scarlett turned away, shifting her attention back to their daughter, clearly upset with him. She didn’t argue nor did she give him her consent either; the tension in the room was palpable, and the silence spoke volumes. Jim howled to himself as he walked away, frustrated by Scarlett’s stubbornness and lack of understanding. With no time to argue, he needed to find a way to a permanent place of safety, and this reality was clearly collapsing as well. He headed straight for the bridge; the ship was on lockdown, and the guard outside had been instructed not to let anyone through.

“Sorry, sir, you cannot go on the bridge; we are at general quarters,” Lieutenant Jed barked.

“Listen, I have information that could help in this situation. Do you know who I am?” Jim asked desperately, trying to negotiate his way onto the bridge.

“Of course, Dr Knight.”

“Thank God! That saves me re-explaining. Look, all I’m asking is that you check with the captain before turning me away, and if he tells you to remove me or he lets me on the bridge, so be it. Think about it for a second; our lives all depend on your actions here.”

"This is what will happen: you can tell me the information and return to your quarters. I'll pass this information on to the captain straight away for you."

Jim had to play his hand; he was afraid his cards were pretty weak. "Okay, tell Captain Malik Dr Knight knows how to control the vortex."

"Sir, I think you better accompany me on the bridge."

"Boy, I knew you were going to say that," Jim replied.

"This better not be airy-fairy, sir, but if you're serious and if there's even a chance the ship could be cold steel, then I have to check."

"Cold steel?" Jim questioned.

"Dead in the water. Navy speak, sir, for finished. Follow me."

"I should be saying FIGMO right about now, sir, and busting your ass back to your compartment. I must be having a brain fart or something; follow me," the officer said, leading him onto the bridge.

"What is FIGMO?" Jim asked.

"Look it up, sir." The officer grinned.

Chapter 36 – Wormwood's Destruction Dawns

On the bridge of the aircraft carrier *Enterprise*, Jim stood frozen, captivated by the cumulonimbus light show unfurling before him—an ink-spilled sky drew in, wind and rain assaulted the ship, and orangey-red sand seemed to be smearing on the portholes as the wipers worked to clear the view. The storm's fury threatened to shatter its reinforced glass.

A rapturous growl echoed from the sky, drowning out even the authoritative voice of Captain Malik. Another meteor streaked across the sky, disappearing over the horizon with a detonation that ruptured the sound barrier. The crew covered their ears as agony engulfed them. Jim, too, fell to the floor, ensnared in a sea of crimson pain.

Captain Malik turned to Jim, demanding an explanation.

"It's Wormwood," Lieutenant Jed answered. "Revelations 8:10: 'And the third angel sounded, and there fell a great star from heaven, burning as if it were a lamp, and it fell upon the third part of the rivers, and upon the springs of waters.'"

"Bible stories? Really?" Captain Malik demanded.

"See for yourself," Jim said, directing the captain's

gaze beyond the meteor's trail to a looming planet in close proximity to Earth, clearly visible to the naked eye. "Do you see that, sir? It could be Nibiru. Keep an eye on the sky—there could be more meteors coming. The same thing happened in the last reality I just jumped out of: we went through the vortex and came back here."

"What are you talking about? You jumped off the ship, and then jumped back?"

"Yes, sir, though I've been through the vortex many times, like I told you before. In fact I've crossed it several more times since we last spoke. I have an idea—if we can make it big enough, I believe we can save the whole ship. This is an extinction-level event; you saw the size of those meteors. We can get out of here, just as I did, the whole ship and crew, sir. If we stay here in this reality, every one of your crew will die. We've seen at least half a dozen of those meteors scream across the sky, since we started talking. How big are those things? What kind of damage can they do? The vortex is a doorway out of here! It's our best chance for survival, sir. It's already here, behind us—we just need to make it larger, big enough for the whole ship to make it through to safety."

"The dinosaurs died out, and now it's our turn—is that it, Doctor?" Captain Malik said, still incredulous.

"Trust me, Captain. Take us into the rift," Jim urged.

Silence descended on the bridge. The air stilled, the

wind calmed, and only the hum of the ship's nuclear engines persisted, pulsing serenely like a newborn child's heartbeat as the crew awaited direction. Captain Malik utilised the lull to order updates on damage and casualties.

"Reactor is stable, sir," reported the chief engineer. "We were reading a power drain when the device was in use, but it's within tolerance."

"And how about now that the collider has been turned off? Have we seen any improvements?" the captain inquired, hopeful for positive news.

"Power drain has slowed, but it's still there. We are capable of maximum speed, still faster than the other ships in her class, sir," replied the engineer, exhibiting pride in the ship's resilience.

"Dr Knight, you told me you fired up the hadron collider. Is there anything you're not telling me?"

Jim hesitated. "If this is the same reality I left, you gave orders to have it reactivated, Captain. If that's the case, it could explain why the rift started so soon after we arrived back on deck. We need to increase the power so it surrounds the entire vessel. I need to get down to the cargo bay to investigate, and we should leave it on now, sir—power it up, in fact. CAG, were you recently rescued by SAR?"

"Yes, Doctor, you know I was, you were there." Balfour replied.

“Great—this is great,” Jim exclaimed, resulting in some rather puzzled-looking responses.

“Before we agree to this, I want a brief with my senior officers in the plot room, you can join us.”

“Yes, Captain. Of course, I understand,” Jim replied humbly.

* * *

The senior officers, and Jim assembled in the plot room to discuss options and status, with the captain.

“We have minimal damage,” reported the safety officer. “A couple of dozen crew members in the infirmary with ear problems, but overall, we’re in good shape, considering the circumstances. I recommend that protective earplugs are used at all times until the crisis is averted, sir.”

“Agreed. Most of those men probably should have been wearing them anyway. Honestly, it’s like looking after a boatload of children sometimes. How many times do we have to tell them to follow safety precautions? Make it happen. Anyone caught not wearing them will face disciplinary action,” the captain ordered. “What does the Combat Information Centre have to bring to the table?”

“We’re picking up multiple contacts, sir—sea and air—in a thirty-mile perimeter. It was five a moment ago, now there are dozens.” reported the CIC officer.

“What’s your assessment of that situation, CAG?”

the captain asked.

“We need more information, sir. A scout plane could verify some of those contacts. I recommend we focus on the closest ones and keep our birds close to the nest, skipper. One of those planes could be our missing refuelling plane.”

“You want to send someone up again in that?” the captain said, pointing into the storm.

“Yes, sir. It’s the only way we can get more answers,” Commander Balfour declared boldly.

“I don’t think so, not this time,” the captain responded.

“Sir, I’ve been through it and survived. Whatever those other blips on the radar are, they’ve passed through it too, the World War II planes I saw, and our IFR plane are still inside. If this is our only hope, I suggest we take it—either with recon first or the whole ship.” Commander Balfour added.

“Thank you, CAG” Captain Malik replied. “Okay, Comm. Your report, please.”

“Very active, sir, with overlapping transmissions. It’s almost gibberish, especially on the emergency channel,” the communication officer reported. When the captain gave him a glare that conveyed his dissatisfaction, he continued, “Right, sir. I need to try and concentrate on one call signal, make contact, and gather more intel. I’m on it."

"Good. Make it happen. Isolate the strongest signal; it should be the closest vessel or craft. Let them know we're not sending a recon plane until whatever this thing is passes—they may need help. Give them our co-ordinates if they can set course to rendezvous—great. If not, we'll work on SAR missions afterwards. Get the comms officers in the nest with Morse code flashlights, to direct any planes in visual range for a safe place to land." the captain ordered.

"Angels and the tactical Aircrew are ready, sir. The first team is on alert, by your command, sir," Commander Balfour reported.

The captain nodded. "Can we rule anything further out?" he asked, but was met with silence. "Based on what we do know, I want each of you to share your opinions on Dr Knight's assessment and any recommendations, please."

The crew hesitated at first, unsure about the risks, but they understood the gravity of the situation. Staying almost certainly meant certain death, and despite their doubts, the vote was unanimous—they were ready to go with Jim's plan.

The captain intervened, redirecting their focus. "Okay, we don't know what we're talking about here. So, since we don't know what it is, let's agree on what it isn't. Have we witnessed a nuclear strike? World War III?"

"No, sir, those were definitely meteors, not man-made nuclear missiles." The tactical officer replied.

The Captain turned to his meteorologist officer. "Well, Cloud Shaman, have you been doing unauthorised storm dances again? What is this, some kind of cyclone? Tornado? Hurricane? A bizarre weather formation, maybe a mirage?" the captain asked.

"No, sir, this is something else, it's nothing we've ever seen before. And mirages don't show up on the radar," Cloud Shaman replied.

"Agreed," the captain replied, "which gives credence to Dr Knight's theories. Can we rule out the possibility of an actual meteor strike?"

"They did look remarkably similar to the meteors that hit Russia in 2013—only bigger sir," the young communications officer boldly spoke up.

"Agreed. Alright, let's recap," The captain said, his tone steady but serious. "This vortex, it looks like an unprecedented storm on the monitors, unlike anything we've encountered before. Coincidentally, meteors are threatening the planet. On top of that, we've got the Wormwood threat—Nibiru—getting closer. We've also got multiple unidentified aircraft and sea vessels, along with our missing refuelling plane, stuck in the vortex. This is escalating." He paused, scanning the faces of his officers. "In that case, the meeting's adjourned, let's move!" he added, clapping his hands together. "We're going with Dr

Knight's plan—boost power to the device. Full speed ahead into the storm. Damn, I never thought I'd hear myself say those words."

The captain rolled his eyes, Jim guessed he was struggling to choose from a list of terrible options. The crew hastily left the plot room, and Jim followed, careful to avoid getting swept up in the anxious scramble.

* * *

Moments later, they flooded back onto the bridge. The command centre buzzed with activity—officers at their stations, eyes glued to the monitors as they co-ordinated their next step. The captain gripped the armrest of his seat as the ship lurched forward, engines roaring to life, just as a powerful wave slammed into them.

"I have made contact, sir," the communication officer reported immediately.

"Good work. Report," the captain ordered.

"On the emergency channel, it's US Navy—Max C. Reynolds, call sign FT-29. He sounds lost, reporting an altitude of two thousand three hundred feet. Matches our radar contacts for five aircraft," the communication officer said.

Jim felt a surge of excitement at the confirmation—Flight 21 was indeed in the vortex. He pumped his fists, a triumphant grin spreading across his face. He knew it, but kept quiet for now.

“You just earned your pay for the week,” the captain said with a smile. “Send them our co-ordinates so they can make their way to us. If not, have them look for our Morse code signals, or, if possible, guide them in verbally. Get some flares launched as well.”

“Sir ...” The officer hesitated. “I checked their call sign. Sir, it’s Flight 21.”

“Flight 21? As in matching Dr Knights dog tag, from the 1940’s? ” the captain asked.

“Yes, sir—one and the same. The planes *are* from the past. It’s confirmed.”

“What the hell is going on here? At least it does support Dr Knights appraisal of the situation at least, and gives me some hope we are doing the right thing,” the captain said.

The young officer continued monitoring, and then said, “This is the aircraft carrier *Enterprise*. We’ve been monitoring your transmissions. Visibility is low, and we stand ready to assist you. Do you read us?” The only reply was a faint voice shrouded in static.

“Captain, we are losing systems. Everything is malfunctioning, sir. We’ve lost track of all the contacts.” The radar officer reported.

“All of them? Interference from the storm?” the captain said, jumping out of his chair to check the sky. His jaw dropped in horror as he saw that it was turning orange at an accelerated rate. The air smelled foul. “Dr Knight, get down to the cargo bay and crank up the power to maximum on the collider. Then call me back on the bitch box. I want to know what the hell is going on down there. We need to make that rift bigger soon or we are all dead,” the captain shouted, accepting the inevitability of the situation.

“Captain Malik, one more thing,” Jim said. “I believe I can control the vortex now, as we increase power to the experiment. But I need you to get everybody on board focussed on a vision of the ship in calmer waters.”

The captain’s eyes narrowed. “A vision?”

“Yes, sir, our combined consciousness should guide us in, through and to safety on the other side.”

Captain Malik nodded thoughtfully. “Very well, Dr Knight. At this point, with all this going on, a little positive thinking from the crew couldn’t hurt right now anyway. CAG, get on the ship-wide intercom and give the command for everyone to stay positive and focus on the ship being in calmer waters.”

“Very well. I will have Lieutenant Jed escort you,” the captain said.

Jim left with a nod and followed Lieutenant Jed out.

Chapter 37 – The Final Frontier of Hope in the Triangle

Jim abruptly halted in the narrow corridor leading to the cargo bay as the metallic walls, adorned with flickering emergency lights, seemed to converge around them. Jim made his way to his quarters, wanting his family close during the experiment enhancements, in case they were pulled through the vortex again. Jed didn't protest. Given the circumstances, he agreed that the family should be together, if it was indeed the end of days.

"Come on, girls, follow me, but leave the cat safe in my quarters for now," Jim said, and grabbed Scarlett's hand as she carried Jerica.

"What's going on, Jim?" Scarlett asked.

"I'll explain more later," Jim replied as they swiftly made their way through the corridors. When he entered the cargo bay with Jed, Scarlett and Jerica, Jim paused in surprise. "Tasha!" he exclaimed.

"Yes, Jim. I guess you can't be mad at me, because this time you followed me, right?" Tasha said playfully, running her fingers through her hair.

Jim, feeling a mix of nervousness and exhilaration, replied, "Oh, my, this could get interesting."

Curious, Tasha and Scarlett inquired, “Why is that?” in synchronicity.

Jim hesitated, glancing back at Scarlett and Jerica before whispering, “My wife is on board. Please, try and be—”

“Be what, Jimmy?” Tasha interrupted in a teasing tone.

Jim coughed nervously, stammering, “W-well, you know...” He cleared his throat. “Anyway, what’s happening with the SHC?”

The rain had eased off, revealing an eerie, orange-red fog outside the portholes that served as a constant reminder of the otherworldly events.

Tasha, turning away from Jim due to her jealousy, explained, “I powered it up again. I figured that you might come back to this reality, and before you arrived, I hoped to get out of here and make a fresh start. And I still do, especially if she’s here.”

Jim tried to reassure her. “Don’t be like that, Tasha, please. Now is not the time for this.”

Tasha’s frustration boiled over. “It’s never the time for us, is it, Jim? There’s always something going on, always some reason, and always there’s *her*. She’s in the way even when she’s dead. What exactly does she have that I don’t, huh?”

“Dead? What does she mean Jim?” Scarlett

frowned.

Jim changed the subject, needing to focus on the situation. "Listen, we don't have time for this. I need to know what has been happening with the device, before this world is destroyed."

"Destroyed? What are you talking about?" Tasha replied.

Jim's attention was drawn to the ominous view outside. "Did you look out of a porthole?"

Confused, Tasha replied, "No, why?"

Jim gestured towards the nearest porthole. "Because there's a vortex closing in on the ship, and my guess is it's our best shot of saving everybody on board. The captain has changed course to take us through it."

Tasha's face paled. "Is it big enough to take the whole ship through?"

"Not yet. We need to increase the power."

Tasha, her anxiety rising, asked, "What should we do?"

"We need to amplify it. If my guess is right, we don't have much time, the storm is pulling us in and we don't have a lot of options." Jim said his voice tight with determination. "The collider—if we push it beyond its limits, tapping into the nuclear power of the ship's core we might have a chance to get the whole ship in, through, and beyond."

Tasha's voice trembled, the weight of the unknown settling in. "But we don't know what might happen, Jim. I'm scared. What if it.. gets out of control?"

"We don't have a choice, "Jim replied, his eyes fixed on the monitors. "We work together, push the limits, and hope we can control it long enough to get through."

"We do have a choice, we could just leave this reality?" Tasha said her eyes widening with fear.

"I'm through running from this thing. It's time we did what's right—not just for us, but for everyone aboard," Jim said.

"Alright, although I'm not sure about this." Tasha replied.

Jim tried to reassure her, "We know better than anyone that another reality will be waiting on the other side, and if we can save a boatload of people, all the better, wouldn't you say? Listen, I know there's a risk. Usually, we're the only ones who can see it, or a select few people we have encountered, and that's why I think this is different. Everyone on the bridge saw it, and they all thought it was a storm of some kind. This is the endgame, and our choices are limited: stay in a doomed world, abandon these people, or trust the path ahead and see where it takes us. Did you see those meteors? That's just the beginning. We have to stay the course."

“What meteors?”

“Christ, well, while you were tinkering with the device in the cargo bay, outside a bombardment has begun. It looks bad, Tasha, really bad.”

Still uncertain, Tasha said, “We’re taking a huge risk.”

Jim pondered the situation, but his determination was unwavering. “Maybe—but we have to find out. It’s been with me ever since I read about Flight 21 as a boy. I saw the vision of it when I was a child through the vortex. Now finally Flight 21 is up in the sky nearby. We need to rescue them too on the other side of the vortex.” He pointed out the porthole nearest to them. “Look—the red-orange mist is surrounding the *Enterprise* now too, just as the communication report with Flight 21 described, just before they lost contact in the 40’s. Now is our chance. They’re here.”

He was interrupted by the internal communication system, and he rushed to answer it, eager for news.

The captain’s patience was wearing thin, and he demanded answers from Jim.

Jim explained, “Sir, I can confirm we have restored the small hadron collider to full working order, just as you ordered.”

The captain pushed further. “Our systems are haywire, we’re navigating visually because we can’t get a fixed reading, and you're sure about us going into that thing?"

"Yes sir, and have you made contact with the planes?"

"Good because it's closing in on us. And what part of our systems are haywire did you not understand, that includes long range communication at the moment. It has me concerned."

Jim decided to play to the captain's ego. "It's a doorway, a gateway to another reality, sir. We have to go through, and if I'm wrong, then it's just a storm, right? Surely sea dogs like you aren't scared of a little storm?"

The captain grudgingly agreed. "I oughta throw you overboard, but okay, let's do this. But if this thing gets out of hand, I want the collider turned off at a moment's notice."

"We need more power down here, sir."

"Do what you can, Doctor. Power levels are balanced as best we can to maintain ship function and helm control. There is plenty of juice left in the second reactor reserved for your experiments," the captain replied, ending the transmission.

Jim looked at Tasha. "There has to be a safe haven, and this is different, I can feel it. It's our only chance. This is the first time we've all been together and Flight 21 overhead as well. It has to be a sign," Jim pleaded.

Tasha was still wrestling with her doubts. "God, I am such a fool. Why do I always listen to you? And here I am about to do it all over again..."

"Let's work together to really crank this thing's power levels to maximum and more, push it over the limits."

"Let's do it," she agreed.

"Scarlett, stay close with Jerica, hold on to that handrail tight, and if you see Tasha and I go through a vortex, let go and follow us through. Got it?"

"Yes Jim, I understand," she cried, holding her daughter in her other arm.

* * *

On the bridge, the captain and his crew continued working frantically, trying to re-establish contact with Flight 21 and their own missing plane.

Petty Officer First Class, communications specialist Sarah Mitchell, had joined the bridge crew. "We just made contact with—" she paused, her brow furrowed, "—a naval vessel called the Cyclops. The ship's computer identified her as a vessel that went missing in 1917, sir."

"What?" the Captain said, still struggling to grasp the unfolding events.

"That's not all, sir. SAR just reported they picked up another civilian in the drink off our port bow."

Intrigued by this new development, the captain said, "Good work."

"Sir, it was Jimmy Trinidad."

"Who?"

"Sir, when I learned we were heading into the Triangle, I did some research. He disappeared in 2006—his boat was found still idling, no signs of a struggle. It was a mystery, and now we've found him. But he hasn't aged a day. By all logic, he should have succumbed to the ocean's whims by now. And one more thing, sir: this orange-red mist has been reported by others who have survived the Triangle."

The captain was now facing a situation he couldn't comprehend. He muttered, "Damn it, the last thing I need is more civilians on this ship messing up the works."

Grateful for something concrete to focus on, the communication officer replied, "Aye, sir. We're heading right towards that thing out there." He pointed at the enigma nervously.

Though the crew on the bridge grappled with their uncertain fate, the captain's reassurance provided them with a sense of purpose. His steadfast attitude was contagious, and the crew refocused their efforts, unsure if they were more afraid of letting the captain down or facing the impending storm.

* * *

Inside the cargo bay, there was an unusual stillness. Jim observed his watch as time slowed down once again.

Jim's gaze remained fixed on the nearby porthole, his heart pounding with anticipation and growing concern they might miss their opportunity, if there even was one. He searched desperately for any sign of what might be happening outside, but all he could discern was the eerie, undulating curtain of orange-red fog.

Time was running out and their efforts to enhance the collider's power were falling short. The ship's energy was maxed out, yet the collider's energy readings barely hovered above halfway. Usually, not long after the time effect, the vortex would close. Jim glanced at their dog tags, infused and glowing with a mysterious energy from their countless journeys across alternate realities. Perhaps they held the key. With a shared glance, Jim felt as if Tasha was reading his mind. They both placed their fingertips on their tags to harness the unique energy contained within. Jim placed his other hand on the collider. Tasha laid her free hand on top of his. Power surged through them, connecting them to the tags and the device.

"Positive thoughts Tasha," Jim said affectionately looking into her eyes, "not for me or us but for everyone here. Calmer waters, keep it simple." They shared a smile, and the collider glowed, indicating an increase in the power intensity, even though it wasn't supposed to do that from what Jim had read—this was a sealed unit. It was no longer playing by the normal rules of logic and science, as he understood them anyway.

"Everybody! focus on the ship being safe in calmer waters." Jim repeated loudly.

Lieutenant Jed called the captain on the bitch box, requesting another ship-wide announcement relaying the message. The captain complied, out of desperation.

As they channeled more energy into the machine, its vibrations intensified, producing an almost hypnotic trumpet-like hum. Jim turned to Tasha, her eyes reflecting a newfound belief in their purpose, and together they waited for the unknown to reveal itself.

* * *

Outside, the interdimensional gateway had expanded, now spanning hundreds of miles. In the heart of the Bermuda Triangle, the vortex was large enough to draw in the lost ships, aircraft, and the massive aircraft carrier—whatever had been swallowed by the Triangle's mysteries could now be reclaimed, if the portal allowed it.

Chapter 38 – The Convergence of Fates

In the cargo bay, tension was thick as Lieutenant Jed and his security team confronted Jim. Despite the chaos, Jed's demeanour remained firm.

"Lieutenant, listen to me," Jim said, holding his hands up, trying to stay calm. "We're in the vortex. I know you're scared, but the captain gave me permission to draw as much power as we need. Everything's under control."

Jed's eyes narrowed. "Under control?" His voice was tight, sceptical. "We're caught in some kind of phenomenon we barely understand. Drawing this much power could destabilise the whole ship, or worse—cause a reactor leak. You're playing with fire, Doctor."

"You fool, look around you, we're getting out of here. I'm working with the captain's consent!"

Jed hesitated, clearly struggling between his instinct to maintain control and his obligation to the ship's safety. He kept his gaze on Jim. "This had better be worth the risk. If you're wrong, this ship will become cold steel at the bottom of the ocean."

Before Jim could respond, the captain's voice crackled through the comms, filling the bay. "What the hell is going on down there? The ship is soaring through some kind of tunnel. It looks like... a tunnel of water—I don't know how else to explain it."

"Great! It's working, sir! We are getting out of here!"

Jed's grip tightened around the mic, his knuckles white under the pressure. He was visibly unsettled by the captain's words. He took a breath, then spoke into the comms. "Captain, are you sure we should continue drawing power? We don't know how long this... whatever it is will remain stable."

Jim glanced through the portal, outside the vortex swirled, growing more powerful with each passing second. The ship was ascending, but uncertainty clung to every moment.

"Security chief, get Dr Knight back to the bridge."

"Aye, sir," as Lieutenant Jed replied, a portal glowing red, opened behind him. Jim instinctively held on to the railings behind the console and grabbed Jed's arm in a fireman wrist hold.

"Calm waters, Jed. Trust me."

Jed closed his eyes, Jim guessed he was trying to visualise the situation, and swiftly the portal shut.

"Thank you, Jim."

"Stay focussed; negative emotions drive this thing to dark places."

“Yes, Sir” Jed replied, and Jim felt he finally understood.

“Wait for me in my quarters, Scarlett,” Jim shouted. “If you’re not sure how to find your way back, Tasha can show you the way.”

“Yes, I bet she can,” replied Scarlett suspiciously. Her concern was not a current priority. Jim knew it would wait.

* * *

They soon arrived on the bridge. The captain’s jaw tightened as he strode forward, his fingers gripping the edge of the console. “Explain how a ninety-four-thousand-ton carrier floats in mid-air,” he demanded, his voice sharp as he pointed toward the window.

“It’s the anomaly, sir. Including the water, I admit I’ve never seen it take anything this big before, but it’s working and that’s the important thing.”

“Dammit, I knew you’d say that!” the captain exclaimed.

“It’s like a black hole, sir, pulling us in. It might be the end, the Rapture. We must have faith we’re chosen, that we’ll make it through to the New Earth,” one of his crewmen piped up.

“Tell my crew to pray for the Rapture?” The captain laughed.

“Do you have a better idea?” Jim asked in support of the young man.

“Yes, you can pray for us all in the brig, how about that, Doctor?”

“I respectfully request that you confine me to my quarters, sir. If this is the end, I would like to see it out with my family in my arms,” Jim implored.

“So be it,” Captain Malik agreed, signalling for the security officer to see to it, with a simple nod.

When Jim returned to his quarters, he watched quietly as Scarlett kept their daughter occupied with simple games on the bed—things like ‘Pat-a-cake‘ and other childhood rhymes. After playing for a while, Jim and Scarlett put Jerica to bed. She requested her favourite story, but the book was missing, of course. Jim began telling her the story anyway, since he knew it verbatim from their many readings. Eventually she was comforted enough to fall asleep. Even the turbulent rocking of the carrier and the ships engines seemed like white noise, helping Jim drift off too. But Scarlett wasn’t about to let him rest. She needed answers.

She kept quiet until Jerica was deeply asleep, then shook him and whispered, “Jim, Jim.”

He breathed deeply, startled. “What? What is it?” he said.

“Shh,” she said, putting her finger to his lips. “You

can explain in more detail what's happening now, about how we got here and why we're on a boat." She spoke quietly so as not to wake up their little one.

"Ship," he corrected her.

Scarlett gave him a stern look. "Don't be a smartarse, Jim," she said through gritted teeth.

"Calm down. We're safe in the vortex, and that's all that matters right now."

"Safe?" Scarlett laughed. "Armed security outside our door? Stowaways on a flipping ship!"

"Aircraft carrier, actually," he interrupted again.

"Honestly, if you interrupt me one more time, you may need those security guards to stop me from killing you, Jim," Scarlett threatened, clenching her fists and waving one of them in his face, which only made Jim laugh.

"Sorry, Scarlett. Yes, we're safe on this ship for now. Forgive me, we just escaped a collapsing reality. And I just had one of the best moments of my life telling a story to our daughter when I haven't seen either of you for nearly two years."

"What is happening?...And *two* years? You were only away from home a couple of months, at the Oxford office."

"For you, maybe. Time has fractured, or split. I

don't know exactly. You'll have to trust me."

"*Trust*," she scoffed. "That's another thing. Who is that woman?"

"I've been trapped in some kind of reality-time trek. Every time I tried to come back to you, we were either estranged... or worse." Jim paused, trying to figure out how to explain without dragging her through the torturous experiences he'd endured. "Tasha has helped me survive. She's been trapped in these reality jumps, too. The ship's going through another vortex into a new reality, but it's taking longer than usual. This is different. Which I hope is a good thing. The final jump, I hope."

"What? You mean we could go through this all again? No, please, not again."

"Listen, everything will be all right now. It took me years to get back to you two, Scarlett. I've been stuck in different realities and traveling through multiverse time loops. I'm not giving up now. I can control the vortex much better than before, and I feel like we're heading somewhere safe. I won't lose you again."

A knock on their door announced Tasha's arrival. She eased the door open, saying, "Jim, are you decent?"

"Yes," he replied.

"Oh, that's a real shame," Tasha said tactlessly as she entered the room.

"Jim?" Scarlett asked.

"Sorry, with all this excitement, we haven't had much time for proper introductions, have we? Scarlett, this is Tasha."

"Oh, isn't he just perfect? He spent a *lot* of time with me, you know, Scarlett?" Tasha said playfully.

"Quit the games, Tasha. What's up?" Jim asked wearily.

"The guard's gone. The ship's gone crazy. A few of the crew are floating off the boat, levitating and then going out of the side of the vortex. There's panic all over the boat, Jim."

"Ship," Jim corrected her.

"What?" Tasha said angrily.

"It—it's a ship," Jim said, looking down, slightly embarrassed and preparing himself for a reprimand.

"Isn't he annoying at times, Scarlett?" Tasha said, pointing a finger at Jim and looking at his wife.

"You could say that, yes," Scarlett replied. "Sometimes I think it's harder to raise a husband than a baby."

They both roared with laughter. Jerica stirred, which, to Jim's relief, quieted the girls.

"Sorry," he said, sneaking a word in. "I'm sorry, both of you. Please continue, Tasha," he added.

"I don't know if they're jumping off, or being pulled out into the vortex, or what's happening, and all you can do is correct my grammar? Anyway, the guard was called away to help with the emergency, leaving us free to roam. In case you didn't know, the captain ordered a guard to keep me confined to my quarters, and he left his post too."

"The *Enterprise* is still at general quarters. I think that means panic stations, red alert, or something. A cruiser appeared out of nowhere off our starboard bow, and panic spread throughout the ship. I heard one of the men shouting, 'look on the starboard side—it's the *Eldridge!*' before it slipped back out of the vortex. It doesn't seem like the *Eldridge* will make it through, Jim. It's gone. I saw it vanish. Security has been reassigned to stop crewmen from going out on deck. So come on, Jim. Let's go see what's happening."

"I'm sorry, Tasha. I'm afraid you wasted your time coming to find me. I'm seeing this through right here with my family."

"What if the crew who are leaving are the ones going to the other reality? Shouldn't we go too? If they're jumping or being pulled out, maybe they're the ones who are safe?" Tasha asked.

"No, Tasha. I believe they're being expelled. Only the righteous may pass."

"You really believe that?" Scarlett asked nervously, looking toward their daughter Jerica. "And who decides who is and isn't righteous?"

"Not me. I'm powerless to do anything about it. If the options are stay on the ship or jump off, I'm staying put, thank you. I want to see where this extended vortex leads us. Ladies, I give you a toast. Here's my hope that Jerica will find her Shangri-La. Here's my hope that we *all* find our version of peace. As to who decides... source energy, perhaps, or God, if there is such a thing, or something else of a divine nature. The point is, I don't know," Jim said, feeling a little confused. "It's this or that, all of the universe or nothing. Which shall it be? I vote to wait and find out."

"The secret of my success, is to never say die," Tasha said determinedly. "Are you coming or staying, Jim?"

"I think you already know the answer to that question. The same spirit lives in me too—I would never give up either, although I did come close a few a times." Jim said with a smile. "Your destiny lies on a different path from mine, Tasha."

"It sounds like you're giving up to me," Tasha said sadly.

"'It is a far, far better thing I do than I have ever done.'" Jim paused, remembering the words from one of his favourite tales. "'It is a far, far better rest I go to than I have ever known,'" he concluded, quoting Charles Dickens.

“Happiness must be earned, eh, Jim?” Tasha said, ignoring his nonsensical quotes.

“Oh, I think I have earned it. All of us have,” Jim said. “And I will wait for Judgement Day here with my family. I have faith that there will be a tomorrow. What about you, Scarlett, what do you want us to do?”

“I don’t really understand any of this. One minute I’m in my house doing normal day-to-day things, the next the world around me is tearing itself apart and I’m on a ship in some kind of vortex. And now I find out my husband and some woman I don’t know have seemingly been on some quantum adventure together. It’s a lot to take on board, but I would like to know more about what’s going on out there.”

“I’m going up to the bridge to speak with the captain,” Tasha replied and swiftly left the room.

Scarlett hugged Jim in a quiet embrace for a few moments before she spoke up. “Why don’t you go with her, Jim? I’ll stay here. I don’t know, she might be right, maybe we should be jumping out of this vortex?”

“So you do trust me,” Jim smiled.

“I am not going to lie and say this isn’t difficult for me,” she looked down at their sleeping child, “but there are more important things at stake here. I will stay with Jerica, you find out what we need to know and come back for us.”

Jim agreed, hugged her and bolted out down the corridor to catch up with Tasha. "Wait, wait. My wife wants me to find out what's going on. She thinks you might be right. Let's go to the bridge and at least find out what they know."

"Okay, let's find out Jim—together."

They made their way up to the bridge and addressed Lieutenant Jed, now on guard duty outside.

"We need to talk to the captain again," Jim stated.

"Aye, the captain said you two might come back. I have to know what's happening here too, so court martial or not, I'm coming in with you."

"Excellent, thank you."

The bridge was bustling with activity. "Doctor!" the captain exclaimed. "Great. Is that infernal machine off?"

"No, sir," replied Tasha.

"I have crew members flying off the deck. If we stop the machine, will it stop this storm?" the captain inquired.

"No, sir," Jim replied. "I don't believe it will stop it now, but it may weaken it, and that could mean losing everything. It's the only reason we have a chance of survival. In my opinion, the device is holding the gateway open much wider and for longer than we have ever seen before. Turning it off now is an unwarranted gamble. What can you tell us, Captain?"

"We've made contact with ships and planes from the past—it's insane. One moment, our radar picks up planes from the 1940s; the next, the USS *Eldridge* appears on our bow only to disappear shortly after. We're working on navigating this chaotic storm, with instruments malfunctioning and seamen flying off the deck; it's a problem we have never faced before. Other than that, not much has been happening—oh, apart from the ship floating in mid-air, defying all the laws of physics. We seem to have levelled out, but we're still in this infernal tunnel."

"What other ships have you made contact with, Captain?" Jim asked curiously.

"T2 tankers that have been missing for decades." As the captain paused and looked out the window, the planes from Flight 21 flew past the bridge. "Did you see that? Those World War II Avengers looked brand new. This is incredible," the captain remarked.

"Captain, when you're going through hell, keep going. This is the *Mandela Effect*," Jim said. "The circle is now complete. I first saw these planes through the vortex. I haven't seen them again until now, and it's all linked to the dog tags from the flight leader of those planes, sir."

"Mandela effect?" the captain queried.

"Yes, multiple different universes have been collapsing; imagine it like bubbles popping in a bath. They don't just collapse, they merge elements with the universe next to them and some people remember the differences from the old reality. At least, that's my theory. It's a phenomenon known as the Mandela effect, because some people remember Nelson Mandela dying in prison years ago in the eighties and others remember him living long afterwards. The ones with different memories are from different universes—and we need a stable one. Keep going, Captain. Trust me."

"At this point, I don't have any choice but to listen to you. We can't escape whatever this storm is. Turning the collider off leaves us in danger, and leaving it on leads us somewhere else. There are seamen who need our help, but I had to withdraw all my crew because they were getting lost in the storm themselves. When the dust clears, we'll be able to resume our rescue efforts. For now, the ship is on lockdown; no one is permitted on deck. That includes you two." The captain pointed to Jim and Tasha, realising that he was having difficulty controlling them.

The visibility outside the window thickened further with orange-red mist. "You had better be right about this, Doctor," the captain said, waving his finger at Jim aggressively.

"I have to be, sir. I have to be," Jim replied wistfully. "If that was the *Eldridge* you saw and they're no longer in the vortex, well, history states they reappeared back in their own time. We know in our reality they return and a lot of the crew died. We can't go back to ours, that world is doomed, your crew will die, you saw the meteors."

The anomaly intensified, and the water all around became turbulent and bright white ahead, visible through the thinning fog.

"Captain, the radar has come back online and we have picked up what looks like a landmass directly ahead," the radar technician reported.

Jim stared out the front windows of the bridge as a huge flying object with a halo above it and wings that extended out of sight rose majestically from the water. Jim looked down at his hand as colours inverted, regretting leaving his family and wishing he was holding their hands. He closed his eyes for a moment to pray for the safety of his family and everybody on board.

All the noise around them distorted, and then there was suddenly quiet apart from the normal hum of the *Enterprise's* engines and systems. Jim opened his eyes and was awestruck by the sight before him. The air had cleared, and the *Enterprise* rode an enormous wave, like a surfer navigating waves towards the vast canyons that had appeared in front of them. The aircraft carrier surged out of the dimensional rift, trailing vast stretches of ocean water visible all around it; the panoramic view from the bridge gave them a stunning surround view. The ship had emerged into the canyon. The vortex was spewing water and filling the canyon with swirling currents, presenting a daunting obstacle course. The ship faced the perilous task of navigating the rocky canyons, like a canoe navigating through wild white-water rapids. Each bend and rapid presented a new challenge, with the risk of destruction lurking at every turn.

"That is an incredible sight, isn't it, Captain?" Jim said.

"It's terrifying, Doctor. Where have you brought my ship?"

"I believe it's Mars. I've seen this on the Discovery Channel," Jim shouted excitedly.

"Mars? How can that be? There's no air or atmosphere on Mars. We'll all die."

"I don't think so, sir, we're getting some help," Jim said, pointing upward at a large unidentifiable craft.

Everybody clung to anything stable they could find. As the water flowed upward, filling the canyons, the speed slowly reduced, and the white river ride slowed to a fast but more manageable pace.

As the ship cleared the canyon walls without incident, the crew exchanged stunned glances, their expressions shifting from tense anticipation to wide-eyed amazement. A collective sigh of relief swept through the crew, their voices hushed as they gazed out at the immense crevasse before them.

"How the hell didn't we collide with these canyon walls or crack the hull under the pressure? And what makes you think this is Mars?"

“I can’t be sure, Captain. This is of course all new to me as well. But look to the west—those three volcanoes erupting. If I’m correct, we’re witnessing something that hasn’t happened for millions, perhaps billions of years,” Jim said.

“What? Volcanoes erupt all the time. What can you tell me that is useful, Doctor?” the captain snapped.

“We’re certainly not in Kansas anymore, Captain. Mars is coming to life again after billions of years dormant.”

“This isn’t Oz, Doctor. Give me some facts.”

“Here are some facts I remember,” Tasha chimed in. “I watched that Discovery documentary as well, Captain. Look at those three volcanoes in the distance. To me, that looks like the Tharsis Plateau. And look at those two objects in the sky, two moons, they must be Phobos and Deimos, irregular-shaped moons just like in the programme.”

“If we’re right, the *Enterprise* is in the Valles Marineris canyon, the largest canyon in our known solar system, which has been dry for millennia. Captain, we are on Mars. This also explains the orange red fog—dust from Mars,” Jim explained.

“Mars? Oz would have been a more believable explanation,” the captain said, unable to accept what he was hearing or believe what he was seeing.

He was knocked off his feet as the water continued to rise, and the ship listed dangerously, nearing the top of the canyon. The canyon wall slumped on the starboard side, and still the water kept coming, but thankfully, the *Enterprise* levelled out enough to prevent it from capsizing.

“If we are on Mars, Doctor, where is all this water coming from?” the captain barked, growing agitated again.

“It’s as though we’ve been adrift in an overflowing paddling pool, cascading over the edge as if an invisible hand held one side down, releasing a torrent of water. Like toy boats careening down a colossal waterslide, hurtling through the dimensional gateway from Earth directly onto the red Martian surface,” Tasha replied.

The turbulent water surged alongside the ship. To the captain’s astonishment, the ship didn’t reach its nadir but continued to ride the ever-slowing wave, skimming above the burgeoning ocean that had formed beneath it. A monumental planetary deluge was in progress, visible all round them.

“The vortex has transported life-sustaining water from our Earth directly into the largest canyon system known to man,” Jim said. “Captain, doesn’t that pique your curiosity?”

Jim gestured again toward the sky as a second colossal spacecraft appeared ahead of them, dominating the Martian sky. Frustration washed over him as he grappled with a sense of helplessness, his mind swirling with the enormity of the situation. He felt like a mere observer, powerless to alter the course of events unfolding before him. The captain shifted his gaze but remained speechless as he beheld the otherworldly vessels above as one of them seemingly projected a beam of light toward them.

"I think they are steering us to safety, Captain. Maybe it's some kind of tractor or energy beam. It's saving the *Enterprise.* Without intervention, wouldn't we have crashed into the canyon walls at the first bend?" Tasha asked.

"Yes, this ship couldn't navigate those turns at these speeds," Captain Malik confirmed.

"Captain, you have your responsibilities, and I have mine. I need to be with my family," Jim stated firmly.

"What? You're leaving the bridge now?" the captain exclaimed.

"Yes, sir. There's little more I can do here. Stay the course and we will be fine. Tasha is as knowledgeable as I am about this situation and can answer any inquiries you may have," Jim said, then left without requesting permission, casting a reassuring glance and smile at a terrified Tasha. He moved his lips to form the words "have faith" for her to lip-read before closing the door behind him.

Chapter 39 – Thoth Conveys Humanities Last Light

Jim reached his family, battered from bouncing off the deck rails as the ship continued to lurch. He was relieved they were together again. Jerica had awoken from the turbulence and they clung to each other, enduring the velocity of the ride, fear etched on their faces. Moopsie, Jerica's cat, had awoken too and was behaving erratically, crying and running back and forth, not knowing what to do with himself. Jim suggested leaving Moopsie in the cabin and returning for him later, as he was now cowering in the corner and hissing at them if they tried to go near him to calm him. They left the cabin and moved to an area with a larger window to witness the surreal scene outside.

The alien crafts above astonished Jerica and Scarlett, who clung to each other. Jerica whispered asking, if it was an angel, and Scarlett murmured a prayer. More alien vessels appeared around Mars, and in tow, Earth's old moon, tethered by an energy beam. Its presence brought a comforting reminder of home.

Scarlett expressed relief as the ship steadied, and Jim reassured Jerica. They marvelled at the moon's now larger size. Jerica noticed a smaller moon on a collision course with it, and Jim urged them to cover their eyes just before a breathtaking explosion filled the sky.

"What now, Jim?"

"As soon as the ship stabilises, we'll make our move,"

The Enterprise jerked to a halt, calm at last and close enough to disembark. The captain's voice came over the speakers.

"Attention, we've anchored the ship in a safe area, away from immediate dangers. We're sending a research party to explore and a recon team to gather intel. Until we know more, stay vigilant and report anything important. We're at general quarters. Flight deck should be prepared for emergency landing protocols. That is all."

Scarlett questioned if they were safer onboard, but Jim reassured her, and they headed toward the disembarkation area. At the cargo bay, Jim deactivated the collider to avoid further disruptions. They were stopped by a guard who blocked the exit.

"Only essential recon personnel may leave," the guard insisted.

"Are we prisoners now?" Jim asked angrily, but before he could argue further, a crowd formed behind them, pressing against the corridor walls.

"Call the captain," Jim shouted, "before we're crushed here!"

After a tense moment, the captain responded with an updated order: non-essential crew could disembark temporarily. The guard unlocked the exit hatch, and the crowd poured onto the Martian landscape. Above, Mars' reddish sky transformed to a vibrant blue, reminiscent of Earth, filling everyone with awe and disbelief.

"I can't believe this," Jim whispered, spotting dense, dark clouds rolling in rapidly. From them emerged another colossal disk-like craft, dwarfing all others. As it descended, Jim noticed a strange whistling noise, speculating the aliens might be harnessing sound energy to power the ship. A sulphurous smell filled the air as the star ship rotated, revealing a holographic face: long, heavy brows, an elongated nose, and owl-like eyes resembling the Moai statues.

The figure began to speak, his voice shaking the ground. "We are the Moai, I am Thoth. We are not responsible for the destruction you've witnessed; it was a celestial event across the multiverse. We saved your solar system in this reality, but not Earth. Scattered across Mars are survivors transported here through dimensional rifts."

He paused, allowing the weight of his words to sink in. "We've visited Earth before, often mistaken as deities, but our messages of peace were misunderstood. In your final acts, your scientists created wormholes and black holes using hadron colliders, leading to this cataclysm. Only the stable rifts allowed you safe passage."

"Listen closely, for this is your ultimate reckoning. Thoth's gaze swept the crowd. "You are one hundred and forty-four thousand souls, each bearing the potential for righteousness within, just as foretold." A collective gasp rippled through the survivors as glowing marks appeared on their foreheads. The names inscribed were familiar to all—Yeshua, Jesus, Jehovah, Allah, Buddha, Krishna, and others, names from the world's many religions, each a beacon of faith from different traditions. The diversity of the names was as striking as it was profound, symbolizing the unity of humanity under a higher purpose—oneness.

Jim scanned the crowd, noticing the vast mix of people from different times and places.

Thoth continued, his voice resonating with conviction. "If you feel unworthy, know that we make no mistakes. None are perfect, but regretful sins done in remorse are forgiven. You must learn kindness and compassion on this New Earth. This mark will soon fade, but its essence remains within. We are not gods, but we are all interconnected. Our people made immense sacrifices to rescue as many as we could from your world whom we deemed righteous. We transplanted the farms and unspoiled landscapes of Terra to this new world. However, our journey came at a cost. Many of our fleet were lost, sacrificed to ensure your survival. The self-destruction of their own ships' drives sealed the collapsing portals. These vessels are now revered as the Guardian Seals. It is important to commemorate their sacrifice each year on this very day."

Thoth paused once more, and a profound silence

enveloped the land once more, interrupted only by the noise of planes landing safely on the *Enterprise* as they had been for some time.

"Hatred has hindered your growth. Let go of fear, anger, greed and embrace inner peace."

"By this stage in your evolution, you should have developed your third eye. I opened your third eye briefly to demonstrate, and so the words of your perceived deities shone through."

Throughout the vast expanse of this new Martian world, the entire assembly of the remainder of humanity stood, united, their hearts and minds synchronised in awe and wonder. Their collective destiny was on the precipice of an unimaginable journey of self-discovery, spiritual growth, and the awakening of extraordinary sensory perception—evolution.

Chapter 40 – New Beginnings Awaken Tomorrows World

Thoth descended gracefully onto the Martian surface, his luminous form casting an ethereal glow against the crimson landscape. Behind him loomed a colossal archway crafted from weathered stone. The doorway appeared carved into the rock, but it was as if it had been sealed shut.

Facing the crowd of survivors, Thoth raised his hand, gesturing towards the monumental structure. “Now, we offer a fleeting offer for the brave,” he proclaimed, his voice resonating across the barren expanse. “The last Guardian has bestowed upon us the means. Who among you dares to venture into the annals of time and rescue those beloved souls left behind? But know this—each traveller may only save three souls, for the gateways are now at their minimal levels to prevent further destruction of our reality.”

A man stepped forward. He was dressed in an ancient, colourful tunic and a priest-like headdress. Thoth approached the man and handed him a gift. “Here is your disk, Muru.” He paused and withdrew the offered disk momentarily. “To all who return here, you must find one of the portals. There are sacred areas on your planet that remain open in time; the disk will lead you to them. Many ancient monuments around the old world will power up the disk."

His gaze swept over the bewildered faces before him, and then he turned, pointing at the ancient structure behind him. "Some of you may have seen a similar structure to this one in Peru. The Puerta de Hayu Marca," Thoth explained, his voice carrying the wisdom of ancient knowledge. "Its power is ancient and sacred, serving as a conduit to your old world. You will find other such structures—pyramids, monoliths, and the like here on New Earth. This world is yours to explore, and each site will link to its counterpart on your old world."

He turned back to address Muru. "Remember, you must only bring the righteous to these locations. Press your palm on the disk and place it into the slot in the gateway to activate the doorway when you are ready to return in the same fashion. You have a maximum of one year. Press it now, Muru, to engage the dimensional portal and travel into your world and your chosen time and reality."

With that, Muru followed his instruction and the solid rock began resonating with a trumpet-like sound echoing across the land. The colour in the rock inverted and then changed into a vortex and Muru vanished.

"If you wish to return to the cursed Earth, you may come and collect your golden disk now," Thoth said commandingly, addressing the crowd again.

Immediately, Jim's thoughts turned to his brother, mother, and father. *Could I put myself through one more jump to save them now that I know Scarlett and Jerica are safe?* he thought to himself. His eyes drifted to Scarlett, carrying Jerica, and to his surprise, in the distance, he saw Jeff and Alex running towards them. Jim leapt into the air, fist-pumping.

"Yes!" he shouted, fists clenched, shaking them with his eyes closed, roaring with appreciation. He ran to them and hugged his brother.

Then he began to panic. "Mum and Dad?"

Jeff replied excitedly, "Yes, they're here in the farmhouse. The Moai transported the entire farm, along with us. We have animals, crops, food—and the underwater well. A lake full of fish—even the petrol tanker and generator."

"That's great Jeff." Jim replied.

Alex continued, "...even my bee hives, and other insects seem to have made it through. Mason and Blake turned up at the farm to collect the fuel tanker from that holiday village colony, but they made it here instead."

Jim led them back to the front of the main group to continue listening to the alien being. Amidst the throng of people, his gaze locked onto Max Reynolds, standing among a group of other flight officers in World War II-era uniforms. He looked just as he remembered from the old photos he found in 1940s news articles online. As Jim approached, he noticed Reynolds posture stiffen, tension rippling through his body. His eyes widened for a moment before narrowing, as if he were searching for something familiar. As Jim introduced himself, Reynolds response was automatic, his voice crisp and formal.

“My name is Captain Max C. Reynolds, serial number 656-5827B.”

Jim reached for the dog tag he had been wearing around his neck since his first encounter with the vortex. He recognised the numbers, but double-checked all the same, and confirmed the match. He had finally met the missing crew from Flight 21. Jim felt his whole body tingle with excitement. To see the man he had read about so often was incredible; Reynolds hadn’t aged a day.

“I believe this is yours. You can relax now, captain. We made it. Welcome to your new home,” Jim said, a smile spreading across his face.

“Thank you. How did you get this?” Reynolds asked.

“It’s a long story I can tell you later. The short version is the dog tags came through a portal, and they led me here.”

Reynolds turned to Thoth, looking for answers. “Why me? I’ve done horrible things. I don’t feel worthy of this New Earth. I’ve killed in the war, and I feel sorrow and remorse for the things I’ve done.”

"You have felt guilt and pain for the lives you took, seeing that as sinful. Yet we saw a brave soul fighting for your nation, a soul who risked his own life for the freedom of others. Some fought in those wars for the opportunity to kill; you fought for a just and noble cause. You no longer need to feel remorse or relive those events. Free yourself of this guilt, Captain Reynolds. Your recompense is to allow yourself this paradise, or you and your people will be destined to repeat your past mistakes. Flight 19 and Flight 21, from different realities are both now welcome among the living here on New Earth."

"Yes that's another thing, I have met the Flight 19 crew, and we seem to have similar stories of how we got here. But these guys have differing memories of certain events. For example they seem to remember me having a wife who by all accounts was pretty mean to me. I have no knowledge of these accounts. They made a wise crack that I couldn't have gotten any further away from her if I tried, and I had no idea what the heck they were talking about." Reynolds queried.

"That's right, you will find most of you are from other realities. That version of you they knew didn't make the journey. It is a universal law no duplicate person can exist in the same reality." Thoth explained.

"What about us? Why are we here?" Jim observed as his old bosses approached Thoth, now dressed in military uniforms instead of their medical gowns.

“You two helped thousands of people, giving them a nurturing place to work, you are good leaders. I know you were not aware of the sinister dark truths behind the experiments with the Hadron colliders and those experiments must never again be repeated. You are good people, and the people here will look to you for guidance and innovation, but be warned: do not lose your connection to nature over science.” Thoth pointed at the golden pyramid in the distance pulsing with power, a glowing orb throbbing with energy seemed to rest on its peak. “You have clean and free energy here, you must create Djeds to harness the power wirelessly, to power your equipment and homes. We shall teach you how to harness the power, in time, and you will build them.”

“But we are dying, we both have cancer.” His wife said desperately.

Thoth placed his hands on both their chests, a white light of energy surged through them.

“Cancer is not something that occurs in nature, only around the archaic and destructiveness of mankind’s own legacy, side effects of your primitive technologies and misuse of chemicals, may it never return again on New Earth. You are cured.”

The crowd gasped in unison, a wave of astonished murmurs rippling through them, their collective awe echoing like a vibrant chorus. Thoth continued addressing the growing crowd, emphasizing the importance of learning from past mistakes and avoiding the return of violence and tyranny. Thoth offered golden disks and guidance to each volunteer, on controlling the doorways and powering up at ancient sites, cautioned against negative thoughts, and emphasised each traveller would have only one return trip permitted, with a maximum time limit of one year. Those who missed this window would never return to New Earth.

"Take heed; fearful thoughts block the power. When you are calm, at peace, then you will materialise within the duplicate monuments we have built here on Mars, the New Earth." Thoth paused for a moment, to distribute more disks to a queue of volunteers.

"And hear this: There is an indigenous race of people and creatures that dwell beneath the surface. You must learn to live in harmony with them. You all form a symbiotic circle now; what happens to one affects the other. A natural transition will occur as a new balance begins. If you destroy them, you will suffer the same fate."

Jim and Scarlett exchanged a glance, the weight of the words hanging in the air. Scarlett's lips parted as if to speak, her eyes wide and dilated in shock. The silence stretched between them, the tension crackling.

"Did he just threaten us?" Jim said.

Scarlett shrugged, nodding at the same time.

"Everything you need from the old Earth is here for

you to thrive, including the great seed banks. And behold, for it shall rain for forty days and forty nights on this planet. After that, the soil shall become fertile. Natural rivers and pure water lakes shall form for you to live from. You should cultivate the remaining freshwater fish in these lakes and become one with nature. Life shall seek life, and new life shall evolve; the circle will then be complete, and you shall be in balance with nature at last."

All but one of the craft in the air vanished at once, leaving what Jim felt would be a lasting impression, something they needed to keep alive and pass down through the generations. Thoth remained, handing out disks and instructions to each of the volunteers.

"I hope he stays a while. I have so many questions," Reynolds said to Jim, who certainly had a bunch of them too.

Jim turned to Reynolds, who was still standing beside him. He caught him staring at his dog tag once again.

"Oh my, I never thought I'd see this again. I lost visibility and couldn't tell if I was over land or sea, so I opened my cockpit, hoping to get a clearer view. Sometimes those blasted things fog up something terrible. The situation felt hopeless—my dog tags started burning against my skin. I saw some kind of energy discharge, like extreme static or electricity, hit them, so I threw the tags out the window. Where's the other one?"

"My friend has it. I haven't seen her since we left the *Enterprise*. I do hope she's okay. She's been travelling through realities as well," Jim said.

"What will you do now?" Reynolds asked.

"Now? Well, I have a family to be with. I need to find Tasha and make sure she's okay." Jim turned to leave, and then looked back. "What about you?" he asked curiously.

"I don't know."

One of the other men in World War II flight uniform stepped forward to take one of the disks.

"Savage—wait," Reynolds shouted.

"Wait for what? I'm the only one in the flight group who is married and a father. I have to go back. I have to try to find my family," Savage replied. "And thank you, Captain Reynolds. You did a swell job, sir. Any landing you can walk away from—"

"—is a good one, even on an alien planet?" Captain Reynolds said, finishing Lieutenant Robert Savage's sentence for him. They both laughed in shared relief, looking over at their planes on the aircraft carrier deck with pride.

"Lieutenant Savage," Jim said eagerly before the lieutenant transferred into the multiverse dimension rift, "in my reality, history considers you all dead, MIA. Be discreet, if you make it back. Stay inconspicuous, find your family, and get them safely to the New Earth. Good luck, Lieutenant." Jim saluted him in respect for his rank and showing his pride at the honour of meeting the legends of Flight 21.

"Who are you, and how do you know me?" Lieutenant Savage asked.

"I've been reading about you and your missions since I was a child, sir. You're all legends—living legends, it turns out," Jim said, beaming.

"Well, take care of yourself old boy," Lieutenant Savage replied, he gave a nod to Captain Reynolds and headed towards Thoth to collect a disk.

Will I ever see him again? Jim thought to himself. He could have stayed chatting for hours about their experiences and the vortex. However, he also had something more important on his mind: his own family. He moved through the ever-growing crowd and watched the clouds form and the ensuing torrential rain with his family by his side.

"Jim, who is this handsome man you haven't introduced me to?" Tasha appeared out of nowhere, tugging on his arm.

"Tasha, where have you been?"

"Amongst the crowd, listening to Thoth or whatever his name is, of course, silly. Anyway, you never answered my question. Who is this young man who looks remarkably like you, only much more handsome?"

Jim smiled. His brother was in for a real treat with this introduction. "Tasha, this is Jeff, my brother. Go easy with him, won't you, please?" he said, giving her a friendly wink.

"Go easy on him, you say, eh?" Tasha said, her eyes sparkling with mischief, teasing both of them. "Oh, I think he can take it. And since you dumped me for your wife, I'm available. Maybe you did me a favour. I had no idea I might get a chance of meeting a younger model upgrade. So Jeff, how would you like to get to know a hot lady on a new planet? Interested in hanging out?" she said in her usual flirtatious manner.

Jeff paused, blushing and gathering his thoughts for a reply. "You'll let me know when one turns up then, right?" he responded, matching her banter.

She huffed and slapped his arm in a playful way, which he obviously liked very much. "Cheeky! Jim, I think your brother and I are going to get along just fine. That's okay with you, isn't it?"

"Of course. Nothing would make me happier than to see the two of you together." Jim turned to his wife, relieved that the tension of the love triangle that never was had finally ended. Though he knew he still had some explaining to do, this would make it much easier.

"Together?" Tasha replied playfully. "Hey, Jeff, your

brother has just skipped us straight into a relationship. Are you scared yet?"

"Me? Nah. Well, maybe a little scared. Hey, are you tripping on me?" Jeff laughed.

"Oh, no, I'm just getting to know you. You seem cute, and nobody ever achieved anything without a little risk, and that's what life is all about, wouldn't you agree?" Tasha said.

Jim smiled, watching the early seeds of love germinate.

As the rain intensified, the crowd gradually dispersed, seeking refuge in nearby Martian caves, as well as the few standing buildings and farm barns that had been transported through the portal. Among them were ancient monoliths and structures, relics from Earth's natural energy lines, including a complete Stonehenge and the one from Alex's farm. In the distance, Jim spotted some familiar buildings resembling the terraced house he had purchased for Tasha's friends. It was a peculiar mix of architecture and structures across the flat area. The juxtaposition of buildings and structures from different eras and locations against the Martian backdrop created a surreal sight, one that beckoned further exploration when the time was right. Determined to reconnect with them when he had the opportunity, Jim made a mental note to visit and check if it was indeed the same terraced houses. He prayed Jana, Ian, Sammi, and Marcus had also made it through. *Tasha would do well to have some friends around her,* he reflected inwardly.

Many of the crew headed back to the *Enterprise,* as their two hours were now up. Jim and his friends and family followed Jeff and Alex back to the farm, and Alex made room in their barn for as many people as he could to wait out the storm.

"Daddy, my cat!" Jerica shouted at Jim.

"Yes, little one, you're right, I forgot about him, sorry. Once we get familiar with the farm's whereabouts, I'll go back to the ship and get him," Jim reassured, lifting her into his arms.

"I want Moopsie now," Jerica demanded.

"It won't be long. Let Daddy find out where everything is, and I'll get Moopsie in a few minutes."

"And don't worry, there are plenty of mice around the farm for the cat to eat." Alex said.

* * *

While overseeing his crew's duties aboard the carrier, Captain Malik distributed supplies to the local colony. Resources from the aircraft carrier, along with other provisions available for sharing, were rationed throughout the community to sustain them during the forty-day ordeal. Meanwhile, farmers meticulously planned for the cultivation and conservation of resources, ensuring the community's long-term sustainability, and town meetings were regularly held on board the *Enterprise,* where all were welcome to attend and vote together on the agreed plans and objectives.

The rain persisted for forty days and nights, a ceaseless torrent beneath dark clouds and a perpetual storm, just as Thoth had foretold. Finally, after the deluge, the morning sun pierced through the clouds. Jim and his family, along with all the inhabitants of the local colony, emerged from their shelters to embrace the dawn of a new era.

“Hmm, that fresh smell after a storm.” Jim groaned, enjoying the familiarity. “It’s the same here. Do you know what that means, Scarlett?” Jim asked, grinning.

“I don’t know, but it smells better,” she replied.

“It’s ozone-energised oxygen; that’s what creates that distinct smell after a large storm on Earth—the fresh scent of the cool upper air mixed with rain. You’re right, it does smell better.”

“Daddy, is it over?” Jerica said, tugging on his clothes, the cat brushing around their ankles, making sure he was paid attention to as well.

“Yes—and look up! Wow, the sky is clearing, what a wonderful vivid blue,” Jim said, looking up at the moon and its new natural satellites, Phobos and Deimos, or what was left of Deimos after its collision, which had left a beautiful but faint ring around the moon.

“What’s wrong, Jim?” Scarlett asked.

“Oh, nothing. I’m absolutely fine,” Jim said, smiling and hugging them both. “I just had the strangest feeling of déjà vu and clarity.” Swiftly changing the subject, he said, “While I was on my own for those two years, I did a lot of reading and research. Did you know the old moons of Mars were named Phobos and Deimos after characters from Greek mythology? Phobos represents flight and Deimos represents fear. They should remind us not to fight, or run from our fears, but to always work together to overcome our troubles. The ancient Greeks believed Selene to be the goddess of the moon. Legend has it she was the mother of the Earth, and now she is the mother of the New Earth, bringing balance once again.” Together, they gazed at their celestial moon, larger than life, tranquil and shining in the sky.

“How do you remember this stuff?” Scarlett’s eyes sparkled with curiosity, her lips curling upwards in a playful smile that hinted at her fascination.

“You know me, great at a quiz. I remember a bunch of useless stuff—my brain thinks it’s interesting and it gets stuck there. Ask me how to make a meal in the kitchen or a bunch of other stuff everyone else knows and I haven’t got a clue.” They both laughed.

The multiverse had served as a portal of self-discovery, a journey of redemption and forgiveness, and a testament to the boundless possibilities of existence. The moon stood as a silent sentinel, its gravitational pull shaping the tides of Mars and nurturing the delicate balance of its ecosystem. Just as the moon had a job to sustain harmony on the New Earth, so too did humanity bear a responsibility to preserve and protect the natural balance.

Jim reflected on Thoth's parting prophecy, envisioning a future where mindfulness and stewardship guided every action, rooted in profound respect for the planet and its inhabitants, even the universe. He pondered the untapped powers Thoth spoke of, waiting to be harnessed through their third eye.

Beneath the surface of New Earth lay untold mysteries, waiting to be uncovered. Jim's thoughts raced with possibilities about the indigenous life forms dwelling below—what secrets were hidden in the shadows? What ancient wisdom might they possess, waiting to reshape their understanding of this new world?

This was not the end, but merely the beginning of an extraordinary path toward interconnectedness—unity with the cosmos, and an adventure of discovering what lies beneath.

Thank You

As we reach the end of this book, I want to say thanks for reading this book.

I want to get this information out to as many people as possible.

If you found this book enjoyable, I would greatly appreciate you leaving me a review. This helps others find the book as well.

Disclaimer

This document is geared towards providing fiction, some topics may be referencing events or places for entertainment purposes only but should not be taken as factual. The publication is sold on the idea that the publisher is not required to render an accounting, officially permitted, or otherwise, qualified services. If advice is necessary, legal, financial, medical or professional, a practiced individual in the profession should be ordered.

This information is not presented by a financial or medical practitioner and is for entertainment, educational and informational purposes only. The content is not intended as a substitute for professional medical advice, diagnosis, or treatment. Always seek the advice of your physician or other qualified health care provider with any questions you may have regarding a medical condition. Never disregard professional medical advice or delay in seeking it because of something you have read.

The information provided herein is stated to be truthful and consistent, in that any liability, in terms of inattention or otherwise, by any usage or abuse of any policies, processes, or directions contained within is the solitary and utter responsibility of the recipient reader. Under no circumstances will any legal responsibility or blame be held against the publisher for any reparation, damages, or monetary loss due to the information herein, either directly or indirectly.

Printed in Great Britain
by Amazon

fd3baf18-88a1-418b-8c0b-6d55b9daa261R01